# PYG

## A NOVEL

## PIP LANDERS-LETTS

ROUXMAUS
PRESS

**Copyright © 2025 Pip Landers-Letts**
**First Edition May 2025**
**Published by Rouxmaus Press**

**Paperback ISBN:** 978-1-7385430-6-9
**eBook ISBN:** 978-1-7385430-7-6

Editing and proof-reading: **Sophia Blackwell**
Cover Design: **Samantha Sanderson Marshall**

**www.pipwritesfiction.com**

*For Sheila*

"The difference between a lady and a flower girl is not how she behaves, but how she's treated."

George Bernard Shaw,
*Pygmalion*

# FUCKING FRAN

*What is that? A cow?* Alice climbed out of her car and peered into the darkness. A large black lump lay in the middle of the road, barely illuminated by the one functioning headlight of her Ford Fiesta. She squinted through the claggy mascara caking her lashes, courtesy of the deluge of tears that had flowed through them earlier. *Courtesy of Fran.*

"Fuck you, Fran," Alice muttered through chattering teeth and took a tentative step closer to the lump. Mist rose from the ground in the low glow of her headlight. The yellow beam sliced through the darkness; not enough for her to make out the full form of the lump in the road, but enough for her to make out the rise and fall of breath. *It's alive.*

"Hello... cow? Are you okay? Can you moo or something?"

Alice shivered and hugged her arms around herself, regretting the decision to wear barely anything under her thin trench coat. But then again, she wasn't meant to be in the middle of fucking nowhere, about to be trampled by a fucking cow. She was meant to be fucking Fran in the cosy hotel room they'd booked for the weekend. But fucking Fran did not deserve her, and Alice did not deserve this. She just wanted to go home, curl up in her bed and forget this evening had ever happened. Forget the last few months and all the hopes Fran had raised and subsequently dashed.

A low groan sounded from the lump, and as Alice teetered closer in her heels, the groaning grew louder... and very un-cowlike. Realisation unfurled and Alice darted over to what was clearly not a cow, but a large man swaddled in a furry black coat, lying in a foetal position on the cold tarmac. Alice knelt by his side, tiny stones tearing into her stockings and cutting her knees.

"Oh my God! Have you been run over?"

The man groaned.

"Okay." Alice stood and pulled her phone from her pocket. She squinted against the bright screen, then held it aloft. No signal. *Fuck.*

"Why me?" Alice muttered, her heels clacking along the tarmac as she paced back to her Fiesta and folded her legs into the vehicle. For a fleeting moment, it crossed her mind to edge the car around the groaning mass of a man and drive on by. *Drive home, make a strong cuppa, and take it to bed. Forget about this evening, forget about this stranger. And more importantly, forget about Fran, once and for all this time.*

But Alice wasn't that person. She could no sooner leave

that poor man in the road than she could forget about Fran, so she pulled her car up as close as possible and lined up the rear doors with the man. The engine ticked over as Alice crouched next to him again.

"I can't just leave you in the road, so I'm going to have to get you into my car. Do you think you can stand?" Alice enunciated each word of the question, as if speaking loud and clear would somehow power the man to his feet.

It didn't, but the man groaned.

"I'll take that as a no." She sighed and tugged at the man's shoulder until he rolled from his side and onto his back. The interior light of the car cast an eerie shadow across his face, and his droopy eyelids fluttered.

"Look, I'm sorry, but I'm going to have to drag you." Alice bent and tucked her hands under the man's armpits, handfuls of his furry, damp coat gathered in her fists. She strained with the effort, panting as she dragged the dead weight as far as she could, stopping just shy of the car. "No offence, but you weigh a ton. I think you might have given me a hernia."

Alice clambered into the rear passenger-side door. She leaned out, grabbed the man's coat by the shoulders and tugged with all her might. After pulling his torso halfway into the car, Alice stopped to gather her strength. Whilst sucking in a few deep breaths, she adjusted her grip then heaved, but the coat pulled up and off the man's arms and his limp body lolled to the side. The man released an anguished cry as his head hit the doorframe.

"Oh, fuck." Alice winced and gawped at the empty coat in her hands. She stuffed it into the footwell and scrambled out of the car and around to the man, kneeling in front of him to survey the fresh gash on his forehead which was trickling blood into his right eye. "Shit, I'm so sorry about that. Okay, let's try this instead." Alice once again latched her hands under his armpits. She cried out as she hauled him up. Then, with an unsteady sway, she pressed her weight into him, and they both flopped into the car.

The man groaned.

Depleted by her exertions, Alice lay panting on top of him.

"This is not how I expected my evening to pan out. And I'm fairly certain I've never spent so much time with my fingers in a man's armpits before." Alice laughed and patted the man's broad chest. "But it's been nice getting to know you."

The man didn't groan.

After a beat, Alice lifted her head, panic soaring as she remembered that nasty gash. "Oh my God, you're not—"

The man's chest heaved again, and Alice puffed out the breath she'd been holding. "You scared me for a moment there."

THE SLIDING DOORS SWISHED OPEN AND EXHALED A gush of hot air.

"Help, please," Alice panted in the doorway. "He's injured."

Heads swivelled in her direction and Alice pointed to

her car parked out the front of the hospital. A split second later, two men in blue scrubs lunged into action and rushed past her. They heaved the man from her car and into a wheelchair, seemingly conjured from thin air. In a trance-like state, Alice followed as the duo pushed through double doors and into a strip-lit room.

"Bay Five is free," said the bearded one. They came to a halt and the fresh-faced man pulled the papery curtain around the bay. Alice fidgeted with her coat's torn sleeve strap as they hoisted the man's dead weight onto a white-sheeted trolley.

*Why did I follow them in here? I'm bloody well stuck here now.*

"I'll fetch Doctor K.," Beardy called over his shoulder as he disappeared through the curtain.

Fresh-face Scrubs gave Alice a closed-lipped smile. "Doctor should be here in just a moment, okay?" he said before swooshing out and leaving her alone with the man.

Not a groan from him now, just the rhythmic wheeze of air in and out of his hairy nostrils. *At least he's still breathing.*

Alice stepped closer and examined the man's crease-laden face in the harsh lighting. Unkempt salt-and-pepper hair, bushy eyebrows, and under his eyes, purple bags that drooped so heavily they looked all set for a backpacking trip around Europe.

"What's your story, hey?" whispered Alice.

The man breathed.

Alice looked down at her scuffed heels and tutted. They had sunk her into the depths of her overdraft, but

Fran adored her calves in heels and insisted Alice wear them to bed. So these beauties had been worth every penny; at least she'd thought so at the time. *Now they're ruined, but then so's everything else.* Suddenly aware of the stinging scratch on her forearm, Alice pulled up her sleeve and rubbed the claw marks etched into her skin.

A woman's voice with a Northern lilt came from the other side of the curtain, snatching Alice from her spiralling thoughts. "Er, why aren't there any details for Bay Five? Seriously, guys..." She released a frustrated groan, and the curtain clattered open.

"Oh, sorry. I didn't expect... you. I mean, there isn't any information for Bay Five, so I assumed they were alone." The woman's dark eyes flicked between her clipboard and Alice. She cleared her throat and extended her hand. "Sorry, let me start that again. I'm Doctor Khurana, and you are?"

"Alice French." She shook the doctor's hand, which was warm and soft. And not smeared with blood and dirt like her own which, once released, she buried in her coat pocket.

The doctor moved around the bedside. She lifted the man's eyelids with her thumb and shone a light into each unresponsive eye. The torchlight flashed over the bloodied gash on the man's forehead and Alice winced.

"So, Alice French. Who do we have here?"

"I have literally no idea. I found him in the road as I was driving."

"Where?"

"Just home after a disastrous evening with—"

"No, I meant which road?" The doctor gave a short laugh.

"Oh, sorry. I'm not sure of the road. I'm not the best with directions. Somewhere between Clopton and Snitter-field, I think. He was curled up in a ball and groaning. I couldn't phone for help as I had no signal, so I somehow bundled him into my car and brought him here."

The doctor paused over the man. She craned her neck around to look at Alice, turning her attention to the scuffed shoes. Her eyes trailed up to Alice's ripped-stocking-covered knees, skimmed over Alice's coat and eventually arrived at her face.

*I must look a fright... like some cheap tart... or a hooker. God, she thinks I'm a hooker.* Alice shifted her weight and cursed the pinch of her toes in her ridiculous heels.

"Right. So you've no idea who he is or how he came to be in the middle of the road near Snitterfield?" The doctor frowned. Her eyes, the colour of dark chocolate, fixed Alice with a hard stare.

Alice shook her head and wondered whether now would be a good time to mention how the man came to get that nasty gash on his head. And that he'd probably have bruised ribs from her falling on top of him too.

"He had nothing else with him?" asked the doctor.

"Er... I haven't been through his pockets, so I don't know if he has a wallet or anything."

The doctor checked the pockets of the man's muddy trousers and shook her head.

Alice folded her arms over her chest, conscious of the scant attire underneath her coat.

The doctor massaged the heel of her hand into her forehead and sighed. "Okay. Well, thank you for your help, Ms French. It was kind of you to bring him in and wait, most people don't bother."

"So, I'm free to go?"

"I don't see why not. It's late and you look like you've had a rough evening yourself."

"Yeah, you could say that."

The warmth in the doctor's eyes betrayed her lips, which she held in a tight, professional smile. "Maybe if I could grab your number?"

Alice grinned. "Oh, er... sorry, I'm seeing someone. Well, at least I was until tonight, but..."

The doctor's neat eyebrows drew together. "I mean, in case we need to get in touch. We'll contact the police and see if anyone has filed a missing person report. They may have some questions for you."

Heat rose in Alice's cheeks. "Oh, sorry. Yeah. Sure. Whatever you need." Alice took the proffered pen and scribbled her number onto the clipboard. "I'm not sure about talking to the police. I mean, I haven't done anything wrong, have I?"

The doctor narrowed her eyes. "You tell me."

Alice swallowed but failed to suppress the surge of panic unleashed by the doctor's suspicious eyes. "I, er... I don't think—"

"Look, it's fine." The doctor reached out. "You've done the right thing bringing him here. You've clearly had a difficult evening. Go home, get yourself... together and have some rest. Someone will be in touch if they need to speak to you."

Something about the warm and reassuring weight of Doctor Khurana's hand on Alice's arm made her want to cry.

"Are you okay?" she asked, her eyes searching Alice's.

For a moment, Alice contemplated telling this kind doctor that she wasn't okay, she really wasn't. She was tired and heartbroken. And aching from dragging the man into her car. She didn't want a phone call from the police; she wanted a hug. And a cup of tea brought to her whilst she lay in a hot bath—

The man groaned.

Alice and the doctor looked at each other and then at the man. His eyelids fluttered, and he opened his mouth.

"He's trying to say something." The doctor rushed to his side and leaned her ear over his chapped lips.

Alice stepped back to the edge of the bed. "What? What is it?"

"It sounds like he's saying... *pig*."

## 1963

### SHE ALREADY HAS A NAME

*W*hen I turned eight and my brother turned five, our mother treated us to an extra-special birthday present. In fact, it was the best present we ever got as kids.

Bernard and I were born exactly three years apart on the second of April. *Not quite fools, but little bastards* — at least according to our grandmother.

Despite being a pretty bright lad for my age, the penny didn't drop until the school Biology syllabus arrived at reproduction and the human gestation period. The enlightening lesson led me to conclude that there must be some significant annual event resulting in our shared birthday. Desperate to get to the bottom of my existential puzzle, I embarked on a detective trail, following clues until the answer became "bloody obvious." Or at least that was how I'd pitched it when presenting the evidence back to Bernard with my chalkboard-pointing ruler in hand.

"Due to the timing, it couldn't have been Father Christmas. And if it were the Easter Bunny, I reckon we'd look a bit different." I bucked my teeth and made my fingers into rabbit ears above my head, which made Bernard burst into giggles.

Very few men visited Charcroft House, but one who had left an impression was Bill, the jolly chap who came to sweep the household's chimneys every July. A filthy job, and thirsty work, and so it seemed that our mother had quenched more than just Bill's need for a drink.

A jaunty smile never left Bill's ruddy face, and we liked him because he could magically produce gold-foil-wrapped toffees from thin air.

"Ta-da!" he'd say and present the sweets to us as our mother smiled on, her hazel eyes twinkling as we basked in the warmth of the kind gesture. Bill smelt like soap, but he always looked dirty — no doubt thanks to the chimneys — and he had a round belly that strained the buttons of his shirt — no doubt thanks to the toffees.

Even if it made no difference to our circumstances, at the time we thought we'd worked out where we'd come from. And by my reckoning, if I knew who my father was, it made me less of a bastard. One day I would shake Bill's hand and thank him for "knocking up my mother... twice" — at least that's how our grandmother had put it.

Anyway, back to the birthday present. As always, we crept down the stairs, and there, in the centre of the drawing room, stood a large box. Bernard and I looked at each other, our eyes wide, eyebrows raised as we did the maths: one box, two boys.

As if a starting pistol had fired, we clambered through

the doorway, elbowing each other out of the way. I, being the older and ever-so-slightly brawnier, arrived at the box first. As I moved my hand to open the lid, a cough came from the doorway, and I spun around.

"George, wait."

I turned to look at our mother leaning against the doorjamb in her paint-spattered dungarees, her wavy nut-brown hair swept back in a yellow bandanna. She raised a thin roll-up to her rouged lips and took a long draw before she said,

"I need you to understand some things before you open that box, boys. It's a joint gift for both of you. You have to share."

Bernard whined.

"Bernard. It's important you understand you're not only sharing the joy of this gift, you'll also be sharing the burden. It comes with responsibilities."

Bernard frowned so hard his forehead almost twisted into a question mark.

"I want you both to understand how much effort is required to take care of another living thing. I want you to appreciate the sacrifices I make to take care of you."

I jiggled with impatience. "What's in the box?"

Mum opened her mouth to speak, but then the box barked.

I looked at Bernard's glee-filled face, a mirror of my own, and we darted forward, pulling open the lid and peering inside. A black and white bundle of fur stared back at us with eyes bright like shiny black pebbles. A tiny pink tongue flapped from its open mouth.

"A puppy!" squealed Bernard. The puppy barked again and jumped up at the side of the box, its sharp claws tearing into the cardboard.

"What shall we call him?" I asked, already shortlisting names in my head.

"*She* already has a name," said Mum. "She's called Pyg."

## 2

## SPRING HAS SPRUNG

*A*lice rubbed her eyes with the heels of her hands and hard-blinked when they came away black with the remnants of her mascara. The pink dawn glow backlit the hospital's multi-storey car park, blurring the straight lines of its brutalist concrete mass. Even her shitty little Ford Fiesta looked almost pretty in this early morning light.

Searching for her car keys, Alice rooted around in her Tardis-like tote bag until her fingers latched onto the source of the jangle. She chucked her bag onto the passenger side, hitched up her coat, and folded herself into the driver's seat. Condensation covered the windows from the late-night drive and the sweaty exertion of lugging the man into her car, but the heater would clear them soon enough and she'd be on her way. A hot cup of tea, followed by a shower. Then bed, where she could sleep away the rest of this disastrous weekend.

Alice turned the key in the ignition.

One false start.

Followed by another.

"C'mon, old girl." Alice gave the dashboard a coaxing rub. She turned her head, squeezed her right eye shut and gently twisted the key again. The engine spluttered and wheezed… then nothing.

"For fuck's sake," Alice screamed and lobbed the keys across the car. She collapsed over the steering wheel as drained as the car's dead battery. Exhaustion washed over her, leaving her too spent to even cry.

A light tapping sound roused Alice back to the present. She raised her head and could make out an outline through the steamy window.

"Alice, is that you? Are you okay?"

*Doctor Khurana.*

Alice groaned with the effort of manually winding down the window. The doctor's face jerked into view with each turn of the handle. She peered through the gap at Alice with tired eyes that radiated kindness.

"I heard screaming and, well… duty of care and all that."

"A spot of car trouble. Nothing to worry about. I'll er, call my brother-in-law in a while. I'm sure he won't mind popping out on a Saturday morning to give the old girl a jump." Alice shuddered at the thought of having to call Markus. *Prick.* And Maggie would be annoyed that Alice had still done nothing about replacing her shitty little car.

"Where are you headed?"

Alice sighed. "Home."

The doctor raised a questioning eyebrow.

"Leamington."

"I probably shouldn't do this, but I'm headed that way too. I can give you a lift, if you like? You look like you could do with some rest, and you could come back for your car later."

"Really?... I mean about the lift, not the rest. I can only imagine I look a state."

"Come on. My car's over there in the staff car park." Doctor Khurana tilted her head. "And you can trust me; I'm a doctor."

"But can you trust me, Doctor?"

One side of the doctor's mouth lifted in a wry smile. "No idea, but I'm not going to leave you stranded out here after you helped that man last night. One good deed deserves another. Karma, right?"

Alice smiled, too weary to put up a fight, hoping karma wouldn't come back and bite her in the arse for cracking the poor man's head open. She fished for her keys in the passenger footwell and scooped up her bag. The doctor creaked the door open and offered her hand as Alice struggled to her feet in her ridiculous heels.

"It's Asha, by the way. Or Ash, if you like."

"Alice."

Ash grinned. "Alice French, I know."

Alice had no idea what make or model it was, but unlike her car, which smelled like a damp dog even though she didn't have one, Ash's sporty little vehicle smelt of vanilla and leather. And unlike Alice's car, it didn't splutter and die, but roared into life when Ash pressed the ignition. Fran would've approved... of the engine's roar, not of Ash.

Fran wouldn't approve of Alice getting a lift from an attractive stranger, even if that stranger was a doctor and she was just being nice. But then, Fran had no right to know anything about what Alice did any more.

*Fran can fuck all the way off.*

Ash gave Alice a sidelong glance. "Are you warm enough?"

Alice nodded, even though she was shivering. Ash fiddled with the buttons in the centre console, and warm air pumped through the vents. "Better?"

"Much. Thank you."

Ash flicked on the stereo and a way-too-cheerful DJ's voice piped through the speakers, which she turned down to a comfortable background hum. Alice blinked through her tiredness and fixed her gaze out of the window. Dewy mist rose from a patchwork of fields in the now orange light of daybreak.

"Looks like it's going to be a nice spring day."

"Mmm." Alice didn't take her eyes off the landscape rolling by.

"I think it's my favourite season, spring. I love the way nature reanimates everything; all that fresh new life... and the longer days are always welcome." Ash tapped her thumbs on the steering wheel to the soft beat of the song on the radio.

Alice turned and took in her profile; her straight nose, the soft curve of her jaw, her glossy black shoulder-length hair now hanging loose and tucked behind her pierced ear.

Ash glanced at Alice and grinned a crooked smile. "What? Why are you looking at me like that?"

"You're way too full of the joys of spring for someone who's just got off a night shift. Aren't you shattered?"

Ash laughed. "I'm used to it. It's my routine. The lighter days really do help, though. I've even been known to hit the gym before going home, especially if it's been an eventful shift."

"And was it?"

"What?"

"An eventful shift?"

Ash's eyes flicked between Alice and the road. Her long, dark eyelashes fluttered as her lips twisted into a smile. "Yeah, it's not every day a mysterious woman turns up with an unconscious man."

Alice stifled a laugh. "I'm not mysterious."

"Well, it was all a bit odd, you have to admit."

"Mmm, I guess so. I honestly did just find him in the road, like I told you."

"I believe you." Ash frowned and bit her lip. "Earlier you said your evening had been disastrous. How so, if you don't mind me asking?"

Alice drew in a deep breath, and released it through her nose. "I think I broke up with my... with my someone."

"You did, or you just think you did?"

"Well, I left. I got into my car, and I drove away. I've never done that before. And I don't feel the desire to go running back, so I'm pretty sure it's over."

"Had you been together long?"

"Long enough. I didn't realise I wanted it to be over... but it really wasn't going anywhere, so what's the point?"

Ash's face set into a frown. "Sounds like you've made a tough choice, but a good one?"

Alice nodded. "I think so. It must be, because I don't even feel sad about it at the moment... I feel relieved, actually."

"There you go then. You've done the right thing if you feel that way." Ash flashed her crooked smile again, and it elicited a flutter in Alice's chest.

*Seriously, Alice? The first person who happens to be nice to you?* She turned and looked out of the window, chewing the inside of her lip. "I'm forty-two, for fuck's sake. It's about time I got my shit together."

"Well, your timing's good; spring's the season of fresh starts."

"Yeah, maybe you're right." Alice gave the doctor a small smile.

"Change nothing, and nothing changes. Someone wiser than me said that, but it's a good way to be. You know, take control and go after the things you want."

"Is that what you do?" Alice asked and bit the inside of her lip again as a punishment for flirting.

Ash didn't answer the question, but a smile flickered in her eyes, and she turned up the volume on the car stereo. "I love this," she said and drummed her thumbs on the steering wheel in time to the beat of an Annie Lennox song.

Alice pointed at the windscreen. "You need to go left after the lights."

By the end of the track, they'd pulled up on the road

outside an imposing cream building, its rendered facade characterised by vast windows and a grand entrance.

Ash whistled. "Is this really where you live? It's dead posh."

"It looks fancy from the outside, but I only have a little one-bed flat in there. I don't even get to use the front door. My place is around the back and up the stairs."

"That's Leamington for you, all fancy from the outside." Ash turned to face her with eyes watering as she stifled a yawn in her palm.

Alice gathered up her bag and jangled her keys in her coat pocket. "Thanks again for the lift... and the chat. It was good to talk about it. I'd invite you in for a coffee, but I don't have any milk..."

Ash raised a polite hand to decline before Alice had finished making an excuse.

"Or coffee."

Ash exhaled a laugh. "Honestly, it was no trouble at all. I hope you get everything sorted with your car... and your life." Her kind smile told Alice she meant the 'sort your life out' thing in a nice way. And there was that little flutter in her chest again.

*Stop it, Alice. Get a grip.*

ALICE LEANED ON THE FRONT DOOR UNTIL IT closed behind her. She dropped her keys on the console table and gasped as she met her reflection in the mirror. Dark smudges circled her eyes, and her bedraggled blonde curls told the tale of a sleepless night. She turned her face to examine a gory smear of blood across her cheek; the man's blood, not hers. Even so, she looked like she'd taken part in some sort of ritualistic ceremony, where she'd sacrificed a virgin or three.

It occurred to her she'd been chatting away to that nice doctor whilst looking completely deranged. Despite her internal chaos, Alice was normally well put together at least. She hiccupped a maniacal laugh, which added to her overall unhinged aesthetic.

What the hell must the doctor have thought of her? And how horrified Fran would be if she could see her now. For a split second, Alice considered whipping out her phone to send Fran a selfie, but she didn't care about fucking Fran any more, so she set her phone face-down next to her keys.

Alice kicked off her heels and wiggled her liberated toes on the Victorian-tiled floor, relishing the coolness on her burning soles. She fixed her gaze on the patent heels; her beautiful, disgustingly expensive Louboutins. *Ruined.* Why had she wasted so much money on them? She had loved them — how they made her feel, how much they'd excited Fran. But now she had to admit they'd hurt her, too; they'd really fucking hurt her. A sob threatened to escape her throat, but she swallowed it down and looked her reflection in the panda-eyes.

"No. No more." Alice snatched up the shoes and fumbled with the front door. When the lock sprung free, she flung it open and launched the heels outside. She pinched her lips together as the Louboutins clattered down the steps and, after one last sorry glance in their direction, she slammed the door shut.

"Right. That's that then." Alice picked up her phone, swiped past the red-dot deluge of missed calls and texts from Fran, and took a photo of her swollen feet as a reminder not to buy any more ridiculous fucking heels.

A reminder not to make herself uncomfortable for anyone else, ever again.

"Spring has sprung."

# FRANCESCA DALTON

## NINE MONTHS EARLIER

*A* giddy ball of excitement bounced around in Alice's stomach as she stepped through the door of The Dog & Duck. Her eyes scanned the room and settled on Fran, sitting in the corner, all pouting red lips and chestnut curls which skimmed the shoulders of her crisp white shirt.

Age had done nothing to diminish the older woman's beauty and elegance — if anything, the opposite was true. At fifty-six, she was practically a goddess, her sculpted olive skin smooth over her high cheekbones and jawline.

Fran tossed her head back and drained the crimson liquid from her glass. She flicked her wrist and stared at her watch, which prompted Alice to glance at her own.

"Where have you been?" Fran's obsidian eyes set on Alice as she approached.

"It's three p.m. You said to meet you here at three p.m."

"I know I did. But I'd hoped you'd come earlier."

Alice felt the smile slipping from her face.

"Never mind. I'm just not used to waiting." Fran stood, gripped Alice's shoulders, and pecked a kiss on her cheek, so hard it almost hurt. Alice inhaled the rich, musky scent of her, which lingered in her wake when she retook her seat.

"Are you going to sit down or just stand there looking pretty?" asked Fran.

"Er, yeah. Of course." Alice smiled. "Shall I fetch you another drink first?"

Fran patted the bench next to her. "Sit."

As Alice slipped out of her coat, Fran waved her arm until she got the barmaid's attention and gestured for two more of the same. "You're fine with the Merlot, aren't you?"

Alice nodded and eased her long legs, courtesy of her heels, under the table.

Fran breathed through her nose and stared straight ahead as she placed a hand on Alice's thigh. "Is this the skirt I bought for you?"

"Yeah, do you think it's a bit short?"

Fran answered by squeezing Alice's soft flesh and edging her slender fingers higher, their French-manicured tips scratching into her skin ever-so-slightly. Heat surged through Alice and Fran grinned, fully aware of the effect she was having.

"There you go." The barmaid placed their drinks on the table and scooped up the empty glass. Fran's hand fell away.

"So, you said you had something to tell me?" Alice lightly tugged at the hem of her skirt.

Fran reached for her wine and took a swig. "Well, that's a mood killer."

"Sorry." Alice sipped from her own glass and winced. She'd never been one for red wine, but she was trying really hard to like it for Fran.

"No, no. It's quite alright. I do need to talk to you." Fran twisted around to face her. "It's about Jeremy." She pressed her lips into a thin line.

"Oh?" Alice took a mouthful of wine, but her throat refused to swallow it. She couldn't spit it back into the glass, so she held the tart liquid in her mouth.

Fran sniffed. "I'm leaving him."

Alice coughed, and her eyes widened with horror as she spluttered wine over Fran's pristine shirt. The muscles twitched in Fran's clenched jaw as she breathed loudly through her nose.

"Oh fuck. Let me..." Like a shit magician, Alice produced a string of balled-up tissues from her handbag and dabbed at the red splotches sprayed across Fran's chest. "God, Fran. I'm so sorry. It's soda water for red wine, isn't it? Or is it salt? I'll get some—"

"No. Leave it. I'm not letting you season me like a hog roast." Fran snatched hold of Alice's wrists and fixed her into place with a piercing stare.

Alice bowed her head as hot tears prickled in her eyes and static fizzed in her ears.

Fran reached up and pinched Alice's chin between her thumb and index finger. Alice peered through her eyelashes and met Fran's dark eyes, surprised to see desire flickering in them.

"How about we go to that little B&B up the road, and I'll get some of your clothes wet, too?" Fran said in a low growl. "And once we're even, I'll tell you all about how I'm leaving my husband."

3

## FIESTA FAIL

lice tipped her head back, relishing the steaming water splashing off her body. She vigorously scrubbed her skin, trying to erase any trace of Fran, holding back the urge to cry as the last of the soapsuds circled and chased each other down the plughole.

After frowning at the discarded tangle of lacy lingerie in the corner of her bedroom, Alice pulled on slim-fitting jeans with a loose grey sweatshirt, quite the contrast to yesterday's outfit.

She thought about the state of herself last night, and flushed with relief that she'd decided against sending a selfie to Fran; she didn't need another regret to add to the pile.

In the hallway mirror, Alice examined her reflection. Her tired blue-grey eyes stared back, but at least she looked herself. She tucked a spiral of curls behind her ear. Even her own hair reminded her of Fran and how she'd once said she had curls like Marilyn Monroe, and the figure to match — a compliment which had made Alice feel like a million dollars.

She sighed and liberally spritzed on perfume, specifically the citrusy one Fran disliked because it made her throat itch. A notification pinged to say the Uber had arrived; Alice slipped on some flats and headed out.

On her way down the steep stairway, Alice bent and scooped up the scattered Louboutins; they'd been rained on overnight and looked sorrier than ever. But even a good night's sleep hadn't changed her mind. Yes, putting them on eBay might fetch her a few quid, but casually depositing them amongst the black bags in the shared bin on her way to the taxi gave her much greater satisfaction.

At the hospital, Alice decided to try the Fiesta again before making a tit of herself with Maggie and Markus. After a promising cough, the engine spluttered and choked. Then nothing. Alice sighed and rested her head on the steering wheel. Behind her closed eyelids, Ash crashed into her thoughts and her lips threatened a smile.

*Stop it.*

Alice's empty stomach growled, so she sat up straight and decided to call Maggie from inside the hospital. *Surely they have a café? Maggie and Markus should not be dealt with on an empty stomach.*

As Alice moved aside to shut the door, she caught sight of something black and furry in the rear passenger footwell. *What the—?*

She dashed around the vehicle and yanked open the passenger door, exhaling a breath and flicking her hands as she summoned the courage to nudge the furry mass with her foot. It moved, and she screamed, jumping back and clutching a hand to her chest.

*Oh! It's a bloody coat.* Laughing, Alice bundled the man's jacket over her arm. *An excuse to see the doctor again.*

"HELLO, AGAIN." ALICE SMILED AT THE MAN AND crossed the room toward the vinyl padded chair next to the bed. "I'm sorry, but in the confusion of last night, I completely forgot your coat was still in my car."

The man lay completely still, aside from the rise and fall of his broad chest, covered in the starched cloth of a hospital gown. The wound on his forehead had been cleaned and his flesh puckered against the sutures, lined up like a crimson track. It would probably scar, but it wasn't as gruesome as it had looked last night.

The man's unkempt hair and beard had been brushed and his face appeared less lined, like the wrinkles had somehow been smoothed out. Not those heavy bags under his eyes though; they still shone the deep purple of plums.

"We're both looking a lot less dishevelled than we did yesterday, that's for sure. But I suppose you'll have to take my word for it."

Alice shuffled the disposable coffee cup between her hands and placed the man's coat over the arm of the chair.

"Well, I suppose I'll leave you in peace." She looked around the room, her gaze settling on the clock above the door. 11:45 a.m.

*What time do the doctors change shifts? It's probably too early and who's to say she's even rostered for today? Oh well, I really ought to call Maggie and beg for Markus to come and help with the car. But begging before midday? So undignified. Unless it were with Fran—* Alice shook her head to halt that line of thought.

"Don't suppose you mind if I sit for a moment?"

The man didn't flinch, which Alice took as an invitation to take a seat. She crossed her legs, angling herself towards the bed, cupping her cold hands around the cardboard cup.

"This coffee is awful. Bitter enough to wake the dead. There's a thought — perhaps I'll suggest they trickle this through your drip?" She chuckled at her suggestion.

"I really should get on my way and leave you to sleep." Alice took a tentative sip of the coffee and grimaced. "I'm putting off calling my sister, to be honest. She'll be annoyed at me for disturbing Markus' Saturday golf plans. He'll be such a prick about it, too." Alice cleared her throat and imitated a plummy deep voice. "For God's sake, Mags, tell me we don't have to bail out your useless sister from her latest disaster." She picked at the edge of the plastic lid with her chipped fingernail. "The worst part is they're not wrong... I am useless. I should've prioritised sorting out a car, and not blowing every penny I earn on ridiculous shit to impress Fran. And she's not exactly easy to impress. Fran is what you'd call *high maintenance*, you know the sort?"

The man didn't respond.

"Women, eh? I'm sure you'd have some sage advice,

Mr..." Alice glanced up at the whiteboard above the bed. *Patient X* had been scrawled in black marker in the box in place of the man's name.

"Patient X? It doesn't really suit you." Alice tilted her head and narrowed her eyes, scanning the man's face. "You know, you look a little like Hugh Laurie... when he'd grown a beard for that role. Quite dapper, in a rugged sort of way."

The man did nothing to receive the compliment.

Alice yawned and slouched into the chair. "Perhaps the X is short for something? How about Xavier?... Xavier, like saviour, although it probably doesn't mean that and actually, I saved you." Alice laughed. "I've never saved anyone before, so thank you for the opportunity to do something useful for once. I mean, apart from causing you a head injury, of course."

An enormous sigh heaved from the man's chest and Alice sat forward so fast her empty cup dropped and rolled across the floor. The man mumbled a string of words, of which Alice could only make out one: *pig*.

## 1963

### COWARDLY SWINE

*M*y grandmother's acidic voice hissed through the gap in the doorway like a gas leak and I pressed my ear between the banisters.

"I don't know what you were thinking bringing that... that thing into my home. It'll be full of fleas or mange. Probably both. Get rid of it, or I will."

Mum laughed, and I scrunched my eyes shut, waiting for the sound of the slap of my grandmother's hand across her face. But it didn't come.

And that was a bad thing as it meant worse was brewing.

"*That thing* is no concern of yours. Pyg doesn't have fleas, and she doesn't have mange. The boys will look after her, so you need not worry."

"Those boys are—"

"Don't."

"I know exactly what you're doing, Eleanor. You think

you're so clever, pecking away at me. You think it'll finish me, don't you? Peck, peck, peck until I'm gone and then you and those little swines will have all this."

Mum scoffed. "All this? Have you opened your eyes in the last twenty years? This place is in ruins because you're too tight to—"

"How dare you! I give you and those little runts a roof over your head. From my own coffers, I fund your life of privilege and comfort."

"A life of shabby-genteel poverty more like. I'm only here until—"

"Until what? Until that dirty lump of a man comes to whisk you into the sunset?" She expelled a wicked laugh, and I could picture the sneer of her lips as they twisted around her spiteful words. "Well, he hasn't come for you yet, has he? You just lay back and let him have his filthy way, you silly little whore."

I didn't know what a *whore* was, but coming from my grandmother, it wouldn't be a compliment.

"Mother, Mother. For the last time, whores get paid. I did it for free and I enjoyed every glorious minute." She laughed, clearly pleased with whatever reaction her words had provoked on my grandmother's face. I could almost see my grandmother's mouth puckering in disgust like she'd bitten into a lemon.

"Imagine, my daughter rolling around with that bit of rough. Could you have sunk any lower? I shouldn't have listened to Father Higgins." Her shrill voice drifted back and forth as she paced. "When you got pregnant, I

33

should've sent you off to Ireland to one of those laundry places for disgusting girls who can't keep their legs shut—"

"Oh, shut up, Sylvia."

My grandmother sharply inhaled. "If your father were still here—"

"What? You wouldn't be such a twisted old recluse?"

My body clenched at the sound of the slap. It must have been a hard one, as Mum gasped. Anxiety twisted in my gut, but then she laughed again; my mother really didn't know what was good for her sometimes.

The stairs behind me creaked, and I spun around. My little brother stood frozen, his eyes wide with horror. I raised a finger to my lips, then patted the threadbare carpet next to me. Bernard tiptoed down and squeezed up close.

"Are they fighting?" he whispered.

I nodded. "Where's Pyg?"

"I shut her in the bedroom like you said to."

"Good lad." I hugged an arm around him.

Bernard jutted his chin towards the kitchen door. "Will she be alright?"

"She always is."

THE DOORBELL CHIMED WITH THREE SHORT RINGS. Bernard and I stood up from where we'd sat on the stairs, awaiting our visitor. Our hair was combed, and we were wearing shirts, shorts, and polished shoes — our Sunday best. Mum hopped down the hallway, muttering something inaudible under her breath, a zesty scent trailing behind her. She stopped for a quick glance in the hallway mirror, scrunching her fingers in her hair and pinching at the edges of her rouged lips. She turned to us as she wiped her palms on her apron.

"Boys, have you shut Pyg in the studio?"

We nodded and stood straight as Mum opened the front door.

"Henry," she said, her voice low and warm.

"Hello, El." The priest stepped inside, his hand grazing Mum's arm as he passed.

"Hello, Father Higgins," Bernard and I said in unison.

"My goodness, have you grown since last month? George, you must be a whole head taller." The priest's face split into a wide grin.

Bernard beamed as Father Higgins patted his head.

"I'll see you both in a while," the priest whispered and gave us a wink.

Mum led him through to the drawing room, Bernard and I followed, but stopped to hover in the doorway. Grandmother's sour face lit up at the sight of the clergyman.

"Father Higgins, how wonderful to see you. Oh, I have been looking forward to our prayers and discourse. Eleanor, fetch the tea, will you? Father must be parched." She flicked her twiggy wrist, dismissing Mum. Father Higgins turned and threw her a small smile, unseen by my grandmother.

Mum playfully nudged me as she passed. Father Higgins folded his tall frame into the armchair opposite our grandmother. The afternoon sunlight streamed through the high sash windows, shining on the priest and making his blonde hair glow like a halo. He leaned forward and took the old woman's hand, which elicited a rare smile from her lips.

"How are you, Mrs Shaw?"

Her fleeting smile fell away. "Oh, Father, I'm grateful you're here. It's been a testing time, what with Eleanor and those little b... boys, and now she's gone and got them a dog, would you believe? My patience has worn thin." She released a haughty groan. "I try, I do try. But they push me to the very edge..." Her willowy voice withered into an anguished sob.

The priest's gaze flicked to us in the doorway, but his face reflected nothing but empathy for the old woman as he appraised her with his blue eyes. He continued to hold her liver-spotted hand.

I clenched my fists as the injustice of it all pulsed through me. *The old witch never tries. She's nothing but vile to all of us. Why does Father Higgins buy this crap?*

"Well, God's will is that we are patient and kind to those in our charge. It's these challenges we're faced with that present our truest test of character. This week, shall we read from the New Testament for a change, perhaps Corinthians?"

The old woman nodded solemnly.

"Excuse me, boys." Mum strode past, holding an ornate tea tray. Grandmother huffed and sat back as our mother placed the cups and saucers on the table and poured the tea.

"Milk, Father?" she asked with a smile that shone through her eyes.

The priest nodded.

"No milk for me. Where's the lemon?"

"I shall fetch it now, Mother." Mum strained her words through gritted teeth.

Grandmother tutted, Mum ignored it and smiled at the priest again.

"I baked, Father. It's a new recipe from the Women's Institute with lemon and poppyseed. Would you like a slice?"

"That would be—"

Grandmother slammed her hand on the table, and the teaspoon clattered off her saucer. "There's no time for all that fuss and nonsense. Just leave us to it, Eleanor. Father Higgins will be out to take your confession afterwards, and to give his lessons to the boys. But this is my time."

Mum nodded and turned to leave.

Grandmother pinched the bridge of her nose and inhaled quick breaths. "On second thoughts, Father, no Corinthians today. I'd like to hear from Isaiah, please. Or anything about adulterers. The Book of Revelation, perhaps? That's the New Testament, yes. Yes, that would—"

Mum clicked the door shut behind her, closing off the conversation.

"C'mon, boys. Let's have some cake in the studio whilst we wait for Father Higgins."

"Can Pyg have cake too?" Bernard asked, as Mum shepherded his slight frame away from the drawing room.

"Of course. In fact, she can have Grandma's slice!"

Bernard giggled.

I couldn't summon a smile with fresh rage pulsing through me. *How could Father Higgins just sit there and say nothing? That cowardly swine.*

# SERENDIPITY

## 1953

"*E*leanor! The door!" Sylvia's screech from the drawing room pulled Ella from her trance, mesmerised as she was by the late afternoon sunlight dappling through the sycamore, its leaves aflame with a glorious display of reds and yellows before winter stripped it bare.

With a sigh, Ella pulled her hands from the soapy water in the sink and dried them on her apron, which she whipped over her head and hung on the hook in the pantry.

"Eleanor!"

"Yes, Mother," Ella called out as she made her way to the front door, tilting her head at the patterned glass panels which distorted the figure waiting beyond — it looked like a real-life Picasso if she squinted hard enough. The person waiting outside stood tall and looked entirely unlike the squat, frumpy outline of Father Harries, whom they'd been expecting.

The door creaked as Ella swung it open, and she raised her arm to shield her eyes from the low sun, blinking into the face of a young man who blinked back at her.

*No, nothing at all like Father Harries.*

"Hello?"

"Hello," he said with a smile that pushed deep dimples into his cheeks. Ella couldn't help but smile back at this handsome stranger.

"Can I help you?"

"Right, yes. I'm from St. Mary's." The smooth, rich timbre of his voice was at odds with his cherubic looks. He extended a hand toward her, and Ella shook it limply, her face no doubt the picture of puzzlement.

"Miss Shaw, is it?"

Ella nodded.

"I've been sent to visit you and your mother—"

"Where's Father Harries?"

"I'm sorry, I should've started with that. I'm afraid he's taken ill, poor soul."

"Oh, is he alright?"

"A suspected stroke." He drew in a sharp breath. "He's stable and they've moved him to the clergy house in Warwick for convalescence, so I'll be taking over his duties at St. Mary's, for the time being, at least."

"But you're..." Ella frowned as her eyes roved over the man's face.

"I'm what?"

"So young." Thankfully, she didn't say *and handsome,* but the implication hung in the air between them.

"Yes, I suppose I am, at least compared to some of my

colleagues. I can assure you, though, I'm fully qualified." He pulled down the neckline of his knitted grey jumper to reveal a dog collar. "See? Bona fide priest. They don't hand these out to just anyone, you know?"

"Right. Well, in that case, we'd better start again. Eleanor, or Ella, if you'd rather." She held out her hand to shake his with a much firmer grip this time.

"Father Higgins, or Henry, if you'd rather."

"Henry Higgins?" Ella giggled, stepping aside to allow him in.

"That's right."

"Like the professor in *Pygmalion*."

"I'm sorry, who?"

"You know, the play *Pygmalion* by George Bernard Shaw?"

The young priest shook his head.

"Never mind. I just thought it a funny coincidence. I'm a Shaw, and you have the same name as the professor, Henry Higgins."

"Ha, yes. Well, I suppose that is a coincidence. Alas, I'm not a professor, just a priest."

*Alas.* They locked eyes and something unspoken passed between them. Colour filled the priest's dimpled cheeks, and he looked away.

"This er, play, Pig...?"

"*Pygmalion.*"

"Yes. What's it about?"

Ella inhaled a big breath. "I'd say it's about a transformation. A young woman realising her self-worth in a flawed social class system."

"I see... And this Professor Higgins, is he a good sort?"

Ella grinned. "He's a pompous twit."

Laughter brimmed in the young priest's vibrant blue eyes. "Oh, right. Well, hopefully you don't think that of me."

"We'll see," Ella giggled and added, "I'll lend you my copy of the play if you like. It's a bit battered, and there's a lot of scrawl in the margins, but I think you'll enjoy it."

"Thank you, Eleanor — Ella. I shall look forward to that." He smiled and his impossible dimples deepened. "It's really quite something, serendipity. It bolsters one's faith in a bigger plot. The grand designer colliding us together in a magnificent plan."

He pointed an index finger towards the ceiling, and Ella's eyes followed the motion before realising what he was referring to. Her own faith had been shaken; you could say that her relationship with God was going through a bit of a rough patch. They hadn't spoken since her father died, and she was still rather cross about all that, but perhaps here stood the answer.

"Sorry, I'm told I can get a little carried away with my theologising..."

"No, I like it," she said, and realised she meant it. So rare was good company that she didn't want to burst this bubble by handing him over, but her mother would be growing impatient so Ella should spare him the wrath. She gestured for the priest to follow her. "Shall we?"

The priest visibly gulped. "Your mother, I've heard she can be a bit... how do I put it politely?"

"Caustic?" Ella smirked.

"Yes, I suppose that's not too impolite."

"You needn't worry. She admires a man of the cloth." Ella chuckled. "Once she's got over the shock of you not being Father Harries, I think she'll be quite taken with you."

The priest's long lashes flickered as if batting away the compliment.

"Papa seemed to soften her sharp edges. When he didn't return after the war, Mother's ferocity took root. She allowed her world to close in, and now struggles with company, mine being no exception."

The priest frowned. "But you, Ella, you're so..." He breathed heavily through his nose, as if trying to puff out the right words to describe her, "...upbeat," he eventually offered.

Ella laughed. "I won't lie. It's a struggle, but I try to hang onto my positivity and sanity as best I can."

"I don't mean to pry, but is there no one else to support you?"

Ella shook her head. "I'm all she has left. Just me and her faith."

"What more could she possibly want?" The priest's smile stretched to his eyes, and he reached out and touched her forearm.

She glanced at his hand as he held it there, his heat emanating through her skin, into her flesh; somehow warming through to her bones.

Sylvia's voice shrieked, "Eleanor! What's keeping you?"

"Right, we'd better..."

"Yes."

The look between them lingered longer than it should have.

"Coming, Mother!" Ella pitched her voice to carry into the drawing room. "Father Harries has taken ill. St. Mary's have sent us Father Higgins instead." With a small smile, Ella motioned for the priest to enter the room.

"Tea, Father?"

1963

PIGTAILS AND LIPS

*Pick of the Pops* scratched out of the paint-splattered speaker of the transistor, and the three of us went about our usual business in the studio.

Mum called it her studio, but it was just a stone outbuilding which she'd transformed into a cosy home away from the place we couldn't really call home. Knitted blankets and scattered cushions dressed the two sagging armchairs, and Mum's colourful canvases brightened the dank walls. On colder days, she served us hot blackcurrant cordial and home-baked biscuits as we listened to the latest songs playing on the radio. The studio smelt mossy and damp, but also like sweet tobacco and oil paints, and we always felt safe tucked away in there because the dragon never left its own cave to enter ours.

The song spun from Gerry and the Pacemakers into the current number one.

"Crank it up, Bernie," said Mum. Bernard dropped his colouring pencil and dashed to the red radio on the window ledge. He twisted the knob as far as it would go, blasting the opening bars of *From Me to You* from the tinny little speaker.

Beatlemania had swept the country, and our tiny corner of it was no exception.

Mum bopped her hips and thrust her hands down to me, where I sat atop a huge, knitted floor cushion with a book perched on my knees. I shot her a sullen look of protest, but still, I let her pull me to my feet.

"C'mon, Georgie. You'll trip over that bottom lip if you're not careful."

I half-smiled despite myself and shuffled my feet as Mum waved mine and Bernard's arms in time to the beat. Pyg jumped around us, her tail swooshing like a bushy black metronome. Bernard sang the lyrics word-perfectly, accompanied by the occasional excited bark from Pyg. I mumbled along, self-conscious, but I felt my bad mood lifting as we all collapsed onto the floor cushions, laughing and breathless.

A light knock at the door snatched our attention.

"That'll be Father Higgins." Mum stood, smoothing her skirt, and reaching up to tidy her hair as she moved to the radio and clicked it off. "Come on in, Father," she said to the door.

The priest ducked under the low doorway and unfolded himself into the room, his presence filling more than just the space he occupied. Pyg bowled over to him, circling his legs, and he bent to ruffle her floppy ears.

"So, how is everyone doing?" he asked as he eased himself down into the armchair.

I shrugged and sank back onto my cushion. I eyed them over the top of my book, somewhat irked that Bernard had rushed to the priest's side and Pyg was curled at his feet.

"Father, do you like The Beatles? They're at number one in the pop charts."

"Bernie, dear, give Father Higgins a moment to settle in. The poor chap has had quite the afternoon of it, no doubt. Can I make you some tea, Father?" Mum smiled and pulled Bernard to her hip, stroking down his blonde hair where it stubbornly sat up at the crown.

"Oh, it's fine. Yes, Bernard. I do like The Beatles, but they're not my favourite band. And I'd love a cuppa, El. If it wasn't a deadly sin, I'd kill for a slice of that cake you were offering around earlier."

"Murder won't be necessary," Mum giggled, her cheeks still flushed from dancing. "But, on the other hand, if you were offering to dispatch a certain person, I wouldn't say no."

Father Higgins raised his eyebrows. "I don't know about murder, but I sent her off into a deep sleep with dark tales of all the hellfire and brimstone awaiting us sinners." A smile quirked his lips.

Mum hummed as she struck a match and lit the camping stove for the kettle. Father Higgins rested his head back and closed his eyes. Bernard, who was still standing by the priest's side, tapped his arm.

"What do you mean, they're not your favourite?"

The priest opened one eye and looked at him. "What?"

"You said The Beatles aren't your favourite band. Who is your favourite, then?"

Father Higgins chuckled. "Oh, I quite like The Beach Boys."

I scoffed from my cushion. "The Beach Boys? One-hit wonders, I'd say."

"I don't know, George. They're pretty cool. I think they'll go far." He puckered his lips and whistled the tune to *Surfin' U.S.A.* Bernard giggled and joined in. *A traitor, like that bloody dog.*

I shook my head, returning my gaze to the book I wasn't actually reading.

"There you go." Mum placed a tray with tea and cake on the priest's lap. "And there's another little slice for you boys too, but don't let it ruin your dinner. Would you be good lads and take it outside, so I can speak with Father Higgins a moment?"

I huffed and Bernard whined.

"Not for long, boys. And then Father will read to you, alright?"

We picked up our cake and slunk outside.

I leaned against the studio wall and devoured the lemony sponge, poppy seeds catching in my loose tooth as I chewed. Bernard, who'd fed half his cake to Pyg, jumped around with her, marvelling at their long shadows in the sinking sunlight.

"Look at the size of our legs, George. We look like giants. Or monsters."

"You look like idiots."

"Oi!" Bernard pouted and raised his arms above his

head with fingers splayed. He growled and stomped towards the dog. "I'm gonna eat you alive!"

Pyg zoomed around in response, bushy tail wagging a frantic rhythm. Her panting mouth resembled Bernard's goofy laughter.

Raised voices from inside the studio pulled my attention and I stepped back towards the door, turning my ear to the gap in the warped frame.

"Why would you provoke her like that, El? I told you getting a dog would be a bad idea."

"The boys deserve at least a little joy in their lives. You've no idea what it's like constantly turning the other cheek. Living this half-life—"

"What are you doing?" Bernard's small voice asked behind me.

Startled, I spun around. "Shh! I'm trying to listen."

Bernard huffed and ran off, his arms out like an aeroplane, with Pyg chasing after him. I pressed my ear back to the door.

"Come now, don't get upset. Try to focus on the future."

"You always say that, but sometimes it's impossible to imagine there'll ever be a way out of here."

"Well, I've made some enquiries about a new overseas mission in Africa. It could give us the fresh start we need."

"Africa?"

"Yeah, imagine the life we could have there. Things won't happen overnight, you know how it is with the church..."

"You really think things could be different for us abroad?"

"There'll be much less scrutiny, so we'll get away with more of this…"

Then came a different sound. No longer voices…

*Wait, was that…?*

I turned my head and closed one eye to peer with the other through the gap.

I didn't know much about kissing, only that in the school yard last week, Felicity Granger had dared me to kiss Emily Fletcher. Emily was okay, for a girl, and I wasn't one to back down from a dare.

"Alright," I'd said and puckered up. I closed my eyes and leaned towards Emily with all her freckles and pigtails and lips, and…

A burst of giggles and I opened my eyes to Felicity holding a dirty great toad up to my face. Now I officially hate girls. And kissing.

Through the gap I spied my mother, her slender fingers cupped around the priest's clean-shaven face, his hands around her waist pulling her close, squeezing her to him.

4

# QUELLE SURPRISE

"*W*ell, hello again, Alice French."

Alice's head whipped from the man to the doorway, where Doctor Khurana stood leaning against the doorjamb.

"What are you doing here?"

"I work here." A smile teased the corners of the doctor's mouth. Instead of scrubs she wore grey denim jeans and a plaid shirt with the sleeves rolled up, exposing her toned forearms. Alice tore her eyes from the doctor and back to the man, who had resumed his regular breathing.

"So, what are *you* doing here?" The doctor's eyes smiled more than her mouth, which Alice read as not being entirely displeased to see her.

"I came to sort out my car and thought I'd pop in to check on Xavier." Alice gestured to the man.

Ash stepped into the room. "Xavier? Has he been identified?"

"No, it's just what I decided his name was."

"Right." Ash shook her head and laughed, the sound of which caused Alice's smile to stretch even wider.

"Surely you're not starting your next shift already?" Alice twisted a finger into one of her curls and pulled it straight before letting it spring back into place.

"No, I was heading to the gym. In all last night's excitement, I forgot my trainers."

"Ah, okay." Alice dropped her gaze back to the hypnotising rhythm of the man's chest.

"So, how is he?"

Alice grinned. "I don't know, you're the doctor."

Ash breathed out a laugh as she moved to the end of the bed and unhooked the metal clipboard from the frame.

"Hmm. Right. Yep. Uh-huh."

Alice looked on as the doctor leafed through the pages, her eyes scanning the notes, about as intelligible as hieroglyphics to anyone not in the medical profession.

"So...?"

"I'm afraid there isn't much to say at the moment. According to the notes, he was awake this morning, but very confused. He doesn't seem to remember who he is."

"Oh no, poor thing."

"They did a few cognitive tests, but he became very agitated and started ranting about pigs again, so they gave him a benzo."

"What's a benz—"

"Ah, it's a sedative. It's sent him off into a lovely deep sleep. He looks like he could do with the rest, so it isn't a bad thing. It buys us a bit more time to try to figure out who he is and get hold of his medical records."

Alice wrung her hands together as her eyes settled back on the man's face. She focused on his forehead, specifically that ghastly cut above his eyebrow. "You know the injury on his head? You don't think that has anything to do with his memory loss, do you?"

"Why do you ask?" Ash's neat eyebrows pinched together.

"I, er..." Alice swallowed against the bilious churn in her stomach; empty, aside from that awful acidic coffee. Static fizzed in her ears.

"It's okay, you can tell me."

"I'm worried this is all my fault. When I found him in the road, lying there and groaning, he was conscious, you know? Incoherent but awake." Alice paused to steady her shaking voice.

"Go on."

"Well, I had no phone signal to call for help, so I had to get him into my car... but he's heavy and... well, I sort of dropped him. That's how he cut his head." Alice blinked back the tears blurring her vision. "This is all my fault, isn't it?"

"Oh, Alice." The doctor moved closer and touched her hand to Alice's back, the warmth from it radiating through her. "There's something called the Good Samaritan Law. Basically, if you've stopped to help someone, you can't be blamed if you unintentionally injure them in the process."

"I'm not worried about being blamed. I'm worried that

I've caused him a serious head injury and now he can't remember who he is and that's because of me. I'm like a disaster magnet."

Ash peered into her face with an earnest look of reassurance. "I can't be one hundred percent certain until we've done some more tests, but I doubt that little cut has caused any major issues."

"Really?" Alice blinked, conscious of Ash's warm hand still pressed between her shoulder blades and the subtle motion of her thumb moving in small comforting circles. *Is this what they mean by bedside manner?* Alice bit hard on the inside of her lip.

"Really." Ash smiled. "It's a flesh wound. It looks worse than it is. He's booked in for some scans anyway, but in my professional opinion the worst you've done is cause him a few stitches."

"Okay, that makes me feel a little better, I guess."

The doctor's hand fell away and in Alice's unprofessional opinion, she thought she should return it immediately. But she stopped herself from saying that.

"Oh, and I found this." Alice reached for the man's coat. "I forgot it came off when I was pulling him into my car."

"Have you checked the pockets?"

Alice scoffed. "No, of course not. Why would I go through his pockets?"

Ash raised an eyebrow and took the coat. "To see if he was carrying anything that will tell us who he is."

"Right. Yes, that makes sense."

Whilst holding the furry mass of a coat by its collar, Ash patted the pockets. First, she pulled out an ancient brick of a mobile phone.

"Bloody hell, is that a Nokia? I thought they went extinct."

Ash pressed the buttons but, much like the man, the Nokia didn't respond. She returned to the pockets and fished out a scruffy leather wallet. "Aha!" She flipped it open and slid out a pastel-pink card.

"*Quelle surprise*, he's not called Xavier."

Alice widened her eyes in mock-surprise. "He isn't?"

Ash laughed and held out the man's driving licence. "No. Here we have one Mr George Shaw." She placed the coat over the end of the bed and waved the wallet. "I'm just going to give this to the team so they can run it through the system." She turned to leave but looked around and grinned at Alice. "Be right back, okay?"

Alice nodded and returned her gaze to the man's sleeping face. She touched her fingers to his warm hand resting atop the blanket.

"Hello, George. Sorry I got your name wrong, and I'm sorry again that I bashed your head."

Ash bounced back into the room, as if unburdened by handing over the wallet. "Okay, that's with the team now. Hopefully, in a short while, we'll be a bit more up to speed on George here. Mystery — almost — solved."

"We still don't know what he was doing in the road like that, poor thing."

"Nope, but we're a step closer to finding out."

Alice nodded and patted George's hand.

"Anyway, I suppose I should get going." Ash gestured to the door.

"Me too." Alice bent to retrieve her fallen coffee cup before she stood.

Ash grimaced. "Oh no, that wasn't from the vending machine, was it?"

Alice nodded with a grim smile.

Ash sucked air in through her teeth. "Blimey, and you drank it?"

"I'm afraid so."

"That stuff is like rocket fuel. I should check you over, just in case." Ash's cheeks coloured as she laughed.

"You can if you want," said Alice, barely suppressing her smile.

"Hmm, well I would, but I'm not on duty, so I'd have to refer you to one of my colleagues."

"Well, in that case... perhaps you could point me in the direction of somewhere that serves a decent cup of coffee."

"Hmm, there's a cute little place just up the road. They have the most amazing muffins." Ash chef's-kissed her fingers. "I'll take you, then at least you'll have a doctor on hand if you need medical assistance."

Alice bit down on her grin. "Lead the way to the muffins, doctor."

THE SHARPNESS OF RASPBERRY KICKED AGAINST the gooey white chocolate coating Alice's tongue. She murmured her pleasure through a mouthful of muffin and closed her eyes, savouring the first taste of something substantial since yesterday lunchtime.

"You weren't wrong... these are delicious. Mmm." Alice swallowed and opened her eyes to see Ash, staring at her display of unbridled pleasure. Amusement ticked up one side of Ash's mouth in that disarming lopsided grin. Alice smiled back and Ash blushed, flicking her long dark lashes down to redirect her gaze at the giant mug of coffee she held in her hands.

"There's a good reason they're my favourite," she muttered into her mug.

"Well, you have good taste." Alice took a sip of tea, the perfect chaser to the rich muffin. She glanced around the small café with its exposed brick walls, reclaimed wooden furniture, and Edison bulbs casting a warm glow overhead. A playlist of lo-fi beats added to the hipster vibe. *Fran would hate it.* Alice smirked and turned her attention to the woman sitting in front of her. "So, you come here often?"

Ash's laughter reached her eyes.

"I try not to come too often; the struggle to resist the muffins is real, and now you know why." She gestured to the crumbs on Alice's plate. "But it's close to work, and it's nice to get out of there from time to time. I used to come here a lot with... my ex."

Alice propped her elbows on the table and leaned in. "Ooh, so this is where you bring all the women?"

"I wouldn't say that, no." Ash snickered. "We used to

come here as it was nice to get away for a coffee together and not be surrounded by gawping colleagues."

"Yes, I can see why that would be appealing."

"Anyway, am I that obvious?"

With a little leap in her chest, Alice grinned because she'd guessed right. She sat back and playfully narrowed her eyes, taking Ash in.

"Let's just say I have a good gaydar."

Ash shrugged. "Well, that makes one of us."

"And your ex, is she...? I mean, do you...? Is it awkward now, working together and not..."

"Oh, no, Sam relocated a while ago." Ash stared into her mug. "A job came up for her in Edinburgh and it was too good to turn down." She took a long sip of coffee and shrugged. "Long distance wouldn't have worked for us, so..."

"But your accent, it's from the North, right?"

Ash's laughter pealed out. "Yeah, but Yorkshire, not Scotland. It'd still be long distance, even if I didn't live all the way down here."

Alice shook her head. "Ah, that's a shame."

"No, not really. There were other reasons it wouldn't have worked, but hey, I've moved on." Ash gave her a small smile. "And you?"

"Me?"

"Yesterday, you said you'd just broken up with someone. Are you doing okay?"

Alice drained the tea from her cup and placed it onto the saucer. "I've been better, but it was time I got real."

Ash placed a surprisingly warm hand on top of Alice's. "If you want to talk about it, I'm a good listener."

Alice threw her head back and drew in a deep breath. *Would it be so bad to get this off my chest?* She hadn't been able to speak to anyone else about it. She'd tried several times with Maggie, but she'd gone all self-righteous when Alice let on that Fran was married, probably because of Markus and his track record... and confiding in Jeremy was out of the question, obviously. There was no one else she trusted, so why not confide in a stranger who was willing to listen?

Alice looked back to Ash, straight into those dark brown eyes, full of concern and kindness. "You really want to know?"

Ash nodded. "Hit me with it."

Reluctantly, Alice withdrew her hand from under Ash's. Her chair scraped across the tiled floor as she stood. "Okay, but I'll need another pot of tea. And I think I'd better get you a muffin."

Ash laughed. "Why?"

"You'll need some sugar to help with the shock."

Ash held up her hands. "In that case, who am I to argue?"

At the counter, Alice ordered another pot of English breakfast tea — ignoring her bladder's better judgement — a large white Americano, "...and two more of those delicious muffins." She pointed at the raspberry-topped cakes in the display and grimaced as the total tallied up on the till, but the present company was more than worth the relatively small outlay, so she tapped her credit card. Plus, a woman had to eat and drink.

As the barista prepared her order, Alice leaned against the end of the counter and glanced at her locked phone screen crowded with notifications. If only she could just block Fran. *If only it were that easy.* Why had she ever allowed herself to get involved in this bullshit?

She sighed and pushed her phone into the back pocket of her jeans, even though she really ought to text Maggie about the car. *Later.*

Alice allowed her eyes to drift over to Ash, who sat mesmerised as cherry blossom from the tree on the street corner caught in the breeze and drifted by the window like pink snow. It was funny observing the things other people noticed; almost as if seeing them for yourself through fresh eyes. Spring really was quite beautiful.

"Alice. Order for Alice." The young barista's voice snatched her from her daydream.

Turning to walk away, Alice almost dropped the tray when in front of her stood Fran, looking as gorgeous as ever and thoroughly pissed off. Alice swallowed hard.

"What are you doing here?"

"I've had warmer greetings, Alice, I must say." Fran chortled before fixing her lips into a smile. "I've been trying to call you, but you weren't answering."

Alice shook her head and Fran's eyes travelled down to the laden tray she was struggling to balance. "You have company?"

"I... I... yes. I'm having tea with a friend." Alice's eyes flicked over to Ash, who was looking in their direction with a furrowed brow. Fran looked around too, her smile faltering as she returned her cold eyes to Alice.

"I see, and who is this 'friend'?"

"No one you'd know. Look, I thought I'd made it clear last night that it's over between us."

Fran stepped closer, blocking Alice's path and placing a hand on her upper arm.

"Darling, sometimes we say things we don't mean in the heat of the moment. I just want to talk things through and see where we get to after that. Where's the harm?" Her voice was low and steady, as if trying to coax a scared animal.

Alice bit her lip as her courage wavered in the face of the woman she worshipped. The woman she *used* to worship.

*No, no, no. It's over.* Her thoughts must have spilled into words as Fran stepped back, shoving her hands into the pockets of her tailored trousers. She inhaled a deep breath before speaking through tight lips, an edge of impatience in her voice.

"Look now, Alice. You're making a scene. Shall we just sit, have a nice cup of tea and talk things through?"

Alice glanced over at Ash again, who gave a concerned smile and mouthed, "Are you okay?"

Somehow bolstered by the doctor's kind eyes, Alice felt her courage restored.

"As you already noticed, Fran, I have company, so I would appreciate it if you would let me pass."

Fran fixed Alice with a steely stare before stepping aside.

*Surely, it wouldn't be that easy.*

With her heartbeat drumming in her ears, Alice placed the tray on the table and composed herself as she set the drinks and cakes in place.

"There we go," she said, retaking her seat.

Ash looked at her with a worry-filled face. "Alice, are you okay? You've gone as white as—"

Alice waved her hand. "I'm fine... I mean, that was my ex."

Ash's eyes popped, and she leaned forward. "Whoa, you mean your ex as of yesterday?" She side-glanced at the other woman, who was now giving a detailed drink order at the counter.

"Yup, that's the one."

Ash released a breathy laugh and sat back with her hands on her head. "Shit!"

Alice focused her eyes on the knotty reclaimed wood of the tabletop, not wanting to look at Ash or over at Fran. Adrenaline pulsed through her, making her hands shake so much the lid of the pot rattled when she poured her tea.

Ash leaned in and whispered, "How did she know you were here?"

The question caused Alice to sit up straight, her eyes searching for an answer. "I've, maybe... I really don't—"

Before she had any longer to think, Fran strode toward them with a mug in her hands. "Ladies, mind if I join you?" She placed the mug on the table without waiting for an answer and shoved a hand out to Ash. "Francesca Dalton, and you are?"

Alice's mouth hung open in shock as Ash clasped Fran's hand in an uncertain handshake. "Asha."

"And tell me, Asha," Fran carefully pronounced the name as if it were a foreign word her tongue might trip over, "how do you two know each other?"

"I, er... we don't really... we met last night. I mean..."

"Oh, I see." Fran's eyes swivelled back to Alice. "So, this is why you haven't been answering my texts and calls?"

Alice said nothing, but her cheeks flamed. She looked at Ash with pleading eyes and mouthed, "Sorry." Fran leaned across them for the sugar sachets and continued her rampage whilst stirring white granules into her mug.

"Tinder, was it? Or some other pathetic little dating app for lesbians."

Ash held up her hands. "Whoa, okay." Shaking her head as she stood, she glanced from Alice to Fran. "You're clearly upset and catching the wrong end of the stick, so I'm just going to—"

"Leave? Yes, that would be best." Fran pursed her lips.

"Ash, please don't." Alice's voice came out tiny and too late as Ash turned to go.

She looked back to Alice and said, "You know where I am, okay?"

Alice nodded, her eyes following Ash as she left. The café door closed, and Alice's shoulders slumped.

"There, that's better. Now we can talk." Fran sat back and cupped her mug.

Alice narrowed her eyes. "How did you know?"

Fran shook her head, a smug smile plastered to her lips. "Know what?"

"Where to find me?"

"Oh, you really do focus on all the wrong things, Alice."

"How did you know I was here?"

Fran tutted and set her mug down on the table. "If you must know, I tracked your phone."

Alice's mouth fell open. "You tracked my phone?"

"Quite right. I like to keep tabs on you. It comforts me to know where you are and that you're keeping out of mischief." Fran chortled, as if it were a cute and perfectly normal thing to do. Alice's jaw clenched as she stared at Fran, brushing this off like it was nothing. Fran slid the plate with Ash's untouched muffin across the table.

"You had no right, Fran." Alice's voice came out in a low growl.

"Come off it. It's only a muffin, Alice. Your little friend has gone, and I don't want it to go to waste." She shrugged and smiled at Alice, then between her manicured finger and thumb she plucked the raspberry from the top and popped it in her mouth.

"Not the muffin. My phone. You had no right to track my phone."

"Shh, keep your voice down." Fran glanced around.

Alice stood, her chair screeching across the tiled floor.

"No, I won't. It's stalking. You're so controlling. I'm done with this, Fran. Leave me alone or else—"

"Or else, what?"

"I'll tell Jeremy about us. I'll tell him everything."

Fran laughed. *She fucking laughed.* The clipped, nasal sound sliced through the air. *Has she always had such an ugly laugh?*

"You wouldn't do that."

"Try me."

"You'll lose your job, and then where will you be?" Fran sat back with a shit-eating grin.

"I don't care any more." Alice snatched the muffin out of Fran's hand, grabbed the one from her own plate, and left with Francesca-fucking-Dalton gawping behind her.

# AMUSE-BOUCHE

## EIGHT MONTHS EARLIER

*A*lice pored over the spreadsheet on her wide-screen monitor. Tiny numbers danced in front of her tired eyes as she tried to finalise the month-end accounts of T&D Counselling and Psychotherapy Services.

As Executive Assistant, the accounts, as well as anything else remotely admin-related, fell into Alice's realm of responsibility. In other words, as their only employee, she performed the role of general dogsbody to both Truscote and Dalton. It could be worse. The pay was okay, and they mostly left her to her own devices, which was why she stayed with them. Well, it was part of the reason — a small part, but still.

Alice rolled her neck and glanced at the delicate gold watch on her wrist — a gift from Fran. 11:36; another forty-four minutes until Jeremy would be finished with his client. Hopefully, this appointment wouldn't run over like the last one, and Alice could shut the office to take lunch.

As if receiving the invitation to her thought party, her stomach rumbled. Last night, she'd congratulated herself on being thrifty by making lunch, but now, the soggy sandwich awaiting her seemed less than appetising. Perhaps she should treat herself to a flat white from Snoots. *And maybe one of those delicious little pastel de—*

An obnoxious burst of sound from the door buzzer jolted Alice from her thoughts; she pressed the button on her desk to release the catch and seconds later Fran sauntered in, her chestnut curls bouncing along with her stride.

"What, what are—" Alice stumbled at the sight of her.

"Oh, Alice. Do close your mouth." Fran pouted. "Aren't I allowed to pop by to bring my little worker bees lunch from time to time?"

"I, er... I have an egg sandwich in the fridge."

From the crook of her arm, Fran swung a Fortnum & Mason picnic basket onto Alice's desk. "I think what I have for you will be much more appealing than your sad little sandwich."

Alice looked over her shoulder, eyeing the door with the brass plate etched 'Dr J. Dalton'.

"I, er..." she glanced at her computer screen. "Jeremy is with a client. He'll be a while yet."

"Well, I'm sure you and I can find plenty to occupy ourselves with before then."

"Sorry, but I just need to finish this." Alice gestured to her monitor.

Fran gave a terse nod. "Fine, I'll entertain myself."

Alice's eyes flicked to her screen, but within seconds

they'd gravitated back to Fran, watching as she stepped around the low coffee table and couch, which comprised the furniture in the waiting room. Fran bent to pick up a glossy magazine and reclined into the corner seat, making a big show of crossing and uncrossing her legs. As Fran leafed through the pages of *Good Housekeeping,* Alice tried to concentrate enough to at least save her work before acquiescing to her brain's desire to be entirely consumed by the other woman.

Fran sighed and tossed the magazine back onto the low table. Standing, she smoothed her hands over her skirt and walked the perimeter of the small room, her top lip curling as she looked around.

"It's always so glum in here."

"The plants are new since you last—"

"Yes, but even so. A little greenery isn't enough to lift the heavy air."

Alice grinned. "Well, Jeremy specialises in bereavement psychotherapy, so a lot of our clients are—"

Fran waved away Alice's words. "Let's change the subject. All this talk of..." She stopped in front of the closed door on the other side of Alice's desk and brushed her fingers over the engraved words on the brass plate. *Dr C. Truscote.*

"Out, I expect?"

"Hmm?"

Fran tilted her head towards the closed door.

"Oh, Doctor T.? Let me see..." Alice clicked her mouse, and her eyes scanned the screen, "...at The Milverton clinic with a client and shouldn't be back for the rest of the afternoon, so you're safe." Alice had never quite understood their vehement distaste for one another, and Fran always shut it down whenever she asked.

"Good, good." Fran strode over to Alice's desk and perched on the edge. She plucked a pencil from the pen pot and rubbed the end over her lips, before leaning in to twirl it in one of Alice's curls. "So, are you hungry?"

Alice gulped, and Fran's lips curved into a satisfied smirk.

"Let me see what I have to whet your appetite." She leaned across and pulled the picnic hamper toward her. Unclipping the wicker fastening, she rifled around before retrieving a breadstick dipped in something smooth and beige. Fran poked it into Alice's willing mouth, and a rich, buttery taste coated her palate.

"Mmm, did you make this?"

"No." Fran scoffed a laugh. "You like it?"

Alice nodded and opened her mouth for more; Fran obliged, this time scooping an extra-large dollop to poke between her lips.

"Honestly, this is the nicest thing I've ever had in my mouth."

Fran arched a dark eyebrow. "This is just the *amuse-bouche*, darling," she said, with a haughty laugh.

"Shh!" With wide eyes, Alice peered over her shoulder at Jeremy's closed door. Heat rose up her neck to her cheeks at the thought of him walking out and seeing Fran perched in front of her, looking all seductive and gorgeous.

Even though Fran was adamant that Jeremy didn't see her in that way, it didn't make Alice feel any better about things. Fran claimed that Jeremy barely noticed when she made an effort, and today she'd made an effort all right. She wore a black, hip-hugging pencil skirt, with a long slit... *oh my God, that slit...* paired with stockings and heels. Fran had topped the cake with a cherry-red silk blouse, unbuttoned to show her full cleavage, which lay nestled in a lacy bra. She leaned over to feed Alice more heaven-on-a-breadstick, and Alice ached to bury her head in that cleavage and inhale her potent musky scent.

You'd have to be blind not to notice a woman like Fran, and practically dead not to be charmed by her. Alice had tried, but resistance was futile. Still, she could really do without losing her job, and sometimes it was almost as if Fran was trying to get them caught.

Fran reclined further on the desk, her arms arching behind her, hips angled upward. Heat ripped through Alice, and she squeezed her thighs against the ache gathering between them, breathing away the reckless urge to push everything off her desk, climb on top of Fran and... just screw it all. *That's what she wants, that's why she's here.*

Fran's dark eyes danced around Alice's face, almost as if she were amused — fuelled even — by Alice's unquenchable want.

"This weekend, I've booked us a room at that cutesy little place in the Cotswolds. I've told Jeremy that I'll be away with the Ivywood tennis girls. I was hoping you might be able to—"

"You've got to be kidding."

Fran cocked her head.

"I can't play tennis. I'm useless at sports or anything to do with balls."

"Goodness, no... I meant, you know... the outfit. There's something about tennis whites. Those little skirts and all that bending over." Fran fanned herself dramatically.

Alice giggled as she flipped the calendar on her desk. "This weekend?"

"What is it? Don't pretend you have plans that you can't cancel for me." Fran flashed a dangerous grin and leaned in to cup her hand around Alice's cheek.

"It's just that I'm supposed to be staying with Maggie. She's planned this whole birthday thing."

"I'm sure she won't miss you."

"Thanks!"

"Oh, you know what I mean." Fran chortled.

"I said I'd be there, and I always seem to let her down lately."

"You're always moaning about your sister and her horrid husband, so what's the big deal?"

"I know, but..." Alice sighed. Why was she even trying to explain this to Fran? *Resistance is futile.* "I suppose her birthday isn't until Sunday, so perhaps I can just spend Sunday with her instead?"

"Attagirl," said Fran, now propped on her elbow with her hot mouth inches away from Alice's, so close Alice could taste the velvety butter of that delicious —

"Ahem."

Alice jerked away, her heart pounding as her eyes darted in the direction of the throat-clearer. In the doorway stood the austere, sharp-cut figure of Doctor Truscote, her steely-eyed gaze flicking from Fran's face to Alice's.

Alice opened her mouth to speak, but before any words came forth, Fran sprang up from the desk.

"Catherine. How lovely to see you! You're looking—" Fran made a show of looking the other woman up and down, and let the end of her sentence hang in the air unfinished.

"Francesca," Truscote said with a nod, then clenched her thin lips into a tight line. The muscles in her square jaw pulsed as her eyes returned to Alice.

"My afternoon session at The Milverton got cancelled last-minute. I'll be in my office dictating the notes for the Liversidge files. I'll need you to type them up ASAP. I'd also appreciate a coffee, when you..." she turned her head slightly towards Fran, but her eyes didn't drift from Alice's, "...when you have a moment." Alice could swear she saw the corners of Truscote's lips twitch with disgust.

"Sure, I'll be right there." Alice's voice came out half an octave higher than usual.

Truscote nodded and strode across the room. When the heavy oak door clicked to a close, Alice released her held breath with a muted, "Fuuuuck."

Fran chuckled.

"Why are you laughing right now?"

"Trusty's got her crusties in a bit of a twist, hasn't she?"

"Fran, it isn't funny. This is serious. What if she tells Jeremy what she saw?"

Fran retook her perch on Alice's desk and steadied Alice's jittering hands with her own.

"And what did she see, Alice?"

Alice looked at her blankly.

"Exactly. She saw nothing." Fran smiled.

*She's actually enjoying this.*

"Just tell the sour old cow I was getting an eyelash for you." She scoffed. "It's not like she'd know affection even if it bit her on the ice-cold arse."

Alice raked her fingers over her cheeks and sank into her chair.

Fran glanced at her watch and hopped off the desk. "Right then, I better be off."

"What? Where are you going?"

"I can't hang around here all day. I have things to do."

"What about Jeremy?"

"Do tell him I said hello. There's a sandwich for him in the basket; the rest of it is for you. Enjoy!"

"But—"

"All good things, Alice, all good things. Besides, I shall see you this weekend! Don't forget your tennis gear." Fran blew her a kiss and disappeared through the door.

"I don't have any tennis gear," muttered Alice.

AFTER A SOFT KNOCK, ALICE PUSHED THROUGH THE heavy oak door with a tray balanced in her left hand.

Truscote didn't look up; her fountain pen scratched rapid notes across the lined paper of her notebook. Alice placed the cup of coffee on the coaster — she'd made it with hot milk, just how Truscote liked it. She'd also added a fancy biscuit from Fran's basket, hopeful that Truscote might notice the gesture and not mention anything about before.

This whole thing with Fran — *should she say* affair?

*Yes, but it sounds so seedy and cliché: the PA fucking the boss, or in this case, the boss's wife.* She didn't know how to make it stop, or even if she could. More to the point, if she actually wanted it to stop. And now that Fran was thinking of leaving Jeremy, perhaps they even had a future together?

Alice swung wildly from being smitten with the woman, to sort-of-despising her for being so... so whatever it was that fuelled Alice's raging desire. Fran was like crack, and Alice the crack-whore — constantly craving the next hit that inevitably left her feeling lower and more desperate than before. *Ugh.* She was disgusted with herself and cursed her weak will and libido because she knew she'd always bend over and take whatever Fran served up.

Alice's insides twisted and the metallic taste in her mouth made her realise she'd bitten the inside of her cheek too hard again.

It didn't help that Jeremy was one of the nicest people she'd ever met, earnest and kind — the opposite of his wife.

Truscote cleared her throat, wrenching Alice from her thoughts. She gave the silver-haired woman a small smile and moved towards the door.

"Alice, wait."

*Shit.* Alice turned.

"Thank you." Truscote combed a hand through her cropped hair and removed her reading glasses.

"For what?"

"The coffee. I was concentrating on my notes. I didn't mean to be rude."

"Oh, it's okay. You're welcome."

"And for the biscuit. I like these. Fortnum's, right?"

Alice bit her lip and bobbed her head.

"Sit for a moment, will you?"

"I should get back to the accounts—"

"That can wait."

Alice swallowed and, accepting her fate, moved to take a seat in one of the two leather chairs facing the desk. Truscote eyed her whilst taking a tentative sip from the steaming cup.

"Mmm, that's good."

Alice stared at the desk, tracing the knots of the dark wood with her eyes.

After a tense moment, Truscote leaned forward and spoke in a soft voice. "You need to be careful with Mrs Dalton. She's—"

"It's not what you think." The volume of her own voice startled her.

Truscote sat back and the corner of her mouth lifted in satisfied affirmation, thanks to Alice's over-reaction.

"Look, Alice. I have no right to tell you how to live your life. But, when it comes to the Daltons, I have an obligation to warn you. Jeremy, he's a good man. But Francesca, she's—"

"She's what?" Alice's fists clenched at the unexpected hurt of hearing someone else ripping into Fran. Alice could think what she liked about Fran, but they were lovers. What right had this woman, this sour cow, got to pass judgement? *Fran is worth a thousand of this frigid old bag.*

Truscote raised her hands. "Just be careful, okay? I don't want you to get hurt."

Alice got to her feet, blood pulsing in her ears as she batted away her intrusive thoughts: the urge to snatch the cup and throw hot coffee all over Truscote's smug face, the urge to take back the fancy Fortnum's biscuit, the urge to tell this old bitch where to shove her job. She breathed deeply to steady herself.

"Thank you for the warning, but I can make up my own mind about Fran. And you'd better not mention any of this... this nonsense to Jeremy."

Truscote puffed a laugh through her nose and shook her head. She replaced her reading glasses and resumed her notes.

Conversation over; Alice dismissed.

Back in the relative sanctuary of the reception room, Alice held out her shaky hands. She could do with a drink after that encounter. She could do with seeing Fran again.

Jeremy's appointment would end any moment now, but she couldn't wait. *Fuck it.*

She scrawled an excuse on a sticky note and stuck it to her screen — Jeremy would understand. *He's good like that.* Her thumbs tapped out a text as she shrugged on her coat and stepped outside.

Still about? Meet me for a drink?

Alice grinned as an instant reply from Fran pinged through.

White Lion. See you there x

# 5

## CHAOTIC LITTLE LIFE

*a* sickening smell of peach air freshener wafted from the vents, as the Uber navigated the tight country lanes and propelled Alice away from Fran and the disaster scene of the muffin café.

Alice groaned and sank down into the back seat, half-hoping that it might swallow her. She retrieved her phone from her pocket and swiped past another wave of Fran-related notifications to dial Maggie.

The phone rang and rang until it didn't, and Maggie's clipped voice spoke into her ear.

"Hey, you've reached the voicemail of Maggie Carter-Mills. I can't take your call right now, obvs. You know what to do. Ta-rah!"

*Shit.*

"Er, hey Mags. Sorry to bother you on a Saturday. I need a little help. My car... it's doing that thing again where it doesn't work. I promise I'll get it sorted after this.

I'm going to sort out everything in my... what do you call it?... *chaotic little life*."

Alice swallowed the lump in her throat, formed at the thought of Maggie, once again, being bloody right about everything, and she hurried to finish the message before it cut off. "Anyway, please call me on the landline in a bit. I er... I need to turn my mobile off. Indefinitely. I'll explain later. Just call me, Mags. Love you."

*Oh God.* That was worse than she'd imagined. Voice-mails were not Alice's friend.

"Are you okay, Miss?" asked the driver in a heavily accented voice.

Alice met his gaze in the rear-view mirror, his bushy black eyebrows raised high on his forehead.

"Yeah, fine. Fine, thank you." She forced a smile. "Actually, I could do with a little fresh air. Would you mind if I—"

"No problem." Before Alice could open the window, the driver had done it for her. "You can close it if it's too much."

Alice shut her eyes to the gush of cool air that rushed in. The afternoon sun bathed the budding landscape in a golden glow. She raised her chin and let the breeze push back her curls as she breathed in the spring air.

The insistent buzz of the phone in her hand snatched her moment's peace. She glanced at the screen, hoping for Mags, but no —

*Fuck off, Fran.* Alice fumbled to reject the call but answered it by mistake.

"Alice, please..." came a tiny impatient voice from the speaker.

In a brief battle lost to impulse, Alice threw the phone from the moving car.

"Oh, shit!" she gasped, and the driver braked to a halt.

"Did you drop something outside, Miss?"

Craning to look from the window, Alice saw her phone nestled in a hedgerow. It'd be easy enough to retrieve. *But actually...* "No, it's fine. It wasn't anything important. You can drive on."

ALICE BOLTED THE FRONT DOOR BEHIND HER, NOT missing the irony of reinforced containment within the minuscule square footage of her flat, when she knew she was about to unleash everything she'd been trying so hard to hold in. She dropped her keys on the hallway table, and as she walked from the front door to her bedroom, she shed her clothes, dropping a trail of them in her stride.

Stripped to her bare skin, Alice wrapped herself in the duvet of her unmade bed and flopped face-first onto the mattress. Cocooned in the sanctuary of her duvet, she buried her head in the many pillows and wept. *Pity-party for one.* No need to hold back; she let it all out, guttural ugly crying wrenching from her core.

Something had shifted within the last twenty-four hours. A conviction concerning Francesca Dalton had cemented inside Alice. This time felt different, not least because Alice's phone was in a hedge, and she couldn't call

Fran even if she wanted to. Over the two years they'd been doing this dance, Alice had tried in vain to be firm, but Fran would always utter the right combination of words and recast the spell.

*No more. No fucking more.*

# 6

# LIFE TRANSPLANT

*a* light but persistent tapping roused Alice from the snot-bubbling stupor she'd stirred herself into. She raised her head from her plush den and listened harder. *Was that the door?*

Barefoot and bundled in her thick duvet, Alice waddled down the hallway, lit only by the yellow street-light glowing through the transom window. She stepped over the clothes she'd discarded earlier and stood by the door.

*Tap, tap, tap.* Quiet, but there was most definitely someone there.

"Who is it?" Alice called out.

A soft voice came from outside. "It's me — Ash — Doctor Khurana."

"Oh." *Shit.*

"I'm really sorry to disturb you, Alice... and I'll leave if you want me to. But I was worried about you after earlier. You seemed distressed."

Alice could picture the discerning face of the doctor, her eyebrows pinched together above those brown eyes, deep pools of concern.

The doctor's soothing voice kept coming. "I tried to call you. I had your number from when you came in with the man... I mean, George. But your phone just rang out and... anyway, I wanted to see that you're okay. I finished my shift and decided to drive by. Your light was on. God, that sounds a bit creepy now, shit. I really shouldn't be here, but..."

Alice listened, almost mesmerised by the way Ash's subtle Northern accent bumped up the ends of her sentences.

"Alright then. Well, you're in there, so I guess you're okay. If you're not, then you know where to find me, or you could call the hospital." The sound of the soft voice faded into footsteps descending the stairs.

"Wait." Alice unbolted the door and pulled it open a crack, enough to peer through, but not enough to reveal her attire, or lack thereof. "Thanks for coming by. That was kind of you. I, er... I lost my phone, but I'm okay—"

"You don't look okay." Ash's face matched the mental image Alice's mind had conjured moments before, her striking features etched with concern.

"No, I don't suppose I do. But I'm fine, really. I just needed a good cry and now I'm all cried out." Alice attempted a smile, but it felt like her face had forgotten how.

"Hmm. I know it's late, or early, or whatever, but do you want to finish that chat we started earlier?"

"I, er…" Alice glanced down at her bunched-up duvet. She looked like a human burrito, hardly fit for entertaining. But here was a doctor on her doorstep, offering to listen, with no apparent agenda other than kindness.

"Look, sorry again to disturb you." Ash turned to leave. "I'll go, but if you want to talk then—"

"No, wait. I, er… I'd like to talk, if you don't mind. I need a moment to put something on under this duvet, though."

Ash puffed out a laugh of realisation, her cheeks colouring ever-so-slightly.

"And you'll have to excuse the state of the place. It's a bit untidy. I need to—"

"Shh! I didn't come to inspect your flat."

Alice grinned. "Okay, but even so — give me two minutes." She closed the gap until the lock clicked and scurried back down the hallway, the puffy duvet tangling around her bare legs, almost tackling her to the floor.

"Shit, shit, shit," Alice muttered. She shrugged off her duvet cocoon and gooseflesh prickled her skin in protest. In haste, she hopped into a pair of dusky pink lounge pants and pulled on the matching sweatshirt. The plush material hugged her curves in all the right places; more flattering than the duvet had been, at least.

Alice darted around the flat, gathering the many items of discarded clothing into her arms, before stuffing the bundle in the overflowing laundry basket in the bedroom. *Tomorrow's problem.*

In the lounge, Alice drew the thick velvet curtain, shutting out the streetlights, and flicked on another low-light to add to the dim glow of the lamp. She plumped the cushions and lit the candle on the coffee table to suck any staleness from the air. Stepping back, she cast an eye over the room and, in a quick move, blew out the flickering flame. *Too much. Don't be too much.* A small plume of smoke curled in the air and Alice wafted it away with her hand.

She released a long calming breath and padded back towards the front door, stopping for a quick check in the hallway mirror —

"Christ!" Alice frantically dabbed at her blackened eyes, makeup smudged around them yet again. She sighed at the useless effort, and put her fingers to better use, scrunching her loose curls; they always bounced back better than she did.

"Oh, bollocks to it, she's seen me worse than this," she muttered to herself.

Alice flung the door open wide this time. "Sorry to keep you waiting." She smiled and stepped aside to welcome Ash into her home. "You weren't wrong before about the state of me."

"Sorry, I didn't mean to be rude, but I could see you'd been upset."

"That's two nights in a row now that you've seen me in a mess."

Ash bent to remove her trainers.

"You needn't worry about that," Alice said, although secretly glad.

"No, it's polite, and besides, my mum would be horrified if I didn't."

A smile spread on Alice's face, at least until Ash held something out to her at arm's length.

"It was on the floor, I, er..." Pinched between her thumb and forefinger was a black thong. Alice's black thong. *Oh, for fuck's sake.*

Alice snatched her underwear and stuffed it into her pocket, her stomach sinking in mortification. "Oh God, see, I told you the place was a state."

Ash chuckled, a warm laugh which Alice couldn't help but echo with her own.

"It's fine. You live here. Stop worrying."

Alice turned and Ash followed. "Welcome to my humble abode. There isn't much to it, but this is me."

"It's nice." Ash's voice came from behind her. "It's really nice. I love the floor tiles. Are they original?"

"Yeah, I think so."

Ash gasped, as Alice had once done, when she took in the height of the living room. "Wow! Look at the ceiling. You could have a mezzanine in here."

"I often wish all that space was down here, not up there. But I suppose it'd just give me more places to leave my underwear lying around for unsuspecting visitors to find."

Ash looked down from the ceiling, her soft gaze settling back on Alice's face. "You need to stop beating yourself up so much."

Alice gave her a weak smile. "Tea?"

Ash yawned. "I thought you'd never ask."

"I'll just go and wash my face and then I'll be right back with a cuppa. How do you take it?"

"Milky please, three sugars."

"Three sugars, but you're a doctor?"

"A doctor with a sweet tooth." Ash shrugged and yawned again.

"Grab a seat." Alice motioned to the couch and Ash sat, resting back and closing her eyes. Despite her confident presence, even she looked small buried amidst the cushions of the oversized sofa.

Alice hovered in the doorway for a moment, adjusting to the novelty of someone else in her space. Fran had only popped by here the once. After an extended visit to the bedroom, where, incidentally, Fran had also admired the ceiling, but for different reasons, she'd insisted they go out for dinner instead of spending an evening curled up with a takeaway, as had been Alice's suggestion.

"My treat," Fran had said, with the air of a dissatisfied health inspector as she looked around the small flat, scattered with Alice's tired possessions.

Alice had simply smiled, shaking off the pinch of Fran's judgement and snobbish disregard. At the time, she chose to take comfort in her knowledge that Fran only wanted her for who she was, not what she had — at the time, she'd thought that had to count for something. And as always, Alice had acquiesced to being wined and dined by the much wealthier woman. After all, Alice's go-to oyster dish from Chopstix, accompanied by a cheap bottle of white wine, had nothing on fresh oysters slipping down her throat, chased by actual Champagne — *Fran's treat.*

Alice wiped away the black from around her eyes and splashed cold water on her face. Her makeup-free complexion wasn't one she normally shared with anyone. In fact, even Fran, her lover of two years, had never seen her bare-faced. But Ash had already seen far worse. And it wasn't like Alice was trying to impress the woman. *Was she?*

*Get a grip, you've just come out of a long-term relationship. You're a mess. And Ash isn't your type... not that she'd be interested in you anyway.*

"I'M SORRY, BUT I STILL DON'T HAVE MILK, SO I made you a black tea, three sugars."

Ash's head snapped up. She inhaled sharply and glanced around. "Sorry, I was just resting my eyes for a minute."

Alice sniffed out a laugh. "You must be shattered." She sat and cupped her hands around her own steaming mug.

"Yeah, more than I thought, and this is a very comfy settee." Ash sat up and ran her fingers through her silky black hair.

"Are you hungry?" Alice asked, but before Ash could answer, she shook her head. "Sorry, I don't know why I asked; it's not like I have any food in. I mean, there might be an old can of tuna in the back of the — oh actually, wait." Alice jumped up.

In the hallway, Alice reached into her handbag and pulled out a scrunched-up paper napkin. Returning to the couch, she unrolled the two muffins from the café, one of which had a considerable bite taken out of it.

Laughter bubbled up from Ash. "What the… how?"

"Sorry, they might be a bit stale now, but I wasn't going to let Fran eat your muffin."

Ash belly-laughed, and it triggered the same response in Alice.

"Wow, I'd have liked to have seen her face when you snatched it away. Was she mid-mouthful?"

Alice grinned and nodded. "Here, you have this one." She passed Ash the intact muffin and took a small bite from the other. "Mmm, still divine."

Ash nodded in agreement whilst devouring the spongy cake.

"I don't normally do this, you know?" she said.

"What, consume muffins in the small hours with strange women?"

"No, I mean I don't go knocking on the doors of random women who just happened to show up at my hospital. I've probably — no, definitely — broken at least ten rules that I can think of by coming here. But I really did want to check that you were okay."

"Well, from one rule-breaker to another, I won't tell if you don't. I'm pleased you came by. You've cheered me up."

Ash chased her mouthful of muffin with a sip of tea. She cupped the mug between her hands and relaxed back, fixing Alice with a thoughtful look.

"Come on then, what rules have you broken, Alice French?"

"Oh, I don't know, a few here and there — perhaps the

worst of which is sleeping with my boss's wife for the last couple of years."

Ash lurched forward, spluttering her tea. "Holy shit. You mean the woman from the café? She's your boss's—"

Alice nodded. Under the spotlight of Ash's wide-eyed shock, the shame of the confession washed over Alice. "I know. I'm the worst."

"Er, no... she is. Bloody hell. No wonder you're upset." Ash leaned across and placed a warm hand on Alice's forearm. Alice stared down at it. She didn't deserve this kindness. She sniffed and swallowed the smarting twist that suddenly gripped her throat.

"Does your boss know?"

"No, Jeremy adores Fran, and I can't bear to tell him. He'd be heartbroken. It's over now, but it looks like she won't let things be, as you saw for yourself."

"That's—" Ash puffed out her lips in the absence of words to sum up Alice's conundrum.

"Yep, I know. I'm totally fucked."

"I hate to agree with you on that, but it sounds like you are indeed... fucked."

Alice laughed. "Is that your professional diagnosis?"

"Yeah, I mean, feel free to get a second opinion, but I've rarely seen a case so clear-cut as this. It's textbook fucked-ness." Ash's lips curved into a smile, which accentuated the fine lines around her tired eyes.

"And can you prescribe a course of treatment, Doctor?"

Ash blew out her cheeks and paused for a moment. "I'd say full transplant... as in, get yourself a new fucking life, Alice."

Laughter erupted between them, and Alice playfully hit Ash's arm with her sleeve before flopping back into the plush couch.

"You know I'm just kidding, right?"

Alice groaned. "That's the thing; you're not wrong. My life's a mess."

Ash stretched up her arms, then slumped back into the cushions, mirroring Alice. They regarded each other, eyes lingering a moment too long.

Alice grinned. "How's George doing, by the way?"

"He's fine. I mean, he's still sleeping mainly. He did wake up for a while, but he really wasn't making much sense, mumbling about pigs again. He became so agitated we had to sedate him again. They've finally found him a bed on a ward, so he should've been moved by now."

"Poor thing. I wonder what all that pig stuff is about."

"No idea. But finding his wallet was helpful. They've got some contact details for his next of kin — his brother, Bernard."

"Oh, great."

Ash stifled a yawn with the back of her hand. "Well, it would be if they could get hold of him. The phone keeps going to voicemail, apparently. But they'll keep trying."

"I hope they reach him, for George's sake. Someone has to know why he was lying in the road like that. And more to the point, someone must be worried that they haven't heard from him. What about his phone?"

"Still dead. No one seems to have a charger for it," Ash gasped through a yawn, which stretched out her words. "Sorry. I can't stop yawning."

"I feel quite invested now, don't you?"

"Mmm, yeah." Ash had closed her eyes.

"Don't you think the pig thing is weird? Perhaps he's a farmer and has a litter of piglets waiting on him to feed them."

"Perhaps," Ash said without opening her eyes or lifting her head from the cushion it had sunken into.

"Maybe George has an award-winning sow that escaped, and he was chasing her down, and that's how he came to be in the road. I mean, he does look a bit weathered like a farmer, doesn't he?"

Ash didn't respond and Alice playfully nudged her with her foot. "Ash?"

"I should go..." she mumbled as her chest fell into a relaxed rise and fall, her features soft in the gentle glow of the lamplight.

Although she barely knew the woman, something about her filled Alice with a sense of calm. Even the steady rhythm of Ash's sleeping breath somehow hushed the rush within Alice.

She reached across, pulled a grey chenille blanket from the back of the couch and covered the sleeping doctor. She moved slowly, not wanting to wake her. Not wanting her to leave.

# PURPLE PICKLE

## SIX MONTHS EARLIER

*A*lice awoke in a king-sized bed, her head pounding with a king-sized hangover and her legs bound in a confusing tangle of hotel bedsheets. Fran's wayward limbs draped across Alice as if she was part of the furnishings, further adding to the suffocating constriction. A fizz of pins and needles prickled under Alice's skin as she tried to extract her numb arm from beneath Fran's naked body.

Fran murmured a disgruntled groan before rolling over and pulling the sheets with her, freeing Alice's legs. Alice tried to shake some feeling back into her hand as her fuzzy eyes squinted into focus on her watch face.

"Shit. Fuck." Alice sprang from the bed.

Fran groaned her displeasure at the noisy commotion.

"Sorry to wake you, Fran... but it's Monday morning and I'm late for work."

Fran didn't stir, so Alice crawled over the bed and stroked her lover's arm. "Fran?... Fran?"

"Yes, I heard you, Alice. And you know this is no way to wake me." Fran shrugged off Alice's hand and snatched the sheets up around her head.

"I'm sorry. I'll make it up to you... but I promised Truscote that I'd—"

"Gaaawd, it goes from bad to worse." Fran voiced her muffled protest from under the covers. "The last thing I want to be thinking about at this time of the day, or in fact any time of the day, is Catherine-bloody-Truscote."

Alice flopped back against the plush pillows. "I know, but—"

Fran arched around and shot her a dangerous look. "Just call in sick. Tell Jeremy you've got your monthlies. He always gets squeamish about that. He'll probably give you the whole week off, silly old fool."

Alice's insides squirmed. "Fran, don't be unkind. Jeremy's good to me."

"Well, if he's that bloody great, why aren't you sleeping with *him*?"

Alice gave her a look that didn't need words.

Fran huffed and retreated under the sheets.

Alice sipped from the glass of water on the bedside table, savouring the quench of her dry mouth. Her eyes darted around the room as she tried to piece together a plan.

Fran was far too precious about her car to let Alice borrow it, so that wasn't an option. Perhaps she could get an Uber? But they'd driven miles to get here, and where exactly *here* was, fuck knows. *Do Ubers even come this far out of town?*

Alice picked up her phone and scrolled. When she looked up again Fran had twisted around to look at her. Her tousled hair fanned across the pillow and a wicked grin lifted her lips, coated in the patchy pink remnants of yesterday's lipstick.

"I'll call Jeremy myself and tell him I've asked you to run some errands."

"No, Fran. I'm not your bloody PA. I'm the Exec Assistant at T&D."

Fran's smile grew wider. "Ooh, Alice, you spicy little sausage. Do you know how sexy you are when you're being salty?" Fran's arm snaked out from between the sheets. With a smouldering look in her eyes, she tiptoed her fingers across the mattress towards Alice, stepping her digits over Alice's thigh and inching towards her groin.

"Stop it." Alice pushed Fran's hand away, only to be betrayed by the stupid smile creeping over her own lips. "Come on, get up. I need you to drive me into town. We came here in your car."

Fran shook her head like a petulant child.

"Stop messing around. Come on, I'm being serious."

"God, you're so sexy when you're all serious." Fran groaned and rolled onto her back.

"Fuck." Alice tipped her head back and pinched her nose.

"Yes, please. I thought you'd never offer," Fran purred and rested her hand back on Alice's thigh, this time sinking her nails into the tender flesh. Alice breathed heavily through her nose and grabbed her phone again; her thumb made quick work of tapping out a text.

Sorry, car troubles...

Technically, not a lie — the trouble being that she was nowhere near her car.

Will be there as soon as I can.

With a swoosh, the message sent to both Catherine and Jeremy. An immediate response pinged back, but without looking Alice placed the phone face-down on the bedside table. She sucked in a deep breath and scooched down the bed until her eyes were in line with Fran's.

Fran smiled her approval and cupped Alice's breast, pinching the already erect nipple between her fingers.

"You're going to get me fired, one of these—"

Fran hushed Alice with a deep kiss, pushing her tongue into her mouth. She released the firm grip on Alice's nipple and her fingers travelled lower, but stopped short of where Alice hoped they were heading. Alice quivered in anticipation of Fran's touch, but Fran wouldn't play nicely; she never did. There would be punishment for the rude awakening — *exquisite punishment.* Fran took Alice's bottom lip between her teeth and bit it.

"Do you want me to touch you?"

Alice nodded.

Fran coiled a fistful of Alice's hair around her hand and pulled her head back, exposing her throat. "I want to hear you say it."

"Touch me," Alice rasped.

"Turn around."

Alice obliged and rolled onto her stomach. Fran straddled her naked buttocks and leaned forward, her soft breasts pressing into Alice's shoulder blades. "I want you to beg," she breathed into Alice's ear.

Fran traced her tongue along the curve of Alice's neck before sinking her teeth into her shoulder. Alice's breath hitched.

"Beg."

"Please." Alice's hips rocked into the mattress, desire ripping through her at the sensation of Fran grinding on her arse cheeks.

"Please, what?"

"Pleeeease fuck me."

Fran licked a trail down Alice's spine and inched herself back until she was between Alice's legs.

"Let's see how much you really want it."

Alice released a low moan as Fran traced a finger along the slick length of her and lingered at her entrance.

"Oh yes. I can feel that you've got your priorities straight now."

Fran's weight shifted from the bed, and she started rummaging around the room. Alice lifted her head. "What are you—"

"Did I tell you to move?" Fran barked.

Alice buried her face in the pillow, desire pulsing through her as she waited, ready for whatever was coming.

Then... *slap.*

Pain seared across Alice's arse cheeks. "What the fuck, Fran?"

"Not okay?" Fran's confident tone was belied by a hint of reticence.

"You know it is, you just... took me by surprise." The stinging subsided, only to be replaced by a throbbing ache between Alice's legs. She wanted this, and everything that was coming to her.

"Good girl," Fran said with a smile in her voice. "That was for the rude awakening."

Alice steadied her breathing, waiting for the...

*Slap.* Tense and release.

"That was for even thinking of going to work before pleasuring me."

"Fuck, Fran."

Fran softly rubbed Alice's buttocks and placed a gentle kiss on each cheek before... *slap.*

Alice whimpered.

"And that was for mentioning Catherine-fucking-Truscote."

Alice felt Fran's weight shift back onto the bed and she moved between her legs again. Alice writhed in anticipation; she'd combust if Fran didn't touch her soon.

"Arch your hips for me," Fran commanded. Alice did what she was told, lifting onto her knees and presenting herself to the woman in charge.

"Good. That's good." Fran reached between Alice's legs and slipped a finger into the wetness she found there. Alice's knees almost buckled at the touch. "Ooh, we like that, don't we?"

"Fran, please..." was all Alice could utter before Fran thrust into her — *she's wearing the strap.* "Fuck," Alice cried out and stars fizzed behind her eyes. Even though she had a feeling it was coming, the penetration shocked her system.

Fran held still inside her, allowing Alice to adjust to the sudden intrusion.

"And this is for being so fucking delicious. You drive me wild, Alice French, but I think you know that." Fran gripped Alice's hips and unrelentingly fucked her. It didn't take long to tip Alice over the edge, the sheets clenched in her fists as she screamed into the pillow with an unholy release.

Fran collapsed, hot and breathless, on top of her. "Now, tell me that wasn't better than a dull morning with Truscote?"

"Truscote couldn't be further from my mind." Alice chuckled. "What is it with you two, anyway?"

Fran groaned and rolled off Alice. "Let's not go there and spoil the moment."

Fran's purple latex protrusion stood to attention in its leather harness. Alice gripped her hand around it and sidled up close, resting her head on Fran's shoulder whilst she ran her fingers up and down the smooth shaft.

"I'm very pleased you brought your purple pickle along for the weekend. That was... a nice surprise."

Fran sighed. "You know I don't like it when you call it a pickle, Alice."

Alice giggled, traced her fingers up Fran's stomach and played with her nipple instead. Fran frowned.

"What's up?"

"It was you mentioning Truscote."

"But you brought her up this time!"

"Either way, it made me think about Jeremy. Do you remember what we talked about before?"

Alice's fingers froze in place.

Fran continued. "You know, about me leaving him... and you and me starting over somewhere new?"

"I thought we agreed that was a bad idea. I'm forty-two and all I own is a shitty car and the tiny flat I bought with the money my mum left me. I can't offer you the life Jeremy does."

Fran twisted her fingers into Alice's curls and kissed the top of her head. "I know, but would it matter? I think about us together and imagine our days like this."

"This isn't real life, though, is it? I need to work; I have bills, and there's my overdraft and my credit card—"

"I have needs too, you know."

Alice rolled her eyes. "Needing to get laid isn't the same as needing to get paid, Fran."

"Shh! Don't be a bore." Fran traced lazy circles over Alice's upper arm with her fingertips. "Just imagine you and me, our own cosy little place somewhere. Not having to do all this sneaking around in hotels. We'll have our own big bed and our own soft sheets... I'd be able to have you whenever I wanted to..."

Alice scoffed. "You kind of do that anyway."

Fran turned and muted her with a fervent kiss.

"But what would I do for work?"

Fran slipped her hand between Alice's legs. "You'd be my little sex slave," she purred.

"That's not a real job."

"I beg to differ. With a body like yours, you could fetch good money."

Alice clenched her thighs around Fran's hand. "That's really offensive, actually."

Fran pouted. "Oh, play nicely, Madame French."

Alice relaxed her legs and Fran pushed on. Alice gasped as Fran's fingers found their way inside her. "See, you're not so offended now," she said and glided a third finger inside.

"Oh fuck," Alice murmured, partly in pleasure, partly in disgust at her body's insatiable appetite for this woman.

"There's a good little sex slave." Fran's cackle trickled through Alice, intoxicating her like a potent cocktail; she'd always want just one more sip of her.

Fran built up the tempo, her fingers curling inside and causing waves of pleasure to crash over Alice; her thoughts scrambled until she latched onto something bright and firm... clarity. Oh, how she adored this woman... *why shouldn't Fran leave Jeremy? Maybe the two of us could make a go of it?*

And *fuck*, here she was again, screaming in release as she toppled over the edge, completely undone by the fingers of her lover, *Francesca Dalton*.

FRAN PULLED UP TWO BLOCKS AWAY FROM THE offices of T&D. She cut the engine and twisted in her seat, watching as Alice applied fresh lip gloss in the visor mirror. Alice craned her neck to examine a deep purple bruise, still visible under the caked-on concealer.

"Did you have to bite so hard?"

Fran's painted lips twisted into a smirk as Alice met her gaze. "Here, wear this." Fran untied her silk scarf and looped it around Alice's neck.

"I feel like such a tramp. I'm literally turning up to work in the clothes I was wearing when I left on Friday evening."

"Yes, I suppose that is a little bit slutty." Fran chortled a throaty laugh and rested a hot hand on Alice's knee.

"I just hope no one notices. It's bad enough that I'm, what..." she shook her watch free from the cuff of her blouse, "...four hours late."

Fran laughed louder. "You'd have to be kidding if you think Jeremy'd notice. And as for Truscote, she's so far up her own arse she can barely see daylight. You look gorgeous and you smell divine. That's all that matters." She leaned in and brushed Alice's lips with her own. "I'm having a hard time not thinking about where those lips were last. Are you sure you have to go to work?"

"Yes," Alice said through a smile. "So don't get yourself all revved up again." She gently pushed Fran away, to which she groaned, slumped back into the driver's seat and closed her eyes. *Obviously tired, and just trying her luck... because Fran always gets what she wants, if she really wants it.*

Traffic buzzed by the intersecting road, but in the peaceful bubble of the car, Alice studied Fran's side profile, as she had a thousand times before. *God, she's beautiful.*

A surge of affection soared through her. Why would she not want to be with Fran?

The truth was, she couldn't really imagine why Fran wanted to be with her. But she did. At least, she said she did. Who did Alice think she was to resist? Even if the future was a hazy blur of complications, they'd have each other.

Alice's thoughts spilled into words and punched through their silence. "You know what you've been saying lately... about leaving Jeremy?"

"Mmm?" Fran remained in position, her features serene.

"I was wondering... are you serious about that?"

A slow smile crept over Fran's lips, and she turned to look at Alice with one arched eyebrow. "Deadly."

"Okay. Well, in that case... I think you should." Alice took one of Fran's hands between both of hers. "Let's make a go of things."

"Is this you agreeing to be my sex slave?"

Alice laughed. "No, but if you seriously want to leave Jeremy and be with me, then let's plan for that. I'll find another job and we can move. Start over somewhere else—"

"Good idea. A nice penthouse in London with a swanky postcode. Somewhere trendy, with wine bars and restaurants—"

Alice scoffed. "Don't get carried away. You know how much PAs earn, right?"

"I thought you were an Executive Assistant?" Fran actioned air quotes around Alice's job title.

"I don't earn that much, Fran. I won't be able to afford—"

Fran waved Alice's protest away. "I'll get a good divorce settlement; don't you worry about that. We'll figure it all out."

"I don't just want to freeload, though, I want to contribute to our lives together."

Fran squeezed Alice's hand. "Oh, you'll do your part alright."

Alice rolled her eyes but smiled in spite of herself. "I better get going."

Fran leaned in and crushed Alice's lips with a hard kiss, mussing her hair and smudging her lip gloss. "Think about me," she purred into Alice's mouth.

Alice pulled back, breathless from the bruising kiss. "Christ, Fran. I barely think of anything else."

# 7

# QUEEN OF I-FUCKING-TOLD-YOU-SO

*A*lice peeked around the doorframe and smiled at the sight of Ash curled up on the couch, adrift in peaceful slumber. She fought the urge to replace the cushion Ash's arm was wrapped around with herself.

For the first time in a long time, Alice's waking thought hadn't been of Fran — it had been of breakfast. But with the doctor sleeping in her lounge, it would be rude to rattle through the bare cupboards, searching for food she knew wasn't there.

Alice tiptoed down the hallway and softly closed the front door behind her. Blinking against the stark sunlight, she gripped the wet railing and focused on the steps down from her flat.

At the bottom of the staircase, she did a double take at the sporty black car in her parking bay, before remembering it was Ash's. Alice's own hunk of junk still sat lifeless and abandoned at the hospital, and Maggie hadn't returned her call. Alice reached into her pocket for her phone and tensed when it wasn't there — *ugh, of course.* Despite the inconvenience, she shrugged off the momentary regret at chucking it from the window of the Uber.

An early morning shower of rain had filled the air with a refreshing petrichor, and Alice drew a deep breath of the earthy scent. *Fresh start.*

She walked her usual route of leafy tree-lined streets and Regency terraced houses in the direction of Snoots and their fresh pastries — the best answer to her stomach's demanding growls.

Hopping over the puddles in the cracked pavement, Alice made a pact with herself to get better at grocery shopping. She'd make a weekly meal plan, write a shopping list — and stick to it. It was time to get some routine back into her life. *Time to grow up,* said the voice of her sister inside her head. Alice shook it away, but the thought of Maggie remained. Maggie would like Ash because Ash was sensible and had her life together — from the little Alice knew of her, at least. Although, to be fair, Ash had just spent the night in the flat of a weird woman she'd only known for two days. Perhaps best not to mention that bit to Maggie if she ever introduced them.

*Calm down, you've only just met her and you're already subjecting her to Maggie and Markus.*

COFFEES IN HAND AND BAKED GOODS TUCKED under her elbow, Alice pushed through the front door. Ash appeared in the hallway, her raven hair tousled with sleep and the chenille blanket wrapped around her shoulders like a cape.

"I'm so sorry. I must have fallen asleep on your couch."

"You did, and it's completely fine. I went to fetch us coffee, as well as some of the best croissants you'll ever taste."

"Snoots?"

"You know it?"

"Oh my God, yes." Ash blushed and reached a hand behind her neck. "I mean, thanks... you didn't have to... it's not like I'm your guest. I totally showed up uninvited and fell asleep mid-conversation."

Alice grinned, handing a coffee cup and paper bag to Ash. "You looked so peaceful. I didn't want to disturb you. Besides, you've been so kind to me. It's really above and beyond what I expect from the NIIS."

Laughter sparkled in Ash's eyes. "I offer a very personalised service."

Alice turned and Ash followed her back to the lounge. With her legs curled beneath her on the couch, Alice devoured the buttery croissant and, with her free hand, brushed the flaky pastry from her chest. She eyed Ash, who was carefully plucking flakes from her shirt and popping them in her mouth.

"Don't want to waste a crumb," she said, becoming aware of Alice watching her.

Alice smiled. "I'm pleased you stayed last night. I mean, I know you didn't intend to, but I was grateful for the company."

Ash scoffed. "I wasn't much company... but I'm

pleased you're okay, Alice. I hope it helped to talk things through with someone. I was thinking perhaps, maybe—"

Four loud bangs hammered at the front door and Alice jumped.

"What the—"

A muffled yell came through the door. "Alice, are you there?"

"Maggie?" Alice jumped up and dashed along the hall. She flung open the door to the scowling face of her sister. "What are you doing here?"

"You leave that weird message, Alice, about your car and your phone. And then I can't get hold of you. The line just rings and rings and what else was I supposed to do?"

Without waiting for an invitation, Maggie marched through to the lounge with Alice in tow.

"Oh, hello." Maggie stopped dead at the sight of the other woman and turned to shoot Alice a filthy look.

"Hi. I should, er—" Ash gestured awkwardly to the door.

"Ash, this is Maggie, my sister. Mags, Ash is my — doctor. I mean, friend. She's not my doctor. She's *a* doctor, who is also my friend…" Alice's words trailed off into an awkward laugh.

"Right." Maggie stepped forward and limply shook Ash's hand before turning back to Alice with a death stare. "And also, she's no doubt the reason you couldn't answer your bloody phone and tell me that you're okay?"

"What? I told you to call the landline."

"I did, Alice. It just rings," Maggie said through gritted teeth.

Alice moved to the sideboard and pulled the phone cord, which came free in her hand. She winced and held up the loose connection. "Shit, I forgot I'd unplugged it. Telemarketers drive me mad."

Maggie threw her arms up. "Oh, bloody hell, Al. Markus is fuming that I made him drive all the way over here on a Sunday morning. What were you thinking?"

"Clearly, I wasn't. I didn't mean to put you out. I just needed a little help."

Maggie shot another sidelong glance at Ash, who was rubbing her neck.

"Well, thank you for coming to check I'm alive. I've had a rough couple of days. I think my car needs a jump; it's been out of action since Friday night. That's when I met Ash."

"I see." Mags darted a third disapproving look at Ash in as many minutes before fixing a hard gaze back on Alice, her blue eyes a shade lighter than Alice's and all the more piercing for it.

"Right, well, you'll have to get yourself together now and we'll get going. Markus is waiting outside. Engine's running, so don't be long."

"Okay, yep. I'll be right there." Alice saluted and Maggie tossed her a look of disdain before retreating down the hallway.

"Nice to meet you, Ashley," she called over her shoulder without a backward glance.

"It's Asha," Alice yelled back as the front door slammed shut.

Ash puffed out a breath. "Blimey, is she always so intense?"

"Yeah, pretty much. We've always been close, but we've not seen eye-to-eye for a while now." Alice massaged her palm into her forehead.

"Don't worry about it. Families, eh? I don't exactly have the best relationship with mine, but that's a long story for another time."

*Another time.*

"You were about to say something before Maggie rudely interrupted us."

Ash scratched the back of her neck. "Oh, just that I need to be heading off to get myself ready for another exciting shift. Thanks again for..." she gestured to the couch, where at some point during the Maggie whirlwind she'd folded the blanket and fixed the cushions; a small gesture that pulled a smile from Alice.

"It's no problem. Really, thank *you*. You were so kind to check in on me and, you know... listen to me. I won't forget that."

Ash smiled. "On behalf of the NHS, you're very welcome." Her eyebrows drew into a frown, and she breathed in as if she was about to say something else, but instead she looked down at her stripy socks and wiggled her toes.

A moment passed before Alice spoke. "Well, I suppose I shouldn't keep Maggie waiting."

The words seemed to tug Ash back from whatever internal battle of indecision she was in and she moved to the front door, bending down to pull on her trainers. Alice shrugged on a coat and tapped the pocket containing her keys.

"Right then." Ash straightened up. She stood a couple of inches taller than Alice without heels, which Alice hadn't appreciated until now. She wondered what it would be like to be wrapped in her arms, and as if reading her thoughts, Ash stepped closer and pulled her into an embrace just like the one she'd been imagining. Ash's strong, capable arms held her tight and, for a moment, everything else seemed insignificant.

"Things seem messy right now, but you're going to be okay."

Alice closed her eyes and inhaled Ash's cedarwood scent. She hadn't noticed it last night, but now it filled her senses.

The obnoxious blast of a car horn sounded from outside, and Ash's arms fell away.

"Introducing my dear brother-in-law, Markus."

Ash laughed and stepped back. "Take care of yourself," she said, looking at Alice with the warm consideration of someone who'd known her for much longer than a couple of days.

IN THE BACK OF MARKUS' BRAND-NEW RANGE Rover, Alice chewed the inside of her lip, biting at a new blood blister until she felt the satisfying pop between her teeth. A metallic taste filled her mouth.

Clearly annoyed that his Sunday morning had been so

selfishly interrupted by his irritant of a sister-in-law, Markus had grunted little more than three words to Alice since she'd slid into the backseat, and two of them were "buckle up."

Maggie fixed her gaze out of the front passenger window and Markus cranked up the volume on Radio 5 Live — where two male commentators were enthusiastically discussing another man's groin injury.

"Well, he should've been pulled off in the first half. Didn't I say that? I don't know why they even put the bloody idiot on." He banged the steering wheel.

Maggie puffed out an irritated breath and flicked the radio off.

"Oi! I was listening to that."

"I can't hear myself think with all that jabbering nonsense and I would like to speak with my sister, please. I haven't seen her for weeks."

"Look, I'm really sorry to put you both out. Hopefully, it won't take long, and you can be on your way," said Alice, meeting Markus's glowering eyes in the rear-view mirror.

*Moody bastard.*

"Why didn't your sleepover friend offer to jump-start your car?" asked Markus.

Maggie scoffed. "They've only just met, so it would've probably been a bit of an imposition."

Markus searched out Alice's eyes again and waggled his eyebrows.

"Classy, Alice. One-night stand, was it?"

"Fuck off, Markus," she muttered under her breath.

"Tinder?... or do you lesbians have your own app?"

Maggie slapped his arm. "Stop it."

"If you must know, Ash is a friend. That's it. We met at the hospital because I found a man in the road who needed help, so I took him to A&E. Ash was the doctor on duty and she popped by to give me an update on how he's doing. That's all. No fucking scandal, okay?"

Markus shrugged his broad shoulders and Alice glared at the back of his priggish head.

"And why does everyone think I'm on Tinder? I was literally in a relationship up until two days ago, so... *fuuuuck*..." Alice scrubbed her face with her palms.

Maggie twisted around to look at her.

"You've ended things with Fran?"

"Yeeeees," Alice said impatiently, her voice on the seesaw edge of cracking.

Maggie reached between the seats and steadied Alice's bouncing knee.

"You must be happy now, Mags. You never approved of Fran. Go on, say it, say *I told you so*... because you were right." Even through her scrunched-up eyes, the tears started to fall. *Fucking hell, not here, not now.*

"Oh, Al." Maggie's eyes softened with understanding. "Markus, pull over."

"What? No."

Maggie thumped his arm. "Pull over," she said through gritted teeth.

With a loud huff, Markus indicated and pulled into a bus lay-by. Maggie unclipped her seatbelt, jumped out and slid into the backseat next to her crying mess of a sister.

"Come here. Let it all out."

Alice folded herself into Maggie's surprisingly comforting arms and sobbed.

"Oh, for fuck's sake," Markus grumbled.

Maggie ignored him and tightened her grip around Alice, gently rocking her. "I'm so sorry, Al. I knew you'd end up getting hurt like this, but I wanted to be wrong."

"No, you didn't. You said before I shouldn't be involved with a married—"

"Well, no, you shouldn't have, but that doesn't mean I wanted you to get hurt."

Alice hiccupped a sob.

Markus thrust a box of tissues towards them between the front seats.

"Don't get snot on my interior," he mumbled.

Maggie gave Alice an incredulous look, and they both burst into laughter.

"What?" Markus said, his forehead creased in confusion.

"You really are a prick, you know that?" Maggie continued to chuckle as she brushed back Alice's curls and planted a kiss on her forehead.

RAIN PATTERED ON THE WINDSCREEN AS MARKUS parked up alongside Alice's Fiesta, his shiny new vehicle somehow making her shitty little car look even more pathetic. Since when had she cared? A car was a car, and she barely needed to use it, but over the last twenty-four hours it had somehow come to represent a metaphor for her self; a bit knackered and rather broken.

As she stood despairing, the reassuring weight of Maggie's arm wrapped around her shoulder.

"C'mon, let's go get a cuppa before we sort that out."

"I know a place," said Alice.

She led them to the quirky muffin café and once inside, she glanced around, a tiny bit hopeful to see Ash, but also not, given the snot-bubbling state of her... again.

There was no Ash, but the spot they'd shared yesterday by the window was free. Markus bought the drinks and delivered them to the table. Maggie offered no protest when he suggested taking his latte back to the car to listen to the rugby so they could have their 'sisterly chat' without him intruding. Alice studied her sister's face, watching her as she watched her lumbering hulk of a husband retreat.

Maggie's asymmetrical bob framed her angular features in contrast to the softer lines of Alice's. When she and Markus had been going through their rough patch, Maggie had taken her frustrations out on her own body, hitting the gym hard and slashing her calorie intake to achieve a concerning deficit. Her 'revenge body', she'd called it. *Skeletal* is the term Alice would've gone for. And Mags did it all to get back at him, to show him that he'd dined out on dog meat (twice!), when there was prime rib at home. *What an unbelievable arsehole he'd been.*

Yet, it was Maggie who believed she'd 'married up.' She'd had the honour of becoming a Carter-Mills and just in time for their mum to witness before she passed away. Maggie proved to everyone that she'd made it. Despite her humble beginnings, she'd bagged a privately educated career man. Still, Alice couldn't help thinking her sister had fallen short — in the lottery of life, Markus hadn't exactly lucked out on looks, and his personality did little to compensate.

With a far-off look, Maggie chewed her thumbnail, which steeped Alice in guilt. She'd been so wrapped up in Fran recently, she'd neglected everything else, even her sister.

"How are things with you two?" Alice asked softly, pulling Maggie's focus back to her.

"Oh, we're fine. He's just... Markus."

Alice narrowed her eyes.

"Counselling dredges up a lot of stuff. It's hard." Maggie sipped her green tea. "Anyway, we're not here to talk about me, Al."

"I haven't been a very good sister lately. I'm sorry... I'm going to get better at... well, at everything now. It's spring." Alice nodded her head and blew on the steaming mug cupped between her hands.

Maggie's eyebrows pinched together.

"Spring, you know... the season of new beginnings."

"Right. Okay. Well, one step at a time. Are you going to search for a new job?"

"Do you think I need to?"

Maggie glared at her with wide eyes. "Aren't you in a bit of a compromised position?"

Alice tilted her head and Maggie leaned in, lowering her voice to a faint whisper.

"You know, the fact that you've just ended a relationship with the wife of your employer. Wouldn't it be better to leave on your own terms? Avoid the risk of it all coming out and destroying your reputation?"

"I suppose, but I don't have anything else lined up. I enjoy the work and I like Jeremy. Truscote's okay too, as long as she keeps her nose out of my business."

"Does Truscote know about the affair?"

Alice nodded gravely.

Maggie placed her hands flat on the rough wooden tabletop and looked Alice square in the eye.

"Al, you need to resign. Francesca Dalton is a woman scorned and she'll lash out when she doesn't get what she wants. If you're serious about ending things with her, then you're probably going to lose your job anyway."

Alice chewed her lip, processing Maggie's words and their implications with a slow nod.

"I'll speak to Markus. Perhaps there are some suitable roles at his place? They're always looking for new assistants."

Alice scoffed. "And why do you think that is?"

Maggie stiffened. "Low blow, Alice. I'm sitting here trying to help you and, needless to say, we both showed up for you today."

Alice raised her hands in apology.

Maggie pursed her lips and fixed her gaze out of the window.

Alice reached across to her. "Mags, I'm sorry. It just came out. I've never forgiven Markus for hurting you." Alice stared up into Maggie's face as she rubbed her sister's palms with her thumbs.

"What about you, Alice? You're no better, carrying on with a married woman all this time. I thought you liked Jeremy—"

"I do like Jeremy. What I had with Fran... you make it sound like some sordid affair, but it was different. I can't explain it."

"It was no different. Why can't you see that? Someone was still being cheated on. Someone was always going to get hurt."

Alice sat back and folded her arms. "Like I said, it's over. So, you were right. Well done, Maggie, Queen of I-Fucking-Told-You-So."

After an impasse, the expressions of the scowling sisters softened. Maggie spoke first, leaning across the table to cup Alice's cheek with her hand.

"Let's not fight, Al. I hate to see you hurting."

"Me too. I'm sorry. I didn't mean to be cruel about Markus, and I am ashamed of—"

"Shh! Don't say it. You've been so brave and I'm proud of you. You'll soon feel better about all of this."

Alice forced a smile. "I hope so, Mags, because I can't feel much worse."

THE KNACKERED FIESTA ROARED BACK TO LIFE.

"Huzzah!" Markus pumped his fist in the air like it was a major triumph of the human race. He unclipped the jump leads from the battery and let the bonnet slam with a metallic *thunk.*

"I'll chuck these in the back for you. You'll need them again before I do." Markus gestured to his shiny Range Rover. *Smug prick.* Then, in an almost overwhelming display of empathy (by Markus's standards), he patted Alice roughly on the shoulder with his bear-paw-like hand and said, "Take care now, won't you?"

Alice opened her mouth to reply, but before any words could be uttered, Markus had once again ensconced himself in his car to resume shouting at the radio.

Maggie pulled Alice into a hug.

"Plug that phone back in, Al. And call me when you're home, okay?"

"Thanks again, Mags. For everything."

Maggie held Alice out at arm's length. "Come over in the week and I'll cook. Markus will be home late on Tuesday. We'll open a bottle and chat, or watch a film, whatever you need. Just don't be on your own when you're like this."

"I'm fine."

"No, you're not."

"I am and it depends on whether the car is—"

"Get an Uber."

Alice opened her mouth to protest.

"I'll pay." Maggie rubbed Alice's arms in a motion she probably intended to be soothing, but if anything, Alice felt like her fur was being rubbed the wrong way.

"Just come. Let me know how you get on at work. Make sure you get ahead of this whole thing, or it'll blow up on you." Maggie gripped the lapels of Alice's coat and peered into her face. Alice squirmed under her sister's harsh focus. There was no escaping this scrutiny.

"Okay. Yes."

"Yes, what?"

"Yes, I'll plug my phone in, I'll call you, I'll quit my job, then I'll come over and I'll bring wine," Alice said in one breath and bulged out her eyes.

Maggie gave a satisfied nod and released her.

"Good, see you Tuesday." She pulled her coat around her knees as she climbed into the car, her small frame dwarfed by the colossal chassis. "Don't bring wine, we've got plenty."

"You mean, don't bring the cheap stuff?" Alice laughed, and Maggie poked her tongue out.

"You know me too well. Love you, Al. Be good."

Alice blew her a kiss and closed the car door. She waved them off and watched the Range Rover's taillights glisten in the persistent drizzle.

Sat in the driver's seat of her Ford Fiesta, the engine ticked over as Alice rested her head on the steering wheel and released a heavy breath. She should drive home, type out her resignation letter, dust off her resume and apply for some jobs. She should check her credit card balance and if the credit fairies deemed it possible, she should order a new phone and buy some groceries — healthy things like kale and chia seeds. And whilst she was at it, she'd sign up to a yoga class and work on her pelvic floor; after all, she wasn't getting any younger.

*C'mon.* She lifted her head and gripped the wheel.

What she really wanted was to check on George. A flurry of cherry blossom splattered onto the wet windscreen.

No, what she *really* wanted was to see Ash.

Alice shook her head. *Ridiculous and completely unnecessary.* She met her own eyes in the rear-view mirror.

*One. Ash is not interested in you.*

*Two. You are not actually interested in her. She was kind when you were feeling low. Don't mistake that for anything else because it's not. Ash isn't your type. You like older women.*

Sophisticated, powerful women with sharp edges to contrast with her own soft ones.

*Like Fran.*

*Fucking Fran.* Alice bounced her forehead on her hands.

A light tapping on the driver's side window roused her. She turned her head to a distorted figure on the other side of the rain-spattered glass, a blur of khaki and black clothing.

"Ash?" Alice cranked down the window, bringing the doctor's quirky grin into focus. Ash leaned her arm on the wet roof and peered down into the car.

"I'm starting to wonder whether you even know how to drive."

Alice laughed a little too loudly; a glow seemed to radiate from inside her, which must have beamed out of her face.

"I was just sitting here having a little think. That's not a crime, is it?"

"Depends on what you were thinking about."

Alice grinned and words escaped her mouth before

she'd had time to vet them. "Are you flirting with me, Doctor?"

Colour rushed into Ash's cheeks, and she stepped back from the car. "No, sorry, I, er... didn't mean to..."

Alice smiled, but disappointment zipped through her at the confirmation Ash didn't like her like *that* and, worse, her flirting had made Ash uncomfortable.

"I was thinking about George, and trying to decide whether to pop in to see him. But if I cut the engine, this old girl might not get going again. Markus left the jump leads for me, but I'm not sure how to use them."

"I do, so I can jump you."

"There you go, flirting again." Alice bit her lip to stifle a laugh.

Ash's blush deepened, and she cleared her throat. "Come on, let's go and see how our patient is doing."

Alice didn't need to be asked twice; groceries and yoga could wait. She twisted the key, silencing the ticking engine.

"How old are you?" The question popped from Alice's mouth before she'd realised she'd said it aloud.

Ash laughed. "Why?"

"I just... wondered."

"Thirty-seven. Rapidly sliding down that slippery slope to forty."

*Not that much younger. And very confident, but not in a Fran way; in a professional, assertive way.* "Hmm."

"What does '*hmm*' mean?" Ash stared at her, looking bemused.

Alice smiled and shook her head. "Forty-two, in case you were wondering."

"I wasn't, but thank you." Ash grinned.

As they stepped over the rippling puddles of the car park towards the hospital, Alice tried and failed not to notice the flattering way Ash's dark jeans hugged her thighs. Flicking her gaze to the large yellow sign listing the parking rates, Alice came to a stop and puffed out her cheeks. "My parking ticket is going to cost a bloody fortune."

Ash touched her arm. "Don't worry, I'll speak to Pinkie. He'll sort it out."

"Pinkie?" Alice laughed.

"Pinkie Pete, the security guy who looks after the parking, too. I'll tell him why you've been stuck in here and he'll sort your ticket out."

"You can do that?"

"Yeah, Pinkie owes me a favour, anyway. I saved his little finger."

Alice blinked at Ash, who was grinning and looking proud of herself. "You what?"

"He had a bit of an accident with a mitre saw."

Alice grimaced, and Ash's eyes widened in relish.

"He came into A&E as white as a ghost, slipped his detached digit — sealed in a freezer bag — onto the check-in desk and then passed out. By the time he came around, I'd stitched it back on and you'd hardly even know." Ash wiggled her little finger in the air.

"Well, there are two things I have to say about that: *ew*, but also *wow*."

A blast of warm air and noise hit them as they stepped through the sliding doors into the entrance of A&E. A hive of activity buzzed in the strip-lit waiting room. Alice surveyed the throng of people in their various states of triage and regretted her decision not to go kale shopping, but Ash took her arm and steered her over to a quiet corner.

"Wait here for a minute. I'll find out where they've sent George."

Alice's eyes followed Ash as she wove through the melee with the confidence of someone who'd done it a thousand times before. The sharp smell of disinfectant stung Alice's nostrils. She could've been sniffing sandal-wood and doing a sun salutation, *but no* — she stood, trying to remind herself why she was here.

Ash returned a few minutes later and guided Alice through double swing doors into an empty corridor. Their shoes echoed a symphony of squeaks off the bare walls as they paced towards an elevator bank. Ash pressed the 'up' button and a red light illuminated around it. She made wide eyes at Alice.

"Looks like it's going to be a busy shift tonight."

"I don't know how you do it."

Ash shrugged. "I don't suppose it's for everyone, but I knew what I was getting myself into. I love the thrill of it. It's totally unpredictable, from sewing a finger back on to literally saving a life. Just helping people and making a difference gives me such a rush."

"I could think of better ways to get a rush." Alice raised her eyebrows, then internally kicked herself for flirting *again,* but this time, instead of being abashed, Ash's lips quirked into her signature grin. They locked eyes for a moment until a thought seemed to snap Ash's attention away and she tapped the pockets of her parka.

"Oh, talking of helping people..." Ash unzipped the left pocket and pulled out a mobile phone, which she held out to Alice. "You lost your phone, and this is an old one I had in a drawer at home. You'll need to pick up a SIM card, but I thought it might do you for now, until you get sorted."

Alice stared at the device in Ash's hand, lost for words... for once.

"Shit. I've overstepped, haven't I?"

"No, it's just—"

Ash's eyes popped. "Oh God, Fran and the tracking?"

Alice nodded. "Yeah, she bought me my last phone and set it all up. I guess that's how she..."

"Alice, I wouldn't do that. I'm not a creep... I mean, it isn't a normal thing to do, is it? It's been factory reset, look." Ash held up the device with its screen looping on the set-up instructions.

"You're being so kind to me, and you don't even know me. And what you do know doesn't exactly give the best impression." Alice bowed her head.

Ash stepped closer and puffed out a breath. "What I *know* is that you stopped to help someone else when you were in distress yourself. And I know that you're coming out of a difficult... complicated relationship, and you're being really brave about it. You're doing your best, Alice."

Ash's words pulled a smile from her.

"Well, if you don't mind me borrowing your old phone, it'd really help me out."

As she took the phone from Ash's proffered hand, their fingers brushed, and a giddying fizz of excitement bubbled through Alice. *Did Ash feel that too?*

Alice looked up and met the captivating depth of Ash's dark brown eyes, noticing for the first time the amber flecks in her irises.

Ash licked her lips and spoke in an almost-whisper. "Alice, I—"

The elevator clunked onto their floor, and with a *ding*, the metal doors rolled open.

"Finally," Ash said, stepping into the bright metal box, leaving Alice wondering what she'd been about to say for the second time in a day.

## 1968

## THE CHANCE TO ESCAPE

*D*aylight lasered through the split in the mothy brown curtains and I buried my face into the pillow, inhaling my own smell. Over the last few months I'd noticed a change in my scent; sometimes musty, sometimes sour, never particularly pleasant. Upon further examination, I discovered clusters of wiry dark hairs sprouting under my armpits and, more disturbingly, in other places. When I'd asked Mum about it, she just chuckled her soft, buttery laugh, kissed my forehead and said, "Georgie-boy, you're nearly fourteen. You're turning into a man. A little extra hair will soon be the least of your worries."

And she wasn't wrong.

Pyg stirred at the foot of my bed. I patted the blanket, and she crawled low, like a ninja, along the bare floorboards and hopped up next to me. Her wet nose nuzzled at my arm until her head poked through from under my smelly armpit.

"Morning, girl." My voice rasped with sleep, but at least it came out low and not squeaky like it often did lately. Pyg leaned in as I scratched her ears, her bushy tail thumping on the bedspread like a bass drum.

Propping myself up on my elbows, I frowned at the empty, unmade bed across the room.

"Where's Bernie, eh?" I whispered.

Pyg cocked her head.

I swung my legs out of bed, stretched and yawned.

As if her strings were being pulled by an invisible puppeteer, Pyg sat up straighter, as I poked my head around the doorframe. All the doors along the hallway were shut, so I tiptoed along the landing with ninja-Pyg silent in my wake — we'd taught her well. *To the right, right, left, right again,* and every third floorboard until the clock. Then *four, six, two* and *breathe.*

We made it to the top of the stairs without a creak. I looked down at Pyg and double-blinked for 'well done'. She double-blinked back; smarter than half the kids in my class at school, but that wasn't hard.

I pointed to my temple. *Focus.* I gestured for Pyg to take the stairs first. At least that way she wouldn't be blamed if I miscounted and made a sound, like the last time.

I clicked the kitchen door to a close behind us. Pyg ran to the French doors, so I let her outside. Still no trace of Bernard. *He must be in the studio with Mum.*

Stretching up, I reached for a glass from the shelf. Only a month ago, I'd had to stand on a chair. I winced as I turned the tap and the old pipes rattled into life. The cold water spluttered out, as it always did, and I drank, relishing the coolness on my dry throat. I wiped the glass with the front of my vest and placed it back on the shelf.

*No trace means no trouble.* Mum's words underscored our mouse-like existence inside this house.

Following Pyg into the garden, I hunched and rubbed my goose-fleshed arms; my vest and briefs were not the most practical attire to face the autumnal morning. I should've thought to grab a sweater, but I couldn't think of everything. The long dewy grass glittered in the pale sunlight and whipped my bare ankles as I quick-stepped down the path towards the studio.

As I neared, I stopped in my tracks because unusually, the wooden door was ajar, and an odd scuffling sounded from inside. I waited, angling my ear to the gap until the scuffling morphed into the timid sniffs of Bernard crying. I pushed through the door, and Bernard lay on the rug with Pyg now curled around him.

"Hey, what's up, Bernie?" I dropped to my knees and stroked Bernard's hair back from his forehead.

"She's... she's—" A sob choked Bernard's words, and he covered his eyes with his forearm, as if it might dam his tears. I rubbed his back.

"Hey, c'mon. What's this all about, lad?"

Pyg whimpered.

"Look, you're upsetting Pyg. It's alright, girl. He's alright."

"No, I'm not," Bernard roared, and he thrust a balled-up sheet of writing paper at me.

Frowning, I smoothed out the scrunched paper on the rug. Between the creases and splodges, presumably tears, I struggled to decipher the intricate swoops and loops of our mother's handwriting until an impatient Bernard found his voice again.

"She's left us, George. She's fucking left us."

With greater urgency, my eyes dropped back to the crumpled missive on the floor, scanning the scrawl. I picked out snippets from the jumble of words.

*I can't live like this any more... it feels like poison ivy, choking the life out of me... A wonderful opportunity has finally presented itself... the chance to escape all this... We'll be able to start a new life... I promise, promise, <u>promise</u> I'll send for you as soon as I can... It'll be a fresh start, for all of us... money is tight, so it may take a while... Boys, please don't be angry with me x*

Then my gaze snagged on a word; a name in the ink that suddenly made sense of everything.

## 8

## PIGS AND DOGS

George's eyes twitched underneath his thick eyelids when Alice walked into the room.

"Hello, George. It's me again, your pal, Alice. Ash is here at the hospital too. I guess you know her as Doctor Khurana. We came to see how you're getting on."

Alice glanced around the small rectangular room and moved toward the plastic upholstered chair in the corner. The functional space was furnished with typical items; a copy-and-paste of pretty much every hospital room anywhere, but outside the large window stood a pretty tree, its vivid green foliage striking against the slate-grey sky.

"Nice room they've given you."

The window was in line with the tree's tallest branches and blossom bloomed amongst its leaves. Alice hadn't really appreciated spring before, but since meeting Ash, she seemed to be noticing it everywhere.

She turned back into the room, eyes adjusting from the

dull daylight to the overhead lighting, and perched on the chair. George's wild hair and beard seemed to get tamer by the day now that someone was taking regular care of brushing them. His hospital gown had been replaced with some paisley pyjamas.

Alice reached out and touched his hand. "It'll be nice to meet you properly when you're awake. Ash, Doctor K., has popped off to see if there's any more information about your brother. Bernard, I think?"

At the mention of Bernard, George's eyes moved rapidly under his eyelids. Alice gently squeezed the man's large, rough hand under her own.

"George, do you know that I'm talking about your brother Bernard?"

The man's eyelashes twitched as if he were trying to open his eyes, but the lids were too heavy.

"You can hear me, can't you?" Alice leaned closer and enunciated each word, as if somehow speaking clearly would rouse him into consciousness. "They've been trying to get hold of Bernard so we can find out what's going on with you and get you the help you need."

A jolly chuckle preceded a rotund Black nurse as she bustled a trolley into the room.

"You won't get much out of Mr George," she said in an accent as rich as ginger cake. She peered at Alice over the top of her gold-rimmed glasses and Alice glanced at the name badge pinned to the nurse's generous chest — *Marjorie Reid. Staff Nurse.*

Marjorie manoeuvred around the room, picking things up and putting them down again.

"George wakes, eats a few mouthfuls in between mumbling a load of nonsense about pigs and dogs. He works himself up and then he goes back to sleep, just like that." She snapped her fingers whilst waving her forearm in the air.

"Pigs and dogs?"

"Yes, yes. Pigs and dogs."

"Oh, well that's new. It was just pigs before, not dogs."

"Today he said, 'the pigs *are* dogs' or some such thing." The nurse shrugged her round shoulders and continued to busy herself in the room. "You're his relation?"

"No, I'm just a friend... I don't really know him at all, actually—"

"Well, it's time for his bed bath, so unless you want to get to know him much better, you might want to make yourself scarce." The nurse chortled and whipped back the bed covers, revealing the man's entire pyjama-clad frame. The bulk of him looked so vulnerable, laid out flat on the sterile sheets.

Alice stood and squeezed the man's hand again. "George, I'll go and find Ash to see what's going on. Enjoy your bath," she added as an afterthought.

The nurse's merry chuckle continued as Alice closed the door behind her and stood alone in the corridor with a faulty strip-light flickering overhead. Alice resisted the pull of the vending machine humming in the corner and eased herself down into the end seat on a row of shiny blue plastic chairs. She pulled Ash's old phone out of her pocket and turned it over in her hand. Currently as useful as a brick, with no SIM card or phone numbers programmed into it, but she smiled at the device and then pressed it to her lips, enjoying the feel of the cool glass screen against her skin.

There had never been a shortage of flashy gifts from Fran — jewellery, perfume, all the latest mobile phones, expensive weekends away and fine dining in exclusive restaurants. There'd even been talk of a trip abroad — somewhere chic and European. But everything with Fran was transactional; she was either buying something she wanted from Alice or paying for something she'd done to her.

With a loud whoosh, Ash burst through the double doors at the end of the corridor. Alice almost dropped the phone as she scrambled to stuff it back in her pocket.

"Hey, sorry I was gone so long. Why are you sitting out here?" Ash slunk down into the seat next to Alice.

Alice nodded towards the closed door of George's room. "Bed bath."

"I take it you didn't want to help?" Ash giggled.

"Funnily enough, no. Any news?"

"Not really. They've continued to try the landline for George's brother. The answering machine must be full now, as it just rings out."

"Oh, that's so frustrating. Poor George."

"Perhaps his brother doesn't like telemarketers either?" Ash playfully nudged Alice with her elbow.

Alice chewed her lip to restrain her smile. "So what will happen if they can't reach anyone for him?"

"They'll keep trying for now. George is scheduled for some scans tomorrow and he has a follow-up with the neurologist, which'll help give us some idea of what we're dealing with."

"But will they just release him without support?"

Ash shrugged. "I guess it depends on what's actually wrong with him. If we don't think he's capable of looking after himself, we'll have to get Social Services involved. It's looking like that might be where we're heading as things stand at the moment."

Alice must have been frowning as Ash summoned a kind smile and placed a hand on her back, that charming bedside manner shining reassuringly through the clouds of worry. *Do they train them to do this in med school?*

"It's hard to say what'll happen, but for now he's in the right place and we're taking care of him." Ash pulled out her phone and illuminated the screen. "Okay, I have a couple of hours until my shift starts. Let's get Pinkie to sort out your parking and I can jump your car if it won't start."

Alice nodded, slowly standing as if compressed by the weight of her to-do-list: *write a resignation, sort out the car, get a SIM card... buy some bloody chia seeds.* Inertia crept in like treacle, molasses in her veins, and she imagined sliding beneath the sheets of her unmade bed and hibernating for a while. *Bears have the right idea.*

For so long, she'd been using Fran as a fantastical excuse to put off real life, but now the illusion had shattered, Alice realised that was all it ever was — a fantasy. Life with Fran was a fairy tale, and like many of the great fairy tales, it was written by a sadist who'd cast their protagonist under the spell of a witch. But instead of a happy ending, the witch had eaten Alice alive.

"Alice? Earth to Alice!" Ash's words crashed into Alice's thoughts.

"Sorry, what was that?"

"I asked whether you fancied a cuppa first."

"Yeah, actually. That'd be nice."

Ash bent her head in a shallow bow and flourished a hand for Alice to lead the way.

Alice laughed. "Er, you're going to have to guide us out of this rabbit warren. I've no idea where we are."

## 1968

### BLACK OUT

*A*s if life wasn't already difficult enough, in the wake of our mother's departure it became invariably tougher. The only reprieve was school — and that was saying something.

"My mother says your mother's a tart." The taunts stung as much as the blows.

"Shut your stupid mouth!" Bernard's anguished yells reached me before I rounded the corner into the playground.

"Oh Christ, Bernie," I muttered under my breath, clenching my fists in preparation.

My brother gripped the collar of pale-faced Johnny Malone and pushed him against the wall. Johnny's thin lips snarled and then he barked laughter in the face of the younger, much smaller boy. The gang of Johnny's mates pressed closer.

"Go on, hit me, you little wimp." Johnny turned his head and presented his pockmarked jaw, feathered with pubescent fuzz. The crowd of boys jeered, and Johnny laughed again.

I elbowed my way through the boys and held Bernard's primed arm.

"Don't waste your energy, Bernie. He's not worth it."

"Get off me!" Bernard's high-pitched squawk prompted a boom of laughter from the boys, gathered and grunting like baying baboons.

"No, come on." I pulled my brother back by the shoulders, his small frame easily yielding.

"Aw, I wanted him to hit me like your mammy's head hits the headboard when she's shagging the priest, and probably anyone else who wants a go."

In one swift move, I shoved Bernard away and swung my arm until my fist connected with Johnny Malone's face. Two cracks followed: Johnny's nose breaking, and his head hitting the brick wall.

Johnny cupped his bleeding nose and slid to the ground; his mates crowded in. Adrenaline pulsing, I weaved and ducked out of the scuffle, grabbing the open-mouthed Bernard by the sleeve and tugging him away from the scene.

"SHIT, SHIT, SHIT." I PEERED AROUND THE enormous oak tree at the edge of the field.

Bernard stared up at me. "I think you broke his bloody nose, George." A smile widened across his face. "I actually heard it crack."

"Me too, but that's not a good thing. We're in deep shit now, Bernie." I swallowed, my mouth as dry as sawdust.

"Yeah, but that'll teach him for talking rubbish about Mum." Bernard bounced on the balls of his feet, fists up as if sparring with an imaginary adversary.

"Not rubbish though, is it?" I muttered.

"What was that?" Bernard threw a right hook.

"Nothing." I huffed and slumped against the tree, watching as my brother bobbed around throwing punches at the air, apparently oblivious to both the truth and the trouble we were in.

Nearly two months Mum had been gone and not a word from her. Not a phone call or letter, or even a message via our grandmother. We'd quickly given up asking to avoid the grim satisfaction that lit up the otherwise sour features of our grandmother's face.

"That's what stray bitches do, abandon their little bastard pups. Just be grateful I'm still willing to put a roof over your heads and food in your stomachs."

*It's the least you can do,* I thought, but kept my mouth shut.

Between us, Bernard and I picked up most of the housekeeping chores, aside from the cooking. We'd tried and failed — resulting in one pot of inedible burned potatoes and one burned finger, Bernard's, which Grandmother roughly lathered in margarine as she snapped at him to "stop snivelling like a sissy."

Thereafter, a dowdy little woman called Miss Bray, who wore a crucifix so big it looked like it might snap her scrawny neck, came in to cook three times a week. She showed up with grocery shopping, purchased from the miserly budget Grandmother afforded her, and left behind a refrigerator full of evening meals, which I heated and served.

The three of us ate together, sitting around the kitchen table in silence, except for when Grandmother lectured us on our eating etiquette and table manners, or lack thereof.

We'd taken to shutting Pyg in the studio during school hours, keeping her out of Grandmother's, and harm's, way. At night we waited until the old woman heaved her creaky frame upstairs to bed and then we'd sneak Pyg into our bedroom; ninja-stealth mode. We fed her scraps from our own lean meals — cold cuts and stale bread — her eyes glistening as she hungered for more.

"Sorry, girl, that's all there is," I would say, stroking the soft downy fur of her head and ignoring the growl of my own stomach. *Where are you, Mum?*

"George?" A voice pulled me from my thoughts. Bernard had slumped down next to me, his back resting on the oak tree and his head on my shoulder. "What did Johnny mean by what he said about the priest?"

"Huh?"

Bernard's light eyebrows drew together as he concentrated. "You know, he said that Mum was—"

"Just stupid rumours, Bernie."

"Did he mean Father Higgins? Because he's been gone a while now, too."

I shrugged. *Fucking Higgins.*

The shrill school bell signalled the end of lunch and stymied Bernard's line of questioning. I jumped to my feet and lowered an arm to pull Bernard up, wincing as he gripped my hand, my bruised knuckles a throbbing reminder of the deep shit we were in.

"Come on, let's get this over with."

I'd barely walked through the main entrance before I was met by Sister Evelyn's haughty voice.

"George Shaw. Father Sutherland's office, immediately." Her words quavered like her jowls.

Bernard shot me a doe-eyed look of apology and slunk off to his classroom. I took a calming breath and trod heavy steps in the direction of Father Sutherland's office. I gulped at the trail of dried blood dotted along the dingy corridor. No doubt Johnny Malone's. And I berated myself for defending our mother's honour.

*Why bother? The rumours were true, weren't they? At least where Higgins was concerned. And now she's off, shacked up with him somewhere.* I shook my head to expel the thought, to dismiss the delirious grin that always lit up Mum's face in the presence of Higgins.

The bloody trail continued past where I came to a stop at the wooden church pew. I sat waiting to be summoned; waiting to receive Father Sutherland's wrath, and no doubt his ruler across the back of my legs. As if my knuckles weren't sore enough, the sadistic old bastard would make sure I couldn't sit down for a week without wanting to cry.

*And all for what? A mother who'd abandoned us.* Still, the crack of Malone's nose had been quite satisfying. I flexed and clenched my fingers.

The heavy wooden door creaked open, and the white-haired head of the priest peered out. "Come on in, Mr Shaw."

With leaden legs, I hung my head and sloped into the office like a dead man walking. But I accepted my fate; I'd always defend my mother and Bernard against bullies like Malone. For that, I wasn't sorry.

The musty room smelt of cigarettes and furniture polish, and dust motes swirled in the light of the low sun streaming from the window behind the priest's desk. I stood by the floor-to-ceiling bookcase, which housed tomes that were probably heavier than Bernard.

"Take a seat please, Mr Shaw."

I tentatively perched on the bench in front of the desk. Already dwarfed by the towering man, in the low seat I felt like I'd been shrunk to Lilliputian proportions. Defiantly, I lifted my gaze to meet the priest's sunken blue eyes. I was surprised not to see a face contorted in anger, like it had been the last time I'd entered this room, but a soft expression.

"I understand that things haven't been easy for your grandmother since your mother went on mission."

"Mission?" My voice came out as tiny as I felt.

"Yes, the Catholics of Mercy Project in East Africa."

"Africa! She's in Africa?"

"Yes, with Father Higgins."

I frowned. "Wait. Isn't this about Malone?"

"Malone?"

"Johnny Malone."

"No, it's about your grandmother." Father Sutherland slowly closed and opened his eyes. "We, the church that is, should've given your grandmother more support. And now, I'm sorry to say, she's had a nasty fall. Earlier today, she was in the garden burning some rubbish—"

"What rubbish?"

Sutherland drew a breath through his bulbous nose. "I don't know. That's not the... listen, she'll be in hospital for some time, I'm afraid. The good news is that Miss Bray has very kindly—"

"The lady from church?"

The priest raised his fingers to his temples. "Yes, Ruth — Miss Bray — is a lay sister. Lucky for you, she's very fond of your grandmother. She's offered to live in and watch over you and your brother, at least until your grandmother is out of hospital. It may be a while, as she sustained some burns on her arm and will need an operation."

I blinked rapidly, my thoughts sprinting too fast for me to keep up with them. I had so many questions, but I could sense the headmaster's thinning patience, so I tried to focus on the most important ones. "You said my mother's in Africa? I'd really like to speak with her. It's been months. Do you know how I can reach her?"

"That's not possible."

"Why not?"

"If I were you, I would save all my thoughts and prayers for wishing your grandmother well. Your mother has given herself to another purpose now. It's unlikely you'll be hearing from her again."

"What? No, she said she would send for us." Panic

143

clutched at my throat, and I sprung to my feet, now the same height standing as the priest was seated.

Father Sutherland shuffled through the paperwork on his desk. When he spoke again, he did so without meeting my eyes.

"You're dismissed, Mr Shaw."

"But—"

"Miss Bray will keep me updated on your and Bernard's behaviour, so ensure it's at its best, or else we'll have to come to some other, less favourable arrangement."

"But—"

"Please close the door on your way out."

Rooted to the spot, I stared at the priest for a moment, but he acted as though I'd already left and continued to busy himself at his desk. I darted out and raced along the corridor, skidding to a stop outside Bernard's classroom. I inhaled a fortifying breath before opening the door. Thirty young heads swivelled in my direction as I edged into the room. I gulped when met with the incendiary glare of Sister Mary Assumpta.

"Yes, Mr Shaw?" said the nun without blinking.

I cleared my throat, which had decided to seal over at the sight of my audience.

"I need to speak to Bernard, please."

"Can't it wait until after school?" She still hadn't blinked.

"No, it can't, sorry. Bernard, get your things. We have to go."

Bernard started to rise to his feet.

"Sit down, Bernard."

"Come on, Bernie," I said. The poor lad stood frozen in a crouch.

The nun's eyes bulged so much I thought they might pop out. Bernard's head whipped between Sister Mary and I, before he made a split-second decision and dashed for the door.

"Get back here."

"Sorry, Sister," Bernard called over his shoulder.

We ran along the corridor and out through the main school doors.

"What's going on, George? We're gonna be in so much trouble," Bernard panted.

"We have to get home. I'm worried about Pyg."

"Shit." Bernard stopped in his tracks.

"What?"

He clutched his arms around himself. "I forgot my coat."

I quickly whipped off my jacket and thrust it at my brother. "Here, have mine."

"Won't you be cold?"

"I don't care, let's go."

I SLID MY KEY INTO THE LOCK, BUT BEFORE I'D turned it, the door edged open. I looked around at Bernard, who stared back with wide eyes. I tentatively pushed my way inside and an eerie silence met me instead of the usual shriek of Grandmother from the drawing room.

Several pairs of muddy footprints had been trodden along the parquet floor and the smell of smoke lingered, like the time we'd burned the potatoes, only stronger.

Bernard followed in my wake as I walked the muddy trail in reverse, along the hallway, into the kitchen, through the unlocked back door and out into the garden, where smoke filled the air with an acrid stench and a swirling grey haze.

*Sutherland said she'd been burning rubbish.*

A lead weight sunk in my stomach with the realisation.

*No, no, no — she wouldn't have, would she?* I put an arm out to stop Bernard.

"Maybe you should wait inside?"

"No," Bernard whined. "I want to check on Pyg. She's my dog too."

I sighed and dropped my arm. We continued along the path together, the smoke growing stronger with every step. Then, through the grey haze, the shape of the studio emerged. The remnants of the door hung from its hinges and the small window had shattered in its charred frame. Thick blue-grey smoke poured out through the gaping holes.

"Pyg," Bernard cried out, darting past me.

"Bernard, wait." I bolted after him, blinking my watering eyes against the smoke and following him into the blackness.

Beyond the charred door, the studio had been gutted. Water dripped from the blackened remains where the fire had been doused. Embers flashed like the eyes of tiny demons, still aglow in the wooden beams, cracking and popping as the fire died.

Everything was gone. Destroyed. Ruined. Our books, the transistor, Mum's paintings, the cushions and blankets she'd made by hand, her smell, the memories. It that instant, it struck me that I'd never see my mother again. *She's gone.* And the hope drained out of me, swirling away like water down a plughole.

"Pyg? Pyg?" Bernard's panicked voice called out. "George, where's Pyg?"

Then he was at my side, coughing and tugging my arm.

*We left her in here to keep her safe... because the dragon never leaves its cave... because the dragon... the dragon...*

*I hope the dragon fucking dies.*

"George," Bernard screamed, but I felt so far away. I wanted to answer. I wanted to tell my little brother that Pyg was alright. That our mother was alright. That I'd light the stove and make hot blackcurrant. We'd turn on the little red radio. *Pick of the Pops* would be on, and I would laugh as Bernard made up dances to the new songs and Pyg would bark and swish her tail. And everything would be alright. Because I didn't know what to do if it wasn't.

And then I stumbled, spluttering, falling. I dropped to my knees. Bernard was crying, and I wanted to hold him, stroke his hair and smooth down the stubborn tufts at his crown, because that's what Mum would do. I wanted to rub those black smudges off his face.

But I couldn't feel my arms. And then, there was black. I sunk into the darkness, swallowed by its depths.

9

## NOT MY CIRCUS

*A*lice twisted the wand to open the vertical blinds and natural light flooded the office. She reached up and opened the sash window — not too far because of the piss-taking pigeons, but enough to let in some air. The blinds flapped and rattled against the windowsill in the light breeze, damp and fragrant from the morning dew burning off in the bright sunlight.

Alice drew in a deep breath and smiled, because the fragrant morning dew wouldn't have even crossed her mind until recently.

So much had shifted since she'd last been in this room. *How was that only three days ago?* Surely, the seismic change she'd experienced needed longer than days? But perhaps it had all started before she'd even realised.

Alice stowed her handbag under her desk and flicked on the computer. As the machine whirred to life, she went to the kitchenette with the supplies she'd picked up on her way in. The tube light buzzed as Alice popped the biscuits in the cupboard and the milk in the fridge — semi-skimmed for Jeremy, oat for Truscote. She tipped last week's milk away, rinsed the containers and left them to drain in the sink.

Alice checked her watch and frowned. Another thing to add to the growing list of 'Stuff to Replace' — she didn't want to be reminded of Fran every time she looked at her wrist.

*8:23 a.m. Jeremy always arrives at precisely 8:30 a.m.* She'd boil the kettle and get a cafetière ready. She'd leave the phone lines off until they'd had their meeting. *Shit, the meeting!*

Alice rushed around her desk, leaned over the keyboard, and entered her login credentials. She clicked straight into Jeremy's calendar, which was thankfully empty until his first appointment at 9:30 a.m.

Alice checked Truscote's diary too; she really should speak to each of them face-to-face, seeing as she worked for them both. For some reason she was dreading the Truscote conversation more, even though it wasn't Truscote's wife she'd been sleeping with.

*Bollocks.* Truscote was at The Milverton all morning.

*Oh well.* She'd have to arrange something with her separately. Perhaps by then the wounds would've had a little more time to heal and Truscote wouldn't be able to pick her apart and scrutinise her real motivations for leaving. Also, in her current state, Alice would likely still react if Truscote were to round on Fran.

Fran was Alice's mistake, and it really was none of Truscote's business.

This was Alice taking responsibility. Claiming her power back and moving on with her life. God, Maggie had really got in her head. But she'd also chatted it through with Ash over coffee yesterday. It helped that Ash agreed Alice resigning was for the best. The triangulation of opinion bolstered her, convincing her it was the right decision, even though she didn't have another job to go to and a mountain of debt looming large.

"You can text me if you wobble." Ash had pulled a pen out of her pocket and scribbled her phone number on a muffin café napkin. "But you're stronger than you think. You've got this."

Alice had picked up a SIM card on her way home and Ash's had been the second number she programmed into the phone, right after Maggie's.

Everyone else, she'd have to message on Facebook with her new contact details; if only she could remember her password to log in.

Whilst waiting for the kettle to boil, Alice watered the office plants. Hopefully, her successor would keep them alive too — they were her plant-babies. And, yes, they may well have come off the back of Fran telling Jeremy he needed to allocate some budget to 'brighten up the dreary place,' but it was Alice who'd picked them out and nurtured them, even if she couldn't actually identify most of them. Now that she could trust herself to keep them alive, she would buy some plants for her flat. First, she needed to get a new job. And write a list to remind herself of the order of things.

*One foot in front of the other; less chance of tripping over.*

Alice returned to the kitchenette and rinsed out the cafetière whilst humming that Annie Lennox song about walking on broken glass which had been stuck in her head for days now. But it felt happy and hopeful, so she didn't mind it spinning on repeat. Despite her trepidation about handing in her notice, the levity of her mood could only be a good thing.

"Morning, Alice." Jeremy's low voice rumbled through from Reception.

Alice popped her head around the doorway. "Morning."

"Can I talk to you in my office, please?"

"Sure, I need to speak to you, too. I'm just making coffee. I'll be there in two."

Briefcase in hand, Jeremy glanced down at his polished brogues and frowned. "Don't worry about the coffee."

"Are you sure? It's almost ready."

"It's fine. I'd just like to talk to you. Please." Jeremy's tone was terse, lacking his normal joviality. He stepped toward his office, his movements stiff and mechanical, like he was going through the motions, forcing himself in a direction he didn't want to go.

*Oh shit, surely Fran hasn't told him.*

Alice stepped back into the confined space of the kitchenette. She clenched and unclenched her fists to dispel some of the nervous energy that now tingled in her limbs. *Deep breaths. In for four, hold for four, out for four.*

"You've got this," she muttered to herself, and made

her way to Jeremy's office via her own desk, where she stooped to collect a small white envelope from her handbag.

Alice entered Jeremy's office, fingering the letter between her hands, uncertainty taking hold with every step. Jeremy had shrugged off his coat and draped it on the back of his desk chair rather than hanging it on the door hook, as he usually did. He sat at his desk with his head cradled in his hands. His face looked pale and drawn, with dark bags drooping under his eyes. Alice had never seen him like this.

"Rough weekend?" she asked and immediately wondered if that was the wrong thing to say.

Jeremy lifted his gaze. His hangdog expression punched Alice in the chest.

"I think you know the answer to that." Foreboding built with each of his quietly enunciated words. "Take a seat."

Alice swallowed, her throat suddenly dry. She perched on the edge of the leather chair, not wanting to recline into it. This situation was anything but comfortable. How could she relax?

"Jeremy, I—"

"I think it's time we ended the pretence, don't you?"

"Sorry?"

"About Francesca."

Alice felt the colour draining from her face.

"I know you've been sleeping with my wife."

Alice's eyelashes flickered down. She looked at the envelope she was turning over in her hands.

"Yes, I have. I'm so sorry, Jeremy. I really didn't mean to hurt you. I know you won't believe me when I say how much I respect you. You've been a wonderful boss, and you didn't deserve..." all her words spilled out at once, tumbling over each other.

Jeremy raised his hand. But she needed to say her final piece.

"It's actually why I wanted to speak to you today. I'm handing in my resignation. It's for the best." She slid the letter across the desk towards him. He stared at the missive for a moment before sliding it back.

"I can't accept this."

"Why? I've been sleeping with your wife!"

Jeremy scoffed. "Well, at least one of us was."

Alice winced. "God, I'm so ashamed. You must be so angry with me."

"I'm not angry with you, Alice. If anything, you should be angry at me because I've known all along."

Alice shook her head. "What?"

Jeremy sat back and folded his arms. "Look, it's pretty uncomfortable for me to talk about. But I owe you this much. It's an arrangement Francesca and I have."

"An arrangement?" Alice stared at him through narrowed eyes.

"I love my wife, and I want her to have whatever she wants, but I can't satisfy *that* part of her. You know, the part that craves... well, you."

The room felt like it had tipped sideways. Alice shook her head again, trying to right herself. "Wait, what — she knew that you knew?"

"Of course."

"But she was always threatening to tell you. Whenever things didn't go her way, she—"

"That's Francesca. She loves like a cat — with her claws." Jeremy laughed, a warm chuckle of endearment, as if Fran were a harmless fluffy creature, not a manipulative toxic viper. Alice glimpsed the insanity of it all. He'd completely rationalised Fran's behaviour. Jeremy loved his wife so much he was prepared to live with every wound she inflicted, not only on him but on anyone else.

"Oh-my-fucking-God," she muttered, slipping back into the leather chair, yielding to the comfort of its warm folds. She stared into the middle distance, trying to process everything she thought she knew but had got so wrong. How had she become so entangled in this web? Truscote had tried to warn her. Why hadn't she listened? *Wait, Truscote — she and Fran... had they?*

"Alice, you see, I can't accept your resignation. I have a predicament, and I was wondering if you would consider helping me out."

"Sorry?"

"It destroyed Francesca when you said you wouldn't see her any more. She came home from your rendezvous in a blind rage, screaming and tearing up the house. And then whatever happened on Saturday... well, she's been distraught ever since. I had to prescribe her something to calm her down. You're not like the others. This is different."

"The others?"

"Yes, it's an arrangement, like I said. We've been

together for thirty-seven years. Married for thirty of those. Of course there have been others. But no one else has ever enthralled her like you have."

Alice's stomach swooped at the thought of the shatter-proof Francesca Dalton in a frenzy of despair over her. *Seriously?* She couldn't quite envision it, but then Fran had always struggled when she didn't get her way. This was clearly just her response to one of those rare occasions.

"She's heartbroken, Alice. I can't bear to see her like this. I need your help."

"I don't know how I can help you fix your wife's broken heart, Jeremy. I think you both need the sort of help that's completely beyond me."

The man in front of Alice seemed to deflate; he sank lower in his seat. His red eyes and tired face drooped like a bloodhound's.

"Don't leave her. Can't you just carry on as you were? We'll *all* just carry on as we were. Pretend like nothing has changed."

"So, let me get this straight, as it were... you want me to continue having an affair with your wife?"

"Well, I wouldn't put it in quite those terms, but yes, I suppose that's about the crux of it. What would it take? I can give you a pay rise?"

"No. Fuck." Alice scrunched her fingers in her hair and massaged them into her scalp. "Why do you people think you can buy me? I'm not a hooker."

"Goodness, no, that's not what I was implying. It's just if I can throw a little money at the problem and secure Francesca's happiness, then I'm more than prepared to do that." Jeremy laced his fingers together on the desk. Alice had seen him do this when he thought he was about to have a breakthrough. "If it's mutually beneficial, who is it hurting?"

"Fran was going to leave you. Did you know that?"

Jeremy paused for a moment. A flicker of sadness passed across his face, but then he chuckled. "Yes. She hasn't, though, has she?" He raised his left hand and pointed to his wedding ring.

Alice stared at him. *I've been told my whole life that I'm the crazy, irrational one, but clearly it's a spectrum and everyone normalises their own insanity...*

*Well, not my circus, not my fucking monkeys.*

Jeremy looked at her with pleading eyes. "Alice, please. If not for me, then for Francesca. I know you love her too—"

"No. Neither of you are who I thought you were. You're both cracked. I wish you well, Jeremy, but I want nothing more to do with this." Alice stood and forcefully pushed her handwritten letter across his desk towards him. "I resign."

Jeremy stared at the white rectangle, the corners of his mouth twitching. Alice felt a pang of pity for him before turning and walking away.

"I don't accept. You're fired," Jeremy shouted after her.

"Whatever," Alice muttered as she scooped up her handbag and left the building with her head held high.

# CHAMPAGNE AND
# STRAWBERRIES

## TWO YEARS EARLIER

"*A*lice?" Jeremy's hearty voice boomed, reaching Alice in the kitchenette where she was loading the dishwasher with the day's coffee cups.

"Be there in a moment," she called out. She quickly set the dishwasher to go and swiped a cloth over the countertops. With a satisfied glance around the room, she flicked off the light. *Final task of the day, tick. In fact, final task of the week — hello, Friday! Ooh, and payday.* She'd treat herself to a Chinese takeaway and a bottle of wine, curl up on the couch and find a decent series to binge on Netflix. Plus, Maggie and Markus were in the Maldives, so she didn't even have to see them on Sunday for their usual visit. All that lay ahead was a whole delicious weekend all to herself.

Alice peered around the doorway of Jeremy's office. He'd left the door open after his final client departed and had since been shuffling papers and tapping away at his keyboard.

"I'm going to head off shortly, if that's okay? Did you need something?"

"Ah, Alice. Yes. Is Catherine still here?"

Alice leaned back from the doorframe to glance around at the closed office door of Catherine Truscote. She'd been ensconced in there all afternoon. With the amount of coffee Truscote consumed, Alice was surprised the woman didn't need the loo more often.

"Er, yeah. She's in her office."

The corners of Jeremy's mouth pinched together. "Fine. Would you come in and close the door for a moment, please?"

"Sure." Alice clicked the door shut behind her.

Jeremy gestured to the chair in front of his desk and fixed Alice with a kind smile. In the three months she'd been working at T&D, she'd really warmed to him. His patient benevolence was a stark contrast to Truscote's manner, which was icy at best.

"Sorry, I know you're keen to get off home. I won't keep you long. I, er..." Jeremy rubbed the light stubble on his chin and broke eye contact. "Do you, er... I was wondering... if you have plans this weekend?"

*Oh, bollocks. Not this again.* Alice shifted in the chair. Had she somehow led him on? Sometimes men got the wrong idea about her, but she could never quite work out how that happened because she'd never once been interested in a man. *And besides, isn't he married?*

Jeremy must have sensed her discomfort as he held up his hands. "Oh, no, sorry, I didn't mean... I just meant, are you busy? If not, then I wondered whether you'd like to do a little overtime?"

Alice cocked her head. There hadn't been any mention of overtime before now.

"Look, it's okay if you're otherwise engaged. It's just that my wife, Francesca, chairs the women's group at our country club. It's their AGM this weekend, but their secretary has let them down." He winced. "Emergency root canal, I believe. Painful business."

"Right, so..."

"Francesca called me in a dither and asked if she could borrow my... well, you. She said she'd met you about a month ago, do you recall?"

Alice nodded. "I wouldn't say we 'met' exactly." She swallowed with the vivid recollection of the uptight brunette who'd waltzed into Reception like she owned the place. Ignoring Alice's attempt to engage, she charged straight into Jeremy's office, closing the door behind her. Alice must have been on her lunch break when the woman left, but the musky smell of her perfume lingered in the room all afternoon.

"Well, it seems you made an impression on her." Jeremy chuckled.

"Oh, really? We didn't even speak."

"Francesca is very astute." Jeremy's pale blue eyes settled on Alice's face, and for a moment he looked lost in thought. "Anyway, what do you say?"

"To what?"

"This weekend. Are you free?"

"I... er..." Before Alice could cobble together a plausible excuse that didn't involve binging Netflix whilst wrapped in her duvet, Jeremy powered on with his pitch.

"It's at Stonehurst Abbey, all expenses paid, and I'll give you double-time for your trouble. They'll need you most of Saturday and possibly some of Sunday. Knowing Francesca, the schedule will be pretty full-on, so you can take a half day Monday to recover. How does that sound?"

"Oh, well... yeah, I guess that'd be..."

Jeremy clapped his hands together, his cheeks flushed with relief. "Fantastic. Fran will be delighted." He slid open a drawer and retrieved a manila file, which he pushed across the desk toward Alice. "All the details are in here. Francesca will fill you in on everything else when you arrive tomorrow."

"Right, great. Thanks." Alice stood to leave.

"Oh, one more thing. Discretion."

"Sorry?"

"Your discretion about this... little favour, would be appreciated."

"How so?" Alice frowned.

"What I mean to say is, please don't mention any of this to Catherine."

Alice nodded and left the room, manila file in hand and head swimming with her new assignment. This was the sort of thing she'd usually run by Maggie. But seeing as her sensible sister was sunning herself on a white sandy beach, Alice would have to make do with her own instincts. And she was more than a little intrigued by Francesca Dalton.

"AS IF THIS PLACE IS REAL!" ALICE BLINKED through the windscreen as the vast expanse of Stonehurst Abbey unfurled into view at the end of the tree-lined driveway. Amidst a thick curtain of ivy, the abbey's weathered sandstone facade glowed in the mid-morning sun.

Alice pulled into a parking spot and cranked the handbrake; her Fiesta groaned with the effort. But it'd just passed its MOT, so there were plenty of miles left in the old girl yet.

Having recently turned forty, Alice felt a bit the same; still roadworthy, but prone to groan, especially when effort was required. She stepped outside into the fresh country air which, if she were honest, smelt a bit like shit, but there was something wholesome about it. Just as there was something wholesome about being out and about at this hour on a Saturday, instead of lying in her pit, doom-scrolling whilst eating Pop-Tarts straight from the box.

By the looks of the abbey, work would be a pleasure. Plus, with the double-time Jeremy had promised, she'd be able to pay Maggie back for the little loan, at last.

The notes in Jeremy's manila file had outlined a smart-casual dress code, but Alice had erred on the side of smart. She'd met Francesca Dalton in the flesh, and she seemed so stuck-up it was entirely possible the woman slept in formal evening wear.

Alice adjusted her blouse where it had ruffled *en route* and smoothed down her charcoal-grey pencil skirt, which hugged her hips, showing off her hourglass figure. She even looked good in the reflection of her grubby car window; blonde curls tumbling around her face, full lips painted deep red to match her blouse.

If nothing else, she'd nailed the part of 'sexy PA', although admittedly that wasn't the part she'd been hired to play. No, essentially she was here to take the minutes for a meeting where a bunch of bored, rich housewives took themselves way too seriously. But as well as overtime, this was a free stay in an incredible hotel she'd never have been able to afford otherwise, so the least she could do was look professional — sexiness was a bonus.

Pulling her small wheelie case behind her, Alice stepped through the stone-arched entrance into a dark, wood-panelled Reception. Archways encircled the room and led to stone corridors spidering in every direction. Enormous pillar candles flickered in elaborate candelabras, and statues in various states of undress adorned plinths everywhere she looked. Alice felt like she'd gone back in time as she wheeled up to the front desk and dinged the bell. A moment later, a concealed door in the panelled wall opened; a tall man in a hotel uniform appeared and eyed Alice over the top of the spectacles perched on the end of his long nose.

"How can I help you?" The corners of the man's thin lips tugged upwards with the hint of a smile.

"Alice French. I should have a reservation."

The man's gaze dropped to the computer concealed within the desk. His frown deepened as he tapped at the keyboard and clicked the mouse.

"I'm with Francesca Dalton. Ivywood Ladies Club?"

"Ah yes." The man stood taller and removed his glasses. "Let me show you to your room." He stepped from behind the desk and took Alice's small suitcase. "This way, please."

"Are you able to let Mrs Dalton know I'm here?"

"Yes, of course. I am to show you to your room first, though."

The clip-clop of Alice's heels echoed along the corridor as she followed behind the man; she glanced about herself, trying to work out how she'd remember the way. They came to a wooden staircase at the end of the hall.

"We have you just up here."

The wooden stairs led to a small landing with two doors facing each other. The man swiped a key card in the door to the right, then stood back to hold it open. Alice stepped into the most luxurious hotel room she'd ever seen. A four-poster bed draped in red linens and plush pillows dominated the centre of the room. From the high ceiling hung an ornate chandelier, its teardrop pendants sparkling in the sunlight spilling through the window.

"Enjoy your stay with us, Ms French."

Alice had almost forgotten the man. He'd deposited her case on the luggage rack, and no doubt looked on in bemusement as she'd gawped at her surroundings, hoping there hadn't been some mistake and this room was actually meant for somebody else.

"Thank you," she smiled.

The man bowed his head and closed the door behind him. Alice released an excited squeal and stamped her feet before kicking off her heels and jumping starfish-style onto the bed. She'd have sent Maggie a selfie if she weren't on a different continent. Besides, she needed to get herself together — she was here for work, not play.

Alice squealed again when she entered the bathroom and saw a freestanding clawfoot tub with its own view of the sprawling grounds. Resisting the urge to strip off and dive in immediately, Alice straightened her clothes again, spritzed on a little perfume, and scrunched her hair.

"I have a date with *you* later," she said to the bathtub.

As she stepped onto the landing, the door opposite swung open, revealing Francesca Dalton dressed in dark-blue high-waisted jeans and a fitted white shirt with sleeves rolled to her elbows. She'd nailed the brief of smart-casual.

Amusement flickered in the woman's eyes as she caught Alice staring, probably with the same levels of awe she'd had for her hotel room just moments ago. If that room exuded opulence, the woman stood in front of her exuded elegance.

"Alice! We haven't yet been properly introduced. Francesca Dalton." The woman extended a hand. Her chestnut hair fell in loose waves, grazing the collar of her shirt.

Alice took her manicured hand and returned the firm handshake.

"Lovely to meet you, Mrs—"

"Call me Fran." She gripped Alice's hand a little tighter.

Alice's breath quickened as the woman's dark eyes stared directly into her own with an intensity she felt had the power to strip her bare if she held the gaze too long.

"Fran," she said in an almost-whimper.

A satisfied smirk spread over Fran's lips, as if she'd just won a contest no one else knew the rules to. "Shall we? Better not keep our Ivywood ladies waiting."

Alice followed Fran into the labyrinth of winding corridors; the woman was clearly blessed with a better sense of direction than she.

"Jeremy shared the file with you?"

"He did, thank you."

"And you're comfortable with the brief? Poor Susan and that molar extraction."

"I thought it was a root canal?"

"Mmm, yes. Probably. Anyway, it's just a case of jotting down who says what in some intelligible way."

Alice nodded, trying to keep pace with Fran, who was now two strides ahead of her.

"I'm sure it'll all seem terribly trivial, but some of these Ivywood women have agendas, and they're not afraid of drawing blood to get their own way."

*Great, now they all sound terrifying.*

Fran came to a stop in front of a door and grasped the brass handle. Before entering, she turned and hit Alice with a sexy half-smile. "Ready?"

Alice inhaled a steadying breath and released it with a nod. As Fran pushed into the room, the conversations hushed. From their chairs along the conference table, a dozen coiffured heads swivelled in Alice's direction. All of a similar age and affluence to Fran, the women exuded a status Alice didn't possess. After a cursory smile at the blur of faces, she took the seat Fran patted next to her.

The lively chatter resumed, and as teacups rattled on saucers, Alice took a moment to buoy herself in a sea of designer dresses, tailored suits, and chic accessories. In contrast to the ripe animal smell outside, a heady fragrance perfumed the air from an arrangement of lilies and lilacs in the centre of the table. Floor-to-ceiling antique walnut panelling adorned the walls, which would have been gloomy if not for the light streaming through the tall arched windows overlooking a topiary garden.

Fran clinked a teaspoon on a glass. "Ladies, shall we begin?"

Alice pulled the printed document from the manila file and set a notepad straight in front of her.

"Firstly, I'd like you to extend a warm Ivywood welcome to Ms Alice French."

Alice held up a hand and returned the polite smiles directed at her from around the table.

"Right, shall we start with…"

Alice reached into her handbag for her pen. *Shit, where is it?*

As Fran started rattling through the agenda, Alice's rummaging became frantic until Fran tapped her arm and she stilled. Mid-sentence and without a glance her way, Fran subtly pushed a silver pen toward her.

Being bailed out before she'd even got started was not the impression she'd been hoping to make. However, the rest of the meeting passed without event. As long as Alice had a task, she could focus and listen. The coffee breaks helped too; Alice used them as a chance to tidy up her notes and clarify any unclear points with the various attendees.

Fran's presence dominated the room; she skilfully steered the discussions away from contentious points and gently edged them in a different direction. On more than one occasion, Alice had to hide a grin behind her hand as Fran dismantled anyone who got above themselves. The woman commanded complete control, and the more Alice listened, the more enraptured she became by Fran's hypnotic voice.

The meeting continued into late afternoon, covering every topic from financial reporting to the election of new committee members — at which point Fran was unanimously re-elected as chairwoman, although Alice suspected the women would have been too afraid not to.

As the final session concluded, Alice had almost filled her notebook. She glanced up at the weary faces around the table. In contrast, she could almost feel the energy pulsing from Fran next to her.

"Well, ladies, that concludes a successful day. Thank you, as always, for your contributions throughout. Also, sincere thanks for the vote of confidence; I look forward to continuing as your chairwoman in the coming year." She glanced at her wristwatch. "As per your schedules, dinner will be served at seven p.m. in The Madison Suite, which allows a little time to freshen up. See you all there."

Noise rose as the ladies gathered their things and started filing out. Alice shuffled the papers back into the file and picked up her notebook.

"Thank you for today, Alice. We couldn't have done it without you. You are joining us for dinner, aren't you?" Fran's red lips twisted into a sultry smile, her dark eyes simmering with a look that brought heat to Alice's cheeks.

Alice cleared her throat. "Er, yes, please, that'd be great." She glanced down at the pen in her hand. "Oh, and thanks for this. I wish I could say I'm not normally that disorganised, but…"

Fran grinned, her fingers brushing Alice's as she took the proffered pen. That tiny connection sent a charge right through her, and the intensity flickering in Fran's eyes said she'd felt it too.

With a tap of Fran's elbow, a pointy-faced woman in a powder-blue skirt suit snatched their attention. Fran looked startled, but with a fixed smile, she spun around. "Harriet, what can I do for you?"

As Harriet reeled off a list, Alice took her leave. Somehow, she navigated her way back to her room. Once inside, she kicked off her heels and collapsed onto the bed, her heart cantering and thoughts swimming with Francesca Dalton. *What a woman!* Everything Alice wanted to be — and do.

*Fuck. Stop it, she's your boss's wife. Only to be admired from a safe distance.*

With no time for a soak in the bath, Alice freshened up with a cool shower. As she lathered the luxurious soap onto her body, her mind teased her with thoughts of Fran, the cold water proving ineffective against the heat pooling between her thighs. She retouched her makeup and decided to wear her little black cocktail dress. She'd been in two minds when packing it and brought two backup outfits just in case, but it was the perfect dress to impress Fran, even though she shouldn't have been thinking like that.

The opulent decor of The Madison Suite shimmered in the swaying candlelight. A waiter showed Alice to a seat at the currently unoccupied side of the table, returning moments later to pour her a glass of Champagne. The other ladies already seated didn't acknowledge her arrival, or perhaps they hadn't noticed. Either way, they chatted amongst themselves, and Alice fidgeted in her chair. She fought the impulse to pull out her phone; instead, she glanced around the room to take in the decadent surroundings. She held a sip of Champagne in her mouth, enjoying the bubbles fizzing on her tongue as she examined the oil painting above the fireplace. It featured a semi-naked woman on a chaise longue clutching a swan in an intimate embrace.

"Do you like it?" Fran's husky, honeyed voice ripped Alice's attention from the painting. Alice turned, drinking in the older woman. Fran was wearing a dark green jumpsuit which fitted and flowed in all the right places over her toned body.

"Er, yeah. It's... interesting."

"It's Leda and the Swan. A controversial piece, but I find some of the depictions, particularly this one, quite... erotic."

Alice swallowed, her suddenly dry mouth thirsting for more Champagne, as Fran took the seat next to her.

Before long, all the empty seats filled, and the food

service commenced. Each delicious course was served with a flight of wine. After the third, the edges of the room started to blur, and Alice had long since tuned out of the various conversations around her. Under the table, something warm and soft brushed against her thigh, snapping her back to her senses.

*What the* — she glanced at Fran, whose head was turned in conversation with the woman to her right. *Perhaps it was an accident.*

*Oh* — the brushing fingers were now tracing circles on her knee, causing tiny explosions to erupt under her skin. Alice poured a glass of water and gulped it down as Fran's hand rode up her leg.

*Oh fuck.*

Alice clenched the napkin spread on her lap. Should she push Fran's hand away? She really didn't want to, *but* —

Before she could decide, Fran gripped the tender flesh at the top of her leg, her fingers sinking into Alice's skin and treading the thin line between pleasure and pain. Alice gasped. No one seemed to notice, and Fran's hand came to rest inches from her now-drenched underwear. Any closer and Fran would know just how aroused she was.

Heat rose up Alice's neck and into her cheeks.

"Excuse me, I need to get some air," Alice said to no one in particular.

With her heartbeat drumming in her ears, Alice stood, and Fran's hand subtly fell away. Fran didn't even look around, but laughed loudly as she touched the forearm of the woman next to her.

Much like Alice's arrival, no one seemed to notice her departure. She stepped outside into a cool evening breeze that carried the scents of honeysuckle and lavender. Alice blinked hard — *no, I'm not that drunk, and yes, that really just happened.*

She glanced over her shoulder, half-hoping that Fran had followed her outside and was on her way to finish what she'd started. But there was no Fran.

To return now would look like she was going back for more, and whilst she was keen to resolve the ache between her legs, there was a time and a place, and perhaps her boss's wife wouldn't be the wisest of conquests. Alice decided to call it a night and meandered back to her room. She drained a glass of cold water and started to undress as a knock came at the door. Alice's chest lurched, because she didn't need to open it to know who stood on the other side.

To open the door would be to invite her in, and to invite her in would be to accept everything that was coming to her. *Fuck.*

Alice shrugged her dress back on and made her choice.

Behind the door, Fran stood with an uncorked bottle of Champagne and two empty flutes held by the stems.

"Well, you left in a hurry. Something I did?" She flashed a wicked smile and tongued her top lip.

Alice gulped as desire ripped through her. "I, er, think you know what you—"

"I'm sorry, did I offend you, Alice?" Fran pouted, but her eyes were full of teasing laughter.

"No, it's just that... well, there's Jeremy, so I thought... you were straight," Alice stuttered.

Fran scoffed. "I thought *you* were intelligent."

"But you're married."

"Oh, Alice, don't be naïve. I have an appetite which Jeremy cannot sate. Besides, I'm sure you've fucked plenty of women who claimed to be straight, but as you know, spaghetti is straight too until it gets wet. Now, do you want to fuck or not?"

Alice nodded; Fran had her at *spaghetti*.

She moved aside and Fran sauntered into the room. She put down the bottle and glasses, then stepped back towards Alice, who was now completely at this woman's mercy.

"This dress..." Fran purred and ran a finger under the strap, letting it fall off Alice's shoulder. Alice shivered at her touch and Fran lowered her head and kissed her collarbone.

"As soon as I saw you in this dress, I knew I had to have you." Fran guided her backwards until Alice was against the wall and then she kissed her, hungry and desperate, almost feral, biting and sucking her lips, probing with her tongue. Fran tasted like Champagne and strawberries, and Alice moaned into her mouth.

Fran ran a hand up her thigh, hitching up the soft material of her dress. When she reached the top, she edged her thumb around to Alice's soaked underwear, stroking her through the lacy material. Alice's breath hitched.

"You're so wet for me," Fran growled, biting Alice's neck as she flicked her thumb underneath the lace, and massaged the precise spot with the perfect amount of pressure.

"Oh fuck, yes. Yes!" Sparks fizzed behind Alice's eyes as her orgasm erupted. She'd never come like this before — so quickly and from so little. But here she was, melting in Francesca Dalton's hands, and it was fucking exquisite.

1 0

## DOCTOR'S ORDERS

*A*lice's hands still shook with adrenaline, rattling the teapot as she tried to pour the hot brown liquid into her mug. Most of it splashed onto the saucer, but that's what saucers were for, right? She tried to steady her shaking hand with the other, but it was just as bad.

She'd texted Maggie as soon as she'd left the office.

> I've done it — I resigned. But I got fired too. So much to tell you, you won't believe it. Call me when you can. A x

She needed to speak to someone. Everything she'd just found out was blowing her mind. Her thumb had hovered over Ash's number too, and even though Ash had said to let her know how it had gone, Alice didn't want to come across as too keen, or too much.

*Less is more, Alice.* Even if that was a lesson from Fran, it made sense. However, Alice wondered whether, now that Fran was getting much less of her, she was craving more?

She shuddered. *Fran and Jeremy were in on it together, all along. How messed up is that?* She shook her head to shake the Daltons from her thoughts. Her phone buzzed on the table. *Maggie.*

> What? Only you could resign and get fired at the same time. Can't talk now but speak later. Proud of you X

Alice smiled at the screen and again scrolled down to Ash's number. *Fuck it.* She tapped out a text.

> Good news, I'm no longer an emotional wreck. I'm now a jobless emotional wreck. Wanna hang out again sometime? Lol xx

Her thumb hovered over the send button; usually she couldn't restrain it, but this time she took a breath and backspaced. *No, not now.* Besides, Ash was probably still sleeping off her night shift.

*Play it cool, Alice... for once in your life.* She scrolled back over their text conversation from last night, her cheeks heating with fresh embarrassment as she recalled it.

She'd texted a breezy,

> Hey. This is my new number!

> Who is this?

> Sorry, should've said that. It's me, Alice.

Just kidding, I figured x

Ash had signed off with a kiss. Alice should've put a kiss, but she was trying not to flirt. Yet the absence of a kiss now seemed conspicuous. *Does a text kiss even count as flirting? People put kisses all the time these days, don't they?*

As Alice tried to think of something else to say so she could add a kiss, another message from Ash pinged through.

Good luck tomorrow x

In her haste to even the kiss score, Alice quickly replied,

> Thanks, you too x

*Shit! No... not 'you too'.*

Lol. Goodnight, Alice. Get some rest,
doctor's orders xx

Alice cringed and took a sip of tea. It was so hot it stung the sore spots in her mouth.

She should use this time for planning her next steps, not for thinking about Ash, or Fran, or *doctor's orders* or anything along those lines... *focus, Alice!*

She rummaged in her handbag and pulled out a crumpled sheet of paper, which she smoothed flat on the table. She dived back into her bag for her pen; a shiny Montblanc ballpoint — courtesy of Fran, of course — gifted to Alice on their second 'date'. It had seemed like such a thoughtful gift, something Alice would hold between her fingers most days and think of her beguiling lover.

*Ex-lover.*

Alice twisted the smooth metallic barrel until the nib poked out, then she crossed through the top line on her to-do list, which said 'Hand in resignation letter', and added 'Buy new pens' to the bottom. She didn't need a fancy pen, especially not this one, as it was another reason to think about the Daltons. She'd dig out the velvet box from the darkest depths of her flat, *probably under the bed or on top of the wardrobe*, and she'd give the Montblanc to Maggie for being such a wonderfully supportive sister.

Alice sighed. Next stop — groceries. She scrawled out a second list on the reverse of the page, otherwise she'd end up with a basketful of crap and only half the ingredients to actually make a meal with. After shopping, she'd head home, put on her comfiest clothes and power up the laptop to tidy her resume.

The phone buzzed on the table, and an incoming text from Ash lit up the screen.

Morning! How did it go? X

Alice grinned. *Big kiss!*

Good, I resigned and got fired X

Three little dots bounced on the screen, then disappeared, to be replaced by an embarrassingly loud ringtone sounding from the handset and causing the — mostly grey-haired — heads of the other people in the café to turn and glare in her direction.

"Sorry," she mouthed and snatched up the phone, nearly knocking over the teapot as she did.

"Hi," she said in a loud whisper. "I wasn't expecting you to call."

"Sorry, not a good time?" Ash's voice sounded groggy with sleep.

"No, yeah. I mean, it's fine. I'm in Snoots having a cup of tea."

"Oh, cool. Speaking's easier than texting when I've just woken up. So, you're jobless then? Well done on going through with it. That was brave."

"You don't know the half of it," Alice grinned. Yeah, she had been brave. It would've been so easy to keep her job, to stay with Fran and fall back into a rut. Jeremy had literally given her permission and offered her a pay rise. But she'd ripped off the plaster, and it was time to heal.

"Wanna fill me in over brunch?" Ash said through what sounded like a huge yawn.

"Er..." Alice looked down at her to-do list.

"I mean, if you have plans, that's fine." Ash gave a sweet, self-conscious laugh. "Tell me to mind my own business, of course, but I'm invested now. I want to find out what happened next, you know?"

"You mean you want the next instalment in my big fat mess of a life?"

"Yeah, it's way better than anything on Netflix."

Alice giggled. "Alright, you're on."

She scribbled down the address of the place Ash suggested, intrigued by Ash's glowing review of Porky's and their 'badass bacon butties.'

The health kick and the to-do list could wait, as could her resume. Today was a cause for celebration because she had been brave. And who was she to go against *doctor's orders*?

STANDING OUTSIDE THE SHABBY CAFÉ ON A QUIET, run-down street, Alice double-checked her phone to make sure she'd got the right place. *Yep, this is definitely Porky's.*

A bell rang overhead as Alice pushed through the peeling door and tentatively stepped inside. Vinyl gingham tablecloths covered square tables, each set with condiments in squeezable red and brown tubes. Large tin cans that once held chopped tomatoes were now stuffed with cutlery and serviettes. The smoky smell of bacon hung in the air and roused Alice's appetite, making her mouth water. Aside from a sumo-sized man reading a red-top newspaper, the only other customer was Ash, sat at a corner table and smiling in Alice's direction.

"I know what you're thinking," she said as Alice approached.

"You do?" Alice grinned back.

"This place, it doesn't look like much... but trust me."

"Because you're a doctor? You already used that line."

Ash laughed. "This was our go-to at Uni. Their bacon butties are a proven cure for any hangover or heartache. We've literally done medical research on it."

"Mmm-hmm." Alice peeled the laminated menu from the table and studied the instructions on how to 'Build your own bacon butty'.

This place was a million miles away from anywhere she'd ever been with Fran. She'd more likely see a pig dance out of the kitchen on roller-skates than she would ever see Francesca Dalton set foot in a place like this, let alone order a 'butty'.

A round woman with cropped hair and a blue apron popped out of the kitchen and hobbled her way over to them.

"Sorry for the wait. It's just me on today. Merv's at the surgery. His hip's troubling him again, poor love. Eh, he should've just let you see to him." She nudged Ash's arm and chuckled. "Is it the usual?"

"Give Merv my best, will you? And yep, I'll have my LGBT special please, on a wholemeal bun. Thanks, Barb."

"Right you are, lovey." Barb scribbled onto the pad she'd pulled from her apron pocket. "And you, dear?"

"Oh, I'll have the streaky smoked bacon, on sourdough please. And mushrooms, lots of mushrooms."

"Is it tea for two?"

Ash looked to Alice, who nodded. "Sounds good."

As Barb returned to the kitchen, Ash leaned over the table. With a grimace, she whispered, "Mushrooms?"

"Yeah, who doesn't like mushrooms?"

"Me." Ash stuck her tongue out. "They're slimy and gross."

"Well, what's an LGBT special?"

"Lettuce, guacamole, bacon and tomato. It's delicious." Ash chef's-kissed her fingers.

Alice raised an eyebrow. "Guacamole has no place outside of a taco."

Ash gasped in mock-horror. Laughter bubbled between them, and they eased into each other's company, which Alice realised was as effortless as slicing through warmed butter. She wasn't on eggshells, scared she'd slip up at any moment. She wasn't even wondering why Ash wanted to spend time with her, which she usually did around other people — always second-guessing their motives and worrying about whether they really liked her or just felt sorry for her. None of the usual mind-buzz seemed to bother her when she was with Ash.

*Until now.* Noticing the absence of mind-buzz seemed to have summoned it. Static fizzed and Alice blinked rapidly as she tried to equalise herself.

Ash tugged her back to the present with a hand squeezing over hers.

"Hey, where'd you go?" The corners of her eyes crinkled with concern.

Alice shook her head and refocused her gaze on that kind, lopsided smile, and after a moment, the fizz faded into the background. "Sorry."

"Don't be. You've had a tough few days, you've got a lot to process."

Their order came quickly, despite Barb being on her

own. Ash agreed to eat a mushroom in exchange for a bite of the LGBT, which Alice conceded was delicious. Ash hadn't been quite so complimentary about the mushroom.

Between mouthfuls, Alice filled Ash in on the conversation with Jeremy, how she'd resigned and been fired. And how all along Jeremy had known about the affair and Alice had been set up.

"That's proper creepy. I can't believe they were in on it together." Ash sat back and wiped a tiny blob of guacamole off her cheek. "And what he said to you, I'm sure there are employment laws against that. You should seek legal advice."

"No, I don't want to go through all that. It's finished." Alice cupped her hands around the giant mug of tea.

"Fair enough. So, what's next?"

"Tidy up the resume and apply for some jobs, I guess."

"But you're going to give yourself the day off, right? Maybe a couple of days to clear your head and get some rest before you dive in."

"Yeah, maybe you're right... are you working today?"

"Afraid so." Ash glanced down with a look of genuine disappointment. Chewing her bottom lip, she met Alice's gaze again. "I was thinking..."

Her pause stretched out. Alice put her mug down, willing Ash to finish her sentence.

"This might be a bad idea, but..." Ash fidgeted with the sports watch on her wrist.

Before she could stop them, Alice's thoughts jumped out of her mouth. "Ash, are you trying to ask me out?"

"Oh God, no." Ash held up her hands. "Sorry, no, it's er…"

Ash's vehement protest hit Alice square in the chest, and the static returned, fizzing furiously in front of her eyes. She bit the inside of her lip too hard and winced. Ash must have registered the recoil.

"Sorry, I know you're going through a difficult time. I don't want you to think I'm preying on you when you're… vulnerable."

Alice folded her arms. "I'm not a fragile little flower."

Ash sighed and hung her head. "I really messed that up. I didn't mean to offend you. I just don't want you thinking I have ill intentions, especially after what you've just been through."

Alice looked at her through narrowed eyes.

Ash leaned her elbows on the tacky tablecloth. "I really enjoy your company, Alice. And hopefully I'm not being too presumptuous when I say that I think you enjoy mine, too." She looked up through her long eyelashes, a shy smile tugging at her lips.

Alice felt herself thawing. She uncrossed her arms, shifting in the wooden chair as she tongued the metallic spot inside her lip.

"I was wondering whether you're free on Wednesday night. It's technically my Friday, and I don't have any plans, so… it's fine if you're not free and it's probably a bad idea, which is what I was trying to say… I'm conscious of how it might come across—"

"I'm free on Wednesday night. And it's fine, we are allowed to just be friends."

"No, wait… I don't want you to think that I'm not—"

"You don't have to explain yourself."

Ash placed a palm over her chest. "Okay. Let's hang out on Wednesday. Your place? I'll bring pizza. And we can watch a movie, or something. What's that one with the bunny boiler?" Ash held up her fist as if clutching the ears of an invisible rabbit.

"*Fatal Attraction?*"

Ash grinned. "Yeah, to help you process your lucky escape."

Alice laughed and playfully nudged Ash's foot under the table.

"Right, well. I'll settle up here. My treat, seeing as you're currently unemployed." Ash winked.

"You don't have to do that, but thank you. Seeing as I'm treating myself to a day off, would you mind if I tagged along with you to the hospital? I'd like to see how George is doing."

ALICE FOUND HERSELF WILLING TIME WITH ASH TO go slower, despite their little misunderstanding at the café, which had been entirely Alice's fault… again. Jumping to conclusions was her superpower. Even though things with Ash seemed uncomplicated, she didn't want to leap from one tangled mess to another, and it'd literally been four days since she'd ended the longest relationship she'd ever had.

*Four days.*

Her chest still ached when she thought about Fran for too long and she was struggling to ignore the fact that time with Ash felt like a magic balm that soothed the ache. Every moment spent with Ash was time not spent in her own head, thinking about Fran or Jeremy. She'd trusted him. She'd felt sorry for him. And now she just felt a bit stupid.

*The Daltons are probably sipping their expensive red wine and having a good old laugh about silly little Alice, far too naïve to realise she was being played.*

They arrived at the hospital and after an awkward hug, Ash left in one direction and Alice in the other, towards the hospital shop. She hadn't yet managed to do her own grocery shopping, but she wanted to pick up a few things for George.

After browsing the well-stocked aisles, Alice checked out with a large bar of Fruit & Nut, a bottle of Lucozade, some green grapes, and a copy of *Countryfile* magazine, with a cute fluffy lamb on the cover. *After all his talk about pigs, hopefully George likes lambs too.* Alice tapped her credit card without pausing to debate it with herself. *Tomorrow's problem.* Today she was visiting her friend. If you could call someone who you hadn't met whilst they'd been conscious *a friend*.

Somehow, Alice navigated her way to George's ward. The nurse from the other day — Marjorie, Alice recalled from her name badge — was exiting the room as she arrived.

"Oh, you're in luck today." Marjorie beamed. "Mr George is awake and making much more sense."

"He is? That's great. Is he okay to have a visitor?" Alice craned to peer into the room. The man sat propped up in the bed, staring into the void.

Marjorie chuckled. "He's been asking for you."

"Me? But—"

She peered over her glasses. "Yes, you're Alice, right?"

Alice swallowed hard and nodded. *Oh, God, he knows I dropped him.*

"You better get in there before he drifts off again."

George turned and fixed Alice with an unblinking stare as she stepped into the room, and she suddenly felt very unsure of herself. *Actually, why am I here?*

"Hi," she said. "I'm Alice."

"I know." His voice was a raspy whisper, and Alice was sure he still hadn't blinked yet.

"I hope you don't mind, but I found you in the road and I brought you here."

"After dropping me on my head." His bushy eyebrows framed his scowl.

Alice preferred him when he was asleep; at least then they got along alright.

"Yeah, I'm sorry about that, but the doctor said it isn't likely to have caused any complications."

George scoffed. "It might explain the skull-cracking headache though."

Alice shifted her weight between her feet and the carrier bag brushed her leg. "Oh, um, I bought you a few things." She held up the bag. "It's not much, but—"

George's frowning face relaxed and Alice puffed out a breath.

"I didn't know what you'd like, so I went with the usual." She pulled the items from the carrier bag and placed them on the over-bed table.

"Is this compensation for the head injury?" George smirked as he fumbled with the punnet of grapes until his thick fingers tore the packaging open and he popped one in his mouth.

"I guess, I..."

"I'm just messing with you. Sit down, will you? Have a grape."

"Apart from the headache, how are you feeling?" Alice took her usual seat.

George touched his fingers to the stitched gash above his eye. "Everything is still fuzzy... and I feel so tired all the time, even though I've never slept so well."

"That'll be the sedatives. Ash — I mean, Doctor Khurana, said you've been getting really agitated, so they've been trying to help you with that. Do you know what happened?"

George frowned and breathed heavily through his nose. "I can't really remember. I'm just grateful you stopped to help a stranger. Only a particular type of person does that."

Alice smiled. "I'd like to hope someone would do the same for me."

"And you've kept coming by. I haven't always been fully conscious, but I knew when you'd been here. Although, if we're honest, I don't think it's been entirely for my benefit." George raised an eyebrow and the corners of his chapped lips lifted.

"I've no idea what you're talking about." Alice felt her cheeks flush, but she couldn't suppress her smile.

"A certain doctor?"

Alice rolled her eyes.

"Before my recent retirement, I was a science teacher, which means I know chemistry when I see it."

"Bloody hell. You've been far more conscious than you've been letting on. I only met her on Friday. We're just friends." Alice laughed and reached for a grape.

"You only met me on Friday, too, but here we are. Me in my pyjamas and you eating my grapes."

"Tasty grapes." Alice plucked another and popped it between her teeth as she relaxed into the chair.

"So?"

"So, what?"

"Doctor K.?" George said with an incredulous nod.

"You don't quit, do you? We're friends, I told you. Plus, I've literally just ended something long-term, and I think I should take a little time to—"

"Ah yes, would this 'something long-term' happen to be 'fucking Fran'?"

Alice's stomach lurched. "How do you know about Fran?"

George chuckled. "You were muttering away to yourself the whole car journey here."

"Oh, so you were awake then?"

"Barely, but enough to hear you twittering on."

"Let's say you caught me at a bad moment."

George placed a hand on his chest. "*Bend when you can, snap when you have to.*"

"Did you get that from a fortune cookie?"

"No, Taylor Swift."

Alice giggled. "I wouldn't have had you down as a Swiftie, George."

Amusement shone through his tired eyes. "She's quite the modern-day philosopher."

"George, you're awake!" Ash's surprised voice came from the doorway.

"Speak of the devil," he said.

Ash pointed to herself, "Me?"

"Yeah, he thinks you're Taylor Swift," said Alice.

George spluttered a laugh, coughing out a bit of grape skin.

"Oohkay," said Ash as she picked up George's file from the end of the bed and flicked through the pages. "How are you feeling?"

George stifled a yawn. "I've been better. Everything is still hazy. I've no idea how I ended up out there, lying in the road. I'm just grateful that Alice stopped."

"Yeah, me too," Ash said without looking up from the notes. George nudged Alice's arm.

"Stop it," she mouthed at him.

"You had your MRI this afternoon?"

George nodded; his eyelids were starting to droop.

"Good. You should get an update tomorrow."

"Thanks, Doc," George said through another yawn.

Alice squeezed his hand. "I'm going to let you get some rest."

George gave her a sleepy smile.

*P*yg charged ahead, pushing through the tall grass in the meadow, her bushy tail swishing like a flag.

"Pyg, wait," George called, breathless because he'd been running after her for so long. The blistering sun beat down and the further he ran, the hotter the sun felt, like he was getting closer to it. His legs powered him on and on, only slowing when the green grass started to yellow.

No longer a meadow, but a crop so tall and thick he could no longer see Pyg's tail. He could hear her panting. Or was that the sound of his own breath?

"Pyg, come back," he yelled and doubled over with the effort.

"George," came a voice from behind. *Bernard?*

George looked around, but the crop was taller than he was, thick golden stems in every direction.

"George," called the voice again. *Mum?*

The crop rustled around him. He spun, trying to locate the source.

"Hello, who's there?" He called out. "Bernard? Mum? Where are you?"

The crop rustled again, and George's nose twitched at the smell of smoke. He looked down, noticing the grey wisps twisting through the stems, curling around his feet and ankles. His ears tuned to the cracks and pops of a fire taking hold.

A black figure in a trailing cloak darted past, caught in the corner of his eye.

"Wait!" George called out, but the figure had disappeared.

Panic rose in his chest, constricting his throat. Or was that the smoke?

The figure darted past again. *Was that a beak? A big black beak.*

George ran, holding his arms up to protect himself from the thick crop that whipped at his face, but it was sharp and sliced into his flesh.

"I can't keep up with you. Please..." George wheezed, but still he ran and ran. His lungs ached with every breath until the air grew fresher and cooler.

He was back in the meadow, but when had it grown so dark? George shivered and goosebumps prickled his skin.

"George." The voice called. *Not Bernard. Not Mum.* But he knew that voice.

George clenched his fists instinctively as anger simmered in his stomach. He squinted into the inky darkness and a tiny light fizzed and flickered up ahead.

"Higgins?" *I'm not calling you Father.*

"Yes, it's me," said the priest. The voice grew closer and the light larger.

George resisted the urge to turn and run.

"I have them all with me, George. They're safe. You can rest."

"Why have you taken them?"

"I didn't take them. They came to me."

"You're a liar. Why would they leave me?"

"One day, you'll see." Higgins turned, striding into the darkness; a trail of spent matches scattering in his wake.

## 1968

### WORMS DON'T HAVE FEET

*L*ight flickered as my eyelids shuttered; black to grey, black to grey, to ankles. A pair of women's ankles in the thick swirling smoke. *Mum?*

*No, too skinny.* Matchstick ankles with black church shoes and thick tights, all bunched at the bottom. Bernard's cries filtered in and out of my consciousness.

"Bernard!" I tried to call out, but my chest lurched violently. I coughed then dry-retched, my eyes burning and bulging with so much pressure I thought they might pop. A searing pain shot through me and then I was on my back with gravel ripping into my flesh and clawing at my spine. It felt like I was being dragged into hell, yet the air grew cooler and clearer, and the sound of Bernard's cries grew stronger.

I reached out a hand and Bernard grasped it, then hugged his arms around me and sobbed into my chest.

*Time to be strong, George. You're all he's got left, not that he knows it yet.*

The voice in my head sounded like my mother's, and pain spasmed in my abdomen.

*She's not here, it isn't her. She'd never wear shoes like that.* All that was left of her was the voice stitched into the fabric of my mind.

*I promise, promise, promise,* she'd sworn in her letter. I'd read it and hoped.

*New life. Fresh start, for all of us.* But the letter was burnt and gone, as good as the promise.

"George. Can you stand?" A soft voice spoke, and a bony hand prodded into my armpit. "Bernard, can you help on the other side?"

Bernard tugged under my other armpit, and I struggled to my feet. We moved at a snail's pace along the garden path, every step making my head spin with a dizzying whoosh.

"Let's get him into the kitchen. I'll heat the water and we'll draw him a bath."

"Will he be alright, Miss?"

"He'll be fine. It's just the shock. I'll fix us all some sugary tea."

In the kitchen, they flopped me into a chair; my body lolled, unresponsive to my brain's commands. I felt boneless and breathless, confronted with a wall of pain I couldn't begin to scale.

A while later, the woman knelt in front of me, her eyes magnified by the thick glasses perched on her beaky little nose.

"George, you're going to have to stand and lean on me so that we can get you into the bath." Her tiny voice sounded shrill as her cardigan-clad arms flapped around me like a frenzy of wings, pulling at my jumper, unbuttoning my shirt and tugging off my vest.

"Are you a bird?" Laughter crested in my throat, and I hiccupped.

She peered into my face and frowned. "What?"

"You're a big bird and I'm a little worm." I laughed again, hiccupping as my limp arms flopped at my sides.

"George, stop fooling around. Bernard?"

Bernard stepped out from behind the bird-woman, his soot-smeared face rumpled in concern. Tears had tracked white lines down his cheeks, and he looked like a clown. I giggled.

"Can you help me get George to the tub?"

"Shouldn't we call for a doctor, miss?"

"No." Her shrill voice pecked the word into the air.

"But miss, he seems to think you're a bird. I think he might've hit his head or something."

The bird-woman fixed her bug-eyed gaze back on me for a moment. "No need for a fuss. I can handle this." She muttered something under her breath. "Come on, or the water will be cold."

She pulled me into a standing position and tugged off my remaining clothes, but thankfully leaving my underpants in place. Even though she was a bird, and I was a worm, I didn't want her to see me in the nude. *What if she pecks off my little pecker?* I giggled again.

With my head still whooshing, I eased my weight onto their shoulders, and they guided me into the small utility room off the kitchen, which doubled as a washroom.

Steam rose from the tarnished copper tub in the centre of the room. Rarely did I get fresh hot water for myself — I was usually second or third in line, after Grandmother and Bernard. Mum would top the tub up with a fresh pan of hot, but the water was always slick with soap and grime and, at best, tepid.

At first, the hot water stung my bare feet and ankles and jolted me back to myself. *I'm not a worm because worms don't have feet.* But the water soon soothed me, and I wanted to immerse myself to feel the relief all over my body.

"George, now that you're in, I'm going to leave. Take off your underpants. Bernard will help you." She left, and soon enough, I submerged my entire body. A gentle, muffled silence enveloped me as the water revived my numb flesh. The heat warmed me through to my bones, because I had bones and was most definitely not a worm.

I held my breath and opened my eyes under the clear water. A bare lightbulb shimmered overhead.

"George?" came the sound of Mum's voice, crystal clear. I turned my head and tiny bubbles floated up, catching the light like miniature silver beads. Then the blackened face of Bernard came into view.

"George?" The sound bubbled into my ears. I yearned to stay submerged in this tranquil realm where I could still hear Mum, but Bernard's worried face tugged me through the surface, and I gasped for air.

Consciousness trickled into my mind, along with an uncomfortable awareness of my very full bladder. Hushed and hurried voices whispered on the landing, and daylight shone through the gap in the curtains. The blankets on Bernard's bed had been tidied, and there was no indication of when he'd last been in the room. Turning to the wall, I gathered my own musty blankets around myself. I curled into a tight ball, hoping my bladder might settle for a while longer and the voices would grow mute.

Seconds later, the door creaked open. Someone entered and stepped on all the wrong floorboards, clearly untrained in stealth, thus not Bernard. Or Pyg. And, therefore, I wasn't interested in speaking to them.

A hand pressed on my blanketed shoulder.

"George," a woman's voice said softly.

I held my breath and lay as still as possible.

She said my name again and her hand gently pulled at my shoulder, trying to tug me out of my cocoon. If I resisted too much, it would give the game away, but if I didn't resist at all, she would see I was awake anyway. I groaned, and it came out as a rasp. I tried to swallow, but my throat felt dusty.

"George, come on now." The soft voice grew stern. "You've been in bed for nearly two days. You need to eat and drink something."

The persistent pressure of my bladder suddenly overwhelmed everything else.

"I need to pee." I whipped around, fighting my way out of the blankets and clambering to my feet, which weren't fully working. Holding my groin, I stumbled like a drunken sailor to the toilet at the end of the landing. After the pain subsided, relief flooded through me.

But now to face that woman... and everything else.

She waited for me, blocking the entrance to my room, and my chances of climbing back into bed. At only thirteen, I already stood taller than her, but despite her bird-like appearance, she didn't seem intimidated.

"Why don't you put on some clothes, and I'll fix you something to eat?"

"Where's Bernard?"

"He's left for school."

"You sent him to school without me?" I scratched my neck, trying to push away thoughts of Bernard dealing with the bullies on his own.

"Well, you've hardly been fit, but there was no reason for Bernard not to go."

How did this odd little woman not understand that our world had been upended? Our mother had abandoned us. Then our bitter, twisted grandmother had burned all we had left and, in the process, murdered our dear Pyg. Our lovely, soft girl, with her bright eyes and clever tricks.

My face must have said it all. As she touched an icy hand to my bare shoulder, I fought the urge to shrug it away.

"Come on now. I know you must be worried about your grandmother."

"You don't know anything."

She removed her hand and gripped her pale fingers on the crucifix hanging around her neck. "Father Sutherland said you might be... difficult. He said, if you give me any trouble, then—"

"Then what? I don't care if you leave as well. I don't care if we get sent somewhere else. Anywhere has to be better than here."

"I'd be very careful if I were you, or you might lose that little brother of yours as well as everything else. Exodus."

I frowned.

"Chapter twenty, verse five. *God will punish the children for the sins of their parents.* It's no small coincidence that some of us have a lighter cross to bear."

*Ironic, given the size of the one swinging from her neck.*

I swallowed what little saliva I had left in my dry mouth against the sickening churn of my stomach grumbling for food. I didn't want to need this woman, but...

"You'd do well to reflect on this little chat."

I flinched as she touched her freezing fingers to my arm again.

"Get yourself dressed and I'll fix you something to eat. We can start afresh."

She flapped her tiny wings and twittered downstairs, humming a churchy tune as she went.

I tugged a scratchy wool jumper over my white vest and a thick pair of socks onto my cold feet. Treading the usual pattern of floorboards, my heart wrenched at the absence of Pyg leading the way. I sniffed and squeezed my eyes shut against the urge to cry.

In the kitchen, I pulled out a chair and sat at the table as the woman busied herself.

"Now then, eat up." She placed down a bowl of creamy porridge with a sprinkle of brown sugar melting on top.

I clasped the spoon and forced a smile.

I would eat my breakfast. I would keep my head down and my mouth shut, because I knew a threat when I heard one, and I wasn't prepared to lose the only thing I had left — *Bernard*.

## 11

# TELL YOUR FACE

*L*eaning over the marble-topped island in Maggie's gleaming kitchen, Alice reached for a caper from the ramekin next to the chopping board.

"Oi," Maggie said, slapping Alice's hand away.

"Ouch! No need to hit."

"Well, no need to be so bloody uncouth all the time."

"I'm starving." Alice stuck her bottom lip out, even though that never worked on Maggie.

"It's almost done. Just drink your wine and keep your fingers to yourself; I never know where they've been."

Alice tutted and took a mouthful of wine, the flavour crisp on her palate. She held the long stem of her glass between her fingers and twirled the pale liquid around.

"This is a nice one."

Maggie sipped from her own glass. "Mmm, it is. That's why I told you not to bring the cheap stuff."

Alice pulled a face. "I'll have you know, I've tasted some of the finest wines."

Maggie scoffed. "Didn't Fran practically force you to drink red all the time?"

"She didn't force me, exactly. But yeah, she isn't a fan of white unless it's fizzing." Alice grinned to herself, remembering Fran's white shirt sprayed with the Merlot she'd choked on that time in The Dog & Duck. And the hot night that followed in the room they'd booked on a whim. They'd ended up staying the whole weekend, and it'd been lovely, at least until Fran's mood had changed.

She'd never been truly at ease with Fran. Their time together, although *mostly* enjoyable, somehow felt make-believe, like Alice was an actress in a play with stunning sets and elegant costumes — and Fran directing her this way or that. Alice had never been in control, merely reading the lines and hoping she didn't fluff them, although inevitably, she always did.

Maggie pulled a steaming dish from the oven and fanned it with her oven glove before prodding at the contents with a knife. "Almost ready."

"Thank goodness. I'm going to pass out if I don't eat soon."

"You pretty much ate a family-sized bag of Monster Munch by yourself when you arrived."

"I've been very active today. I went to the gym."

Maggie tilted her head. "You joined a gym?"

"No, I said I *went* to the gym. I took one look at the membership prices and left. But it's the thought that counts, right?"

"Um, I'm pretty sure that doesn't apply to working out."

Alice waved away Maggie's reasoning. "When I got home, I did a YouTube workout."

Maggie raised an eyebrow, as if waiting for the punchline.

"Seriously, I found my old yoga mat under the bed, as well as a lot of dust, which I vacuumed whilst I was down there. And I did a HIIT workout."

"Wow! I'm impressed. You're going to ache like a bitch tomorrow."

"No, I should be fine. I stretched before and after."

Maggie gave her a smug grin. Alice wasn't going to tell her that she was right, that the muscles in her thighs and arse cheeks were already burning in protest against her deciding to use them again. Alice shifted her weight, grateful for the plush cushioning on Maggie's counter chairs.

"I can add you to my gym membership if you like?" Maggie offered.

"Really, you'd do that?"

"Yeah, of course. It'll make me feel less guilty about all the times I don't go. And when you get a new job, you can put something towards it."

"You know I probably won't, though."

"Yeah, I know, but isn't it the thought that counts?" Maggie chuckled and nodded to Alice's empty glass. "More wine?"

Maggie passed Alice the bottle from the fridge and turned her attention to serving up their meal. Alice's phone screen lit up, and her heart bounced. She grinned at the screen as she read Ash's text. Despite refraining all day from texting her, and resorting to exercise to distract herself, Ash hadn't strayed far from her thoughts.

> Hey! Hope you've had a good day. Did you get some rest? Remember doctor's orders! Just about to start my shift. I'll try to check on George and let you know how he's doing. Looking forward to our non-date tomorrow X

*Big kiss.* Even though they were just friends, it was good to have someone new around. Someone new, who felt like they'd always been there. And unlike Fran, Ash actually made Alice feel good about herself.

> Good day, thanks. I rested a bit, but also did a workout and I'm about to eat some broccoli. Isn't that what doctors like to hear?

*Best not to mention the wine and Monster Munch.*

> Have a good shift and say hello to George from me. See you tomorrow X

*Big kiss back at her*, but the energy of something left unsaid thrummed through Alice's fingers. Was it weird that she'd missed her? Seriously, how could you miss someone you hadn't even known existed five days ago? ... or perhaps it was Ash who'd always been missing?

*No, stop it.*

She had missed her though, and the urge to tell her

was strong, which was ridiculous because Ash had made it clear she just wanted to be friends. Still, Alice couldn't shake the sensation of the spark between them. George had only been half-conscious and he'd noticed it too, so...

"I know that look, Al. Please tell me you're not texting Fran."

Alice snapped her head up and took in Maggie's concerned frown. "What? No! She doesn't have this number and I'm not a complete moron... it's just Ash."

"*Just* Ash?"

"You know, the doctor you met at my place the other day."

"Oh, I thought you said that wasn't anything?"

"It's not."

Maggie raised her eyebrows and chuckled. "Tell your face that."

Alice flushed with heat. "Stop it. It isn't like that. Ash just wants to be friends."

"And you?"

"Yeah, me too. I could do with a friend right now."

Maggie passed a full plate over the counter and Alice's mouth watered as she took it, inhaling the delicious aroma of baked salmon.

"Just be careful, Al."

"I am house-trained, Mags!"

Maggie rolled her eyes. "Not with the plate. With your heart. Give yourself some time. Fran was toxic. You need to heal from that."

"I know, and I am. I honestly feel so much better already, and it's only been a few days."

After the initial heartache, followed by the shock of Jeremy's revelation, something inside Alice had lifted. Even when she'd been considering a future with Fran, it hadn't ever felt real. There was always something hazy and intangible about it. But now, at the point where everything was so uncertain, possibilities were blooming inside her.

She'd just denied it, but she felt an undeniable pull towards Ash, with her kind nature and buoyant confidence, which would never be too much because she was also adorably bashful. And there was the soft lilt of a Northern accent Alice hadn't even known she found attractive until it came from Ash's very kissable lips. She'd thought about Ash's strong arms more than once and how they'd feel wrapped around her, whilst those capable hands explored her body.

"Mmm," Alice groaned.

"You like it?"

"Huh?" Wide-eyed, she looked at Maggie across the table.

"The salmon?"

"Oh, yeah. Delicious." Alice speared another forkful and steered it into her mouth.

Of course, her older, wiser sister was right — she should slow and steady herself, not yield to her tendency to dive headlong into situations and relationships... wasn't it that which had made her such easy prey for Fran?

## 12
# FULLY FUNCTIONAL ADULT

*A*sh had seen Alice at her worst. Despite that, the intriguing doctor still wanted to spend her first work-free night since they'd met in Alice's company.

For some reason, this incredibly generous, caring, funny... *very cute* doctor wanted to be Alice's friend. As such, Alice wanted her *new friend* to see that she was a fully functional adult. She wanted to show her that she lived a tidy, ordered life, which only by exception involved panda-eyes, stray thongs, broken-down cars, lost phones, job quitting, and general chaos. In the short time they'd known each other, it was entirely possible Ash had got the wrong impression of her, but more likely that she'd glimpsed the real Alice because she hadn't had a chance to put her guard up yet.

Waking early Wednesday morning, after a coffee in bed — made with fresh milk from her fully stocked fridge — Alice threw open the curtains and windows. She ached like a bitch from that workout, but sore muscles aside, now seemed like the ideal time to spring clean her flat. The space wasn't big by any stretch, but the high ceilings needed de-cobwebbing, and everything needed dusting. She vacuumed the entire flat, bleached the kitchen, and washed the floors.

Momentary panic gripped her when she stripped the bedsheets — would Ash realise she'd changed them? And if so, would she think Alice was being presumptuous? *Promiscuous, even?*

Wait, if Ash made it to the bedroom and got close enough to the bedsheets to realise they'd been changed, then surely Alice had a right to be presumptuous — *stop overthinking, your sheets are dirty so change them like a normal person.*

Her tummy flipped at the thought of them between the covers together, but she blinked it away.

*This isn't that kind of date — friends, Alice. Just friends!*

The problem was, aside from Maggie, who was under sororal obligation to be her friend, Alice didn't have many female friends.

*...Any* female friends.

*...Any friends.*

It was partly by choice, partly by circumstance. A few had come and gone over the years — mostly gay men who were, in her experience, flaky as fuck. Just like her past relationships — fun while it lasted, but nothing had endured. Alice was okay with that; it suited her personality not to be stuck with the same people for too long. They either annoyed her or she annoyed them and so they all moved on with their lives.

Before Fran, Alice's longest relationship had been with a jar of mayonnaise in her fridge. Of course, after a while, even that turned sour. And it wasn't until Fran had planted the seed that Alice had hoped for anything more than the arrangement they had. Before that, the idea of waking up next to the same person day in, day out, struck her as tedious. Yet Fran's suggestion of something more had unlocked a desire for domesticity — mornings dancing around each other in the bathroom, a smiling face to come home to at the end of a difficult day, rainy Sunday afternoons curled up on the couch, legs entangled... and the most basic yearning of all; someone to bring her a cuppa in bed without having to ask how she liked it.

And whilst Alice would miss the heat and the feeling of being desired by a woman with the gravitational pull of Francesca Dalton, she realised it wasn't the loss of Fran specifically that stung; it was the loss of the possibilities of a future with someone.

When Alice finished scrubbing the bathroom, the bathtub beckoned. After all the exertion, her muscles were screaming for a soak and a cheeky glass of wine to help stop her over-thinking the whole Ash thing.

Alice reclined in the deep tub, where she lay for nearly an hour, inhaling the zesty scent of the steam infused with the lemongrass oil she'd added to the water. When the water went cold, she added more hot, twisting the tap on and off with her toes. She'd long since finished her wine —

a glass of the nice white she'd shared with Maggie — but she couldn't bear to leave the sanctuary of the bathroom to dash along the hallway in a towel. And besides, she didn't want to spoil her clean floors with drip marks.

A faint knocking noise pulled Alice from her meditative state.

She wasn't expecting anyone or anything; perhaps she'd been soaking for longer than she'd realised. Alice sat up and leaned over the side of the bath to dry her hands on a fluffy towel. As she picked up her phone to check for messages, the faint knock became an obnoxious hammering at the door. Alice tutted. *Bloody delivery drivers.*

If it were Maggie, she'd have called, and Ash wasn't due for hours yet. In the time it would take to get out of the bath and dry herself, the unexpected visitor would have left, anyway.

"Just leave it outside," Alice yelled, although it was unlikely they'd hear her through two closed doors. The banging continued. Alice groaned and re-submerged herself, relishing the hot water enveloping her entirely. As her ears filled, the hammering morphed into a distant thudding. A warbling sound filtered through the water, muffled and far-off —

"Alice! Alice!"

Alice gasped and bolted upright, splashing through the surface.

"I know you're in there. You can't keep avoiding me like this." Fran's voice sounded strained and desperate.

*Fuck, why is she here?*

"Alice, please open the door. I just want to speak with you."

Alice's stomach clenched into a tight ball.

"Well, I'm not leaving. You'll have to come out at some point." The letterbox snapped shut.

*Bollocks.* Alice pulled the plug and reached for her towel. When getting to her feet, she slipped, stumbling, and grasped for something, anything — the shower curtain. The metal rings gave way as she tumbled out of the tub, twisting in the material and bashing her knee on the side of the bath. She landed with a thud on the cold floor tiles and her wrist bent painfully underneath her.

"Fucking oils," she screamed and winced as she tried to move her arm. After drying the soles of her feet, Alice tentatively stood, blood pounding in her ears. Swelling bloomed over her knee already and she yelped when she tried to apply pressure to it.

The plughole sucked and slurped the bathwater and Fran's hammering resumed. Alice opened the bathroom door a crack and shuddered as cool air rushed in.

"Just give me a minute," she screamed in a tone she'd never used with Fran before, and the banging ceased.

Alice padded across the hallway to her bedroom and threw on the pink robe that hung from the back of the door. With one hand she towel-dried her curls as best she could, then released a shaky breath as she fingered her injured wrist to assess the damage. "Ow, ow, ow," she whimpered, tears springing to her eyes.

"What on earth are you doing in there?" Fran shouted through the letterbox.

With a steadying breath, Alice unlocked the front door and stepped back at the sight of Fran. She was dressed well as always, but her face looked pallid. Makeup did nothing to conceal the dark bags encircling her eyes.

"Alice, at last. Thank goodness." Fran smiled, revealing a smudge of dark lipstick on her front tooth. As she crossed the threshold, a deep frown wrinkled her forehead. "Oh, darling, don't cry."

Alice sniffed. "I'm not."

"Yes, you are."

Alice inhaled a ragged breath. "I fell out of the bath."

"Oh, you silly thing. Lucky I'm here, isn't it?"

Fran's frown dissolved into a smile, and she pulled Alice into a hug.

Alice yelped as sharp pain from her wrist and knee bolted through her.

"Come on, let's sit you down and look you over."

Fran shepherded Alice into the lounge and sat her on the couch. She removed her light jacket, placing it over one of the dining chairs, and knelt before Alice.

"Now, tell me what hurts." Fran's dark eyes stared up at her.

"I banged my knee and fell onto my wrist."

"Okay, I'll take a look at your wrist first."

Alice held out her right arm, and Fran took it. She touched her thumbs around the area and tried to move the joint.

Alice hissed. "Fuck, that really hurts."

"Hmm, I don't think it's broken. Perhaps just sprained." Fran softly traced her fingers up Alice's bare forearm, then lowered her head and tenderly kissed along the same route.

Alice breathed heavily and closed her eyes.

"And you said you hurt your knee too?"

Fran pulled back the lapel of Alice's robe and let her fingers resume their slow dance, tracing over Alice's skin. She lowered her head and kissed Alice's knee, before licking her way to her inner thigh.

Alice swallowed as her own body started to betray her. It would be so easy to let Fran consume her, and the ache starting to pulse between her legs would appreciate that very much. Fran's tongue moved higher up Alice's thigh and Alice whimpered.

"Sounds like somebody missed me," Fran purred, heat smouldering in her eyes as she looked up from between Alice's legs.

"Stop. I don't want this." Alice panted with the effort of pushing out those words.

Fran pulled back and glowered. "You actually want me to stop?"

Alice nodded and pulled her robe closed, flinching as it grazed her throbbing knee. "Why are you here?"

Fran huffed and rose to her feet. She sat next to Alice on the couch.

"I don't understand you, Alice. Was I not giving you enough attention before? I don't know what you want from me."

Alice considered her for a moment, then stood and limped to the kitchen. She poured a glass of cold water and punched two ibuprofen tablets from a blister pack. She gulped down the pills and drained the water.

"I need to lie down. You can see yourself out." Alice limped to her bedroom and crawled between her fresh sheets. She drifted, latching onto the image of Ash's warm brown eyes, as if they were life rafts in this maelstrom.

# JEKYLL OR HYDE

## SIX DAYS EARLIER

"*S*hit," Alice muttered, dropping her car keys after locking the door. She bent to pick them up and, conscious of the next-to-no-clothing underneath, held her coat with one hand over her arse to stop it riding up. She dropped the keys in her bag and glanced at the time on her phone screen. *Over half an hour late. She's going to be livid. But I come bearing good news and she'll approve of my outfit, at least.*

Trying to focus on the positive, Alice pulled her small suitcase behind her and into the reception of the boutique Cotswolds hotel — one of their frequent haunts, and certainly not one she'd even dare to consider if Fran wasn't paying. Not that Alice would've minded them spending the weekend holed up at her place, but Fran never seemed keen on that.

"It's too domestic, too mundane," she'd once said, which Alice shrugged off, but she'd never really understood how it was any different. And besides, Fran needed to get used to the idea of domesticity between them now they were planning to live together.

The young receptionist looked up from her computer and beamed. "Welcome back." Her high ponytail bobbed like the swishing tail of a golden retriever. "Mrs Dalton checked in earlier. She said for you to go right up. It's 201, the usual. Do you need a separate key?"

"No. Thank you." Alice smiled at the young woman.

Standing outside room 201, Alice smoothed her hands over her coat and drew in a couple of steadying breaths before tapping the solid oak door. Fran opened it, a glass of red wine in her hand and her lips set into a firm pout.

Alice took a breath. "Sorry I'm so late, I—"

Fran held up a hand. "Just come on in, will you?"

"I did text you to say I was with the estate agent and running late."

Fran walked to the sideboard. Grabbing the open half-empty bottle of red, she splashed it into a glass and held it out to Alice.

"Er, thanks."

Fran swigged the contents of her own glass and refilled it.

"Cheers." Fran took a gulp and slouched into the wing-back chair, her usual composure as awry as her legs; one was hooked over the arm, the other jiggling.

Alice stood, unsure what to do with herself as Fran surveyed her from her leather throne. This wasn't really the seductive entrance she'd planned. And now she couldn't really take off her coat until she'd sparked the mood. She took a tentative sip of the wine — so sour, she might as well be drinking vinegar.

"So, as I was saying, I was with the estate agent. He was really positive about my flat and thinks it'll sell quickly in this market. His valuation was way over what I paid five years ago, so we'll have a nice sum to put towards—"

"Oh, Alice, I'm not interested in any of that."

Alice tilted her head. "What do you mean?"

"I mean, I'm not interested in your little flat."

"But I thought we were going to..."

Fran frowned and swished the crimson liquid around her glass.

"Fran, you can't seriously be this angry with me because I'm a little late."

"No. I'm angry with you because you expect me to upheave my life to fit in with you."

*What the fuck is happening?* Alice placed the glass down, not wanting to swallow any more of that shit as well. "You leaving Jeremy was *your* idea. Us getting a place together was something *you* suggested. If you don't want to do that any more, that's your choice, but we need to have a conversation about what we're doing here." She drew an invisible line between them with her finger, surprised by how calm she sounded considering the panic sirens screaming inside her head.

Fran shifted in the chair and glanced up. With a sigh, she rose to her feet and stepped towards Alice.

"I care about you deeply. I don't want to lose you." She traced a finger under the lapel of Alice's trench coat.

Alice frowned. "I don't want to lose you either."

Fran peered into her face, a saccharine grin spreading over her lips. "Okay, well, that's settled. Let's kiss and make up, shall we?" She closed the gap between them. With her fingers twisted in Alice's hair, she kissed her with a fierce intensity, hungry and desperate, but not in a good way.

When she pulled away, Fran inhaled sharply through her nose. "Why don't we get you out of this silly little coat? Then I can show you just how much I care about you." Fran tugged at the waist belt, and the coat fell open, revealing Alice's lack of attire underneath; a lacy black bra, matching panties, stockings, and suspenders.

"Oh, hello gorgeous," Fran purred.

Alice touched a finger to her lip, throbbing where Fran had bitten it. "So, just to be clear. We're making up?"

"Yes, of course."

"But is anything actually resolved?"

"Oh, Alice. Please, let's not go over it all again." Fran moved closer, her hot hands pawing at Alice's underwear.

"No, this is important. Are you or are you not leaving Jeremy?"

Fran's mouth twisted into a sneer. "That's all you really want, isn't it? For me to leave my husband, so that I'm as alone and pathetic as you are. Struggling to get by, and grateful for handouts from kind benefactors, like a pigeon pecking up crumbs."

*Ouch.* Fran's words were a verbal slap across the face.

Again, Alice's voice came out calm and at odds with the confusion and anger swirling inside her. "Like I said, it was you who suggested it in the first place, Fran. How have you forgotten that? I thought we—"

"*I thought we, I thought we...*" Rage rattled through Fran's words, like they were shutters in a storm. "You thought we *what?* That we'd live out our days in luxury, sipping Champagne on yachts and fucking in expensive hotel rooms. Is that what you thought, Alice?"

"We talked about getting a place together, and being—"

"Oh, get real. That isn't going to happen, is it? Where will we live? Another dreary little flat. What will we live off? A PA's meagre salary. Surviving on tinned soup and pre-sliced bread? Fat chance even of that when you're fired for fucking your boss's wife." Fran panted, breathless from her tirade.

The air stilled. Alice pulled her coat around her and tightened the belt. As she moved towards the door, Fran grabbed at her arm, her manicured nails scratching Alice's flesh like talons.

"You're not leaving, Alice."

Noticing how that wasn't a question, Alice stared down at her heels. Earlier, when she pulled on her stockings, she'd felt sexy and desirable; now she just felt cheap and ridiculous. *As if an affair with my boss's wife wasn't sordid enough.*

Fran sniffed and stepped toward her. "I'm sorry I hurt you. Can I kiss it better?"

Alice looked on in a trance-like state, as Fran lifted the forearm she'd just clawed to her lips, dark, apologetic eyes searching through thick eyelashes. *How does she change so quickly?*

"Come on, let's have a nice weekend together."

"I can't do this any more, Fran." Alice turned and gripped the door handle.

"Stop being so ungrateful. After everything I've given you." Fran spun her around and gripped Alice's shoulders. "Why don't we just—"

"You're hurting me. Stop it!"

"No, you stop it." Fran's fingers dug into Alice's biceps. "The sooner you realise that I'm the best someone like you will ever get, the better."

"Let me go." Alice pushed her and Fran stumbled backwards, shock registering on her face. She gritted her teeth and her lips twisted in a savage sneer as she lurched forward and grasped Alice's arm, clutching her coat. Alice snatched it away and the sleeve strap tore.

"Look what you've made me do. Happy now?" Fran screamed.

Hot tears stung in Alice's eyes. She didn't dare blink because she didn't want to give Fran the satisfaction of making her cry. She didn't want Fran to think she'd won, because she hadn't, far from it.

"It's over, Fran. I don't want to see you again." The words came out quiet but steady, and because of this, they both realised she meant them. And as if her rage had just evaporated, Fran's face fell. A mixture of sadness and hurt flickered across her features as she reached out and took Alice's hands.

"You don't mean that, Alice. We have a good thing going on. Let's not over-complicate it. Why don't we—"

"No."

Fran tilted her head. "You didn't let me finish."

"No. I meant what I said."

"Just because you got a little scratch and your coat got ripped. I'll buy you a new one, a better one. Don't you think you're being a bit petty?"

Alice breathed out a laugh. "You really don't get it, do you?"

Fran released Alice's hands and held up her own.

Alice searched Fran's face for any sign of self-awareness, any hint of remorse. *Nothing.*

"You're a husk, Fran. You're incapable of love." She turned, opened the door, and stepped through it. Such a simple and obvious thing to do, but in the two years she'd been intimate with Fran, she'd never walked away from her before. Throughout their affair, she'd been enthralled by the woman. Yes, she could be cold and haughty, but never had she been so cruel, and in that moment, Alice realised that was who she really was. It hurt like hell, but the spell had been broken.

With her heart thundering in her chest, Alice paced out of the hotel, her little suitcase clattering behind her. She made it to her car before the tears fell. Ugly tears, as she turned the key in the ignition. Anguished tears, when the Fiesta didn't start the first time. She stroked the dashboard.

"Come on, old girl. Not now, not now."

Relieved tears, when the Fiesta coughed and spluttered into life. Imagining Fran charging into the road after her, Alice pulled out of the space and sped off, her one functioning headlamp lighting the way. She really needed to get that fixed. She really needed to replace the Fiesta, full stop. But first, she needed to pay off her ridiculous credit card balance and sort her fucking life out.

She really needed to stop thinking for just a minute. She twisted the knob on the stereo. Of all the billions of songs in the world, that insipid track about being in love and giving it your all sang out of the tinny little speakers. The tears came hard. Alice sniffed and wiped her nose on her torn coat sleeve, Fran's look of wounded confusion in the front of her mind.

*Was I too hard on her? Fran had tried to apologise and make amends, hadn't she?*

"Fuck off, John Legend," she screamed and pushed a tape into the deck, which clicked and whirred until an angry, wronged-woman song filled the car.

*That's better.* She turned up the volume, singing along through her snot bubbles.

A jarring mechanical clunk sounded from the deck, then the song distorted as the tape snagged and crinkled into the machine's inner workings.

"No, no, no." Alice glanced down and rapidly punched the eject button with her finger. "You ate Madonna already. Don't take Alanis from me too."

The tape deck ignored her pleas and devoured the cassette, crunching until it whined a high-pitched scream of mechanical distress and the reels pulled the mangled tape through. Alice flicked her eyes down and pumped the eject button again. *Fucking jammed.* A truck horn honked like an angry goose.

"Shit!" She swerved back onto her side of the road,

slowing to a near stop as she clasped the steering wheel with both hands. The truck's taillights shone like demonic eyes in the rear-view mirror, thankfully shrinking into the distance.

After a couple of calming breaths — in through her nose, out through her mouth — Alice accelerated again and took the next left off the highway and onto a back road, her favoured shortcut. Her mind whirred in the absence of any musical distraction. The buzz of her mobile phone sounded from her pocket. After the near-miss she'd just had, she resisted the urge to fish it out and glance at the screen, but she didn't have to look to know it was Fran. Would it be Jekyll or Hyde at the other end of the line? Perhaps both? The buzzing stopped, and seconds later came the *ding* of a voicemail.

Curiosity gnawed at her, but Alice drove on into the inky night. Her headlight illuminated something in the road. A large, dark lump. She leaned towards the windscreen as she drew closer to the obstruction. She glanced in the rear-view; no sign of any other vehicles, so she came to a stop.

Alice climbed out of her car and peered into the darkness.

*What is that? A cow?*

## 13

# GASLIGHT GODDESS

*A*lice stirred, squeezing her eyes shut and opening them again, trying to adjust to the low light. The curtains were still open, but daylight had faded to dusk. She tried to sit up, but was immediately reacquainted with pain; a sharp stabbing in her wrist that radiated up her arm, and a dull throb in her knee. Alice slowly attempted to flare her fingers and recoiled with the pain of it. With her left arm, she flicked on the bedside lamp to look for bruising and turned to see the indentation of where someone had been lying next to her. *Fran?*

So strange that Alice had, until recently, yearned for the woman to occupy her space. She'd imagined a life where they'd wake up and fall asleep alongside one another as part of a normal routine. But this — this felt like an invasion. She'd asked her to leave, hadn't she?

Alice glanced at the closed door and noticed the strip of light underneath. She got to her feet and, with her pain-free hand, pulled her robe around her as best she could. Her hair would be a frizzy fright, but she wasn't trying to impress anyone. With a steadying breath, Alice hobbled into the hall and followed the light to the lounge. Fran smiled up at her from the couch, where she was sitting with a glass of wine in one hand, her phone in the other.

"Hello, sleepyhead. You've had a good couple of hours. Feeling any better?"

Alice shook her head. "No, not really. My wrist, it's—"

"Let me see." Fran placed her glass on the coffee table — *no bloody coaster* — and stood. She took Alice's arm and glanced at it for a moment, before peering into her face. "You do look a bit of a fright, you poor thing. You know, I don't think I've ever seen you makeup-free."

"What?"

"Well, you know we're usually done up and out and about, aren't we?" She rubbed Alice's upper arm, in what was probably intended to be a tender gesture, but it made Alice's insides squirm. Fran swung around, taking in the room.

"I was wrong about your flat before. Having spent the afternoon here, it's actually quite pleasant. A lick of paint here and there, and perhaps some new curtains, it could be —"

"Fran, why are you still here?"

Fran scoffed. "Charming! I wanted to see you. Patch things up after our little spat."

Alice closed her eyes and breathed in through her nose. "What world are you living in?"

"Oh, Alice. Don't be so melodramatic!"

Alice tensed her jaw to clamp down on the scream building inside her. *Why won't she fucking leave?*

"Sit yourself down and I'll pour you a glass — it's delicious, for a white. And let's just have a little chat. If you don't feel differently afterwards, I'll go. I promise."

With a shaky exhale, Alice conceded and limped to the couch. Moments later, Fran shuffled up next to her and passed her a glass, which she clinked with her own.

Alice took a large sip and swished it around her dry mouth.

Fran leaned in, arranging her lips into a conciliatory smile as she rested a warm hand on Alice's thigh. "Look, I'm sorry you got upset with me. I really am. I didn't mean to—"

Alice growled in frustration. She moved to clench her fists, but pain shot up her arm. *Fuck.* Fran bristled and sat up straight, widening the gap between them.

"Are you going to continue behaving like a petulant child, or will you hear me out? What I'm trying to say is that I'm sorry you got the wrong end of the stick about everything."

Alice chewed her lip.

"It's possible I led you to believe that I was going to leave my husband. And, whilst Jeremy may drive me wild, he and I... well, let's just say we have our arrangements."

Alice scoffed. "Arrangements?"

"Yes, I understand you've been clued in now. Jeremy appreciates that I have certain needs... and I've smoothed things over with him about all this, so you needn't worry.

You can have your little job back. No rush, take some time — whenever you're ready."

Alice's eyes widened, and she shook her head. *Is she for-fucking-real?*

Fran leaned in and rubbed Alice's thigh again.

"Oh, and there's another thing. Jeremy has agreed for you and me to go on a trip together. So, let's get it booked up before you go back to work."

The material of Alice's robe bunched under Fran's hand as it crept higher.

"Imagine us sitting out at sunset, sipping a Barolo amongst the Italian vines. Dipping our toes in the delicious pool, swimming... naked, under the stars. I can't wait. It's all arranged. You just need to book the flights with Jeremy's credit card." Fran inhaled and closed her eyes. "Mmm," she murmured as if transported there already.

Alice stared down at Fran's hand, the platinum band on her ring finger glinting in the light. She'd always felt so guilty when she caught sight of it before, but now she saw it for what it was — *Fran's meal ticket. Jeremy's collar.* Fine if it suited them, but Alice wanted no part of it.

She cleared her throat and Fran's eyes flickered open. Her serene smile faltered when she saw it wasn't reflected on Alice's face.

"Have you finished saying what you have to say?" Alice asked with a confidence she didn't realise she had, especially in the presence of Fran.

Fran sat up, her hand falling away from Alice's inner thigh.

"You've really got gaslighting down to a fine art, haven't you? You're like the fucking goddess of gaslighting. Believe it or not, I don't want my *little* job back. I don't want you back. And I don't want anything to do with whatever twisted shit you and Jeremy have going on."

Fran stiffened and sniffed. "You're skating on very thin ice, Alice. You know I'm not a patient woman."

Alice laughed, surprising herself almost as much as Fran. *How had I ever thought this woman had it all together? That a life with her would be anything but chaos and heartache?*

A knock at the front door snatched Alice's attention, and she sprung to her feet, flinching as pain seared through her knee. She looked down at Fran's face, scrunched in confusion.

"Well, thanks for the chat, but I don't feel any differently."

Fran's lips puckered.

"I have plans this evening. So, if you don't mind." Alice motioned to the door, but Fran didn't move. Another knock, and Alice released an exasperated sigh. She limped along the hallway and opened the door. Her heart squeezed at the sight of Ash, brandishing two large pizza boxes and a bottle of wine.

The smile fell from Ash's face as she took Alice in. *So much for being a fully functional adult. It went from bad to worse.*

"You better come in." Alice hobbled aside, cradling her wrist. "I've had a bit of an afternoon."

"What's happened?" Ash asked as she stepped out of her trainers.

Alice grimaced and jutted her chin towards the lounge. "Fran," she mouthed.

Ash's eyes widened. "Has she hurt you?"

Alice sniffed a laugh. "No, not physically, anyway. I fell out of the bath and—"

"Shit, Alice. I should check you over."

Alice grinned. "Steady on, Doc. First things first." She shuffled along the hallway with Ash in her wake.

Fran stood facing the window, her wine glass empty on the coffee table. Alice gestured for Ash to put the pizza boxes in the kitchen.

"I'm not leaving, Alice. Not until you see sense," Fran said without turning around.

"Er, Fran. I have company. I told you, I have plans."

Fran remained fixed in place at the window, as if turning into the room would force her to face reality. "Well, you better un-plan your evening. We're sorting this out, once and for all."

Alice looked over her shoulder. Ash stood awkwardly behind her.

"Fran, I really would like you to leave now, please."

Fran spun around, red-rimmed eyes brimming with tears. She whipped her jacket from the dining chair and rushed past Alice. Then, coming to a halt in the hallway, she turned, nostrils flaring, and screamed,

"Why is it so difficult for you to understand, Alice? I love you, you stupid girl. This isn't over."

Alice's mouth hung open as Fran stormed out, slamming the front door behind her. Alice cradled her wrist and collapsed onto the couch. Ash darted to her side.

"Bloody hell, Alice. Are you alright?"

Shock waves rippled through Alice, and her whole body trembled.

"May I take a look at your arm?"

Alice held out her arm and Ash carefully pulled up the sleeve of the pink robe, the frown lines deepening on her brow as she gently examined Alice's wrist.

"Okay, I hate to tell you this, but I think you might've fractured it. We need to get you to A&E."

"No, no, no..." Alice whined, as tears welled in her eyes.

"Come on, it'll be alright. Is it okay if I have a look at that knee, too?"

Alice nodded and Ash knelt in front of her and swept the robe aside, revealing a large bruise blooming over Alice's knee.

"Ouch! Alright." Ash covered the knee and looked into Alice's face with such tenderness that Alice burst into tears. "You've had a traumatic afternoon, but I'm here now and I'm going to take care of you, okay?" Ash reached up and touched Alice's chin. "Stop chewing your lip. You'll make it sore."

And at that moment, Alice wanted nothing more than someone capable to take charge of the situation, to take care of her and make it all better. Yet again, she'd proven nothing to herself, nor anyone else — she was an unmitigated disaster, a dysfunctional fucking mess. She hiccupped a sob.

"I'm sorry, Ash. The last thing you want on your day off is to go to hospital. I'll call Maggie instead."

"No. Don't be silly. You're hurt and I'm a doctor. I have a duty of care to look after you."

"But you're off duty."

"It doesn't matter. I made an oath. Now stop procrastinating, get dressed and I'll drive you. I might even be able to pull some strings and get you seen quicker." Ash winked and helped Alice to her feet, supporting her as she limped to the bedroom.

"I'll, er... just wait out here. Shout if you need me."

Alice grimaced. "I feel a bit pathetic, but I think I'll need your help."

"Er, sure. Okay. I can do that."

Alice pulled some underwear and leggings from a drawer. Turning her back to Ash, she shrugged out of her robe, yelping as it snagged on her arm. Ash rushed over and took the weight of it, then lingered so close that Alice could feel the heat of her.

She bent and stepped into her underwear — the first thing she'd pulled from the drawer — lacy red pants. She tugged them up with her good hand and wriggled them over her hips. Her breath hitched as Ash's fingers curled into the flimsy waistband, setting it straight across her lower back.

Sparks flickered behind Alice's eyes — was it the proximity of Ash to her near-naked body or her broken wrist causing her vision to falter?

Alice picked up the matching bra and slid the straps up her arms. Ash moved closer, her breath warm on Alice's bare skin as she hooked a finger under each strap and pulled them into place. Her hand trailed over Alice's back with a feather-like touch as she clipped the clasp shut. Alice stilled, all her nerves alive to the presence of the woman behind her — she didn't know it was possible to be so aroused by someone putting clothes *on* her. Forgetting the pain in her wrist, she wanted to turn and cover Ash's mouth with her own, to press their bodies together and fall into the clean sheets with her...

"Do you have a shirt or something with a zip that might be easy to undo... at the hospital, I mean?" Ash's voice came out in a hoarse whisper.

*Fuck.* Alice cleared her throat. "Er, yeah, there's a hoodie in the wardrobe... thanks."

A LITTLE UNDER THREE HOURS LATER, THEY WERE back in Ash's car with Alice's wrist strapped into a splint. With Ash by her side, Alice felt like she'd been whisked through the system at record speed. The X-ray showed her broken wrist, a distal radius fracture, which thankfully wouldn't require surgery, but would need a cast in a few days once the swelling had reduced. Her knee, although throbbing along with her pulse, was fortunately just bruised and swollen — no skirts or heels for her for the time being. They'd given her some more drugs and strapped her arm.

Despite Alice's impromptu afternoon nap, tiredness seeped through her. She rested her head back and closed her eyes against the headlights of oncoming vehicles blurring in her vision.

"You okay?" asked Ash.

Alice gave a sleepy nod, her head heavy with the effort.

"You look shattered. I'll have you home soon."

"Thank you. I'm sorry again that I ruined your night off. I'm clearly a walking disaster. You should keep well away." Alice coughed to hide her voice cracking.

"Nonsense." Ash laughed. "You know I love the bustle of the hospital; any excuse, eh?"

Alice opened her eyes and gave the grinning doctor a sidelong glance.

"Oh, I forgot to tell you, I popped by to see George."

"When?"

"Er, when you were called for your X-ray, and I went to get us tea and snacks."

"How's he doing?"

"He's okay. He sent his love and told me to tell you that you're a klutz — smashing his head and breaking your bones all in one week."

Alice laughed.

"He saw the neurologist today, but he hadn't really understood what they'd told him. So, I went to find out more, but when I returned, he was asleep."

"Bless him. What did you find out?"

"I shouldn't really be telling you..." Ash's grip tightened on the steering wheel, as if wrestling with her better judgement. "But seeing as I've already broken so many rules and I don't want you worrying... The scans came back normal, so it isn't neurological. They think George experienced some sort of dissociative fugue."

"A what now?"

"It's like a temporary amnesia. Typically, when it happens, the person ends up somewhere completely unexpected and can't remember who they are."

"Wow, yeah, that fits. Have they any idea what caused it?"

"With George's confusion and tiredness, it's hard to pin down anything definitive. But that sort of thing is often triggered by something traumatic. Given how worked up he was when he first came in, that tracks."

"They still haven't reached his brother?"

Ash shook her head. "And we've still had no luck finding a charger for that damn phone of his either. It's a relic."

"So, what'll happen to him?"

"They need to make sure he isn't a risk to himself, and that it won't happen again. I mean, he could've been killed if you hadn't found him and brought him in."

"I'm glad I did."

Ash's eyes flicked from the road to Alice and back. "I'm glad it was you, too."

Alice swallowed, recalling the way her body had responded to just the hint of Ash's touch earlier; every nerve ending alive and alert to her proximity. Alice would've detonated in her hands if there'd been more... but Ash didn't want more. *Did she?*

Ash cleared her throat. "Back to George. He'll probably need to see a psychologist, but I'm sure you're familiar with NHS waiting lists — things are stretched, so I don't know how soon that'll be."

Alice puffed out a breath, her mind immediately turning to Truscote and Dalton's pro bono caseloads. But she hadn't exactly left things on good terms. It'd be a bit cheeky to ask for a favour right now, and the thought sickened her.

"Speaking of trauma, what happened earlier with Fran, that was... pretty intense. Do you want to talk about it?"

Alice looked out of the side window. Black hedgerows blurred against a deep indigo sky. "I'm not really sure what to say. I've never seen her like that. And what she said.... well, she's never said that to me before."

And that was the truth. Fran's words had bounced around in Alice's head ever since she'd screamed them at her. *I love you, you stupid girl.*

It had been vaguely terrifying, yet also electrifying. Alice knew if Ash hadn't been there, she likely would've ended up in bed with Fran after that outburst, because being wanted with such violent passion was insanely erotic.

Ash sighed, as if reading Alice's mind for the second time in as many minutes.

"No one's ever said that to me before," Alice said in an almost-whisper of something she'd never spoken aloud, but always held in the back of her mind.

Ash glanced across, her face scrunched in confusion. "What?... really?"

"Yeah, really... well, aside from Maggie. And my mum when she was alive. No, no one else."

Ash frowned. "I find that hard to believe."

Alice laughed. "Why? Because I'm just so lovable?"

Ash glanced at her again, her face serious, like she was about to deliver difficult news to a patient. "Yeah, you are. Even more so because you don't see it yourself."

Alice looked into her lap and picked the Velcro on her splint with her good hand. She didn't know what to say to that. Apparently, Ash didn't know what else to say either, as only the low hum of the radio sounded between them until Ash pulled up alongside Alice's Fiesta.

The amber light from the streetlamp cast a warm glow in the car and dark shadows on their faces. Ash sharply inhaled. She unclipped her seatbelt and twisted around, harpooning Alice with that serious gaze.

"I'm sorry that the first time someone said it to you, it was full of anger and derision." Ash flung her hands up. "I mean, she literally chased it with an insult and a threat. I barely know you, Alice... but you deserve so much better than that."

Alice's heart squeezed in her chest. She had to look away, or she'd cry.

After another sharp inhale, Ash continued. "And I'm probably overstepping here, but that didn't look like love from where I was standing; it looked like control."

Alice nodded slowly. Ash was right, but what if that was it? What if Fran's love was the best she'd ever have? What if it was the *only* love she'd ever have? Wasn't something better than nothing? And besides, isn't love like water? When you're thirsty, who cares where it comes from? You'd drink from the gutter if you were desperate enough.

Ash smiled. "Lecture over; you're tired, and hopefully hungry because I bought two ridiculous pizzas. Let's get you inside and comfortable. I'll have a couple of slices and then I'll leave you in peace."

"Mmm, I'm stuffed. That was delicious." Alice patted her stomach and flopped back into the couch cushions.

"Told you! Fat Tony's makes the best pizza in town. I'm ashamed to say I'm very well acquainted with most of the takeaways in Leamington. I've tried them all!" Ash leaned over the box as she bit into another slice, mozzarella stretching from her mouth to her hand.

"It must be difficult with your work schedule."

Ash nodded as she chewed. "I guess it's laziness, but it's hard to get the motivation to cook for one."

"Oh, I hear you! But to be honest, even when I do cook, it isn't great."

"I love cooking. I'll cook for you sometime — that'll solve a problem for both of us."

"You're on." Alice grinned. Amazingly, Ash still wasn't sick of her or scared away by her *chaotic little life*.

Ash beamed her wonky smile and closed the pizza box, stacking it on top of the other empty one. "And we have leftovers!"

Alice laughed. "I should think so. You bought enough to feed the entire street."

"You can't beat a slice of cold pizza for breakfast! I always buy extra for that exact purpose. Right, I'll get these tidied up. Do you want a cuppa?"

"My bladder won't thank me later, but yeah, I'd love one." Alice shuffled to get up. "You're my guest though, I should—"

Ash held out a hand. "No, I insist. Patient trumps guest."

Alice sniffed out a laugh. "For the last time, you're off duty, and I'm not your patient."

Ash raised an eyebrow. "Just shut up and let me take care of you, alright?"

Alice grinned and settled back into her nest of cushions.

"And call your sister. Or text her, or whatever. You said to remind you."

Ash moved into the kitchen and Alice pulled out her phone. A quick call was easier than trying to text with her left hand. She scrolled to Maggie in her contacts and hit the call button, for once hoping for voicemail. Maggie picked up after two rings.

"Darling sister! How are the achy muscles? Or should I refrain from rubbing the — *I told you so* — salt in the wounds?"

"Oh yeah, I forgot about that, actually. I'm still a bit sore, but achy muscles aren't a patch on my broken wrist and bruised knee."

"Come again?"

"Er, yeah... so, I had a bit of an accident earlier. Long story short, I fell out of the bath. I'm fine, just a bit broken, I guess."

"Oh Al, why didn't you call me?"

"Well, Fran was here—"

"Oh, bloody hell, Alice—"

"She just showed up, Mags. It wasn't planned and she's long since gone. That's a whole different story for another time." Alice glanced over at Ash as she moved around in the kitchenette like it was her own.

"Do you need me to come over? Markus is at a client function tonight anyway, so I can stay if you want."

"No, it's fine. Ash is here."

Maggie huffed a laugh. "Of course she is. Well, remember what I said? Be careful. Give yourself some time."

"Yeah, I know. I will. I am. And it isn't like that, I told you."

"Sure, keep saying it and you might convince at least one of us."

"Stop it," Alice hissed through clenched teeth, trying to fight the grin overtaking her lips. Warmth spread through her as Ash returned with a mug in each hand. "Maggie says hi."

"Hey, Maggie," Ash called out towards the phone.

"Anyway, I gotta go, Mags."

"Call me if you need me, Al. And behave — not that it sounds like you'd be much use to anyone in bed right now anyway."

"Maggie!"

Maggie laughed and Alice ended the call, shaking her head as she smirked at the phone.

Ash raised her eyebrows. "White, no sugar. Did I get that right?"

"Spot on, thank you. I know it's late, but do you fancy watching something?"

"Yeah, I'd love to, if you're not too tired?"

ALICE WOKE UNDER THE GREY CHENILLE BLANKET in a nest of cushions. Triumphant music played over rolling credits and the light from the screen flickered in the low-lit room. Noticing something soft and warm under her feet, she lifted her head to see Ash reclined next to her. Alice's feet were resting in Ash's lap. *Bollocks.*

"Oh hey, you're awake. Sorry, was it too loud?" Ash reached for the remote control.

"No, no, it's fine." Alice stretched and moved to sit up. *Fuck, wrist... knee.* "Ow, shit. Sorry, I must have fallen asleep on you."

Ash smiled. "Now we're even."

"Did I miss much?"

"Yeah, only most of it." Ash laughed. "It's time for you to have some more painkillers. Let me sort that out and I'll head off." Ash peeled herself from the couch, yawning as she stretched up. She padded towards the kitchen.

"Ash?"

She spun around. "Yup?"

"Will you stay tonight?" Alice asked, and the question

hung between them, along with all her vulnerability and doubt. She didn't mean *like that,* because this evening hadn't been *like that.* It had been two friends sharing a pizza and hanging out. Literally, *Netflix and chill* — if it didn't mean sex, but what it said on the tin. "Please?" she added as an afterthought, as if she didn't sound needy enough already.

Ash stepped back towards her, an unreadable look on her face. She perched on the edge of the couch.

"I'm really pleased you asked. I've been worried about leaving you tonight, but I didn't want to sound like a creep by asking to stay."

Alice released the breath she'd been holding.

"Can you lend me a T-shirt? I'll sleep on the settee."

Alice shook her head. "No. I mean, yes, I can lend you a T-shirt, but no, you'll sleep in with me. It's a king-size bed, there's plenty of room and we're just friends, right?"

Ash's cheeks flamed. "Yeah, I mean, of course. If you're sure? I don't want to intrude."

"You're not intruding, you're doing me a favour. I don't want to be alone. No funny business. Besides, I'm hardly in any fit state." Alice held up her splinted wrist.

Ash exhaled a breathy laugh. "No, I don't suppose you are."

WHILST ALICE HUNTED AROUND IN THE BATHROOM cabinet, Ash scooped up the fallen shower curtain and draped it over the bath.

"I'll have a go at fixing that for you tomorrow, if you like? Should be easy enough, I'll just have to grab some new hooks."

"Doctor *and* handywoman. Is there no end to your talents?"

Ash's cheeks flushed. Alice grinned and presented her with a new toothbrush.

"Help yourself to anything else you need."

Alice's stomach flipped as she returned to the bedroom, the king-size bed looming in front of her like a pool of possibilities. She quickly smoothed out the rumpled duvet and flipped the pillow where Fran had lain earlier — *uninvited.*

With the fleeting thought of Fran came the echo of *"I love you, you stupid, stupid girl."* Alice shook the words from her head and undressed, which was manageable until she reached her bra. Twisting her good arm behind her back, she could reach the clasp with her fingertips, but couldn't flick it open.

"I think that's a job for me." Ash's voice came from behind as she stepped up and uncoupled the bra's clasps. Alice held the cups in place on her tumbling breasts, and craned to look over her shoulder, but Ash had already retreated.

Alice pulled on a T-shirt and some striped pyjama bottoms, then set out an oversized T-shirt for Ash — she picked one of her favourites for sleeping in. She offered pyjama bottoms too, but with a blush Ash declined.

"My legs get hot. I prefer to just sleep in my pants, if that's okay?"

Alice swallowed hard. *Of course she does.* And of course, Ash's pants turned out to be fitted boxer-briefs that hugged her so perfectly around her hips and arse that Alice had to fight the urge to reach out and pull her close enough to run her fingers beneath the tight fabric. She tried to look away, but her eyes wouldn't obey. Watching Ash get ready for bed did little to quench her desire, and it was charging the air between them with want. *Surely it isn't just me feeling this.* Ash had gone awfully quiet.

Alice couldn't recall a time when she'd had another woman in her bed and not slept with her. Maybe this was why she didn't have any female friends? But not everyone had this effect on her; this was something else. *Oh, get a grip.* The voice in her head sounded suspiciously like Maggie, throwing a cup of cold water over her libido.

"Do you need anything else before I jump in?" Ash had untied her hair, and it hung loose to her collarbones.

"No." Alice smiled. "Thank you."

Ash pulled back the duvet and slipped underneath. So close, yet so far away — a tundra of bed between them. She lay on her back and looked up at the high ceiling.

"Shall I turn out the light?" asked Alice.

Ash turned her head on the pillow and glanced over with those chocolate-brown eyes. "Yeah, go for it."

Alice flicked the switch, plunging the room into darkness. She couldn't see her, but she sensed Ash was still looking in her direction.

"I, er, I haven't done this for a long time," said Ash.

"Done what?"

"Stayed over with someone."

"No?"

"Not since Sam, actually. I'm sorry if I've made things awkward at all, it's just—"

"You haven't. I mean… it's not awkward, is it? Like you said, we're friends." Alice reached across, searching for Ash's hand amidst the sheets. She eventually found it, laced their fingers together and squeezed. "I really appreciate everything you've done for me over the last few days."

"I, er… I meant what I said earlier."

"Which bit?"

"When I said you don't realise how lovely you are."

And at that, guilt clenched in Alice's gut.

*She thinks I'm some sort of saint, and all I can think about is getting in her knickers.*

Alice freed her fingers and rolled over. "Night, Ash."

## 14
# THAT'S WHAT FRIENDS DO, RIGHT?

*A*lice surfaced from sleep with the weight of an arm wrapped around her, a leg hooked over her thigh, and the rhythmic rise and fall of sleeping breath warm on her neck.

At some point, whilst they'd been sleeping, Ash had rolled into the space between them. Alice clearly hadn't resisted, so they now lay entwined like lovers. Alice closed her eyes again, her senses awakening to the woman embracing her. Even if it was unintentional, it felt so good to be held like this.

Ash snuffled in her sleep and snuggled up closer, her pelvis rocking into Alice. The movement triggered an involuntary response, heat rising between Alice's legs as she gently pushed back into Ash. Their hips rocked together, and Alice moaned out loud before she could mute herself.

*Fuck.*

Ash inhaled sharply and rolled away.

Alice held her breath, not wanting Ash to realise she'd been awake and enjoying *whatever that was*. And to her shame, she wished she were still enjoying it as the throb between her thighs desperately needed some relief. Ash got out of bed and padded to the bathroom, and Alice silently screamed into her pillow. *This friendship business is fucking torture.*

On hearing Ash rattling round in the kitchen, Alice dashed into the loo. Whilst peeing, she touched the bruise on her knee, which had blossomed into a rainbow of colours.

Alice scoffed at her reflection in the bathroom mirror; her hair was a mess of wild curls that she'd have to tame later — goodness knew how with a broken wrist, besides, Ash had already seen her looking much worse than this.

Alice stilled at the sight of Ash moving around her kitchen. Ash reached for the cafetière on the top shelf and the loose T-shirt rode up, exposing those tight boxer-briefs that left nothing to the imagination. Alice chewed her lip, biting down on the urge to saddle up behind Ash and run her hands underneath the T-shirt. The desire to kiss that soft brown skin. Just the thought of cupping Ash's breasts and nibbling her neck was making her wet. Alice sighed.

Ash spun around and flashed her a broad grin. "Hey, morning. Sorry, did I wake you?"

"Er..." *Oh my God, yes! And I still haven't recovered.* "No, no. You're all good."

"Coffee?"

"Yeah, that'd be great." Alice swallowed.

"Cool. If you want to go back to bed, I can bring it through."

"Sure."

"How's your wrist feeling?"

"Not too bad." Alice glanced at her splint, remembering it was there. With how they'd woken up this morning, she hadn't even paused to consider her pain.

"Good, I'm pleased it isn't giving you too much trouble. You should take these anyway." Ash dropped two white tablets into Alice's open palm and handed her a glass of water. "It's ibuprofen, so you'll have to eat something. Is cold pizza okay, or do you fancy something else?"

"Ash, you don't have to run around after me, really—"

"Shh! Cold pizza it is then." Ash turned back to the kitchen and busied herself finding plates.

Alice laughed and shook her head. *How was this woman even real? And why hadn't Alice found her years ago?*

The extraordinary thing about the day that followed was how ordinary it was. After chatting over coffee and cold pizza in bed, Ash got dressed and nipped out to get some new hooks to fix the shower curtain. She returned with groceries to cook dinner and an overnight bag.

"Just in case," she said, putting it down next to her trainers in the hallway.

Alice played it cool, but a bubble of happiness rose in her chest at the thought of another night with Ash, because time with her was already moving too fast.

They lay under a blanket and binge-watched a whole series on Netflix. Alice managed to stay awake, and somehow, during their Netflix marathon, she sneaked her feet onto Ash's lap again. It wasn't at all subtle, but friends could get cosy together, *couldn't they?* Ash didn't seem to mind. In fact, she rested her hand on Alice's calves, and it was all Alice could concentrate on. Desire soared through her, before dipping into guilt that she was enjoying Ash's touch far more than she should have been.

Ash cooked a Thai green curry, with big prawns, heaps of fresh vegetables and enough chilli to make Alice's eyes water; it was delicious and better than anything Alice could have made or ordered from a takeaway. And, of course, it got late, and Ash stayed over again. Bedtime had been more relaxed. After chatting for a while with the lights out, they'd fallen asleep holding hands, because that's what friends do, *right?*

## 15
## PINK, OBVIOUSLY

*A*lice blinked awake as the bedroom door nudged open and Ash entered, with a steaming mug of coffee gripped in each hand.

"It was my turn to make you coffee this morning," said Alice, her voice thick with sleep.

"Next time." Ash grinned, and Alice did too, at the possibility of *next time.*

She sat up and took the proffered mug from Ash, who slipped back into bed beside her.

"So, I gotta go to work today."

Alice groaned.

Ash laughed. "I know. I don't want to go either. But if you want to come with me, I could probably fit your cast if the swelling looks good. It'll save you a trip later in the week." Ash blew on her mug and took a sip. "And you could visit George, if you wanted to, that is?"

"If you don't mind, that'd be great. I can't believe you're not sick of me yet."

Ash frowned and shook her head. "Why would I be? I've loved hanging out with you. I'd like to do it again sometime if you want to?"

Alice smiled and nodded. Right now, she wanted nothing more, because time spent with Ash was like a tantalising tonic. *Perhaps all medical professionals have this effect? They're trained to make people feel better after all.*

*No.* She'd never felt this way in the presence of any other doctor, especially not her fusty old GP, Doctor Scrivens, whom she had to come out to every time she so much as needed a repeat prescription.

"Is there any chance you might be pregnant, Ms French?"

"No."

"You're not sexually active?"

"Yes, I am."

"Well, we're not prescribing birth control, so what methods are you using?"

"Lesbianism," Alice answered the last time and perhaps Doctor Scrivens had finally got the message, as he nudged his thick-rimmed glasses up his nose and said,

"Jolly good. That'll do the trick."

*Make a note on my bloody file, it'll save us both the blushes,* she'd thought, but been too embarrassed to say.

A few hours later, a very different doctor sat in front of Alice; she removed the splint and examined Alice's bare wrist. Black with bruising, but only a little swollen, it looked pretty good, considering.

A deep line etched between Ash's brows as she concentrated. She traced her fingers up Alice's forearm, and Alice's breath hitched. *Fuck.*

"Sorry, did I hurt you?"

"No, no. Not at all." *Pull yourself together, she's only touching your arm.* But since when had Alice found scrubs so damn sexy?

*Since right now, looking at Ash. God, she's actually gorgeous.*

*Stop. It. You. Fucking. Nympho.*

Ash looked at her and smiled. "Red, blue or pink?"

"Huh?"

"What colour cast would you like?"

"Oh. Pink, obviously," Alice said.

Ash grinned. "Obviously."

A loaded silence filled the air as Ash worked methodically, applying the cast to Alice's arm. When it was dry, Ash plucked a black marker pen from the breast pocket of her scrubs and flashed Alice a mischievous grin.

"May I?"

Alice laughed. "You want to sign your handiwork?"

Ash nodded and pulled off the pen lid between her teeth. Alice held out her arm and Ash cradled it in her lap as she set to work, neatly printing small letters across Alice's palm. Alice's body tingled with the proximity of Ash's warmth and her scent; coconut shampoo and cedarwood.

She swallowed. "Do you deface all your patients like this?"

"No, just you." Ash lifted Alice's hand towards her lips

and blew on the ink. Alice's heart raced with the sensation of Ash's breath on her fingers.

"There, all done." Ash grinned.

Alice glanced down at the inscription.

### HANDLE WITH CARE X

DESPITE HER BROKEN BONE AND PAINFUL, BRUISED knee, Alice left Ash with a spring in her step and made her way to see George. In the corridor outside George's room, she smiled at the familiar face.

With big eyes popping over her glasses, Marjorie glared at Alice's bright pink plaster cast. "Tsk. What scrapes have you been getting yourself into now?"

"Oh, this..." Alice suddenly felt a bit foolish. Why had she opted for a pink cast? It announced her injury like it was some sort of achievement. "I, er... fell out of the bath," she mumbled.

The nurse chuckled.

"Is George awake?"

"Mmm-hmm, but he's a bit quiet today. Perhaps you and your Barbie Girl arm can cheer him up?" Marjorie's laugh punched through the air again and her hips swayed as she bumbled away.

Holding a plastic mug in his hand, George stared into the void, his face as blank and pale as the surrounding walls.

"Hey," Alice said softly, not wanting to scare him into spilling his drink. George blinked hard and squinted to focus in her direction.

"Hey there, klutz." He conjured a half-smile that seemed to take a lot of effort. "You look awfully happy with yourself, all things considered."

The warmth in Alice's chest must have been radiating into her smile. "Yeah, well, karma took a bit of revenge on me for bashing your head. How are *you* feeling?"

George blinked and turned his gaze back to the spot he was staring at before. "I've been better."

Alice considered him for a moment and reached into her vast bag, rummaging as she stepped towards the visitors' chair. "Now, I didn't know what you'd like. I was trying to figure out whether you'd be more of a custard cream or a Hobnob type guy. It was a tough call."

"What did you go with?"

"Jammie Dodgers."

George puffed a laugh through his nose.

Alice placed the packet on the over-bed table and pulled out a box from her bag.

"And chocolate fingers because you can't beat a chocolate finger, can you?"

George's lip ticked up with the hint of a smile.

"Oi, I didn't mean it like that, dirty old man." She tore open the box and held it out to George. "Dip one in your tea?"

George glanced down at the cup in his hand as if he'd forgotten it was there. "It's gone cold."

Alice shrugged and popped a chocolate finger in her mouth, holding it like a cigar. "I hear it was good news about the MRI. No brain injury, after all?"

"No, apparently not. Even so, I'm stuck in here and I'm not really sure why." He sighed. "It was my birthday."

"When?"

"The night you found me."

"Oh, I'm sorry, I didn't know."

"How could you have known? To be honest, I didn't remember until yesterday."

"Well, happy birthday, George." Alice continued to suck the chocolate from the biscuit finger. "Well, whatever you were up to, it didn't end so well, did it?"

"That's the thing. I have this terrible feeling about it all. I just can't quite..." George clenched his fists.

"I'm not sure whether anyone told you, and you might've just been dreaming, or whatever... but before you woke up, you kept mumbling about a pig."

George looked at her, his thick eyebrows drawn down towards his eyes. "A pig?"

"Yeah. And Marjorie told me you were saying something about a dog, too."

"Ah." George's eyebrows shot up.

"What?"

"Was I saying Pyglet?"

Alice frowned. "No, just pig."

"Oh, well, I must have been talking about Pyg then."

"Yes, that's right, you kept saying pig."

"No, you don't understand — Pyg."

Alice looked at him through wide eyes. *Maybe they should do another MRI?*

"P-Y-G. Pyg, she was our dog. Such a beautiful girl." George smiled as if seeing her in his mind's eye before his forehead rumpled into a frown. "But why was I talking about Pyg?"

They both pondered the question for a moment; it seemed as impossible for George to answer as it did Alice.

He turned to look at her again. "I was going to ask you a favour before you broke your arm. But I'm not sure it'd be fair of me to ask you now."

"Just ask." She shrugged and pulled another chocolate finger from the box.

"I wanted to ask if you'd go by my house and see if everything's in order. I've been wondering whether there'll be any clues as to why I was out and about that night."

"You'd be okay with me doing that? How do you know I won't steal everything?"

"Because one, I don't have much to steal and two, you brought me here and you keep coming back. So, either you're in it for the long game, hoping I'll write you into my will and promptly pop my clogs, or you're genuinely a good person."

Alice giggled. "You got me. I'm in it for the will."

"Plus, you brought my coat and wallet back, and there was still money in it."

"Oh, damn, I missed that. Yeah, I'll go to your house. Maggie, my sister, is picking me up in a bit. I can ask her to swing by there before taking me home. I'll give Ash a call if I find anything."

"Really, you don't mind? I feel awful putting you out when you've already done enough for me. If I didn't have this nagging, right here…" He touched a hand to his stomach. "Something isn't right."

"Sounds ominous. I'm in. Now, eat your Dodgers and cheer up, birthday boy."

# 1968

## CHRISTMAS MIRACLES

*T*ime ticked by; the months after Mum had gone, and the weeks after losing Pyg. Our grandmother remained convalescing in hospital, recovering from the fall and the burns she'd effectively inflicted upon herself. And we settled into a quiet, ordinary routine with Ms Bray — or Ruth, as she eventually relented to us calling her.

Whilst the loss of the studio, along with all our treasured possessions, had been traumatic, with Ruth at least there was less of a need to retreat. Unlike Grandmother, Ruth didn't seem to mind when Bernard and I sat at the kitchen table to do our homework. Neither did she mind us chatting quietly between ourselves. From time to time, she even joined in. Her company wasn't entirely discordant, at least when she wasn't quoting biblical verses, which seemed to spill out of her randomly, like a pot bubbling over.

Ruth was the polar opposite of our mother. She

appeared to be around the same age, but unlike Mum, she was an austere woman of the church, dowdy in cardigans and thick brown stockings that bunched around her ankles. If Mum was a gloriously sunny afternoon in May, Ruth was a dreary grey morning in January. Despite all that, she wasn't cold-hearted; her kindness could be measured in small gestures — the sprinkling of sugar on our porridge, or the occasional hand on the shoulder or pat on the head. Lukewarm, but warm nonetheless. And infinitely better than living with Grandmother.

The only remarkable thing that happened in the weeks that passed was an alarming sight I glimpsed one morning on my way downstairs. On hearing a gasp and noticing Ruth's bedroom door ajar, I'd been unable to resist the urge to peer through the gap. There she stood with her long black skirt hitched high and one leg up on the bed. She sucked air through her teeth and yanked tight a chain-link belt around her upper thigh. It looked like a medieval torture device.

*What the—*

She spun around, and I darted away from the door and had the good sense not to ask her about it. But, unable to shake the mental image of either the spikes cutting into her flesh, or her bare leg exposed, I hadn't been able to look Ruth in the eye for a good week afterwards.

Our first Christmas without Mum looked to be a sombre affair. Bernard and I chopped down a small spruce and between us, we dragged it inside and propped it up in the drawing room. We rifled in a box under the stairs and pulled out a string of fairy lights and a few dusty baubles.

Without Mum's artistic flair and her handcrafted decorations, the tree looked a sorry state. But still, it was more festive than no tree.

Christmas Eve started with a forced visit to our grandmother in hospital. Scrubbed and in our Sunday best, we stood by the old woman's bedside for thirty minutes listening to her moan about her ills and chastise us for our sins. All the while, I seethed with indignation and Bernard stared down at his polished shoes. The hospital visit was followed by the second of our mandatory obligations for the day, church. We attended mass and listened to Father Sutherland preach about the ills of the world and condemn the congregation for their sins. Once again, I seethed, and Bernard stared at his shoes.

For supper, Ruth served a watery parsnip and potato soup and even though it was lumpy and tasteless, my stomach rumbled for more. Then she permitted us to sit by the tree. It'd been one of our Christmas Eve traditions, except it used to take place in the studio. We'd pull up cushions and huddle around our little tree, sip from mugs of cocoa and munch homemade biscuits, whilst reading each other Christmas stories from a heavy old book, which Mum had told us was her most treasured possession.

The book had been burned, along with so many of the things we loved, so we sat by the tree, watery mugs of cocoa in hand, and I hummed a Christmas song I'd learned from the older boys at school. Quite a lot of the lyrics were inappropriate, so I mumbled those, but Bernard giggled because he knew the words.

"Why not sing a nice carol, boys?" Ruth sat in our

grandmother's wing-backed chair, the low-light casting sinister shadows on her face and her eyes closed behind her glasses. "*O Come All Ye Faithful*, perhaps? Or *Away in a Manger*?"

Bernard looked at me and scrunched up his nose. But we indulged her with our finest rendition of *Silent Night*. She smiled on, tapping her foot like a metronome, and after the second refrain puffy snores emanated from her beaky little nose.

"I, er... I've got something for you, Georgie," Bernard whispered. He got up and scurried out of the room, then returned with a parcel crudely wrapped in brown paper. He retook his place on the rug and presented the package to me.

"Don't get mad at me, alright?"

I frowned. "Why would I be mad?"

"You just might. But don't be because I was careful."

As I tentatively pulled at the corners of the brown paper, a bitter burnt scent wafted from the package. I peeled the paper away, revealing a book, its spine and cover charred and blackened. I looked from the book to my brother.

"I told you not to go in there. It isn't safe."

Bernard held up his hands. "I know what you said, but when Bill came to clean the gutters because of that leak, I asked him to help me. I wanted to see if there was anything worth saving."

"You could've come across anything in there. What if... what if you'd seen Pyg?"

"Well, I didn't see Pyg. But I did find this." Bernard

touched his hand to the book in my lap. "I cleaned it up as best I could. I couldn't save the cover, but I think it protected the inside a little bit." Bernard's eyes shone with enthusiasm. "Well, go on, open it. You'll see."

I carefully opened the cover. The spine creaked and black flecks chipped off onto the floor. Water lines rippled down the page, but there inside the cover, intact and legible, were our years of Christmas messages. Tears prickled my eyes as I ran my finger down the decades of words, a sort-of scrawled family timeline.

*1935. Dearest Eleanor, Merry Christmas. All my love, Papa x*

*1937. I think you're starting to enjoy these stories, darling! You giggled at the ghosts. Or maybe it was my silly voices for them? Papa x*

*1940. It isn't Christmas without you. Wish you were here. Eleanor x*

*1945. It's all over, Papa, but not for us. E x*

*1953. I couldn't pick this book up for a long time. My heart forgot joy, but lately my cup is full. I read our stories, Papa, and giggled, remembering your voices. I still miss you, Ella x*

*1955. Oh Papa, I've made the happiest mistake of my life. Merry Christmas, Ella & George (...and H, but he's being grumpy about writing his name) xxx*

*1956. George is one! I've started him off early. He already giggles at the ghosts. I realise now that you did the voices to make them less scary. E&G xx*

*1957. H isn't happy... another accident. I'm delighted. I've tidied out your old workshop, Papa... I'm painting again, and it gives George somewhere to play away from the house. Ella & George xx*

I scanned down the words, zooming through the years until the writing changed to my own juvenile hand; and large, capitalised letters announced my name with all the self-importance of a five-year-old.

*1960. GEORGE HENRY SHAW... and Ella and Bernard xxx*

I could almost hear her chuckling as she added their names too; blue smoke curling from the thin roll-up pinched between her fingers, as she frowned and carefully scratched the ink into the book. Then the writing switched to Bernard's hand. He'd scrawled his name, but I'd crossed through it and put mine first, a battle I'd conceded by 1964.

*1964. Pyg ate all my biscuits and George wouldn't share his. Bernard, aged six and a half. Love from the rest of us too, Ella, George and Pyg (the piggy little biscuit thief) x*

I sniffed and swiped away my tears with the coarse sleeve of my jumper. Tracing my fingers down the years, I landed on the final one; written in Bernard's handwriting and finished by Mum. I recalled how I'd been sulking and too stubborn to join in with the fun, and how she'd poked me in the ribs when I wouldn't do the voices.

"You do them best, Georgie," Bernard had whined, and so I relented and did the damn voices, my brother's giggles rising like bubbles of pride in my chest.

*1967. My brother does the best ghost voices, ever. Merry Christmas, Bernard, George, Mum and Pyg (the dog) xxxx*

My heart lurched as I blinked at the message underneath written in the swooping, elaborate loops of our mother's handwriting, but scrawled, as if written in a hurry — perhaps an afterthought as she dashed out the door and abandoned us.

*Boys — If things have gone to plan, then we'll be reading this together, enjoying our first Christmas in our new home. If not, then know that I love you so very much and I'll be back for you soon. You have my word. Merry Christmas, Mum x*

I looked at Bernard through tear-filled eyes. "Did you read it?"

Bernard pinched his lips together and nodded. "She did say she'd send for us."

"But when? She hasn't yet. We haven't heard a thing from her."

Bernard reached out and rubbed my arm. "What is it they're always saying at church? *Have faith*."

I scoffed. "You really believe in all that stuff?"

"No, but I believe in Mum." Bernard smiled, and it reached my heart. The book fell from my lap as I threw my arms around him.

"Thank you, Bernie."

Bernard sniffed, and I held him tighter.

"Shall we read a story?"

"Only if you do the ghosts."

I grinned. "Alright, I'll do the ghosts."

"BERNARD, DID YOU HEAR THAT?" I SAT BOLT upright and blinked into the darkness. Bernard grunted and from the clanging protest of his bedsprings, it sounded like he turned over and burrowed himself further into his blankets.

I cocked my head to listen out. *Nothing. Perhaps I dreamt it?*

With a teeth-chattering shiver, I lay back down and pulled the blankets up to my chin. I closed my eyes and patterns swirled in the blackness behind them. I concentrated on breathing the way Mum had taught me to whenever I woke from a bad dream. *In through the nose — hold — out through the mouth. In, hold, out. In, hold —*

My eyes snapped open, not that the blackness in the room was any different to the darkness behind my eyelids. *No, there it was again.* Urgent scratching — claws on wood. And not the scurrying little paws of mice in the attic, but much bigger paws.

"Bernard, wake up. There's a noise."

He groaned, and sleepy words drawled out of him. "Whassit you want?"

I pulled the feather pillow from behind my back and lobbed it across the room. It hit the target with a heavy flop.

"Oi, what d'you do that for?" Bernard lobbed the pillow back. It missed my bed and landed on the floorboards with a whoosh.

"There's a noise. I think it's downstairs. Listen."

The scratching grew louder, and the monster grew in my mind.

"Perhaps it's Father Christmas?"

I scoffed. "Seriously?"

"Well, what else could it be? It *is* Christmas Eve."

"I guess we better go take a look." Fighting the urge to hide under them, I flung back my blankets and swung my feet out of bed. "Come on, I'm not going on my own."

Bernard whined but shuffled to his feet. "Shall we bring a weapon?"

"Like what?"

"I dunno."

"We'll just have to rely on our wits. Failing that, our fists."

"Alright, but you first, because you're bigger... and smarter."

I scoffed a laugh. "That's the first time you've ever admitted that."

With practised stealth, we crept out of our room and past Mum's room, currently occupied by Ruth. I stilled halfway down the stairs when the scratches came again, this time accompanied by a loud whine. Bernard took a deep breath, which made me realise I'd been holding mine.

"It's at the back door," I whispered and continued my descent.

With the kitchen door shut behind us, Bernard flicked on the light, blinding us both. "Bloody hell, why'd you do that?" I shielded my eyes.

"I thought it might scare it off."

"Or advertise that there's someone in here?"

"I didn't think of that. Shall I turn it off?"

"Bit late now."

Another scratch came at the door, and for a horrifying

moment, we just looked at each other. Before I could change my mind, I swung the back door open, admitting a gush of frosty December air and a filthy, matted black dog.

"Pyg!"

We dropped to our knees and wrapped our arms around our girl, her bushy black tail swishing in reciprocated joy.

"She's alive," squealed Bernard, his voice still able to reach a pitch that mine couldn't.

I held her head in my hands and looked into those trusting round eyes. "Where have you been, girl?"

Pyg responded by licking my face, licking away the tears that I hadn't realised were running down my cheeks.

"Oh my God, she's so much better than Father Christmas. All we need is Mum to come back and—"

"Don't get your hopes up about that, Bernie. Let's just be happy we've got our Pyg back."

Bernard's face fell, but seconds later, it lit up with a goofy grin. He ruffled his fingers in the dog's greasy fur. "You're so stinky, Pyg!"

"We'll bathe her in the morning, but for now let's get her some food. We can sneak her upstairs and I'll explain everything to Ruth tomorrow."

"What if she doesn't let us keep her?"

"It's not up to her," I said with a confidence I wished I felt.

"AND YOU'RE SURE THAT YOUR GRANDMOTHER
doesn't mind a dog being in the house?" Ruth blinked at us
through her thick glasses.

Bernard and I shook our heads in unison as if we'd
rehearsed it.

"When we go to the hospital next time, I will check
with her." She sniffed. "And if you're lying..."

"We're not, Miss, promise," blurted Bernard. I elbowed
him in the ribs.

She narrowed her eyes. "Alright. Well, you better give it
a bath. It smells putrid. And you can scrub the tub when
you're done. I don't want to see a speck of dirt, you
hear me?"

Ruth wasn't wrong. The stench was the first thing that
had struck me when I woke; musty and sour, like rotting
garbage. I'd covered my nose and breathed into my blanket
with a smile stretching across my face as Pyg's tail thudded
on the floorboards, where she'd slept.

"She must've been sleeping in the same bins she was
eating out of," said Bernard, screwing up his face.

We led Pyg into the washroom and filled the tub with
cold water. I didn't dare ask for some to be heated on the
stove; that request was only grudgingly upheld for our own
bath time. Pyg didn't seem to mind. She jumped into the
tub with a splash, panting as her eyes shone with
excitement.

The harsh antiseptic smell of the red carbolic soap cut
through Pyg's stench as we lathered it up and massaged it
through her thick fur. We rinsed her until the water ran

clear and our laughter erupted when Pyg shook, spraying everything and soaking us.

"That doesn't sound very much like washing the dog," Ruth called through the door.

We giggled again, and Pyg wagged her tail, flicking water with every swish.

I ruffled an old towel over her, but although clean, her fur was badly matted.

Bernard disappeared, returning minutes later.

"I got this from Grandmother's room. Do you think she'll mind?" He produced a hairbrush from behind his back and I whooped a laugh.

"She'll kill you if she finds out. But I'm not gonna tell."

Bernard brushed out Pyg's mats as best he could whilst I cleaned up. When we left the washroom, we were shivering in our damp clothes, so I offered to light the fire, which thankfully Ruth agreed was a good idea.

Not wanting to take our eyes or hands off Pyg for a moment, we sat beside her on the hearthrug. She curled into a tight ball between us and slept, drying in the warm glow of the fire.

The church had gifted us a stuffed goose, which Ruth roasted, and the house filled with a mouth-watering aroma. Come dinnertime we were famished, and after a drawn-out grace, during which our stomachs rumbled louder than Ruth's chants, we stuffed ourselves as much as the goose, filling up on roast potatoes, carrots and parsnips, and feeding the pink tender goose meat under the table to Pyg when Ruth wasn't looking.

"St. Mary's sent us another treat, boys—"

The shrill tone of the telephone in the hallway cut into Ruth's sentence, leaving us hanging as she flitted off to answer it. Bernard shot me a wide-eyed look, and for a moment I allowed my own hopes to rise too. *Could it be?*

Ruth turned her back and spoke into the receiver. Mirroring Bernard, I tilted on my chair and listened in, my hopes dashed with every overheard word and soon replaced with a sickening swirl that wasn't agreeing with the rich dinner.

"Yes, speaking...

Right, I see...

Oh, goodness, how awful...

Prepare for the worst?...

Yes, I'll break it to them.

Our thoughts and prayers are with her."

Ruth returned to the kitchen, the colour leached from her cheeks. "I'm so sorry to tell you this, boys, especially on Christmas Day. Your grandmother suffered a stroke this afternoon."

"Is she dead then?"

"No, Bernard." Ruth glared at him until he hung his head. "But she's not at all well. We need to be brave and send all our thoughts and prayers." Ruth placed a hand on each of our shoulders, which I suppose she meant as a comforting gesture, but her bony fingers were freezing, even through my woolly jumper.

Bernard and I eyeballed each other as Ruth chanted a prayer at double-speed and punctuated the "Amen" with a wet sniff and the sign of the cross.

"Good boys. Now, Father Sutherland sent us a

Christmas pudding. Wasn't that kind of him? I'll make some custard to go with it. George, clear the table, please." She fluttered to the stove and set to work.

Bernard tugged my sleeve as I stacked the dirty plates. "What now?" he mouthed.

I could only shrug because I honestly didn't know. It didn't feel like entirely bad news — suffering, a stroke or otherwise, was no less than our grandmother deserved after everything she'd inflicted on us. But it didn't feel like good news either — our fate and future hung in the balance of whether a sick old woman survived. With no Mum around, what would happen if Grandmother died?

Adding Christmas pudding to the mix in my twisting gut suddenly felt like a bad idea.

## 16

## WHY WOULD IT BE DODGY?

*S*tanding in front of the hospital, Alice shivered and hugged her arms around herself. As the daylight faded, so too did the warmth of the spring afternoon, and she regretted not grabbing a coat, but it had seemed like an added faff with her cast. Besides, with all the heat blazing through her in Ash's presence, extra clothing hadn't been necessary at the time. The toot of a car horn snapped Alice out of her thoughts. A green Mini pulled up to the curb, and she jumped in.

"What are you like?" Maggie grinned, shaking her head.

"Walking disaster, that's me."

"You didn't have to go to such extreme measures to avoid further exercise."

"Haha, very funny. Now, thank you for coming to get me, but I have another favour to ask as well."

Maggie rolled her eyes. "What now?"

"Come on, Mags, don't be a bore. Don't tell me you

have to rush home to cook dinner for your darling husband?"

"Fuck off, Alice."

Alice smirked.

"It's Friday, so Markus is cooking tonight. He makes a real effort in the kitchen these days."

"So he bloody well should."

Maggie pouted and considered her sister for a moment. "Out with it, then."

Alice pulled her phone from her pocket and scrolled to the note she'd made with George's address and instructions for finding the spare key. "It shouldn't take long. I've checked and it's only fifteen minutes away. We need to go here." She tilted the screen at Maggie.

"Why?" Maggie's perfectly pruned eyebrows pinched together as she looked at the address.

"Because I said I would."

Maggie narrowed her eyes. "Is this anything to do with that doctor you fancy?"

Alice tried to bite back her smile. "No, stop it. I don't—"

"Too easy." Maggie laughed as she typed the address into her satnav.

"It's for George, actually."

"George?" Maggie shook her head, her sleek bobbed hair swaying with the motion.

"Keep up, Mags. George, the man I found in the road last week."

Maggie dropped the handbrake and took off. "Oh great, because now it's all so much clearer."

"I want to help him."

"You can barely help yourself, Al. Look at you." Maggie gave her a sidelong glance, her lips twisted in disapproval.

"That's not a reason not to help someone else."

"This better not be anything dodgy."

Alice scoffed. "Why would it be dodgy?"

AT THE END OF A ROW OF EIGHT HOUSES STOOD George's cottage. Set back from the road and standing apart from the other taller properties, it resembled a lonely old man, hunched over a pint. The roof sagged under the weight of its years and the windows reflected the dying daylight like black, lifeless eyes.

"I really don't like this, Alice." Maggie glanced over her shoulder at her Mini parked on the grass verge. She clicked the key fob and, with an orange flash from the indicators, the doors locked. "Are you sure this is the right address?"

Alice shrugged. "It's what George gave me."

"And tell me, why has he asked you to come here, exactly?"

"No one can get hold of his next of kin, and they don't know what triggered George's dissociative fugue—"

"His what?"

"It's like a temporary amnesia, possibly caused by something traumatic."

Maggie held up her hands and spun around to face Alice. "So, what... you've brought us here to find out what traumatised a man so much he ended up in hospital?"

"Well, when you put it like that." Alice bit her lip.

"We're literally in the middle of nowhere. What if—"

"Don't be so dramatic. It's not the middle of nowhere, there's another house right there." Alice pointed to the two-story house beyond the tall hedge bordering George's property.

"Why did I let you talk me into this?"

"Look, we're here now. We may as well have a look around and see what's what. And don't worry, I have a weapon!" Alice waved her plaster cast in the air.

"Oh terrifying! You're going to wield your broken Barbie arm like a club, are you?"

"Huh, that's what Marjorie called it too."

"Who?" Maggie scowled.

"George's nurse."

"Well, if Barbie were to pick a plaster cast..."

"The colour options were limited."

"Sure they were."

"Come on, let's get this over with." Alice linked her arm through Maggie's, and the sisters stepped towards the cottage. At the front door, Alice bent down and tipped back a terracotta plant pot full of blooming narcissi. "Hold this a sec, will you?"

Maggie tutted and bent to hold the pot. Alice used her good arm to feel around underneath until her fingers grazed something cold.

"*Et voila!*" She held up the key, before turning it in the lock. The door creaked open into a dark hallway.

"Of course, the door creaks like we're in a fucking horror movie," whispered Maggie.

Alice turned and glared at her. "Do you want to just wait out here?"

Maggie looked as if she were seriously considering it. "No, because you have the weapon."

They laughed and ventured inside. With Maggie's near-hysteria ramping up the tension, Alice flicked on the light, half-expecting to see a body face down on the floor, but all that covered the floorboards was a well-worn rug.

"Alice, look," Maggie whispered.

"Why are you whispering?"

"I don't know. But look." She jutted her chin to a pile of post stacked on a console table. "Someone must have been in here. They've been picking up the post."

Alice frowned. "George didn't mention anyone else."

They walked through the unremarkable rooms together. Nothing seemed unusual or out of the ordinary. Having chatted to George, the decor and furnishings were, as Alice expected, functional yet comfortable. She'd even go as far as calling the place cosy, with the log burner and the shelves stacked with books. She could imagine George in this space; and, much like his face, she would describe it as 'lived-in.'

In the kitchen, Alice filled a jug to tend to the thirsty houseplants, some of which she recognised as the same variety she'd had in the office. However, as she went to pour the water, she saw the soil was already damp.

"Al," Maggie called from the lounge. "I think there's a voicemail."

Alice joined Maggie by the phone where a red light rapidly blinked on the answering machine.

"Should we listen to it?"

"It feels a bit intrusive, but yeah, I suppose that's why we're here."

Maggie pressed the button and a robotic voice chirped from the speaker, "You have one new message and two saved messages. New message, received Saturday the third of April at oh-one-thirty-six."

First, came the sound of shuffling and heavy breathing into a receiver. Then, "George? Are you there?" The heavily accented voice hitched and stumbled with emotion. "Please, you must call me back. Again, I will try your mobile." A click and the message ended with a loud beep.

The sisters looked at each other.

"That didn't sound good, whatever it was."

"Shall we listen to the saved messages? Maybe there's more?" Maggie pushed another button and the robotic voice moved onto a different script.

"First saved message, received Friday the second of April at seventeen-twenty-seven."

"Happy birthday, dear brother. Thank you for the card. Can you believe it?" the voice gasped, then chuckled. "Me? Sixty-six. But you, you're almost seventy, dear boy. We're old men. Sorry I didn't call you earlier. Juan whisked me off for pancakes at The Langham before we caught a matinee — *My Fair Lady*. Of all the shows." A phlegmy cough wheezed at the end of the muffled line. "Sorry about that, still haven't recovered fully from that blasted chest infection, nothing a drop of whisky won't cure, eh?

Oh, and he's pouring me one now, the darling. Better dash. Speak soon, dear." *Click, beep.* The message ended.

Alice looked up from the phone, meeting Maggie's eyes. "That must have been Bernard — the next of kin no one can get hold of. But I'm confused, do they have the same birthday?"

"He sounds a bit—"

"Gay?"

Maggie hit Alice with a hard glare. "I was going to say *eccentric*, actually. The first voice was different, though. I wonder who that was?"

"There's one more message." Alice clicked the play button.

"Second saved message received Friday the second of April at twenty-fourteen."

"George, it's me, Juan."

Juan — the man with the accent. The words that followed were rushed and panicked, punctuated with rhythmic beeps and whooshing. Muffled voices spoke in the background, but it was impossible to make them out.

"It's his heart, Bernard's heart... it's not good. We're in the ambulance and he is, how you say, is cardiac arrested? I think it's my fault, I just wanted him to have a — George, you can speak with him, please? George, I will pass the phone—"

A different voice cut into the recording. "Sorry, sir, but I'm going to need you to move back." The sound of shuffling brushed over the receiver, followed by a series of erratic beeps. Then one continuous, high-pitched tone pierced down the line, but not enough to mask the sound of Juan breaking into a sob. "No, no, Bernie, no—"

*Click, beep.*

Alice stared down at the machine; for such an unassuming little black box, a whole lot of drama had unspooled from its recordings. George had heard this message the night she found him. Clearly it had triggered his catatonic state. But why had he ventured out into the night? Where was he trying to get to?

"Poor George." Alice stroked the machine as if it might somehow comfort him.

"Poor Bernard, by the sounds of it."

"Yeah, well, that too. And now we have to break the news to George again because I'm not sure he knows that he knows. I mean, he knows that something isn't right, but this is—" Alice blew out a long breath.

"What about this Juan fellow? Do you think there's anything sinister?"

"How so?"

"He said, *I think it's my fault.*"

"I guess I need to speak to George about that. I can't just call Ash and leave her to do it."

"Really, tonight?" Maggie looked at her watch. "It's late. Doesn't he need to rest?"

"Yeah, perhaps you're right. I'll go tomorrow. Let's round up some bits for him. It might help him piece things together. Oh, and I need to find his phone charger too."

Alice spun around and almost screamed at the sight in the window. A face framed by a shock of frizzy ginger hair pressed against it, peering through the glass.

"Who the fuck is that?" Maggie whispered, with round eyes like a frightened bunny.

"How should I know? Come on, let's find out." Alice led the way, with Maggie trailing behind. She steeled herself with a breath before unlatching the door — Barbie arm at the ready behind her back, should it be required.

"Who are you? Where's George?" The short squat woman, owner of the face and frizzy hair, barged past the sisters and turned, putting herself in a position to shoo them out.

"Whoa! I should ask you the same thing."

"I'm Trisha Summers, friend and neighbour of George. And who might you be?"

Alice released a breath. "Trisha, did you say? Sorry, yes, I'm Alice, and this is my sister, Maggie."

Trisha glanced between them, her fierce little face still scrunched with suspicion.

Alice spoke slowly in the hope it might help the scary little woman to relax. "George is in hospital, he had a bit of an accident and we, well, me — I've been visiting him. He asked me to pop by and check on things here."

The woman's face fell. "What? But he knows I keep a check on things for him here. He knows he can always call me." Then, as if struck by an afterthought, she said, "Why's he in hospital then? He didn't say nothing about going to hospital."

"It's a bit of a long story, but he's doing much better now. We came by to pick up a few things for him, including his phone charger, and then he'll be able to give you a call... if he wants to." Alice could already think of several reasons why he might not. She glanced at Maggie, who looked like she was thinking the same.

"Well, I suppose you don't look too much like burglars, so that should be okay. Shall I help you find what you're looking for?"

"Yes, please. That'd be a big help."

Alice caught Maggie's eye as Trisha beckoned them through to the kitchen like she was their host.

"So, Trisha, do you know George's brother?" Alice continued to speak slowly, judging that it might be the best approach.

"Oh yes, Bernie," she said, filling a jug at the sink and watering the already-saturated plants.

"And Juan?"

"Lovely Juan, Bernie's husband. He comes from Spain, you know?"

"Yes, I heard... and, er, have Bernard and Juan been in touch recently?"

Alice glanced at Maggie's frowning face, choosing to ignore her as she mouthed, "What are you doing?"

Trisha dried the water jug and put it away. "Oh no, we don't see much of them. They live in London. I come by here when George goes to visit. I keep an eye on things. But, most importantly, I take care of his Pyglet."

"What, he has an actual piglet?"

Trisha laughed and gave a funny little snort, which actually resembled that of a piglet. "No, no. Pyglet's a dog, of course."

"Of course," Alice grinned, flicking her eyes to Maggie.

"Pyglet doesn't strictly belong to George. She's a stray, a

free spirit. George found her, and he named her too. At first, I said, 'that's a strange name for a dog', but George insisted and it's stuck."

Maggie glared at Alice and tipped her head towards the front door. Alice nodded.

Trisha continued to potter around the kitchen, lost in an invisible list of chores. "Although Pyglet seems to spend more time at mine than here. She has a dog flap, so she comes and goes as she pleases." Trisha chuckled.

"I see. Well, shall we get that phone charger, Trisha?"

"Oh yes." She held up a plump finger and charged forward with it in the air, like it was a jousting stick. "Right this way."

## 17

## IT'S COMPLICATED

George sat in the armchair by the wide hospital window. Dappled sunlight filtered through the budding leaves of the tree outside and danced in patterns across his face.

"Hey, how're you doing?" Alice asked quietly, not wanting to startle him.

George turned and his face crumpled into a smile. "Ah, it's both of you! That's what I like to see."

Alice tried to suppress her grin as she sideways-glanced at Ash, who was seemingly oblivious to George's teasing, or else just ignoring it.

"I popped by your house, like I said I would." Alice swung a small brown holdall onto the end of the bed which, with the help of Trisha, she'd packed a few things into — fresh clothes, clean pyjamas, slippers, reading glasses, a well-worn sudoku book and, most importantly, the phone charger.

George smiled. "You really are an angel, you know that?"

Ash nudged her arm. "I've been trying to tell her that."

George gave Alice a sparkly-eyed look and she bit down on her grin.

"You didn't warn me about your neighbour."

"Ah, you had the pleasure of meeting Trisha?" George raised his bushy eyebrows and smiled. "Her heart's in the right place, and she makes a wonderful pork casserole."

"And co-parents your dog, by the sounds of it," said Alice.

He chuckled. "Pyglet is a free spirit. She comes and goes as she pleases."

"So I've heard."

"Was there anything out of the ordinary? At the house, I mean?"

Alice opened her mouth to speak, but George got there first.

"Something's happened to Bernard, hasn't it?"

Alice gave a solemn nod. "I think so, George, I'm sorry. There was a message on your answering machine. It didn't sound positive. Your brother-in-law was trying to get hold of you."

George closed his eyes, his eyelids creased like elephant skin. "I know it isn't good news."

Alice unzipped the holdall and rifled around for the charger. "You should call."

George groaned as he stood up from the chair and went to the bedside locker. From the top drawer, he pulled out his old phone and plugged it in. Within a few seconds, it chimed into life. George put on his reading glasses and peered at the small green screen as messages started to ping through.

"Yes, there are a lot of messages from Juan."

Alice looked on as foreboding shadowed George's face. She felt the urge to wrap him in a hug to shield him from the news somehow, but Ash's voice held her back.

"We'll leave you alone to make the call, George." She placed a gentle, guiding hand on Alice's lower back. "We'll bring you a cuppa, okay?"

George silently nodded, distracted by the flurry of messages still pinging through.

Ash nodded to the door and mouthed, "Let's go."

"Poor George," said Alice, out in the corridor.

"Best to leave him to make the call, then we can support him once he knows for sure."

"Yeah, I guess." Alice sighed.

Ash pursed her lips and narrowed her eyes for a moment, as if battling with a tough decision. Drawing in a breath, she said, "Come with me. I want to show you something."

ALICE FOLLOWED ASH ALONG THE CORRIDOR AND into a stairwell which seemed to wind upwards forever. After four flights of stairs, Alice had to catch her breath.

"Where are you taking me?"

Ash looked over her shoulder. Realising Alice had

stopped, she jogged back down to her. "Trust me, it's worth the hike."

"Look at you, you're not even out of breath." Alice panted. "I'm clearly not as fit and I've got a broken bone." She held up her arm.

Ash laughed. "I don't think that's making any difference. There are only a couple more flights to go. Come on."

"You're indefatigable," Alice puffed and marched on.

"You should've saved your breath on that big word," Ash called after her, laughter bouncing in her voice.

At the top of the stairwell, they came to a fire exit. Ash pushed the bar, and the doors clattered open, flooding the stairwell with fresh air and sunlight.

"No one really comes out here. I think people assume it's alarmed." Ash wedged the door open with a brick, seemingly left close by for just that purpose.

Beyond the doors was a small terrace, with a waist-high industrial railing. Weeds poked through the cracks between the paving slabs, but there was little reason to look down. Beyond the squat brutalist buildings, fields of rapeseed bathed in brilliant sunshine rolled into the distance.

"It's lovely," said Alice, lifting her face to the sun.

"It's a good place to take a breather."

"You need it after all those stairs."

"I tried to talk Facilities Management into putting a bench out here, and some plants to make a proper little garden out of it. I pitched the wellbeing angle; it'd be somewhere for people to get away for a bit."

"It'd be perfect for that."

"Unfortunately they knocked it back for health and safety reasons, but I suspect it was funding."

"Shame."

Ash nodded. "I usually bring a cup of tea up here."

"Mmm, yeah, a cup of tea right now would be perfect."

"Best I can offer you is a couple of fingers."

Alice whipped around so fast she almost caused herself another injury. "Sorry, wha—"

Ash's lips quirked into her wonky smile as she held out a red wrapper. "Kit Kat. Do you want half?"

"Right, yes." *Of course, that's what she meant. Christ, Alice.* "Thank you."

Leaning on the railing and looking out over the vista, Alice nibbled the chocolate off the wafer fingers, whilst Ash crunched hers.

"Mmm, delicious, but so much better after it's been dipped in tea," Alice said.

"Yuck, I don't do that."

Alice looked at her, mouth open in mock outrage. "What? Come on, at least tell me that you've used a Crunchie as a straw?"

"What? No!"

"Doctor K., you haven't lived. I'm going to have to buy you a Crunchie now, aren't I?"

Ash smiled as she gazed into the distance, squinting slightly in the sun. Alice scanned her profile. A few strands of Ash's glossy black hair floated in the light breeze, fluttering around her face. Alice resisted the pull to reach out and gently tuck the hair behind her ear, as well as the urge to touch her face and curl her fingers around

Ash's jawline, to caress her soft, smooth skin. Alice's eyes dropped to Ash's lips, which lifted into a smile as she turned to face her.

"What?" Ash asked.

"Huh?"

"You're staring at my mouth. Have I got chocolate on my teeth or something?"

Alice breathed a laugh. "No, no... it's just..."

"Just what?"

Alice felt the heat rising into her cheeks and turned away. "Did you used to come up here with your ex?" *Why did I ask her that?*

"Yeah, it was Sam who showed me this spot, back in the day."

*Great.*

"Does being up here still remind you of her?" Alice asked, hoping for an immediate, "No," which would've paired nicely with an, "All I can think of at the moment is you," and she wouldn't have declined a, "Let's go back to yours and get naked," to finish off with.

But none of that came and Ash looked so lost in thought that when she spoke again, it startled Alice a little.

"I wasn't entirely honest with you about Sam."

"Oh?"

"My life is more complicated than I perhaps implied."

Alice raised her eyebrows. "Sam's not an ex?"

"No, she is. It's just... complicated."

"Tell me you've got a husband and five kids, but you're battling with latent lesbianism, and we have *complicated*. But otherwise..."

Ash winced. "You're not too far from the truth."

*What the* — Alice's face must have said what she was thinking as Ash quickly filled in the gaps. "No, not me. Sam. I only told you half the story. She *did* move to Edinburgh, but it wasn't for a job... she had a different offer she couldn't refuse. Her family found her a good match."

Ash's accent took on an Indian lilt as she said, "A very nice boy, from the right caste." Her brown eyes found Alice's, the hurt visible behind them. Ash looked away.

"So, yeah. She's married now."

"Oh, Ash." Alice touched her arm, but she wanted to pull her into a hug and squeeze away her sadness.

"It almost broke me at the time. She was my everything, you know?"

Alice nodded.

"She just chucked us away, like we never really mattered. I knew she wanted a family. I'd have liked to have given her that one day, but she said she wanted to do it properly, in the right way... as God intended it."

"Ouch."

Ash inhaled, her knuckles going white as she gripped the railing.

"But that's her, not you. You're not complicated."

"I am, because I've been hurt. I couldn't go through that again. And I've had to distance myself from my family, as they want all that for me too. You know, husband, kids — *in the right way.* It's a lot of pressure and I don't think they'll accept anything else."

"So, it's either lose yourself, or lose them, potentially?"

"Yep, that pretty much sums it up."

"Shit, so you're seriously thinking of going along with that?"

"Oh, hell no! I'm not like Sam. I couldn't live a lie, well, not completely — I do have a beard for family gatherings, but that's just to make my life easier."

"You're not out to your family at all?"

"Sort of — My brother knows and some of my cousins, they're cool with it. My mum hopes it's just a phase." Ash widened her eyes. "She said she'd die of shame if anyone else knew... hence, the beard. I spare everyone's blushes and the only grief I get is about why I haven't married him yet."

After a moment, Ash turned to her and something other than sadness flickered behind those dark brown eyes.

"I don't really like talking about it, but I wanted to be honest with you and tell you the whole story."

"Why?"

"Because you asked." Ash's gaze dropped to Alice's mouth. "And because I—"

The doors rattled open behind them, and two nurses appeared, lighters sparking under cupped hands before they'd even made it outside.

"What a pile of shite that we're working on such a gorgeous day. As soon as I get a day off, it's nothing but feckin' drizzle," said the younger nurse with a thick Irish accent.

"It's not like your skin can take the sun. Surely, you'd just turn into one giant freckle?"

"Now, Eileen, that's what you call an Irish tan."

Eileen laughed through a smoker's cough before eyeing Alice and Ash. "Sorry ladies, we're not interrupting anything, are we?"

"No," said Ash, although the pained expression on her face said the opposite. "We were just leaving."

Alice sighed.

"We should get back to George," Ash said and led the way through the doors. "Bloody smokers. I bet that's the other reason Facilities ruled out a terrace garden. It'd only encourage more smokers. Not that it's even allowed on the hospital grounds."

"Why didn't you say something to them?"

"It isn't worth it. I don't want to get on the wrong side of the nurses."

Ash paced ahead and Alice willed her to slow down or, better, stop. She wanted Ash to turn and finish what she'd been about to say... or do, because even though it didn't make sense after the conversation they'd just had, Alice could've sworn Ash had been about to kiss her.

"It might be best if you go in on your own first. I don't want to overwhelm him." Ash buried her hands in her pockets and leaned against the wall.

As they stood in the corridor outside George's room, Alice's mind spun with questions about everything unsaid between them.

"You're the doctor. Wouldn't it make more sense for you to go in?"

"He doesn't need a doctor right now; he needs a friend. And you've been there for him from the start."

"So have you."

"Yeah, but I was being paid. You were just there because you're a good person." Ash visibly swallowed. "The best per—"

"Coming through," the bearded one of two porters called out, as they rushed down the corridor wheeling a bed.

Without a thought, Alice pressed closer to Ash to let them by, but in the whoosh of them passing, she stepped off balance and stumbled into her.

"Whoa, easy." The hands previously stuffed in Ash's pockets were now on Alice's hips, her fingertips in contact with the flesh under Alice's T-shirt. Alice looked up into the slightly taller woman's face.

"Sorry, I—"

"It's okay, I got you," said Ash.

The peril was over. The porters had long since passed, but Ash's hands stayed put. Alice's heart galloped. Neither of them made to move away. *Ask her, now...*

"Before, on the roof. You were going to say something else."

Ash's mouth twitched into a grin. "Yeah, I wanted to tell you—"

"Sorry to interrupt, Doctor K.," Marjorie's voice boomed, shattering the moment.

Ash's hands fell away from Alice's hips. She stood up straight and cleared her throat. Alice stepped back, her heart pounding and skin tingling from Ash's touch.

"Nurse Reid?"

"I know you're not on duty yet, but can we borrow you for a minute? We need a quick second opinion on a complex care plan."

"Sure. Be right there."

Marjorie turned and swayed back towards the nurse's station.

"Sorry, I better..." Ash pointed in the direction of the departing nurse. "You go into George, and I'll grab you both some tea, okay?"

Alice nodded, disappointment replacing the hope that had risen in her chest only moments ago. Ash must have read it on her face as, before she sprung off, she shot Alice her disarming grin and said, "We will get to finish our chat soon, I promise."

"I think I'll implode if we don't," Alice muttered to Ash's retreating figure.

Alice tapped on George's door and entered. Still sat in the chair facing the window, he didn't turn with the swoosh of the door, nor when Alice softly called out to him. She pulled up a blue plastic chair from the corner of the room and sat alongside him.

"Bernard's dead." George's voice came out croaky and raw.

"Oh, George, I'm so sorry. What happened?"

"Juan said it was a heart attack. He died in the ambulance."

Alice reached across and squeezed his arm.

George sighed. "I'm not at all surprised. Bernard liked

to live large. Juan and I were always telling him to slow down. Sixty-six though, that's no age, is it?"

"No age at all."

"Poor Juan is distraught. He's blaming himself because he'd plied Bernard with rich food and alcohol. And he bought him a birthday cigar and let him smoke it even with his bad chest. But it was his birthday. Our birthday!" George's voice cracked. "It isn't Juan's fault."

"No, poor guy. Had they been together long?"

"About six years. They both work in the theatre business. Bernard cast Juan in one of his plays and they fell in love. I was a bit sceptical at first as Juan's so much younger. He's around your age, but he was good for my brother. He made him very happy."

"Not all of us youngsters are gold-diggers, you know?" Alice smiled.

George scoffed a laugh. "I didn't mean to imply that. Bernard was my little brother. I always looked out for him. We didn't have the easiest childhood."

"The answering machine message, I think it was when Juan and Bernard were on the way to hospital. Do you think when you heard it, it triggered your fugue?"

George nodded. "My mind has been scrambling through flashbacks over the last couple of days, but now I quite clearly remember hearing the message and turning to see a flash of black fur in the front garden. I thought it was Pyg, so I followed her."

"Pyg — as in your childhood dog?"

George nodded.

"I don't mean to be insensitive, but surely Pyg must be long gone?"

"Mmm, you're right. She died a long time ago. But I don't sleep well — chronic insomnia. If it's been an especially bad patch, I sometimes see the shadows of things that aren't really there."

Alice rubbed his arm through the thin paisley fabric of his pyjama shirt.

"Perhaps with the shock of hearing Bernard... my mind was playing tricks on me? Or it could've been Pyglet I saw? It's the only sense I can make of everything. Pyg was there when Bernard and I went through a particularly difficult time as kids. She was like a beacon when all other hope had faded."

"Do you want to talk about it?"

"Bernard died without knowing the truth. I just wanted to protect him, but I should've told him." George squeezed his eyes shut and a tear rolled down his cheek and into his beard.

Alice drew closer, moving her hand from his arm to his back. His chest heaved with the weight of his sorrow. There was something unsettling about witnessing fragility in a person as sturdy as George, almost like watching a crack appear in a mighty dam.

# 1978

## SKULKING IN SHADOWS OF THE PAST

*A* sense of melancholy weighed heavy on me as I stood in the front garden of the only home I'd known as a child. Despite the warm spring day, a strong smell of damp earth and decomposing leaves filled the air. The vibrant flowerbeds our mother had once tended were now choked with weeds, and the hedges surrounding the property formed a twisted, impenetrable mass which cast long, dark shadows.

I glanced at my watch; Bernard was over twenty minutes late. I hadn't wanted to be here alone, that's why I'd asked him to come all the way from London. But I should've guessed at Bernard's tardiness and planned accordingly. I paced the broken concrete path that led to the front door and kicked a chunk of moss.

"Shit!" I said when it left a muddy mark on my new leather brogues. I bent and brushed the dirt away. They'd cost me a decent chunk of my first pay packet, but a respectable teacher should have a nice pair of shoes. And that's just what I was now, *a respectable teacher.* Pride swelled in my chest at the thought.

Finally, I was earning an income and no longer reliant on handouts from the church or money from my grandmother — not that that would be happening any longer.

"Georgie-boy!" Bernard's bellow pulled me out of my head and instantly dispelled my low mood. He rounded the hedge looking like a rock star, with aviator sunglasses and a pencil moustache, which he smoothed with his finger and thumb. He wore a pair of purple flares and a colourful shirt with a ridiculous floppy collar.

"Bernie, didn't you leave the circus years ago?" I laughed.

"Ha-fucking-ha! It's called fashion, dear. Perhaps you should try it sometime?"

"You look like a peacock!"

"Better than a dull grey pigeon." He pushed his aviators back into his long hair.

We went in for a back-slapping hug and I clutched him to me like it had been much longer than three months since I'd last seen him.

"Right. Shall we get this over with?"

I swallowed. "Yeah, I would've made a start, but I didn't want to go in without you."

Bernard draped an arm around my shoulder and steered me towards the house.

"Cheer up, Georgie. Ding-Dong, the witch is gone. We can sell this old wreck now and put it all behind us, can't we?"

"Do you think she'd mind?"

"Who, Grandmother?"

"No, I meant Mum. Do you think she'd mind us getting rid of it?"

"I think she'll be fucking delighted. This place was nothing but a prison for her. And if she ever shows up again, we'll take care of her, won't we?"

I looked into my brother's bright blue eyes and nodded.

Even now, Bernard held onto a hope that I'd long since let go of. And the solicitor's letter that landed on my doormat last month diminished any glimmer that had remained.

*Dear Mr George Shaw,*

*I am writing to you in my capacity as a solicitor handling the estate of your late grandmother, Mrs Sylvia Shaw, who passed away on 13th November 1977. Please accept our heartfelt condolences for your loss. Regrettably, our records indicate that Mrs Shaw did not leave a valid Last Will and Testament. As a result, the estate will be administered under the rules of intestacy. You have been identified as one of two surviving relatives entitled to inherit from the estate...*

And it continued, but my eyes kept drawing back to the same words: *one of two surviving relatives.* I contacted the solicitor to ask if they had any more information, but if they did, they didn't tell me. Thus far, I hadn't had the heart to tell Bernard, and fortunately he hadn't received a letter of his own, probably owing to his inconsistent living arrangements. *How had he put it?*

"Why be tied down when I can flit from one wealthy fucker to the next? Saves me paying rent and I get to have a bit of fun whilst I'm at it."

I didn't entirely agree with Bernard's lifestyle — not on moral grounds, more safety concerns. Bernard had been hurt on more than one occasion, physically and emotionally. And whilst he always laughed it off, I couldn't help but worry for him.

But here we both were, ready to recover any valuables before we had our childhood home cleared and put on the market. Living there hadn't ever been a consideration for either of us.

I twisted my key in the lock and pushed, but the door had swollen with damp. I took a step back and barged it with my shoulder, it inched inwards a little but didn't budge.

"Shit," I said rubbing my arm.

"Here, let me." Bernard smoothed his moustache and sniffed.

I grinned. "Don't ruin that nice shirt, Bernie."

"Oh, fuck off," said Bernard with laughter in his voice. He clenched his fists and his technicolour sleeves tightened around his biceps. Clearly, my little brother was not so little any more. With a run-up and a grunt, he crashed through the front door.

I stepped inside and coughed as the dust swirled around. The place smelt musty and damp. Cobwebs draped from the ceiling like spooky bunting. No one had been in the house since the church had moved Ruth on. When she left, she must have pulled all the curtains shut, and now they kept the light of the spring day from penetrating the thick gloom.

Bernard flipped the light switch up and down, but nothing happened.

"They must have shut off the electricity," I said.

"Better get finished before it gets dark then, hadn't we?"

"Yeah, can't imagine it'll take long. There probably isn't much worth keeping."

"No, you're not wrong. The old witch was such a tight-arse you could've used her shit for shoelaces."

"Bernard!" Grimacing, I glanced around.

Bernard snickered. "It's not like she can hear us."

A scuttling scratched above us. Bernard squealed and leapt behind me. "What the fuck was that?"

"And you're supposed to be the brave one." I laughed. "Probably just mice."

I threw the curtains open wide in the drawing room and sunlight filtered through the dirty windows. I tried to open one, but the wooden frames were as swollen as the front door.

"Do you reckon this place is even worth anything?" I asked.

"I wouldn't buy it. Someone might if they fancy a project."

All the drawing room contained was a filthy hearthrug and an eclectic array of sagging old furniture.

Bernard shrugged. "Nothing worth keeping in here."

In the kitchen, he opened the back door and stepped

outside to smoke a thin roll-up he pulled out of a tin. "You want one, Georgie?"

"No, thanks. It makes me lightheaded." I rinsed and filled the kettle. After clicking the ignitor a few times, the hob flamed to life. "Bingo! Fancy a cuppa before we venture upstairs?" I looked over my shoulder. Bernard was no longer leaning by the back door. "Bernard?"

I peered through the grimy window and watched as he strode up the overgrown garden path, kicking at the weeds as they pulled at his ankles. He stood at the blackened entrance of the studio, and with a hand pressed on either side of the doorway, he poked his head inside.

I couldn't bear it. Ever since the day we thought we'd lost Pyg, I'd kept away. Nothing good could come of venturing in there to see the charred remains of our childhood skulking in shadows of the past.

Bernard was back at the door. He pulled the last drag from his roll-up and crushed the butt under his shoe. "I still can't believe the old witch burned down the studio. If it wasn't worth something, I'd take great pleasure in burning this fucking house down."

"Do you want tea?"

"Yeah, go on. Is there any sugar?"

I scoffed. "What do you think? I thought to get milk and biscuits, though."

Bernard opened and banged shut the cupboard doors. "Nothing in here but mouse shit. Ooh, what about this?" He held up a dusty decorative glass vase.

I shrugged. "I don't want it."

"I'll have it then. And these too," he said, opening a box of tarnished fish knives.

I raised an eyebrow.

"Dinner parties, darling," he said.

We took our mugs of tea upstairs. Mum's room was devoid of everything but a stripped bed, dressing table and wardrobe with empty hangers swinging on the rail. For the longest time, it had been Ruth's room, anyway. The only trace of its former occupant was a cardboard box, unceremoniously shoved at the back of the wardrobe. It contained the few items Mum had left behind. I pulled it out and rifled through the contents: a cracked handheld mirror, an old pair of stockings, and some tatty paperbacks, including a dog-earned copy of *Pygmalion* by George Bernard Shaw. Nothing of any value, sentimental or monetary, but I shoved the play in my satchel anyway.

"Oi, oi! What's this?" Bernard pulled a chain-link belt from a drawer.

I grimaced. "I'd put that down if I were you."

Bernard whipped the belt around in the air. "Why? What is it?"

"I dunno, but I saw Ruth putting it on once."

"Oh, did you now?"

"Not like that. Jesus! She'd left the door open, and I was passing. She had it around her thigh. I think it's some sort of Catholic thing, you know, like as a punishment or something?"

Bernard turned his nose up and flung the spiky belt onto the bed. "Sounds fucking kinky to me. And they call my lot perverts!"

"Ruth wasn't so bad in the end, was she? As long as we kept our heads down."

"Yeah, bit like living with a big mouse, I suppose. Maybe it was her shitting in the kitchen cupboards?"

I laughed. "Yeah," I said, although she always reminded me more of a bird than a mouse.

As we exited Mum's room, I put out an arm to halt Bernard and raised a finger to my lips.

"Shh!"

Bernard's brows crumpled in confusion until he caught my drift. We hopped along the landing towards our room, retracing our childhood steps. Bernard stumbled and landed on a squeaky floorboard. We looked at each other with wide eyes and burst out laughing.

"Ah, do you remember how Pyg used to do it, too?"

"Such a clever girl. I miss her, Georgie."

"Me too."

"Oh my God, it stinks in here." Bernard covered his face.

I managed to crack open the window and fresh air spilled into the room. "Eau-de-teenage-boy-and-stinky-dog."

"It's disgusting." The springs loudly protested as Bernard flopped back onto his bed and stared at the ceiling.

I knelt and pulled a shoebox from under my bed. After blowing off the dust, I opened the lid. Inside were a few treasured possessions, including the Christmas book. I smiled and held it up.

"Remember this?"

Bernard bounced onto his side and grinned.

"I wrote in it after you left." I opened the cover, looked down at the long list of markings on the page and read the final one aloud. "Three miserable Christmases without you, Bernie. And one without Pyg."

"I couldn't come back here. I'm sorry."

"Don't be, I get it. This place sucked the joy out of everything. You're right, we should bloody torch it."

"Nah, she'd be more pissed off at the thought of us enjoying her money."

I laughed and closed the book back in the box of keepsakes.

Bernard swung his legs around and stretched up. "I'm going out for a fag. I'll make us another cuppa."

I CLASPED THE DOORKNOB OF GRANDMOTHER'S room, my imagination feeding my mind with images: sunken eyes latching onto me through the darkness, a puckered mouth twisting into a sneer, sagging flesh hanging from skeletal arms, and claw-like fingers reaching out from the bed. I took a steadying breath and pushed into the room. A cool draught gushed out, and with it, I could've sworn I heard the hiss of "little bastards".

After Grandmother's stroke, much of her speech had been lost, as was the use of her right-hand side. Her lips could no longer pucker in disgust, but the phrase "little bastards" somehow still came out of them loud and clear.

Thankfully, Ruth had stayed on as Grandmother's

primary carer after she'd been discharged from hospital, over a year after she'd burned the studio and injured her hand in the process. She lived the rest of her days in this room, wallowing and alone, apart from Ruth. She even refused visits from the priest.

I stepped to the window, tugged the curtains open and daylight bathed the room. Only then did I allow my gaze to drift to the bed and dispel the workings of my imagination. *No withered corpse passing judgement from between the four posts, just worn, dusty old bedlinens.*

The wardrobe was stuffed full of clothes that hadn't been worn for years, most of them so moth-eaten they'd likely end up in landfill. I pulled out the seat at the dressing table and sat in front of the mirror, its surface cloudy and de-silvered with age. The dressing table drawer rattled but didn't budge — *locked.*

I opened Grandmother's jewellery box and started as a ballerina sprang up and creaked out a full turn to a few eerie notes before stopping. The treasure she'd been guarding amounted to no more than a few tarnished rings and a pearlescent brooch in the shape of a feather — *oh, and a key.* I turned it in the lock of the drawer, and it clicked open. At the front was a velvet box containing a gold pocket watch inscribed with the name of the grandfather I'd never met. Another box contained a set of military medals.

Tucked away at the back of the drawer were two stacks of letters, each tied with red ribbon. I untied the first stack. The coarse yellowed envelopes were addressed to Sylvia and Eleanor in a hand I recognised from the Christmas book — *Papa*. I retied the stack and picked up the other, noting an untidy handwriting I'd never seen before. I squinted at the envelope, postmarked October 1968 with a foreign stamp, and addressed to *George & Bernard Shaw*.

My fingers fumbled with the ribbon. In haste, I pulled the top letter out of the envelope and narrowed my eyes at the scrawl on the page.

*Dearest George and Bernard,*

*It's with the heaviest heart I'm writing this letter to you. I'm truly stricken, and I don't know where to even begin. I've tried to reach you on the telephone, but as yet, I've been unsuccessful. I'll keep trying and do whatever I can to get this news to you as you have a right to know.*

*Your mother and I were involved in a terrible car accident in Ethiopia. Two days later, she died in hospital from her injuries. I was with her, holding her hand. The last words she said were your names.*

*This won't bring your mother back, but I wish it had been me. I wish I could take her place and she were home with you now. But God took her as my punishment.*

*I'm so sorry. I should've been a better man. But that's just it, I'm weak-willed and flawed. We were going to send for you. We had so many plans.*

*Please know that I loved her with all my heart, and I love you both too, my sons.*

*Your father,*

*Henry Higgins.*

Blood rushed in my ears as I scrunched my eyes and glanced at the words again. The inked characters scrawled across the page confirmed what I thought I'd known all along. *Higgins was our father. That was obvious.*

*But our mother had died in Africa, and Grandmother had known. All these years, she'd known and kept it from us. The fucking church knew, too —*

"Whoa, Georgie-boy! You're brave. You ventured into the dragon's den without me?" Bernard's voice on the landing snatched me from my thoughts. With shaking hands, I shuffled and shoved the letters back into the drawer.

"Found anything interesting?"

"Oh, just these." I gestured to the pocket watch and medals. "And there's some jewellery in here. You think it's worth anything?"

"Oh nice!" Bernard eyed off the feather brooch and slid one of Grandmother's rings onto his pinkie finger, holding it up to inspect it in the light. "Do you a deal? You can keep the watch and medals if I can have these bits and pieces?"

"If you're sure that's what you want." I laughed as Bernard pinned the brooch onto his shirt and pouted at his reflection in the mirror.

"I, er, found some old letters too. Do you mind if I take them and have a read?"

Bernard waved his hand in the air. "Sure, you know I can't be bothered with all that. Right, what delights did the old witch have hidden away in this wardrobe?"

Gulping down my guilt, I retrieved the letters from the drawer and tucked them into my satchel.

"Holy shit! I think this is real fur." Bernard held a hideous brown coat against his body and twirled around, summoning memories of Mum and the studio and dancing to *From Me to You* as it blared from the radio.

*I will tell him. When the time's right, I'll tell him.*

## LITTLE BROTHER

"I never had the heart to break it to him."

George's eyes glistened with tears as he fixed his gaze on the tree outside, its budding leaves swaying in the light breeze.

"I can't believe you lived with the burden of that secret for so long. Even if I wanted to, I couldn't keep anything from Maggie. She always sees right through me."

"I shouldn't have kept it from him. I let Bernard live in false hope. He believed our mum was out there some-where, living her best life. And I don't think he ever gave up on the idea of her coming back one day."

"Wasn't he angry with her?... I mean, didn't he feel like she'd abandoned you both?"

George sniffed and shook his head. "Quite the oppo-site. Bernard worshipped Mum. I think he saw her great escape as something to live up to. I'd say it's what gave him the courage to leave home at sixteen. Bernard couldn't have achieved his full potential in the stifling space we'd grown up in, so he left as soon as he could. Joined the bloody circus, of all things."

"The circus?"

"Yep. Our grandmother was so apoplectic when she found out, I think she nearly had another stroke." George chuckled. "My little brother, the clown."

Alice laughed. "Perhaps it was for the best. You kept the truth from him to protect him. You can't beat yourself up now. Did Bernard know the priest was your father?"

"He figured that out easily enough. Bernard was the spit of him."

"And were you too?"

"Bernard, more so. But yeah, me too, a bit. That's why I grew a beard."

"Very saintly."

"You reckon? I was going for rugged wrong'un. The opposite of a priest."

"Did you ever see him again?"

"No, I was so angry with him. I was afraid of what I'd do. For many years, I blamed him for Mum leaving us, and then for her death."

"That's understandable."

George sighed. "It's another regret that I've lived with. Poor Bernard just followed my lead, so effectively I denied him the chance to grieve for our mother, and the chance to get to know our father."

Alice reached across and placed a hand on George's shoulder. "You were trying to protect him. And you were so young yourself, it wasn't your place to build bridges. He was your father, he should've—"

"Oh, he'd written many times. I found a stack of letters in our Grandmother's room."

"She kept them from you?"

George's hand clenched the paisley material of his pyjama bottoms. "She was a bitter old woman. But it wouldn't have made a difference, even if she'd passed the letters on I wouldn't have wanted any contact with him. From what I gathered he never returned from Africa. He was a coward."

George shook his head. "I don't know if Higgins ever came clean about us, but if he did, then the church turned a blind eye."

"Yeah, that seems to be the way, doesn't it?"

They sat in silence for a thoughtful moment, until George spoke again.

"Thank you, Alice."

"For what?"

His lips formed a sad smile. "For being so wonderfully curious and letting me get this all off my chest. I can't make it right with Bernard now, but I feel better having told someone the truth, at least."

"Do you think maybe you didn't tell Bernard about your mother's death because it would've made it real?"

"What do you mean?"

"As in, perhaps Bernard's hope kept a light on for you too? And that light went out when you realised you were losing him last week?"

George frowned as he considered her words.

A small knock came at the door. Alice looked around as Ash pushed into the room, carrying a tea tray.

"Hey, you two," she said softly. "I made you some tea. And Nurse Reid rustled up some biscuits. She must like you as she's given you the chocolate ones."

"Thanks, Ash." Alice smiled and looked back at George, who was still deep in thought and scratching his beard. "Can I have a word outside?"

Ash nodded and led the way. Alice closed the door behind her, but still spoke in a whisper.

"We were right about the voicemail; it was bad news. George's brother passed away last week. Heart attack. The same day I found George in the road."

Ash's face crumpled in concern. "Oh no, poor George."

"When do you think he'll be able to get out of here?"

"I'm not sure. I'll need to speak to his doctor. I think they're still waiting for a psych evaluation to make sure—"

"But you said yourself there's a waiting list. Can't he be seen as an outpatient?"

"Alice, I think they need to make sure that he wasn't trying to hurt himself."

"He wasn't."

"But you don't know that for sure, do you?"

"I do, Ash. He wasn't."

Ash sighed, her kind eyes scanning Alice's face. "Look, I'll have a word and see what I can do, but no promises. There are protocols and—"

"What if I could help?"

Ash tilted her head, her silky black hair falling forward from behind her ear. Alice yearned to tuck it back into place. But they hadn't finished their chat yet and things between them were fuzzy. Warm and fuzzy, but still fuzzy.

"I could speak to Jeremy."

"Your old boss? Fran's husband?"

"Yeah, he specialises in bereavement therapy."

"Do you really want to be asking favours from someone who—"

"I think they owe me a favour, don't you?"

Ash held up her hands. "It's up to you, but I'm not sure you should put yourself in that situation. Like you said, they're manipulative and messed up."

"Well, if it helps George, it'll be worth it."

"Just be careful, okay?" Ash rubbed Alice's arm and a surge of heat ran through her. Ash nodded to the door. "Your tea will be getting cold."

"Do you mind if I stay with him for a while? I think it's helping him to talk through things with someone."

"No, why would I mind?"

"Oh, just because earlier... you said we'd finish our chat."

Ash blushed. "Oh yeah, that can wait. It wasn't important."

Alice's face must have revealed her disappointment, as Ash quickly picked up the thread.

"Shit, I'm really not good at this. I mean, it is important, but it'll keep. George needs you now, and I start my shift soon, so... are you free to meet me for lunch tomorrow?"

The smile Alice felt lifting her lips was the opposite of playing it cool, but she couldn't hide it. "Yeah, I'm free," she said, in the hope Ash might finally tell her what she'd been trying to say.

# LAYING AN EGG

*A*lice checked the directions on her phone as she strolled through the park, which hummed with activity. She looked up from the map to where the dot on her screen stood in all three dimensions. A beautiful café with intricate black and white ironwork framing its eaves, like a fancy Victorian bandstand. Alice turned and half-expected Dick Van Dyke to pop up and sing a cheerful song amongst the tulips.

All the outside chairs and tables were full, so Alice waited in the shade of a willow tree. She pulled out her phone for something to do with her hands and resumed her research on Kegel exercises. After scanning an article called 'The Big Squeeze', she clicked a link on technique.

Alice clenched and tensed, breathing in for the count of *one, two, three, four... fuck*. She looked up at the smiling face of Ash, curiosity sparkling in her brown eyes. Alice fumbled with her phone, locking the screen as Ash reached her.

"What an earth were you doing just now? Because from a distance it looked like you were laying an egg."

"Just practicing some… er, breathing exercises."

"Doesn't that come naturally to you?" Ash laughed and went in for a hug.

Alice grinned, trying not to notice the way Ash's woody scent lingered in her wake or how the sleeves of her black T-shirt flexed around her biceps. *Nope, definitely not noticing the soft curve of her breasts under the fitted material, either.*

"This place is lovely. How have I lived here most of my life and never come across it before?"

"I guess you weren't looking hard enough." Ash's grin pinched a dimple into her cheek and it was so damn cute Alice had to tear her eyes away before she did something she might regret.

"Ooh, table." Ash sprung over to where a young couple with a grizzling baby were rising from their seats. Her phone trilled as they sat and she glanced at the screen. "Shit, sorry, Alice. I have to get this."

As Ash stepped away, Alice picked up the menu and tried not to listen, but couldn't help overhearing when Ash's normally even tone rose with irritation.

"Seriously, Indi. You can't let me down, you promised."

She paced along the path, interjecting with, "Uh-huh. Right, well, you owe me big-time," and "Yeah, I guess that's my problem to figure out," as she raked her fingers through her glossy hair.

Ash caught Alice's gaze and rolled her eyes as she said into the phone, "Yeah, yeah, love you too, just a little bit less than I did before." She hung up the call and made her way back over, groaning as she slumped into the bistro chair. Alice placed the menu down.

"Okay, that's not a happy face. Who's this Indi and what's she done to upset you?"

Ash glanced up through her long eyelashes and sighed. "Indi is a *he*. And the answer to every gay Indian girl's dreams."

"Tell me more."

"Remember, I told you I had a beard?"

Alice nodded.

"Well, that's Indi, my gay best mate. Incredibly, we make each other appear straight at family gatherings. He's like a very flamboyant invisibility cape."

Alice laughed. "So, what's he done to upset you?"

"Only gone and bailed on being my plus-one to my brother's engagement party next weekend." She added a "for fuck's sake," under her breath.

"I'll go with you," Alice said before pausing to breathe... or think.

"Oh. Er, I mean, the idea is to get through it somehow by passing as straight, so I'm not sure..." Ash shrugged, but then narrowed her eyes. "Fuck it. Maybe you should come with me?"

"Really? I don't want to make anything worse for you."

"They'll all love you. You're so glamorous, you'll divert attention that way instead."

Alice swatted away the compliment. "I'm hardly glamorous. And with some of the states you've seen me in recently, I've never looked such a wreck."

"Seriously, have you seen yourself? Panda-eyes and ripped stockings notwithstanding... you're stunning. I mean, you know that, right?" Ash blushed.

"Yeah, that's me, a hot mess." Alice crushed her lips together to stop herself from smiling too hard.

Ash cleared her throat. "So, do you know what you want?"

"Well, you're the one who keeps getting interrupted as you're about to say something intriguing. What do *you* want, Ash?"

"To order, I mean." A teasing grin played on Ash's lips. "You've been staring at the menu for ten minutes. I already know what I'm having so..."

*Oh. My. God.* "Surprise me. And a large glass of white wine..." *...so I can fucking drown myself in it.*

As Ash walked into the café, Alice tried and failed not to notice how her stonewashed denim jeans hugged her arse. Her thoughts spiralled into a vision of cupping those pert cheeks as Ash topped her.

"You look lost in thought," Ash said as she returned with their drinks.

Heat rose up Alice's neck and she gulped a mouthful of wine. "I think we need to finish our chat."

"Yeah, we do." Ash swigged from her bottle of beer.

Alice's heart squeezed. *This is it.*

"It's been nearly two years since things ended with Sam. I've really struggled to get over it. Like when she messages me, it's as if everything comes crashing down again." Ash frowned, and started peeling the label from her beer bottle.

*Hmm, not where I hoped this was going.* "Oh, you're still in touch?"

"I try not to be, but sometimes she pops up on my phone, out of the blue, saying how much she misses me. Sometimes she says she wishes things were different." Ash sighed. "But she let me down, not the other way around."

Alice reached over the table and covered Ash's hand with her own.

"Sorry, I didn't mean to make this about Sam." Ash stared down at their hands.

"It's okay, you can talk to me about it."

"I just wanted you to know that I understand what you're going through with Fran."

"Yeah, well about that, I—"

"It's hard for me to open up to people usually. And this will sound so clichéd, but I feel like I've known you forever."

"Yeah, me too." Alice's voice came out higher than usual.

"I really enjoy your company, Alice. I'm glad that we met and that we're friends."

Alice guzzled another mouthful of wine, swallowing down the feelings she'd been hoping were about to be aired. *Friends. Just good friends.* She forced a smile.

"So, tell me more about this party. When is it? Where is it? What the hell am I supposed to wear?"

Visibly relieved that the conversation had moved on, Ash sat back.

Alice tried to concentrate as Ash reeled off the details of the party, but her mind whirred. Why did she have this yearning to over-complicate things with Ash? Had she been so desperate to fill the void left by Fran with something other than loneliness and self-loathing, she'd kept misreading the signs? Ash presented the thrill of something new, and she was unlike anyone Alice had ever met before. *But Ash has been more than clear about what she wants, hasn't she? She needs a friend, and you need one too, so don't mess this up.*

"Are you even listening to me?"

"Sorry, what?" Alice's eyes dropped to Ash's grinning lips as they exhaled a laugh.

"I asked whether you'd mind if we share a room? I can try booking a separate room at the hotel, but I doubt there'll be any left since the party's next week."

Alice waved a hand between them. "It's not as if it'll be the first time we've shared a bed."

"No, I know. I didn't want you to think I was trying to..." Ash's cheeks flamed.

"We've established that we're just friends, right?"

Ash bobbed her head.

"And we've managed to keep our hands off each other so far." Alice drank the remaining wine in her glass, trying to swallow with it the memory of waking up wrapped in Ash's arms, stirred by the soft push of hips. "Well, at least I have," she muttered.

Ash planted her palms on the table. "Oh God, the other morning, you were awake?"

Alice tried to squash her grin. "I might've been."

"I'm so sorry. I haven't slept beside someone for so long, I—"

Alice placed a hand over Ash's. "It's fine... I'm teasing you. It was nice just being held. I miss that."

"Mmm." Ash stared at Alice's hand atop hers and nodded slowly. A line etched between her brows, and she opened her mouth, but instead of speaking, she tipped her head back and drained the beer bottle, its shredded label curling over her fingers.

Alice tapped her empty glass. "Fancy another?"

ALICE LAY SPRAWLED ON HER COUCH, AN ARM hanging over the edge as she flicked through the Netflix menu, looking at the screen but only seeing Ash's face; her gorgeous, confusing-as-fuck face. She couldn't get enough of her new *friend*, but for all the wrong reasons... and now, where was fucking Maggie when she needed to talk to her?

Alice groaned and let the remote roll out of her hand onto the plush rug. The television flickered with the looping trailer for *Baby Reindeer*.

*God, am I like that poor deluded woman? Ash felt sorry for me, and she was just being kind, but now I'm obsessed and following her around like a stalker.*

No, Ash had sought Alice out and made plans to begin with. Ash had decided to sleep over two nights in a row. And yes, she may have been asleep, but it was Ash who'd rolled into Alice's bed-territory and humped her, not the other way around. Alice had enjoyed it, but she hadn't initiated it. And okay, Alice had checked Ash out on more than one occasion, and she'd flirted, big time, but that was just what Alice did.

At least all the energy expended on trying to figure out Ash hadn't been spent mooning over Fran.

Alice reached for her phone on the coffee table and called Maggie again. Her sister's droll tone answered after three rings.

"What tragedy has befallen you this time, dear sister? Wait, don't tell me, dead car, shattered heart, lost phone, broken bone?"

Alice pouted. "None of those, actually. But if it was, you'd only be finding out three hours later, and you'd feel pretty bad right now."

"No, not really, darling. You are a grown woman." The sound grew muffled. "Yes, those. Not the cheap ones."

"Where are you?"

"In Waitrose, picking up a few groceries. You should try that sometime."

"I'll have you know, my fridge is fully stocked right now."

At the thought of her fridge, Alice swung her feet off the couch and padded over to it. The sound on the line grew muffled again.

"No, Markus. You know we don't get that brand. Honestly. Yes, the hot ones."

"Shall I try you again later, Mags?"

"No, just a sec. Christ, Markus. A chunk of the Beaufort and maybe the Morbier, too. You know what *you* like."

Alice stood in the yellow glow of her fridge, considering its contents.

Maggie breathed into the phone. "Sorry, Al. He's bloody useless. Don't ever marry a man, okay?"

"I think we're safe on that count." Alice chuckled and snapped off a yoghurt pot from a six-pack.

"Right, I've left him in the queue at the cheese counter. What's up?"

"I really can call you back later, if it's not a good—"

"Now is fine. Speak. I'm standing near the quinoa, so it's quiet."

"I'm fucked, Mags. Totally fucked. You were right, as always. I've gone and caught feelings for Ash."

"The doctor?"

"Yeah. I mean, I really like her. I can't stop thinking about her. It's driving me fucking nuts." Alice licked the spoon.

"And does she like you?"

"I thought she did. I'm normally good at picking up that sort of thing, but maybe I've read it all wrong. Every time I think she's about to say something or make a move, it fizzles into nothing. And worst of all, she keeps saying that we're friends."

"Right, okay. Well then, it sounds like you've got to stop being such a trashy lesbo-nymph."

"Oi!"

"You said yourself that you could use a friend right now. So, this is your chance."

"There's a reason I don't have any female friends apart from you."

"Yes, because you sleep with them all and fuck it up."

"No, I mean that women typically don't get to know me for the friendship. I don't really know how to—"

"Well, whatever you're doing with that doctor seems to be working. She wants to hang out with you all the time, doesn't she?"

Alice agreed through a mouthful of creamy yoghurt.

"You can just enjoy someone's company without having to sleep with them."

"Yeah, I know, but I can't get *that* out of my head. Perhaps I need to go out and get laid to take my mind off Ash's amazing ar—"

"Please don't finish that sentence."

"Arms." Alice chuckled. "I was going to say *arms*. Honestly, she has very toned biceps." Even though Maggie couldn't see her, Alice flexed her muscle to demonstrate.

"Right, okay. Perhaps you should give yourself a break. Think of it like a sort of detox. You've just come out of something pretty intense with Fran, so take some time to cleanse your body. Clear your clogged chakras and it'll open your heart and mind to something truly transformational."

"Jesus, Mags, are they handing out samples of space cake at Waitrose or something?"

Maggie laughed, and Alice grinned into the phone.

"No, you know what I'm saying, though? Perhaps you're just trying to fill the void with someone else, when actually, you need that space for yourself?"

"I had wondered that."

"So a little distance between you and the doctor would be good. It'll help you get some perspective, hey?"

"Hmm, yeah, but I'm going to her brother's engagement party with her next weekend."

"Really?"

"Yeah, it's at some swanky hotel in Yorkshire. I've no idea what to wear, but I'll figure it out. Shame I ruined my Louboutins, they'd have been ideal."

"Okay, well, those sorts of occasions can heighten emotions, so try to keep your head. And you can always call me if you need to."

Alice scoffed a laugh. "What, and you'll answer three hours later?"

"Yeah, something like that. Right, I better make sure Markus hasn't got lost. Love you, Al."

"Love you too, Mags."

Alice cleaned the yoghurt pot with her tongue and wondered how her sister always managed to be so right about everything in Alice's life, and yet somehow, she herself had ended up married to a prick like Markus.

## 20

# TRUSCOTE & FUCKING DALTON

*A*s per her new weekday morning routine, Alice sat in bed with a cup of coffee and scrolled through job listings. So far all she'd received in return for her efforts was a handful of copy-and-paste rejections — *over-qualified, under-qualified, more suitable applicants, blah, blah, blah*.

At this rate, she'd be begging Maggie to ask Markus if there was anything going at his firm before the end of the month, but she wasn't quite prepared to sink that low just yet. Alice could sit comfortably on her high horse, at least until her next round of bills were due, and even then, she reckoned she might ask Maggie for a loan before she asked Markus for a job. She'd sooner put up with her sister's scowls than a workplace full of toxic masculinity, which she imagined involved a whole lot of backslapping, mansplaining, and general grunting. *No, thanks.*

Alice's laptop dinged with an incoming email, which

immediately grabbed her attention, seeing as it was from Catherine Truscote. Her eyes rapidly scanned the screen... 'Haven't been able to reach you on your mobile.'

*Yeah, because it's in a bush somewhere.*

'There are some urgent matters I need to discuss with you... Please come by the office. I have a clear afternoon today, if that works for you.'

Alice sat up straighter and placed her half-full mug of coffee on the bedside table.

*Urgent matters?*

She'd resigned, or been fired, or whatever — but given the grounds, surely Truscote couldn't be annoyed that she'd not served her notice period? Or perhaps Truscote hadn't been made aware of the truth? Alice really didn't fancy digging into it all with her, especially after her warning about Fran. And even if Jeremy had enlightened his colleague, it was unlikely he'd painted a pretty picture of Alice.

"Ow, shit." Alice grappled for a tissue to stem the blood flowing from a hangnail she'd ripped off her finger whilst wondering about Truscote and *fucking* Dalton. She popped her finger in her mouth and for a moment considered not going. *Why should I?*

But, principles aside, Alice couldn't deny the nagging urge to set things straight, and then there was that biting curiosity about these *urgent matters.*

Two hours later, Alice was buzzed into her old place of employment. They'd hired a new receptionist already, a mousy young thing called Stephanie, who looked out of her depth and far from the sort that Jeremy would be looking to ensnare for Fran. Still, the thought turned her stomach.

"I'll let Doctor Truscote know you're here," Stephanie squeaked.

Alice gave her a small nod of thanks and turned to the plants she used to lovingly tend, annoyed to see them wilting. She fingered one of the long skinny leaves of the yucca and gave it a sorry smile.

"You should really water these."

Stephanie looked startled. "Sorry?"

"The plants. They need watering."

"Er…" The young receptionist made to stand, but Truscote's office door opened, and the woman's formidable figure filled the frame.

"Alice, please come on in." Her thin lips tugged into a smile that didn't reach her eyes.

Alice swallowed. She didn't know why she suddenly felt intimidated by her former employer, but that was the feeling tightening her chest as she stepped across the carpet tiles and into Truscote's office.

"Goodness, what did you do?"

Alice glanced down at the pink plaster cast that had captured Truscote's attention. "Oh, this? It's a long story. I'm fine."

"Okay, good," Truscote replied, thankfully not pursuing the details. "Stephanie, fetch some coffees, please. Don't forget to heat the milk this time."

Truscote glanced at Alice and rolled her eyes as she closed the door. "She's a temp. Started a week ago. As nervous as a mouse, but we needed someone to answer the phones at least, after..."

"Yes, about that. I'm hoping Jeremy explained why I left so suddenly."

Truscote tilted her head, her steely gaze narrowing with such barbed intensity Alice felt as if she were wilting like the office plants.

Alice rolled her shoulders back to remind herself that she actually had bones. Truscote motioned for her to sit and stepped behind her desk.

"Jeremy didn't need to explain. I'm more than aware of what happened between you and... Francesca." Her lips puckered as if the name had a bitter taste.

"Oh God, don't tell me you were in on it too?" Alice covered her face with her palms.

"No, of course not. Let's just say this isn't an isolated incident. I tried to warn you."

"You said Jeremy was a good man."

Truscote leaned forward and steepled her fingers. "I didn't say he was without his flaws, Francesca being the greatest of them."

Alice pointed to the wall in the direction of Jeremy's office. "He knew all along that I was sleeping with his wife. And when it came out, he offered me more money to keep it going. How depraved is that?"

Truscote cocked her head. "Well, can you blame him?"

"Sorry?"

"A woman like that is fire; capable of burning every-thing around her if not contained. Did she tell you she wanted to leave Jeremy for you? Did she say she wanted to make a go of things?"

Alice nodded. "How did you know that?"

"Isn't it obvious?"

Alice frowned and Truscote sniffed at the inconvenience of having to spell it out. "Francesca once told me the same thing. She promised me everything, but it wasn't real. You're just another cycle in a Francesca Dalton shitstorm."

"Wait, when were you and Fran together?"

Truscote waved a hand in front of her face. "A very long time ago. Our university days. Francesca was seeing both Jeremy and I for a while. It was... challenging."

"I can relate."

"As the story goes... in the end, Jeremy won, or should I say, *his trust fund won.*"

"I guess I should've listened to you."

Truscote looked at her with a sad smile. "Alice, I didn't invite you here just to say, 'I told you so.'"

"So, why am I here?"

A small knock came at the door and Stephanie entered with a rattling tray. The two women watched in loaded silence as Stephanie set down the cups with shaky hands. Alice stifled a giggle as the young woman curtseyed before backing out of the room. When the door clicked to a close, Truscote steepled her fingers over the desk again.

"Jeremy and I have sought legal counsel."

Alice shrugged. "For...?"

"Regarding the termination of your employment."

"You're suing me?"

Truscote chuckled. "No, no. Quite the opposite. We wanted to make sure that we do the right thing by you, and by the firm, of course." Truscote slid a desk drawer open and pulled out a thin manila file. "As such, I'm putting this confidentiality agreement to you. You'll see that it includes a settlement figure."

Alice frowned as she struggled to keep pace.

"Basically, if you sign this agreement, you're giving your word that you won't take the whole Dalton escapade any further." She waved her hand again as if dispelling a bad smell. "Think of it as a non-disclosure agreement. The terms are negotiable, of course, but I think you'll find we've been more than generous with the settlement amount we've proposed."

Alice scoffed. "Jeremy couldn't buy me for his wife, so you're buying my silence instead?"

Truscote's thin lips moulded into an uncomfortable-looking grin as she passed the file over the desk. Alice wondered how many times Truscote had done this before as she tentatively lifted the cover of the manila file and glanced at the white paperwork. Her eyes widened when she read the proposed sum. *Holy shit.*

"Do take the time to read it properly." Truscote lifted her mug and sipped the hot coffee.

"But… this is more than you used to pay me."

"As I said, we've been generous."

Alice's mind spiralled. Should she feel elated at being offered this life-changing amount of money or outraged at the suggestion she could be bought off? Although this felt different to Jeremy's offer, it still made her feel cheap, and with that thought, she thrust the file back to Truscote.

"Keep your money. I wasn't even going to say anything to anyone about the Daltons, anyway."

Irritation flickered over the older woman's face. She fixed her cold eyes on Alice, staring at her like a puzzle she couldn't solve. Alice glared back defiantly until Truscote exhaled the breath she'd apparently been holding.

"Look, Alice, you've been wronged quite badly. I probably shouldn't say this, but if you had the motivation, you could take this further and probably get more. You'd ruin T&D's reputation and put us out of business, no doubt."

"Yeah, but I—"

Truscote held up a hand. "I know you don't want to do that, and I'm grateful. But I want you to take the money. It'll give me peace of mind, and compensate you for the inconvenience of... well, everything. It can't have been easy for you."

Alice sat back. The money would be breathing space. She could pay off her credit card, sort out a new car — new to her at least — pay Maggie back in full, at last, and still have some left over to save. Maybe a little to spend, too. But she really should run it by Maggie first to make sure she wasn't doing anything stupid.

"Can I take this away and think about it?"

Truscote nodded. "Yes, of course. I expected you to do that."

"And you said that the er, terms... are negotiable?"

Truscote narrowed her eyes.

"I don't mean the money. I just wondered whether there were a couple of other things we could agree on."

"Like what?"

"Well, firstly there are the office plants. If no one is going to take care of them, then I'd like to give them a good home."

"Yes, you can have the plants, Alice." Truscote's lips lost their battle to hold back a grin.

"And I have this friend. He's in hospital at the moment, awaiting a psych assessment before they'll even consider discharging him. There's a waiting list, so they've no idea when it'll be. Poor guy, he's just lost his brother. I know you have a lot on, but would you be willing to take the case pro bono, as soon as you're available?"

Truscote nodded slowly as she drew in a breath. "My caseload is pretty heavy at the moment, but I'll see what I can do."

Alice nodded and looked down at the file she was now clutching in her lap. "For what it's worth, I think you still have a hold on her. Even after all this time, she still—"

"Don't." Truscote pursed her lips. "Please."

Alice shrugged and got to her feet. "Okay, then. I'll be in touch."

"WHOA, ALICE. SLOW DOWN. BREATHE, WILL YOU?"

"Sorry, it's just... you're not going to believe this. Are you free? I'll come over. It'll be easier if I show you," Alice panted as she powered along the street, as fast as she could, whilst hoisting a large yucca plant under her good arm. Thankfully, she hadn't bumped into Jeremy. She couldn't stomach even the thought of facing him right now.

"I'm just finishing up at work. Markus is in town though, shall I ask him to swing by yours and give you a lift? Assuming your car is still knackered."

"That's a very fair assumption, Mags." *Bloody Markus though.* She'd rather fork out for a taxi than share an uncomfortable car-ride with the prick, but she shouldn't spend money she didn't have... yet. "A lift would be great, thanks."

"I'll text him to pick you up from yours. I'll be home by the time you arrive."

ALICE REACHED THE TOP OF THE STAIRS AND frowned at the large bouquet propped against her front door. Her mind flickered to Ash as she placed the yucca on the top step and picked up the decadent arrangement of roses and orchids. *But why would Ash leave flowers?*

Alice's heart plummeted as she pulled the card from the cellophane and read the message written in Fran's familiar looping handwriting.

*'I'll be at The Dog & Duck*
*tomorrow, 12pm x'*

"Good for you," she muttered and turned over the slip of card. Something was also scrawled on the reverse.

*Please come, I'll explain everything.*

Alice looked around, assuming the woman who'd been brazen enough to track her phone was probably watching her from somewhere. She tucked the card amongst the flowers and dropped the bouquet on the doormat.

Inside, Alice watered the yucca and popped it on the dining table to bask in the remaining daylight.

"Welcome to Chez Alice." She touched one of the waxy green leaves. "I hope you'll be happier here."

In the bedroom, she switched her blouse for a comfortable sweatshirt, tugging her cast through the sleeve and tracing her finger over the words Ash had written in black marker.

### HANDLE WITH CARE X

Ash would be starting her shift soon, so Alice tapped out a quick text, even though she was trying to heed Maggie's advice and put a little distance between them. Her phone pinged with a response right away, and a stupid grin tugged at Alice's lips.

> It's been a VERY quiet day without you in it. In other words, I've missed you. Can't wait to hear your news. I'll call you on my break X

A car horn honked outside. *That'll be Markus. Lazy prick.*

Alice spritzed on some perfume and scrunched her curls. On her way to the front door, she paused, then dashed back to the kitchenette to grab a bottle of wine from the fridge; the one Maggie liked. Three loud knocks sounded on the front door, which she opened to Markus. *Impatient prick.* He grinned and presented the bouquet to her.

"Thanks, you shouldn't have," she said flatly.

"Er, I didn't, they were out here and…"

Alice rolled her eyes. "Yeah, I know."

"Waste not, want not. If you don't want them, I'll give them to Maggie."

"Yeah, whatever," she said, locking the door behind her. *Cheap prick.*

Markus glanced over as Alice slid into the passenger seat. "Need any help with your seatbelt?"

"No, why would I?"

He shrugged. "Because of your arm. Sorry, I was just trying to—"

"Not every woman needs a man to save her, Markus."

Markus huffed and shifted the car into reverse. Talk-Sport radio chattered in the background as they navigated the rush-hour traffic, a blur of traffic lights and taillights, then fading skies yawning over dusky fields as they rolled out of town.

Markus pulled up at the gate, but instead of pressing the button to open it, he cut the ignition. After a minute or two, Alice looked at him.

"Aren't we going in?"

"In a minute."

"Oohkay." Alice widened her eyes and looked down at the bottle of wine she'd wedged between her knees. Markus unclipped his seatbelt and twisted around to her.

"What?" she asked, shaking her head.

"I know you don't like me very much, Alice. And yes, I understand it's for good reasons."

Alice scoffed and traced her finger through the condensation on the bottle.

"Just hear me out, alright? I fucked up a couple of years back. Big time. I nearly lost Maggie over it, and fuck…" He slapped the steering wheel. "We all make mistakes, right?"

Alice speared him with a death stare. "You don't deserve her."

"I know I don't. But I love her."

"If you loved her, you wouldn't have fucked your intern and your fucking secretary."

"Yeah, alright. I messed up, I know. You're not exactly snow-white, are you?"

Alice narrowed her eyes. "Why are we having this conversation?"

Markus sighed. "I want to put things right with you, too."

Alice stared out of the passenger window, willing this bullshit to be over.

"As you know, Maggie and I are going through counselling. I'm seeing a therapist, too. I'll do whatever it takes to fix our marriage because I love your sister and I'm so sorry I hurt her."

Alice turned and glared at him. "Good, because if you ever hurt her again, I'll..."

Markus held up his hands. "I won't. You have my word."

"Fine. Can we go inside now, please?"

"HEY, YOU TWO WERE AGES. WAS THE TRAFFIC bad?" Maggie greeted Alice with a hug and kiss and took the wine. "Ooh, you've bought the good stuff. Are we getting all fancy now that we're hanging out with a doctor?"

"Oh, do shut up, Margaret." Alice grinned.

Maggie ignored the swipe and turned to Markus, who held out the flowers to her.

"What's this in aid of?"

"Can't a chap bring his wife flowers from time to time?"

Alice scoffed, and Markus shot her a sheepish grin as Maggie took the bouquet. *Thick prick.*

"They're beautiful, thank you. Oh, what's this?" She pulled out the card from between the stems and glanced at it, then with a sharp inhale she thrust the flowers into Markus's broad chest and stormed off.

He looked at Alice, bewildered. She smirked and followed Maggie into the kitchen, where she was frantically uncorking the wine.

"So, Fran is still on the scene, then?"

"If that's what you call leaving flowers and cryptic messages on my doorstep, then yes."

"Are you going to meet her tomorrow?"

"I don't know. Hadn't thought about it. Probably not, no."

Maggie tipped the wine bottle and straw-coloured liquid splashed into the glass. "Maybe you should."

"Really? I thought that'd be the last thing you'd say."

"Closure, perhaps?"

Alice shrugged.

"It could help you get that perspective we were talking about."

"How so?"

"If seeing Fran stirs up all the old feelings, then maybe your crush on the doctor isn't as serious as you thought?" Maggie offered Alice a glass and clinked it with her own. "Perhaps just try not to sleep with her again?"

"Mags, it's over. I don't want Fran. She's fifty shades of fucking nuts."

Still clutching the flowers, Markus padded into the kitchen and guffawed. "Shouldn't it be fifty shades of cray?"

Maggie shot him a filthy look before turning her attention back to Alice.

"Ooh, talking of nuts..." Maggie rifled through one of the kitchen cupboards and pulled out a bag of salted peanuts, which she poured into a bowl.

"How's your friend, by the way? George, is it?"

"Not so good. His brother died, that's why he ended up

337

having an episode which landed him in hospital. Now he's waiting for a psych assessment, which he has to have before they'll discharge him. Poor guy, I really feel for him."

Maggie raised her eyebrows. "A psychiatric assessment?"

"Yeah, someone needs to check him over to make sure he's not a risk to himself." Alice reached for the nuts. "Anyway, would you mind looking over this, please? It's why I called you earlier." She slid the manila file across the marble counter.

Maggie opened the file, sipping her wine as her eyes scanned the pages.

"Markus?" she said without looking up.

"Huh?" He lifted his eyes from his phone.

"Can you look over this, please?"

"Uh, yeah, what is it?"

"An NDA and settlement offer Alice got from T&D. What do you think?"

Markus flicked through the paperwork and whistled. He glanced up at Alice.

"If I were you, I'd accept this. It's a substantial offer. Unless you have the time and energy to take them to court? I think you've got grounds, but it'll be a lot of hassle."

Alice blinked at him and looked back to Maggie. "I didn't ask for any of this. I'm not taking them to court. I mean, I'm in the wrong too. I was literally screwing my boss's wife."

"Yeah, but he lured you into it. Surely, that's got to be a form of sexual harassment?"

Markus nodded. "One hundred per cent."

*Because he'd know all about that.*

Maggie scooped a handful of nuts into her mouth. "And he fired you when you refused to sleep with his wife for money. Truscote knows how fucked they'd be if it all got out."

"I suppose when you put it like that…"

Markus placed a heavy hand on Alice's shoulder and squeezed. "Take the money, Al."

# PERSPECTIVE

*U*nder a threatening slate sky, Alice hesitated in the doorway of The Dog & Duck. A morning consumed with panic about what to wear had left her feeling flustered. She obviously wanted to look good to make her ex-lover acutely aware of what she'd lost, yet not so good that Fran would assume the effort had been made for the wrong reasons.

After emptying the contents of the wardrobe onto her bed, Alice had opted for jeans and a light blue blouse, with ballet flats instead of heels. It looked like rain, so when heading out the door, Alice flung on her trench coat. Now, fingering the torn sleeve strap, she recalled the last time she'd worn it, and how little she'd been wearing underneath.

According to her watch, the woman who'd had her heart and fucked her around for the past two years was waiting inside the pub. And as frustrated as Alice was with

Fran, when she saw her a week ago, she'd told Alice that she loved her. Fran had paired the declaration with an insult and a threat, but even so, it was a first. And even if, according to Ash, Alice did deserve more, what's to say that she'd ever find it?

The sky rumbled and rain started to spot from the dark clouds, so Alice dashed inside, ducking her head under the wooden lintel, and emerging into the cosy, familiar pub. She glanced around the room, almost empty aside from an old man nursing a pint at the bar and a middle-aged couple sharing a bowl of onion rings. Sitting at their usual table in the corner was Fran. She'd already clocked Alice and beckoned her over with a wave of her manicured hand.

As Alice approached, Fran stood.

"You came." Fran's painted lips stretched into a smile, but sadness flickered in her dark eyes. "I didn't know if you would, after... everything." She held out her arms, and despite herself, Alice stepped into the embrace. Clutching her tightly, Fran turned her face into Alice's neck and breathed her in. "God, I've missed you."

Alice's insides wrenched. "Okay, well..." she dropped her arms to her sides and pulled away. Fran looked mildly affronted, as if suddenly remembering that things between them had changed, but she shook it off with a flick of her hair.

"Right, let's get you a drink. Wine?"

*Alcohol would be a bad idea.* "I'll have an orange juice, please."

"Of course. Be right back." Instead of summoning the bar staff, like she usually did, Fran actually went to the bar, which gave Alice a moment to settle in.

Rain hammered at the wonky little windows as Alice shucked off her coat and sat in the seat opposite the one Fran had taken, with a table between them to reduce the opportunity for Fran to grope her, and for Alice to let her.

Returning with their drinks, Fran's eyes settled on Alice's pink plastered arm. "Oh, so it's actually broken, then?"

Alice nodded. "Afraid so."

"Oh, darling." Fran reached out for Alice's fingers poking from the end of her cast, but she moved her arm away, glimpsing Ash's inked inscription as she did.

"Why did you ask me to meet you, Fran?"

Fran lifted the glass of wine to her lips and tipped her head back, taking what Alice assumed was a fortifying mouthful. The idea that Fran needed liquid courage was absurd, yet here she was drinking barely after midday.

"Right, I'll get straight to the point, shall I?"

Alice sipped her juice and nodded.

Fran leaned in. "I meant what I said. At your place. Last week."

Alice blinked. "Which bit?"

"The bit where I said l love you, of course."

"Oh, that."

Fran's dark eyes bored into her. "I thought that's what you wanted to hear, Alice. I hoped that if I told you how much you mean to me, then maybe we could—"

"It doesn't change anything, Fran." As they came out of her mouth, Alice realised those words were true.

"Don't you love me?" Fran reached for Alice's hand again. This time, Alice didn't move away, and watched as Fran laced their fingers together.

Alice lifted her gaze, not to Fran's eyes but to her slender neck. The gentle curve of her jawline to her collarbone summoned thoughts of the way Fran moaned when Alice kissed and caressed the hollow of her throat, and how she'd always been amazed by Fran's willingness to expose such a delicate part of herself. But then, if either of them was going to rip a throat out, it wouldn't be Alice, would it?

"Alice?"

"Sorry, what?"

"I asked whether you love me."

Alice looked into those dark eyes that had once sucked her in like black holes. She'd lost herself in those eyes, in this woman, and she'd thought that maybe it was love, at one point, *but—*

"No, I don't."

Fran flinched and slumped back. "Is this because of Jeremy? I don't think you understand why I can't leave him, Alice."

Alice narrowed her eyes. "I never asked you to leave Jeremy. That was your idea, remember?"

Fran stared at her wine glass.

"I even said it was a bad idea, but you were insistent, and you made me want that too...it's like when you don't realise you're hungry and someone suggests chips, then suddenly you're starving and all you can think of is the taste of hot, salty chips. Well, that was me... I didn't even know I was hungry."

Fran looked up, her thick lashes shuttering over her dark eyes. The corners of her taut mouth twitched, but she said nothing.

"I started dreaming of a life with you. I was even going to sell my flat to make that happen. It's all I have, Fran, and I was prepared to give it up for you, but when it came to it, you wouldn't leap for me." Alice leaned forward, peering into the older woman's face. "That isn't love, is it?"

Fran squeezed her eyes shut, and a tear trickled down her cheek. Alice resisted the urge to reach out, clasp her hands and comfort her. Had she been too harsh? Too cruel with her words? *No, she was speaking her truth.* Alice felt behind the chair for her coat and pulled out a balled-up tissue from the pocket, which she held out to Fran.

Fran took it and dabbed her eyes. "I'm sorry, I can't—" With a deep sigh, she kneaded her fist into her chest, as if massaging away indigestion.

The wind howled outside, rattling the windows in their frames. Alice turned her attention back to Fran, who was still rubbing her chest. "What did you mean when you said I don't understand why you can't leave Jeremy?"

Fran released a shuddering breath. "Everyone thinks Jeremy is this wonderfully kind, caring man who'd do anything for his beloved wife. But no one really knows what he's like."

Alice's resolve was crumbling with the rare sight of

Fran's vulnerability. She covered Fran's hand with her own. "Then tell me."

Fran sniffed. "As you're aware, there have been others before you. Jeremy has always been a good sport about it. He's asked very little of me yet given so much. And that arrangement worked for us. At least, until you."

Fran glanced at Alice with such smouldering intensity that an unexpected ripple of desire shot through her. Alice shook her head to recalibrate, and a fleeting grin swiped over Fran's lips. She leaned in and lifted a hand to touch Alice's face.

"I knew I had to have you, from the first moment I saw you in that dreary little office, like a beautiful wildflower growing in the cracks of a pavement. And Jeremy being Jeremy, he helped to make it happen."

"I don't really want to hear about how you both manipulated me. It's humiliating and a bit twisted, don't you think?"

Alice's raised voice attracted the turned heads of the middle-aged couple. Fran glared at them until they turned back around, muttering between themselves.

"Look, I'm telling you because I fell for you hard, Alice. Before you, it was always just a bit of fun, until I got bored, and it fizzled out. Then I'd move on to the next lover."

"Wow!" Alice's lip curled in disgust. "What about Truscote?"

Fran scowled. "Ancient history, we were barely adults. She's never let it go." The fine lines around Fran's eyes creased as she narrowed them. "Don't you hear what I'm saying? Things were different with you. You made me dream of some other life that I was willing to leave Jeremy for. Willing to compromise on the lifestyle I'm accustomed to. That's why I suggested it to you."

"So, what changed?"

"I told Jeremy that I wanted a divorce. I said I wanted to be with you, and it was high time we went our separate ways. Only then did he reveal the tight web he'd woven for me." Fran's voice cracked over the words.

"What do you mean?"

"If I ever leave him, Alice, I'll get nothing." Fran chopped her hand through the air. "Not a penny. Zilch. Diddly-squat. He had it all tied up right from the start of our marriage. He said that because of my nature, he'd put provisions in place to protect himself. It's probably Catherine-bloody-Truscote I have to thank for that, given it was her I was seeing at the time."

Alice frowned. "So what? You'd have got nothing from Jeremy, but you'd have had me, Fran. I don't have much, but it's not nothing. We'd have had each other."

Fran scoffed and fixed Alice with a withering glare before draining the last of the wine from her glass.

Alice recalled how insanely Fran had behaved the night her coat got torn; the night she found George and met Ash. That night Fran had ranted about living off soup and pecking up crumbs, and now the truth about Jeremy made sense of Fran's change of heart.

*What was it Truscote had said?* 'In the end, Jeremy won, or should I say, his trust fund won.' Money and status were Francesca Dalton's true loves, and nothing would ever come before them.

Fran sniffed and nodded to Alice's empty glass. "Shall we have another?"

Alice glanced at her watch. "No, I think I should—"

"Can't we just go back to how we were before? You and me, and all our wonderful weekends spent escaping to lovely places and enjoying each other."

Alice considered Fran's proposal for a moment, rolling it around in her mind like a hard-boiled sweet, until it cracked and she could digest the pieces. Sweet at first, but ultimately it left a sour aftertaste. It would never be enough, *not now.*

"Thank you, but no. I was happy with that once, but I feel like I've been shaken awake. I need more from someone than you're prepared to give."

"I thought once you'd had a taste of the finer things you'd be reluctant to give them up."

Alice smiled politely. "I've realised that you and I have vastly different definitions of *the finer things.*" Her mind flashed with the thought of being curled up on her couch with Ash, eating Chinese takeaway straight from the cartons, or tucking into buckets of tea and bacon butties at Porky's.

She looked back to Fran, pity overriding her other emotions. This woman who'd once held so much power over her would never be truly rich, but Alice could be. She stood and struggled to pull her coat sleeve over the plaster cast as Fran looked on, bewildered.

"Well, thanks for—"

Fran slid a key card across the table towards her.

"What's this?" Alice asked.

347

"I'm staying at the usual. I didn't know if you'd fancy... you know, for old times' sake?"

"Fran—"

"No strings, Alice. One for the road... if you like." Fran cocked her head.

Alice considered the key card for a moment. "Thank you, but no."

"Right, well. That's that then."

"You'll be okay, won't you?"

Fran's cold, dark eyes set a hard stare on Alice. "Yes, of course. Why wouldn't I be?"

Alice smiled and shook her head.

AT SOME POINT DURING THE RENDEZVOUS WITH Fran, the storm had blown over, and vast patches of blue sky yawned between fluffy white clouds. Alice hailed an Uber with the app and walked out to the main road and out of view of the pub, to avoid any possibility of a Francesca Dalton epilogue. She had nothing left to say. They were officially done, and Alice felt... relieved. Fran could *move on to her next lover,* as she'd put it, and Alice could move on with her life.

Alice leaned against a wooden post. Overhead, the hand-painted sign for The Dog & Duck creaked on its hinges in the light breeze. The Uber app showed the car on its way with a six-minute wait, so she dialled Maggie.

"Sister dearest," Maggie answered in a droll tone.

Alice laughed. "Just wanted to let you know you were right again."

"Of course I was. What was I right about this time?"

"Fran. I met her, like you said. It was good closure. And I didn't sleep with her, even though the offer was there."

"Well, thanks for sharing that."

"Are you alright?"

"Why wouldn't I be?"

"After the little mix-up with Markus and the flowers?"

"Ah, that was nothing. He doesn't think sometimes. The silly bastard sent an enormous bouquet to me at work this morning. Bloody mortifying."

"Ah, at least he's trying, Mags. Give him a chance."

"Hmm, since when did you join his cheerleading squad?"

Alice puffed out a laugh. "I haven't, but he actually does love you, you know? He might be a clueless, toffy twat... and in my unqualified opinion, you could've done much better for yourself. But you chose him for a reason, and he's hanging in there, fighting for you, despite all your prickliness. That has to be worth something, right?"

Maggie mock-gasped. "Oi! You're supposed to be on my side."

"I am and I always will be. But, you know... perspective."

Alice let the words land, watching as her torn coat strap flapped in the breeze.

Maggie cleared her throat and changed the subject.

"So, are you going to tell that cute doctor how you feel about her?"

A grin stretched across Alice's lips. "You think she's cute, too?"

Maggie's eye-roll was almost audible. "Yes, Alice. She's hot. And single, right?"

"Yeah, she's single."

"Well, go for it, if that's what you want."

"But what if she doesn't want that and I blow the chance of having an actual friend?"

Maggie chuckled. "You're going to blow the friendship part if you keep drooling over her when you think she's not looking anyway, so you may as well tell her how you feel."

"Okay, I will. Maybe at the weekend. Like you said, emotions are heightened at these events. Oooh, talking of the party—"

Maggie groaned. "Oh, here it comes."

"Don't, Mags, you know I'm going to be good for the money. I've signed that settlement and I'm on my way to drop it off to Truscote now. Then I was going to look for something to wear. Please, just a little loan until the money comes through."

"Christ, you're bloody hopeless, but alright. I'll transfer some money now."

"Thank you, darling sis. You're the best. I'll pay back everything, I promise. Now I just have to find something that either goes with or goes over this bloody cast."

"I'm sure a sparkly pink number will do the job, Barbie."

"Shut up, you. Ooh, my Uber is here, gotta go." Alice pinned the phone to her ear with her shoulder as she opened the rear door of the white car that pulled up alongside her. "Love you, bye... and don't forget the money," she added before hanging up.

Through the tinted window, Alice looked back at the pub, imagining Fran seated inside, scowling into a glass of red wine.

"Goodbye, Fran," she said under her breath as the Uber sped off.

2 2

ONESIE

*T*he rest of the week passed in a blur. Alice collected her remaining office plant-babies and hand-delivered the signed settlement agreement. A very relieved Truscote confirmed she'd juggled her diary to accommodate an appointment with George. Alice relayed the news to a delighted George when she dropped by with a cheerful bouquet of daffodils and hyacinths.

Alice enjoyed a couple of lunch dates with Ash, and on Ash's night off, she invited Alice over. Her place turned out to be the spacious top floor of a Regency townhouse, and it looked like a show home, which Ash had brushed off by saying, "It's only tidy because I'm never here." Once Alice had finished gawping at everything, they ate Thai take-away and binge-watched half a dozen episodes of *Friends* — seriously, *Friends*. Then Ash drove her home just before midnight, muttering something about an early morning suit fitting in the next county.

If this was friendship, and all Ash had to offer, then

Alice would gladly take it. Yet, ever since their meeting in the park, when Ash had talked about her ex, things felt a little less comfortable between them. Alice tried not to overthink it, but wondered if her own unspoken feelings were the problem. Needless to say, she was having doubts about airing them now.

Just three days after delivering the signed agreement, the settlement money landed in Alice's bank account. First things first, she paid off her credit card, and then she repaid all the money she owed her sister. As a thank-you, she booked a spa weekend for Maggie and Markus, and even though she suspected Maggie might enjoy it more, she had to admit they'd both been there for her when times were tough.

Following two unsuccessful shopping trips, Alice found the perfect outfit online; a sparkly black jumpsuit with long puffy sleeves that would cover her pink cast. Of course, she hadn't been able to resist the perfect strappy heels to go with it. Or the matching clutch bag.

She'd tried everything on when it arrived, but now, all done up and twirling in front of the mirror, she really admired the fit — the jumpsuit hugged her waist and flowed around her curves perfectly. She wanted Ash to see her put together properly for once, so she'd taken her time getting ready, cajoling her curls into shape and putting on her face.

When Ash knocked on the door, Alice exhaled a long breath before opening it.

"Wow," they said at the sight of each other, and nervous laughter burst from them. Ash looked more done up than Alice had ever seen her. She'd swept her hair back in a way that accentuated her striking features, especially her eyes. *Fuck the party.* Alice wanted to close the door and push Ash up against it.

"Alice, you look…" Ash breathed heavily. "Like a movie star. I'm, just… wow, look at you."

"I could say the same to you." She reached out and touched the velvet fabric of Ash's embroidered longline jacket. "I love this."

"Yeah?" Ash looked down at her outfit. "I had it made especially."

"That's why it looks so perfect on you."

Ash held Alice's gaze for a moment, then released a breathy laugh. "We better get going if we're to miss the traffic."

"Yeah, of course. Let me just grab my bag."

"I'll take this for you." Ash picked up Alice's small wheelie suitcase and laughed. "Bloody hell, Alice. You know we're only going for a night, don't you?"

By the time they hit the motorway, the coffee Ash had made for the trip was at perfect drinking temperature.

"Mmm, thanks for thinking to bring coffee." Alice sipped from a reusable mug with a university logo printed on it.

Ash smiled but kept her eyes on the road. "You're welcome. I think I remembered how you like it?"

"It's spot on."

Ash muttered under her breath as she indicated and accelerated into the inside lane to get around a middle-lane-hog. Her knuckles turned white as she gripped the steering wheel.

"How are you feeling about seeing your family?"

Ash sighed. "Oh, you know. It would've been easier if Indi hadn't let me down."

Alice winced. "Perhaps I shouldn't have come?"

Ash glanced across and flashed her a big smile. "No, sorry, I didn't mean it like that. I'm delighted you're my plus one, Al." Her grip on the steering wheel tightened. "It's just what I was explaining before... how the weight of everyone's expectations can be pretty heavy."

"I get that, but hopefully having a friend on your arm will make it easier than facing everything alone."

Ash inhaled sharply, then opened her mouth as if to speak, but she said nothing.

"So, tell me about your family, and anything else I need to know. I don't want to come across as a total moron."

Ash laughed and spent the rest of the journey filling Alice in on the who's who, including all the people to avoid.

"Not that you'll be leaving my side," Ash said with a wide-eyed look which said, *please, don't let that happen.*

After a while, the tension eased in Ash's arms. She rolled her neck and relaxed back into the driver's seat with the air of a woman on her way to a party rather than an inquisition. Alice listened attentively, repeating and, no doubt, mispronouncing the names Ash reeled off. She wasn't good with names at the best of times.

Ash snickered. "Don't worry, there won't be a test. All you need to remember is that my brother is Nik and he's engaged to Sukhi. They've been together since they were kids, so it's about bloody time they tied the knot."

ASH'S CAR CRUNCHED TO A STOP AT THE END OF A sweeping gravel driveway. Alice peered through the windscreen at the magnificent venue, its weathered facade bathed in the warm hues of the setting sun. She turned to Ash, who was already looking at her with the hint of a smile.

"You ready?" Alice asked.

Ash puffed out a laboured breath. "As ready as I can be." A deep line appeared between her eyebrows, so Alice reached over the centre console and took her hand.

"Don't worry, I'll be right with you the whole time and I'll do my best to deflect any unwanted conversations, okay?"

Ash nodded and looked up through her lashes. "I'm pleased you're here. Plus, Indi wouldn't have looked anywhere near as good as you do in that sparkly onesie."

Alice gasped. "It isn't a onesie, it's a jumpsuit!"

"Well, whatever it is." Ash grinned. "You look incredible. It took my breath away when I saw you this morning." She turned Alice's hand over and traced a finger across her palm.

*Friends don't say things like that.* Heat crept from Alice's chest to her neck as she stared back into those dark brown eyes.

"Ash, there's something I—"

A loud rap of knuckles on the driver's side window caused them to jump apart.

"Oh my God, Nik!" Ash scrambled for the door handle and jumped out, hugging her brother. "Look at your beard! You almost look like a proper grown-up!"

"Almost? I'm thirty-two." He honked out a laugh.

Alice shuffled her feet by the front of the car, trying to stop her heels from sinking into the gravel. Ash turned to her and held out an arm.

"Nik, this is my friend, Alice." Nik reached out and shook her hand. "Alice, meet my annoying little brother, Nikhil."

"Thanks for coming along, Alice."

Alice smiled politely, trying not to stare too hard into the brown eyes that were a copy-and-paste of his sister's. "Congratulations on your engagement."

Nik beamed a smile full of pristine white teeth, then turned on his heel to head back inside. "Right, let's get this party started."

Alice and Ash followed on until Nik spun around.

"Oh, Ash, there's something..." Nik stepped back toward her and whispered into her ear.

The colour leached from Ash's face as she searched Nik's with narrowed eyes.

"Why are you only telling me this now?"

Nik shook his head. "Sorry, I didn't know until I saw her arrive. Mum must have invited her, or Sukhi, you know they're still in touch." Nik scratched his beard. "I've not really been in control of the guest list."

Ash's mouth hung open as she reeled from whatever blow she'd been dealt.

"I'll, er... give you a minute. See you inside, yeah?" Nik grimaced at Alice before bouncing on his heels and jogging off.

Alice moved closer to Ash and placed a hand on her back. "What's the matter?"

Ash stared down at her loafers. "Sam's here. Mum must have invited her."

"Oh, shit."

"Yeah, shit! This is bad. I mean, I haven't seen her since she left for Edinburgh."

"She's married now, right?"

Ash nodded. "I knew today would be weird, but I didn't expect this."

"Okay, well... it's your family gathering and you have more of a right to be here than she does. So, you can go in with your head held high and with your gorgeous friend on your arm." Alice tried to coax a smile from Ash's frowning face.

Sucking in a breath, Ash stood up straight and proffered an arm to Alice. "Yeah, you're right. Come on."

"Wow!" Alice's eyes popped when they entered the reception room. Mags and Markus had had a flashy do when they tied the knot, but this was next level, and it was only the engagement party. Lush, white floral arrangements adorned the tables and fairy lights suspended from the ceiling twinkled like a starry night. A polished dance floor gleamed centre stage as the DJ spun songs to an empty floor.

"Welcome to your first Desi party." Ash held out her arms. "We go big."

"Yeah, you sure do."

Ash seemed to stiffen as she looked around the room, bustling with party guests. From a gaggle of women chatting in the corner came a loud squawk, and one woman threw her arms in the air.

"Ey up! Here comes trouble," Ash muttered to Alice as the squawking women made a beeline for them.

"And you suddenly sound very Yorkshire!"

"Yeah, that tends to happen when I'm around this lot."

"Asha, you're here at last." The woman's accent was a lively mix of Yorkshire and Punjabi. She took Ash into a rough hug. Pulling back, she looked at her with eyes full of adoration and touched her face.

"Look at you, all skin and bones. You've not been eating enough and you're working too hard." She tutted and rolled her eyes.

Ash laughed. "I'm fine, Mum."

An armful of gold bangles jangled as the woman waved her hand. "You're here now. But what is this you're wearing?" She stood back, eyeing Ash's outfit.

"You like it? I had it made at that place in Leicester you recommended."

Ash frowned as her mum fingered the embroidery, taking her time to assess the fabric and needlework.

"Mmm, yes. The Leicester place. Very good." She touched a palm to Ash's cheek again. "It suits you."

"Oh, I'm being rude. Alice, this is my mum, Rani."

Rani turned to Alice, her flushed round face crinkling in a smile. "Lovely to meet you, Alice. Thank you for making sure Asha arrived in one piece. Did you know her name means *hope*?" Rani's head swayed as she chuckled. "More like hopeless sometimes, especially when she hasn't got Indi with her."

"Mum!"

"Sorry, I didn't mean to embarrass you in front of your friend. Oh, did you see that Sam's here?"

Ash visibly gulped.

"She's brought that lovely husband with her. I hoped she would, and you'll see that there's hope for you yet. Hope for the hopeless."

"Mum, you know that I'm—"

Rani narrowed her eyes.

Alice softly touched Ash's elbow. "Shall we get a drink?"

"Yeah, I think I need one."

"Priya! You made it," Rani screeched, turning her attention to a woman across the room and dashing away.

Alice squeezed Ash's tense arm, the velvet material of her jacket soft under Alice's fingertips.

"Are you okay?"

Ash nodded, but she looked the opposite of okay.

As they cut across the centre of the room, Ash waved and smiled at a blur of faces, but didn't stop to speak with anyone. They jostled through a knot of rowdy blokes and sidled into position at the bar.

"Sorry to ask, but I can't help wondering, which one is Sam?"

Either Ash didn't hear, or she didn't want to answer, as she remained focused on trying to catch the bartender's eye.

Alice's eyes glided around the room, trying to pick out anyone she could imagine Ash with. Then she saw her. At least, she noticed there was *something* about the pretty woman in the electric-blue sari. Her arm was looped through that of a tall man with more hair on his face than his head. They stood chatting to another couple, but whilst she smiled and nodded, her eyes betrayed her attentiveness, darting around as if searching for someone. *Ash, probably.*

Alice turned back to Ash, who was now staring so hard at the bartender it looked like she was trying to levitate him.

"I think I know who she is."

"Huh?"

"Sam. I know which one she is."

"How?"

"I told you before, I've got a good gaydar. Ten o'clock. Blue sari. Hanging off the bald man."

Ash peered over her shoulder. A deep frown formed between her brows, and she groaned.

"I'm right, aren't I?"

Ash tried to suppress a smile. "Yeah, but no one likes a smart-arse."

The bartender finally turned to them. "Two gin and tonics, please... yeah, you better make them doubles."

Drinks in hand, they moved away from the bar to a quiet corner just as the DJ took to the microphone and introduced the bhangra band. A chorus of cheers echoed around the room as the dhol drummer started up and party guests flooded the dance floor. Their vibrant clothing shimmered in a kaleidoscope of colours as they danced around a couple in the centre; Nik and a stunning young woman who Alice assumed was his fiancée. The throng moved in time, winding their hands in the air and bumping their hips.

"Well, that got the party going." Alice tapped her hand on her leg to the beat, and glanced at Ash, who was scowling into her drink. Despite the confusing churn in her stomach, Alice knew what to say. "You should try to speak to her."

"Sorry, what?" Ash turned her ear towards Alice.

Alice leaned in, catching the woody scent of her. "I said, you should speak to Sam. It might help clear the air between you. Maybe it'll give you some closure?"

Ash grimaced. "What if she doesn't want to speak to me?"

"I think it's clear that she does. She hasn't stopped looking at you."

Ash's eyebrows peaked. "Really?"

Alice tilted her head in the direction of Sam. "Am I wrong?"

"Er, no. She's looking this way right now." Ash slowly raised her hand in a discreet wave at the woman across the room. "Right, well. Yeah. Maybe I'll speak to her after I've had another drink. Would you mind?"

Alice shook her head and gave Ash a small smile.

"I'll introduce you to some nice aunties so you're not on your own."

Alice waved a hand. "I'll be fine. I'm on a friend-making streak at the moment."

"Yeah?"

"Well, there's you, and George. Oh, and that nice nurse, Marjorie."

Ash spluttered a laugh. "Nurse Reid isn't your friend. She tolerates you at best, like she does everyone."

"How rude!" Alice grinned.

WITH ANOTHER G&T IN HAND, ALICE WATCHED AS Ash walked towards the pretty woman in blue. The woman's heavily made-up eyes fixed on Ash, her lips parting before forming a smile. As Ash drew near, Sam turned to say something to her husband; he gave a brief nod and continued his conversation with the other couple.

The two women stepped away together. Ash's shoulders looked rigid as she manoeuvred through the entrance, gesturing for Sam to go first.

And then they were gone. Off having a cosy chat in a quiet corner, where they'd no doubt talk about how much they missed each other and how nothing compared. Alice's heart sank to her heels at the thought, but she had no right to feel like that. She was here as Ash's confidante, her emotional crutch — *her friend.*

An emotional outpouring from Alice was the last thing Ash needed right now, *wasn't it?*

With a deep sigh, Alice pulled out her phone and tapped out a response to an earlier text from Maggie.

> We've arrived in one piece, although I'm not sure I'll be leaving that way.

She deleted the words and typed out something a little less melodramatic. No wonder Maggie always thought her life was a trash fire; she didn't exactly paint the best picture. Not wanting to be anti-social, she slipped her phone back into her clutch and peered around for someone to chat to. She didn't have to look far as Nik was striding over, his bearded face beaming.

"Ey up! She's gone and left you on your own, has she?"

The sound of Nik's accent made Alice's chest flutter, although admittedly she preferred it on Ash. Same went for those kind brown eyes, rich and warm like molten chocolate.

Alice breathed a laugh and swirled the liquid around her bulbous gin glass. "She'll be back. She's just nipped off for a chat with someone."

Nik glanced around and looked back to Alice. "Not Sam?"

Alice nodded. "Yeah."

He scratched his beard. "Sam really did her over, you know?"

"Yeah, Ash told me a bit about it. But I think it'll do them good to talk."

Nik gave her a curious smile. "She talked to me about you."

"She did?"

"Yeah, well at least I think it was about you. You've not known her long, have you?"

"No, not really. Only a couple of weeks, but—"

"Feels like longer?" Nik laughed. "Yeah, that's what she said."

Alice's stomach swooped. She took a long sip of her drink, the gin all but diluted by the melting ice. "So, did she say anything else about me?"

"Maybe." Mischief flickered in his eyes.

A loud cheer went up from the crowd and snatched their attention. A row of waiters filed into the room, wielding trays piled high with steaming dishes. The aromatic smell of onions, garlic, and spices filled the air.

"Ah, grub's up. I better dash or she'll divorce me before we're even married." Nik smiled and touched Alice's arm. "Make sure you get some food, alright?"

"I will, thank you. It smells delicious."

He started to walk away but turned back mid-stride. "In case I don't catch you alone again, I just wanted to say, be careful with her, won't you?"

"Sorry?"

"Ash acts all tough and like she's got it all together. But she's as shit-scared as the rest of us. I just don't want to see her broken again, like she was before."

"I understand, but we're just—"

Nik held up his hand and smiled. "Gotta dash."

## 23

# BIG MISTAKE, DOCTOR

*A*sh sauntered over as Alice shovelled in her last forkful of chicken curry.

"Mmm," Alice moaned as she devoured the mouthful. "You've got to try this. It is, without a doubt, the tastiest curry I've ever eaten."

"Well, we are known for our curries." Ash laughed as she took the vacant seat next to Alice.

"Yeah, but this was..." Alice chef's-kissed her fingers and reclined in the chair. "Sorry, I didn't wait for you, the smell was driving me wild."

Ash batted away the apology. "No, I'm glad you ate. I was gone for ages. There was a lot to say, I guess. But I see you made friends, so I don't feel so bad."

"I told you I would."

In the queue for the buffet, Alice had got chatting with a woman who turned out to be Ash's second cousin. She'd complimented Alice's outfit and guided her to avoid the extra-hot dishes so they didn't blow her head off. Alice was sitting with her and two older women, who insisted Alice call them 'auntie', plus an elderly man, who only had three teeth but a lovely big smile.

"So, how did it go?" Alice asked.

Ash drew in a breath. "Yeah, good. Really good, actually."

*What does that mean?* In what she thought was a subtle move, Alice peered over Ash's shoulder to see if she could spot Sam.

"She's gone. She told Navi she had a headache and they left."

"Oh. Do you want to talk about it?"

Ash frowned and shook her head. "I mean, yes, I want to talk to you... but not about Sam. Do you fancy getting some air?"

"Sure. Don't you want to eat first?"

Ash puffed out a laugh. "No, maybe later... I can't just yet."

Ash led Alice away from the party, until they were outside on an empty terrace, barely lit aside from a few flickering lanterns. In the daytime, there'd likely be a stunning view of the hotel grounds. But only darkness stretched out ahead of them now, a parallax in shades of night.

A cool breeze caused Alice to shiver and rub the chill from her arms.

"Are you warm enough?"

"Yeah, I'm fine, just adjusting. It's pretty hot in there, so it's nice to cool down."

"There's a bench over there." Ash gestured to a shadowy corner.

Alice tried to ignore the bite of jealousy at the realisation that this was where Ash had been with Sam earlier. They sat for a while, their eyes adjusting to the low light. Music and voices bled out from the function room, but the enveloping night seemed to absorb the sound into a hushed muffle.

Alice broke their silence. "So, are you going to tell me what happened with Sam?"

Ash exhaled. "We had a good chat, put a few things to rest. She said she's happy, but she misses me and would love to spend some time together again."

"Oof, the classic stab and twist to hook you back in." Alice gestured with her hand.

"Yeah, but it didn't work. It's taken a long time, but I've finally moved on. I'm not willing to be dragged into any games." A tendril of hair fell over Ash's face. She tucked it back and turned to look at Alice. "Besides, I told her I've met someone."

Alice stilled.

"You're the first person I've met since Sam, who I've had any sort of feelings for. And I've been trying so hard to just be a friend to you. I didn't want to be the person swooping in to take advantage of a situation."

"I never thought that—"

"I was crushed when Sam left. All I needed was a friend to pull me out of the hole I'd fallen into, not someone trying to get into my pants."

Alice chewed her lip. "Well, as much as I've liked having a friend…"

Ash scratched the back of her neck. "I feel like a total creep saying this, but I was drawn to you from the moment you walked into my A&E department looking completely deranged. It's only been two weeks, but every moment we've spent together has been… I mean, I literally crave your company. When I'm not with you, you're all I think about." Ash raised her hands. "And I know I should've backed off to give you space…"

"Ash—"

"But I've just been falling further and further. And now, I couldn't stay away, even if I wanted to."

"I don't want you to stay away. I like you too, you know that, right?"

Ash slow-blinked. "I know. The way you look at me sometimes, it takes every ounce of my restraint not to just…" Ash growled, and it sent heat coiling through Alice.

"But the thing is, I don't want to be just a rebound for you. I like you way too much for that, Alice. You're still so raw—"

"No, I'm not. My mind has never been clearer. These past couple of weeks, I realised everything I ever had with Fran was fiction. I loved her power and her appetite for me, but beyond the fantasy, there was no substance." Alice took Ash's hand, threading their fingers and clasping it in her lap. "So yeah, I got fucked over, but it felt more like a violent awakening than the heartbreak you went through with Sam, because I wasn't ever really in love with Fran."

Ash gulped. "How do you know?"

"Because now I know what it actually feels like."

Ash looked at her with such intensity, Alice thought she might combust.

In the swaying candlelight, Ash's eyes dropped to Alice's mouth, and she leaned in. Warmth bloomed in Alice's chest as their lips pressed together in a heart-stopping kiss that left them breathless.

"So, does this mean we can be more than just friends now?" Alice whispered.

"I think you know we were always more than *just friends*, Alice."

Alice smiled so hard it hurt her cheeks. "Well, you better kiss me again then."

Ash didn't have to be asked twice.

AFTER THE JOY OF THE TERRACE AND THEIR FIRST kiss, Alice and Ash returned to the party.

Nik and Sukhi summoned them to the dance floor, but they managed to escape after a couple of songs. They did the rounds, smiling and making polite conversation, Alice helping Ash to navigate away from intrusive questions about her love life. Even Rani, seemingly overtaken by the joy of the occasion, gushed about how proud she was of her daughter — the doctor.

In truth, since the terrace, Alice was finding it difficult to concentrate on anything but Ash. The smouldering looks passing between them had lit a fire within her. Alice couldn't wait to kiss her again; butterflies erupted in her stomach at the thought that soon they'd be alone together. Ash must have read her mind, as she leaned in and whispered. "I can't wait to get you out of that onesie."

Alice wanted to kiss that delicious grin right off her face.

"Do you think anyone would miss us if we left?" Ash asked.

They stood at the perimeter of the room, so close that no one would have noticed as Ash's fingers curled between Alice's.

"Definitely not." Alice squeezed Ash's hand.

"That's what I hoped you'd say."

It was unlikely that anyone cared when they left, but they'd treated it like a covert mission, slipping out the door, dashing to the car, grabbing their bags, and sneaking back inside when the coast was clear. Behind the closed door of their hotel room their laughter burst out. When Ash caught her breath, she moved in front of Alice, tucked a tendril of loose curls behind her ear and harpooned her with a look of pure want.

If their first kiss was sweet, then their second was spicy, and loaded with passion. Their lips crushed together, Alice opened her mouth to let Ash in and groaned as their tongues slipped together. Alice pushed Ash towards the bed, but as they neared, Ash spun her around and lifted Alice's legs around her waist.

Alice giggled. "You're stronger than you look."

"Oh, thanks. I'll have you know I go to the gym every day. These are arms of steel. Unlike your silly breakable arms." Ash lowered her onto the bed, still wrapped between her legs as they collapsed back, lost in another kiss.

"You've made a big mistake, Doctor."

"Huh?"

"The 'onesie' zip is at the back." Alice wrestled Ash around with her thighs until she was straddling her. Ash sat up between Alice's legs, reaching around to the zip. After freeing her arms from the sleeves, Alice let the jumpsuit drop to her waist. Ash whimpered at the sight of her breasts all wrapped up in their lacy bra, and she buried her face in Alice's cleavage.

"I've wanted to do this since I watched you eat that muffin." Ash unclipped the bra and pulled it away with her teeth until Alice's breasts bounced free. "Oh, fuck. You're so beautiful."

Alice moaned, rocking herself into Ash's lap as Ash licked and nibbled at her skin.

"You know that first morning we woke up together?"

"Yeah?"

"I was having the most incredible dream about us." Ash traced her fingertips up Alice's bare back. Alice arched with the sensation, thrusting her breasts forward. Ash captured a nipple in her mouth and sucked it hard.

"Yeah, well I was wide awake and enjoying you grinding me."

Ash looked up with a devilish grin. "I shouldn't have stopped then?"

"I didn't want you to. Perhaps we could try it again in the morning?"

"I don't intend to wait until the morning." Ash pulled

Alice down to her, and in one quick twisting manoeuvre she was back on top with Alice frantically pawing at her shirt buttons. When the shirt finally fell open, Ash yanked it from her arms and flung it across the room. Alice let her hands wander over Ash's smooth skin. She wanted to explore every inch of her, first with her fingers, then with her tongue.

"May I remove the rest of your onesie?"

Alice laughed. "Yeah, but only if you stop calling it that."

Ash knelt up to liberate Alice's legs. "Oh my God, you are so incredibly—" she growled and lowered her mouth to Alice's curves. Alice arched her back with want and pleasure as Ash trailed a finger along her stomach, down to the moist fabric of her underwear.

"Oh, hello. Someone's excited to play!"

"You better believe it." Alice gasped as Ash firmly cupped a hand over her aching sex, then added pressure with her knee between Alice's legs.

"Can I touch you too?"

Ash whimpered her consent and Alice reached between them and pushed a hand into her trousers.

"Shall I take them off?" Ash gasped.

"Later, but right now, don't stop what you're doing to me," Alice panted as she worked a hand into Ash's under-wear. "I'm not the only one who's excited to play."

As Alice slipped inside her, Ash released a guttural moan, and in one swift move, she pushed aside Alice's lace panties and entered her too. They rocked together until Alice's noisy climax pulled Ash over the edge with her, and they collapsed next to each other in a semi-naked, breathless heap.

Alice turned her head on the pillow and met Ash's gaze, her eyelids heavy with post-coital lust and that wonky grin dimpling her cheek. This time, Alice couldn't resist kissing it right off her gorgeous face.

"Right," Ash purred, "let's get you out of those wet clothes."

## 24

# HANDLE WITH CARE

*A*lice stirred, stretched and smiled, cosy in the afterglow of the night she'd spent with Ash.

Daylight strained into the room, but it felt far too early to be awake yet after the night they'd had.

"Are you awake?" she whispered.

"Yeah." Ash squeezed her closer, hooking a leg over her thigh. "Are you hungry?"

Alice hummed. "Yeah, a bit. I think there are some biscuits by the kettle."

Ash's sleepy voice croaked with a laugh. "I was thinking more about proper food. They'll be serving breakfast soon. If we go down early enough, we'll avoid my family, and we can come back here for a bit until checkout. You know, maybe get a little more sleep?"

Alice twisted around in Ash's arms to face her teasing grin.

"I can think of better things to do alone with you than sleep." Alice traced her fingers over the small tattoo inked under Ash's collarbone. Three words printed in perfect capital letters like they'd been stamped instead of tattooed:

## HANDLE WITH CARE

"I got it as a note to self after Sam. A reminder not to be reckless with my heart again."

"And do you feel like you've been reckless with me?"

"No, not at all." Ash kissed the tip of Alice's nose. "Even if you were just using me for a night of hot sex, it was worth it. I don't really know why we wasted two weeks."

"I mean, by lesbian standards, we should've already moved in together."

"No, I'm never moving in with you."

Alice gasped. "Why?"

"Because I'd die of sleep deprivation! You'd keep me locked in the bedroom, feeding me miniature packets of biscuits and demanding orgasms."

Alice chewed her bottom lip. "Would that really be so bad?"

Ash answered with the sort of kiss that made Alice grateful she was horizontal.

## 25

# CASSEROLE

"*A*ll set then, George?"

With a small smile, George patted the holdall full of the things Alice had brought from his house, as well as half a dozen packets of biscuits. Dressed in the furry black coat he'd been wearing the night Alice found him, he unfurled his tall frame from the chair.

Not for the first time, Alice wondered how on earth she'd managed to drag him into her car that night. He'd got off relatively easy with just a minor head injury.

"Thanks again for breaking me out of here, Alice. Your formidable friend, Doctor Truscote, said you pulled a few strings to speed things up. Who knows when they'd have let me out otherwise?"

"I'm pleased I could help. Was Truscote okay with you?"

"No nonsense. That's what I like in a doctor. She's let me out for good behaviour on the proviso that I attend a course of follow-up sessions to work through everything that led up to..." His bottom lip trembled, and Alice squeezed a hand on his arm.

They stopped by the nurses' station so George could thank them and say goodbye. Marjorie even stepped out and reached up to give him a hug.

"You mind how you go now, George," she said, her words almost smothered by his coat. Pulling away, she swiped her damp cheeks and wagged a finger at him. "I don't want to see you back here again."

George looped an arm through Alice's and they walked the corridor towards the lifts. "I called ahead to let Trish know I'll be home."

"Will she have got some groceries in for you, or should we stop—"

"Wait up!" A voice called out.

They spun around to Ash, jogging up behind them.

"Good... I didn't... miss you," she said, bending to catch her breath.

Alice tried to suppress the smile sweeping over her lips before George saw.

She and Ash had been inseparable for the remainder of the weekend. They'd enjoyed most of it horizontally. They'd missed check-out by over an hour, then somehow lasted the entire drive home before reuniting on Alice's couch, finally ending up in her bed, where they'd woken with limbs entwined that morning.

They'd kissed goodbye in the hospital car park and had no further plans to see each other that day. Alice had practically floated to George's room. Despite all that, they'd agreed to take things slow, which meant keeping it just between themselves for now. A secret affair, but this time without all the bullshit that had come with Fran.

If Ash's stupid grin and flushed cheeks were anything to go by, the whole ward would know within seconds. George glanced between them and released a low whistle, but perhaps reading the room, he didn't pass comment.

"I, er... swapped shifts. It means I'll get a sucky double later this week, but I didn't want you having to get an Uber. So, I'll drive you."

"Really?" Alice's voice came out so high there'd be dogs howling in France.

George raised his bushy eyebrows.

"Yeah, really. Come on," Ash laughed.

THE CROOKED LITTLE COTTAGE LOOKED LESS creepy, more quaint than when Alice had come by with Maggie just over a week ago. *How had that only been a week ago?* As they clambered out of the car, the front door swung open, and Trisha came trundling down the path with a wiry black dog yapping in tow.

"Pyglet!" George held his arms open, and the dog jumped into them, yelping as it snuffled into his beard.

Trisha buried her hands into the pockets of her baggy brown corduroys. "She's missed you, she has."

"I've missed you too, haven't I, girl?" George chuckled and tucked the dog under his arm like a rugby ball.

"Well, the cottage was a little chilly, so I lit the burner

and I've got a pork casserole on the hob too. I hope you're hungry."

"I'll always make room for your casserole, Trish. Thanks for holding the fort whilst I've been indisposed."

"Glad to have you home, George."

"Sorry, I'm being rude. Trisha, this is Alice—"

Alice raised a hand. "Hiya, Trisha. We met last week, remember?"

Trisha raised an eyebrow. "I thought I recognised you. You're the burglar who wasn't a burglar." She turned to Ash. "You look different to the other one though?"

George laughed and put an arm around the funny little woman. "Trisha, this is Doctor Ash. She's been looking after me, too."

Ash held out a hand, and Trisha gave it a tentative shake. "Oh, the doctors drive you home from hospital now, do they? No wonder them waiting lists are so long."

Trisha frowned, but the rest of them laughed.

"It's okay, Trish, I'm off duty."

"Right then, shall we go in for a cuppa? I've got plenty of biscuits to go around," said George.

Two pots of tea and one hour later, Pyglet was curled up asleep by the fire. Alice and Ash bid their farewells, with promises to visit again soon and stay for casserole next time.

Stepping outside into the fading daylight, Alice glanced across at Ash, wearing the grin that had barely left her lips all afternoon.

"Do you think he'll be okay?"

"He'll be fine. Trisha will keep an eye on him. And he's got us too now, hasn't he?"

Alice nodded, the swirl in her stomach easing with Ash's words. "Thanks for swapping your shift to do this. It was really lovely of you."

"It wasn't entirely altruistic." Ash gently swayed into Alice as they walked along the garden path. "If anything, I'm being greedy. I wanted to steal a little more time with you."

Alice turned to face her as they reached the car. "Oh yeah? So, what now?"

"Back to mine? I'll rustle up something tasty for dinner."

"Mmm, yeah. Sounds good. Then what?"

"Netflix and chill?"

"You know what that means, right?"

Ash laughed. "Yeah, I know what it means!"

"You sure?"

"Yeah, I'm sure. It starts a bit like this..." Ash tilted Alice's chin up and closed the gap between them. She captured Alice's lips in a deep kiss that comprehensively confirmed her grasp of *Netflix and chill*. Lost in the moment, they pushed back against the car, Ash's hands tangled in Alice's curls, Alice's hands cupping the delicious curve of Ash's denim-clad arse.

They pulled apart at the sound of George whistling from his front door.

"About time," he yelled and gave them a wave.

Ash giggled and wiped her lips. "Shit, I didn't know he was watching us."

Alice grinned and grabbed the front of Ash's plaid shirt, pulling her in for more.

# PYG TRACK

## SIX WEEKS LATER

*A*lice focused on the crunch of one foot in front of the other, trying not to pay too much attention to their elevation and the view. With a dizzying effect, the hazy horizon seemed to stretch further with every step.

Trailing behind made it easier; every now and then, Alice allowed her eyes to wander up from her new hiking boots to Ash's Lycra-clad rear.

Ash's calf muscles rippled with the effort of the incline and Alice grinned with the memory of running her tongue along that smooth skin, which tasted just as delicious as it looked.

"Alright back there, Al?" Ash's voice snapped Alice out of her daydream, and she looked up into the gorgeous face peering down at her. Ash pushed back her shiny dark hair with her aviators and flashed Alice a thousand-watt smile.

"Is there much further to go?" Alice asked, whilst trying not to pant like a dog.

Ash stood, hand on her hip, and squinted at the vista.

"Not too far now. How are your feet?"

"Yeah, great." Alice winced at the reminder. Even her ridiculous heels were more comfortable than these blister-inducing boots.

"It'll take a few hikes to break them in."

Alice laughed. "You think I'm doing this again?"

"You wait. It'll be worth it when we get to the top." Ash rummaged in her backpack and pulled out a flask, which she offered to Alice when she reached her side. Alice gulped a mouthful of cool water before handing it back.

Ash nodded to her boots. "Did you wear them around the house like I told you to?"

"Yes, Doctor," Alice said with a grin, which anyone fluent in grins would realise meant, *no, of course, I fucking didn't*. Although, it wasn't technically a lie; Alice had worn the boots — fresh out of the box, whilst lying on her bed, talking to Ash on the phone. She'd held her feet aloft and clicked her heels together like a hikey-dykey Dorothy.

Alice still preferred her calves in stilettos, and despite saying she'd never wear uncomfortable shoes ever again, she was willing to give hiking boots a go. *For Ash.*

"What are you grinning at?" Ash scanned Alice's face, a bemused smile tugging at the corner of her mouth.

"Nothing." Alice laughed, and Ash squeezed her side in a playful tickle. Alice squealed and reached out to retaliate, but Ash stole herself away, bouncing on her heels and striding ahead like Julie-fucking-Andrews.

Ash's unexpected touch left Alice wanting more; the ache in her boots had moved a little further north. *Pull yourself together.*

"Come on, Frenchie. Keep up," Ash called over her shoulder.

*Frenchie? That's new.* Alice smiled to herself and settled back into the rhythm of her steps. She thought back over the past few weeks. How when one door was slammed shut, plunging her into darkness, another door she didn't even know existed creaked open and let in a shining shaft of light.

Everything was still so new with Ash, but so far, so good. *Actually, scrap that. It was so much better than good.* The last few weeks had been some of the best of Alice's life.

Keeping things quiet had been a big fail. Obviously, George had figured it out right away and Alice hadn't even needed to tell Maggie; her sister took one look at her face and knew everything in an instant. But to be fair, keeping it in was like trying to stop a cola bottle from exploding after shaking it up.

It'd been difficult to pump the brakes, especially after the intensity of the engagement party weekend and the days that followed. But they'd made a real effort not to conform to the stereotype and take things slow. They were getting to know each other properly and letting things blossom.

Sleepovers were reserved only for Ash's days off, and Ash's nightshift schedule suited Alice's night-owl tendencies. Pillow talk had fast become their dawn ritual, albeit in their own beds, at the end of a phone. Alice stayed on the line, listening to Ash breathing long after she'd fallen asleep. She supposed that was kind of creepy, but the gentle in and out of Ash's sleeping breath was as soothing to Alice as waves lapping a shore.

They hung out on Ash's days off, relishing each other's company and concocting plans, like the one which had brought them here to hike this mountain... or *hill*, as Ash called it.

Originally organised as a trip to celebrate the removal of Alice's cast, by the time it came around, there was bigger news to celebrate. Alice had accepted a job offer as an Executive Assistant at a respected firm with an actual HR department.

And now that she had a *girlfriend* — yes, they were officially calling themselves that — there was zero chance of her sleeping with her boss's wife.

At the brow of the hill, Ash stood sentinel with her hands on her waist, surveying the view like she'd just conquered Wales. Alice panted, heaving her weary limbs up the last few steps. She doubled over, her breaths puffing in gusts.

"It's a good thing... you're a doctor... I think I need... medical attention."

Ash laughed and settled a hand on Alice's back.

"When you've remembered how to breathe, just look at this view."

Slowly revived, as if by the doctor's touch, Alice unfurled her torso and looked ahead. The view stretched for miles. In the distance, the rugged hills disappeared into the morning mist. A patchwork quilt of lush shades of green lay in the valley, nestled up to an expanse of water, shimmering in the sunlight.

"Wow," gasped Alice.

"I know, right?"

Alice turned to see Ash staring at her with a hungry look. Ash reached out and tucked some wayward curls behind Alice's ear. The lustful way her eyes dropped to Alice's mouth made her stomach flip. She cupped Alice's cheeks in her hands and leaned in, capturing Alice's lips with her own in a tender yet urgent kiss. Ash tasted sweet and salty, and Alice couldn't get enough.

"How fast do you think we can get down this mountain?" Alice pulled back, that ache from before now back with a vengeance.

"Depends how much those hiking boots are hurting you."

"They're fucking killing me."

Ash laughed. "I knew it. Well, the good news is that just over there is a café with a bar. I'll get you a medicinal glass of wine and then we can catch the train down."

"Oh my God, there's a train?"

"Yeah, I already booked us tickets because I knew you wouldn't break your boots in like I told you to. Do you want the other good news?"

"There's more?"

"Yeah, I booked us a cabin with a hot tub, so we can enjoy the view as we soak away our achy muscles."

"I love you, Ash." The words tumbled out of Alice's mouth before she could stop them. Panic gripped her as she waited for the impact to land.

Ash stilled, staring through wide eyes, her lips frozen in a half-smile, like they weren't sure what to do.

"Shit, sorry. I didn't mean—"

Ash's kiss swallowed the rest of Alice's words. She snaked an arm around her waist and pulled her close until there was only heat and a layer of flammable clothing between them. Ash pulled back, her eyes shining with the same glow Alice felt radiating from herself.

"I love you too, Alice French," she said.

Forget the blisters. Alice was walking on air.

# ACKNOWLEDGMENTS

Firstly, a big thank you to you… yes, YOU!

I really appreciate you taking a chance on an indie-author. I hope you enjoyed this book and it encourages you to seek out more indie-authors. We are the wild ones with voices we refuse to hush. We write our stories and publish them ourselves without asking permission. Don't ever let the big 'guy' tell you that the little 'guy' is less than… it's a sneaky lie.

I owe massive thanks to the following:

*Sophia* – I'm so pleased you agreed to work with me again! Thank you for all your brilliant tweaks and suggestions. You brought the sparkle and the commas… who knew I needed so many? You did, and that's why you're awesome!

*Sam* - I literally couldn't be happier with how the artwork has turned out — it's stunning. You've been a lot of fun to work with and I hope we can do it again!

*Team Beta* – (*Carrie, Lisa, PD, Janie, Jenny, Chery, Kim,* and *JoJo*) for all your feedback and enthusiasm at such a critical stage of the process. Plus, a very special mention to *Sharan* and *Jas*, for your sensitivity read, and helping me pour a bit more Desiness into Ash.

*Team ARC* – You lot got to crack the Champagne open

on the side of the ship before she set sail. It wouldn't have been a very good send-off without you, so I'm very grateful you all showed up with your cheerleading and encouraging words.

*Everyone* who has supported me in ways both big and small... I can't tell you how much I needed all those little nudges. From ordering a book (or ten – thanks 'Kathy'), dropping a kind review, or even just asking me about my writing... It keeps me going.

*Mum* — for being so uniquely you and inspiring a few of Alice's 'quirks'. Also, for pretending really hard not to be asleep that time I was reading out loud to you.

And last, but definitely not least... *Shannon* — for your endless patience and lending me your ears and eyes. Also, for that time you tried but failed to do Ash's Yorkshire accent and it came out Irish. I probably could write a book without you, but it wouldn't be anywhere near as much fun and the end result wouldn't be even half as good. Thank you for being my person for twenty years... hopefully you'll put up with me for at least another twenty!

# ABOUT THE AUTHOR

Pip lives a in the UK with her wife, Shannon and their two 'kids' Mouse (the cat) and Roux (the dog). When she's not hanging out with her imaginary friends, Pip loves travelling, being in the mountains, making delicious food – and eating it, pouring good wine – and drinking it. Yes, Pip is her real name. And no, she's not Dutch.

.

ALSO BY PIP LANDERS-LETTS

The Weight of What Was

# WAIT, BEFORE YOU GO...

## WANT TO SUPPORT AN INDIE-AUTHOR?

Great news! You've taken the first step — you've read my book, or at least you're reading this bit (*who starts at the back?)* Here are **THREE** more simple steps you can take that'll help me out BIG time:

### 1. DROP A REVIEW

If you enjoyed this book, please drop me a review on Amazon, Goodreads, or wherever you normally review things. Even just adding a star rating (5 would be great!) and saying, *'I loved it, what an incredible read!'* could be enough to encourage someone else to take a chance on my books.

### 2. SHARE THE LOVE

Let other people know you enjoyed my books. Sing a little song about them on social media (please tag me if you do that)! If you enjoy my books, you'll likely know other people who will too. Books make great gifts... just saying.

## 3. FOLLOW ME

Pop onto my socials, like and (even better) share my posts to make the algorithm really fall in love with me. Also, don't forget to sign up to my mailing list to receive exclusive content and stay up to date with all my latest news.

*Pip x*

www.pipwritesfiction.com

Printed in Dunstable, United Kingdom